Praise for *Kit McBride Gets a Wife*

"A sweet, laugh-out-loud romantic comedy set in the wilds of Montana, *Kit McBride Gets a Wife* will have readers smiling from ear to ear and set their hearts all aflutter. Maddy Mooney is a plucky, endearing heroine, and Kit McBride is the ideal frontiersman hero. With a cast of delightful secondary characters, including the irrepressible younger sister, Junebug, this charming romance is guaranteed a place on your keeper shelf."

—Elizabeth Everett, author of A Perfect Equation

"Heartfelt, humorous, and sweetly romantic, *Kit McBride Gets a Wife* kept me smiling to the last page."

—Mimi Matthews, USA Today bestselling author of
The Siren of Sussex

"This first installment in a planned series will leave fans ready for a return trip to Buck's Creek." —*Library Journal* (starred review)

"Barry's snappy prose and standout scene setting make Buck's Creek a destination readers will want to return to."

—Publishers Weekly

Also by Amy Barry

KIT McBRIDE GETS A WIFE

MARRYING OFF
Morgan McBride

AMY BARRY

BERKLEY ROMANCE
NEW YORK

BERKLEY ROMANCE
Published by Berkley
An imprint of Penguin Random House LLC
penguinrandomhouse.com

Library of Congress Cataloging-in-Publication Data

Names: Barry, Amy, author.
Title: Marrying off Morgan McBride / Amy Barry.
Description: First Edition. | New York: Berkley Romance, 2023.
Identifiers: LCCN 2022034440 (print) | LCCN 2022034441 (ebook) |
ISBN 9780593335598 (trade paperback) | ISBN 9780593335604 (ebook)
Subjects: LCGFT: Romance fiction. | Western fiction. | Novels.
Classification: LCC PR9619.4.B3746 M37 2023 (print) |
LCC PR9619.4.B3746 (ebook) | DDC 823/.92—dc23/eng/20220721
LC record available at https://lccn.loc.gov/2022034440
LC ebook record available at https://lccn.loc.gov/2022034441

First Edition: May 2023

Printed in the United States of America
1st Printing

Book design by George Towne

For my grandmother Tess,
and for my grandfather Gordon,
who was the love of her life.
I miss you, Grandma.

WANTED

Wife for a bullheaded backwoodsman with a surfeit of family.
A secretly gumptious woman with a mind of her own and a
bit of backbone is required for wifely duties. Must be able
to soothe a fractious temper and not expect cosseting.
But he will mend your boots and give you unwanted advice.
And he has it in him to make you laugh—mostly not on purpose.
Bad cooks need not apply.

One

Buck's Creek, Montana, 1887

Junebug drummed her fingers against the trading post counter. She
was perched up on the stool, watching the store while her brothers
were over in the meadow, building Kit and his new wife a house.
Junebug had been banned from the building site, which was just
plumb unfair. It wasn't her fault the doorframe got split. Beau
should never have left her in charge of it in the first place. He was
nothing but a lazy, no-good shirker. Still, Junebug didn't want to
be out there in the soggy old meadow nohow, sweating up a stink
while they all growled at each other. She was quite happy here,
with her pot of coffee and her complaints book. She'd filled up two
whole pages with complaints—*It makes me sick the way Beau flops
out of work like a boneless rabbit; they got no right keeping me prisoner
up here and not letting me off down to Bitterroot on my own—why, some
gals are married by now and spitting out kids of their own, and I cain't
even go for a walk by my ownsome; if I have to do laundry when I don't
want to, I don't see why Maddy gets out of it, just because Kit's all kicked-
in-the-head over her . . .*

Last year, Junebug had got the bright idea of ordering up a mail-
order bride to help her with the chores. Hell, she had four enormous

hungry men to look after up here—she needed help. And she *had* found a wife, after some trial and error . . .

Junebug remembered the first woman she'd hooked with her advertisement with no small measure of horror. Willabelle Lascalles had been the wrongest kind of woman possible for a McBride. Especially for Kit, Junebug's great big hulking blacksmith of a brother. Willabelle Lascalles had been like a china doll, all frilled and fancy, with pale pink kidskin boots not at all fit for the muddy mountain meadows of Buck's Creek. Worse, she was a *mean* china doll. The kind that wanted cosseting. Or else.

Thank goodness Junebug had been able to head *that* off. She didn't need a china doll. She needed a cook. And someone who could deal with the caterpillars who kept infesting the vegetable patch. And maybe someone to do the laundry too . . .

She'd thought she'd found her answer in Willabelle's maid. A maid was *perfect*. And Kit had been good enough to fall in love with her and everything. It should have solved all her problems. Junebug scowled at the ink-scratched pages of her complaints book. But, in actual fact, things were worse than ever. It turned out Maddy the Maid could only cook colcannon mash and pandy—and Junebug was sick to death of potatoes in all their mash, as were her brothers. Which meant Junebug was stuck back in the cookhouse, cooking for them all. And she *hated* cooking. Almost as much as she hated laundry. Which she still had to do, because Kit had declared that he and Maddy were setting up house and Maddy was only responsible for the two of them. Ugh. Which left three whole brothers Junebug had to launder for.

And then there was the problem of Morgan . . .

Damn Morgan. The blockiest, bullheadedest brother of all. No one beat Morgan for stubbornness, or bossiness, or flat-out infuriating contrariness. He acted like he owned the world. Or at least this patch of it. Junebug bet he even bossed her around in his dreams.

But as irritating as he was, she loved him. And he was making noises about leaving again, which gave Junebug an awful feeling in her stomach. A swampy feeling, like things were crawling away down there. Lately he'd been poring over catalogs again, dog-earing the pages that advertised new saddles and tack. She knew Morgan pined for his days as a cowhand, for the time before he got burdened with his orphaned siblings. When he told stories about being a cowboy, his voice got a dreamy tone that was so out of character that it sent chills down her spine. Since when did *Morgan* talk that way about an orange sunset, and the way it cut through trails of dust, glittering with gold? Or the way the mountains rose blue and violet on the horizon, like a dream of what was coming? This was *Morgan*. Who had as much poetry in him as a cook pot.

But now that Kit was hitched, and there was a woman on the scene to mother Junebug, Morgan was waxing all poetic. And he seemed to think he could saddle up and head back out running cattle, leaving Junebug behind to cook for everyone and to launder Beau's and Jonah's pestiferous underthings. Junebug didn't like it. Not one bit.

It didn't matter how many times Junebug hid or destroyed the catalogs; he always seemed to get his hands on more. It made Junebug sick how much he pined to leave her. They had a good life here in Buck's Creek. Look at the place! It was goddamn *picturesque*.

Through the open door of the trading post, Junebug could see the creek (which was really more of a river) tumbling by, silvery in the sunshine. The thick meadow grasses were spring green and feathered with larkspur and balsamroot, and the chokecherry was waving wands of white blossom. The blue-blue mountain sky was fluffed with clouds so white they looked like new snow and the air was pine fresh and carrying the smell of sap and bloom. What more goddamn poetry could he want?

And aside from all the bucolic waxing on about the mountains, wasn't *she* enough?

Morgan had been a parent to her—a bossy, griping, captious

parent, to be sure, but he had been *there*. He was constant, as solid as the ancient gray rock of the mountains, predictable and sure. Morgan just *was*, and Junebug felt something very like raw panic at the thought of him leaving. Hell, she'd lost a mother, and a father, her brother Charlie and a bunch of sisters—did she have to lose Morgan too?

He seemed to think she didn't need him anymore. Which was just plain wrongheaded. But so much of Morgan was wrongheaded. It was in his nature.

Junebug was scrawling angrily in her complaints book about that exact topic—*Why in hell won't Morgan let me take the train to Butte? Thunderhead Bill says they got a saloon with dancing girls, on a real stage and everything. Morgan says dancing girls ain't no sight for a kid like me, which is the dumbest thing I ever heard; surely the whole point of a dancing girl is to be looked at?*—when Purdy Joe came by with the mail.

Purdy Joe was new to these parts. He was a broad-faced midwesterner from somewhere down on the plains; he had wheat-colored bangs and a big gap between his two front teeth. His name was Jensen or Hanson, or something along those lines, but all anyone ever called him was Purdy Joe. He was up in the Elkhorns prospecting for silver and he was bright with expectation, like a kid on the hunt for candy. Beau and Jonah were prone to button-holing him to ask about the prospecting—those two idiots had a mind to go looking for silver themselves. Purdy Joe had got familiar enough with them that he volunteered to run the mail up from Bitterroot to Buck's Creek whenever he was passing through, to save the McBrides a trip.

Bitterroot was four hours down the mountain and was shaping up to be a proper town. It had the post office, the rail spur, a mercantile, a hotel, a saloon, a cathouse and now a butcher shop (well, it was a tent more than a shop), run by a man named Hicks, who had arrived on the train and decided that the miners would probably spend their coins on beefsteak. He wasn't wrong. As far as Junebug could see, miners liked spending their money on pretty much everything.

Up here in Buck's Creek, in the high mountain meadows, there wasn't any butcher, tented or otherwise; there was only the trading post and Kit's forge. Junebug didn't see that it was ever going to be much of a town—it certainly wasn't getting the railway, not up a mountain this steep. Junebug thought it would be fine to have a railway station on your doorstep. Why, just think. You could hop aboard and go just about anywhere. Butte, for starters. But there was also Billings, Miles City, Bismarck . . . and places she'd only read about in past-date newspapers. Places like Iron County, Missouri, or Wichita, Kansas. There was a whole world down that mountain.

But mostly Junebug would settle for heading down the hill to Bitterroot, the biggest town she'd yet seen. So Junebug was of two minds about Purdy Joe's kindness in bringing the mail up from Bitterroot. She *liked* going down to get the mail. It was a whole day away from the sound of pounding hammers and grumpy brothers. And she could go visiting, gathering up town gossip and letting people ply her with coffee and (if she was lucky) cake. Purdy Joe was depriving her of all that, keeping her stuck in the trading post or the cookhouse, where there wasn't any cake, unless she made it herself. And she hated baking with a passion. Especially since she'd blown up the last cookhouse.

She also wasn't keen on Purdy Joe handling their mail. It was too risky. What if he found out about her secret mail-order bride business? She'd gotten in enough trouble over it last time. And this time would be worse, because this time she was bride hunting for Morgan. Who, let's face it, was the front-runner in the grumpy-brother stakes.

Still. Even if she was conflicted about him bringing the mail, at least Purdy Joe was company. Might as well look on the bright side.

"Mail for you, Junebug!" Purdy Joe stuck his head in the door and held out the pitiful handful of mail. It was only a single letter and one of Morgan's cursed catalogs.

Junebug slid off her stool. Purdy Joe knew not to go in the trading post while Junebug was there alone, so he didn't take so much as a step beyond the porch. It was annoying. Junebug's brothers were big, and they could get mean if anyone got too close to her. Which was dumb as a bag of hammers, since they kept leaving her to mind the trading post. How in hell was anyone supposed to trade if they couldn't come inside when she was here? Spit, her brothers were blockheads.

Purdy Joe grinned as she took the catalog and the tattered splat of an envelope from him. "Who you been writing to, Junebug? You got a suitor?" He wasn't in the slightest bit serious. People always underestimated her that way. It was 'cause she looked like a mite of a thing in these old coveralls. But she could get a suitor if she wanted to, she was sure of it. She could do anything.

So long as her brothers kept out of the way.

"Ha. Sure." Junebug played along, glad of the conversation. "The only way I'm getting courted is from a great distance." Junebug liked the prospector. He was young and cheery, and he minded his own business. The suitor line was just a throwaway comment. He had no desire to stick his beak into her letter. Not like Thunderhead Bill or old Roy—if they'd brought the mail up, they would have pestered her mercilessly, until her brothers got wind of what she was up to. She was glad they were off with Sour Eagle on one of their long hunts, so she could get on with finding a wife without them meddling. Even if she did miss them a little . . .

"You want some coffee, Purd?" Junebug offered. She'd not spoken to anyone but her kin in days and Purdy Joe was a novelty. If she couldn't go visiting in Bitterroot, at the very least she could play host to Purdy. She bet he was full of good stories.

"Best not," Purdy Joe said, backing away from her once she'd taken the crumpled envelope from his hand. He gave her a rueful smile and jerked his chin in the direction of the din in the meadow. "I got no mind to tangle with Morgan." He just about tipped his hat as he said goodbye, straining to be as polite and proper as could be.

Spit. Her brothers ruined everything. Now she couldn't even talk to a damn prospector without him turning tail and running for the hills. She scowled as she watched Purdy Joe head across the meadow to the raw timber frame, which was starting to resemble a house. Seriously? He'd visit with *them* but not with her? It just wasn't fair.

She needed a new wife *now*. There were too many men up here by half. Once she'd watered them down with a couple more women, things were bound to improve . . . *surely?*

Junebug looked down at the catalog and the envelope.

And if she got Morgan the *right kind* of wife, one he could get all kicked-in-the-head over, the way Kit was over Maddy, then he would stop this talk of leaving, wouldn't he? And he'd stop ordering these stupid catalogs.

Junebug rolled up the catalog and tucked it under her arm. She'd burn the darn thing before she'd ever give it to him. She considered the letter. Lucky she'd been here when Purdy Joe came by; somehow, she'd managed to keep her bride hunting a secret the whole season long. She had an excuse prepared, should her brothers ever get suspicious about the mail she received (because who the hell ever wrote to Junebug): she was going to tell them it was all part of her letter-writing business. They'd ask questions, because they liked to inquisition her, but she had a handful of decent answers up her sleeve, so she wasn't too afeared. But she might also just tell them to get their beaks out of her business.

Sometimes she whiled away a good couple of hours having imaginary shouting matches with Morgan over these letters. She sighed. It was a crying shame to waste all that good material.

This letter wasn't making a great first impression, she mused as she turned the envelope over. Postmarked Nebraska, it was a travel-stained splat of a thing. She didn't have much hope as she opened it. She'd advertised for a mail-order bride for her brother Morgan months ago, and none of the responses had yielded the right kind of wife. It wasn't that there weren't takers; there were. There were passels of women looking for men, and in particular men with a patch of land to work. There were widows and spinsters, women of means and women of none, tall women, short women, stout women, thin women, women who wrote with charm and others who could barely write at all. They promised fidelity and loyalty, labor and love, honesty and hardiness. But they were all just too . . . well, *girly*.

While she needed a woman with wiles, and a measure of feminine charm (to achieve the kicked-in-the-head bewitchment), she also needed a worker, and one with a stern backbone. Junebug didn't like the simpering some of these brides were prone to in their epistolary endeavors. Simpering never got you nowhere with a Mc-Bride man. You needed the capacity for combat.

The letter itself was hefty, Junebug noted as she pulled it from its sleeve. The woman had covered both sides of more than a few pages. She was the wordy sort, that was for sure. Junebug counted that in her favor. She was starved for conversation up here. Her brothers were prone to doing little more than grunting at her. When they weren't bossing or complaining, that is.

To whom it may concern, the letter began, all formal and stiff-like. *I never pictured myself the type to be answering an advertisement like this . . .*

They all said that. Why, Junebug didn't know. Hell, she wanted them to answer the ad, didn't she? Or she wouldn't have placed it. So why did they all act like answering an ad was a bad thing?

At least this one was more direct than most when she finally got past the "I'm not the type" coyness. *You've done the courtesy of being honest in your advertisement, which my Granny Colefax says is an admirable quality, as most men are arrant liars.*

Arrant. That was a good word. Junebug would look that up in the dictionary next time she stole it from Kit's trunk of books. Still reading, she wandered back inside to collect a fresh cup of coffee. Then she settled in on the porch of the trading post to ponder this woman.

Since we're founding this correspondence on the promise of honesty—
Junebug pulled a face. Well, sort of. The ad in the *Matrimonial News* had been honest enough about Morgan; it just wasn't honest about who had placed it. The words *surfeit of family* were the only suggestion of Junebug's existence.

I shall tell you my qualities plain, Miss Nebraska promised.

Junebug rolled her eyes. This was where they waxed lyrical about their charms or the contents of their glory boxes. Most of which were completely useless to Junebug. What did she need with a good soprano voice or a wholecloth quilt? Let's hope Miss Nebraska included pies and cakes in her list of qualities . . .

I'm a tall woman, and strong. No one has ever labeled me beautiful, but I'm not homely neither. I always wished I looked like my sister Naomi, who is pretty as a picture, but my mother says it's not right to wish for what we don't have and that at least I don't have to fight the sin of vanity, like Naomi does. So, I'll tell you that I'm well-formed and not vain, and grateful for both.

This Naomi sounded like she might be a woman in Willabelle's vein. Junebug felt a stab of sympathy for Miss Nebraska, and then she flicked to the end of the sheaf of pages, looking for her name. *Miss Epiphany Hopgood.*

Epiphany. Hell, that was a name and a half. Junebug had a vague memory of the word. It was akin to getting hit on the head hard with an idea, she thought.

Promising.

I'm hardy and not prone to illness and, forgive the bluntness, according to Granny Colefax I'm built for bearing children.

Children. Let's not rush things. Junebug felt an irrational flare of jealousy. Of course marriage led to children, but not yet . . . she wasn't ready for Morgan to be parenting anyone but her.

I've all the necessary skills of housekeeping, including cooking, which I note is one of your necessary requirements.

This was getting good. Junebug sat up straighter.

My specialties . . .

Lord, she had specialties! That's what Junebug needed.

. . . include corn fritters, corn bread, sweet and salty roast corn . . .

They must have a lot of corn in Nebraska.

. . . pork chops, ham steaks, fried chicken regular and southern style . . .

Junebug had no idea what southerners did to chicken, but she was willing to give it a try.

. . . also southern fried catfish, and fish pie, although I do believe nothing beats throwing a bass or a walleye straight from the stream into a skillet of butter and frying it nice and simple.

Junebug wouldn't complain about simple fried fish, so long as she wasn't the one doing the frying.

I will confess to a sweet tooth and so also make more than my share of desserts. I'm not sure if you consider this an asset or a failing of character (my mother declares it the latter, as she is not one for self-indulgence and she says I am profligate with sugar).

Definitely an asset, Junebug thought fervently. This woman was the answer to her prayers! Her mouth watered as she read the list of sweets, which Miss Epiphany Hopgood couldn't seem to stop herself from adding (even though her mother would disapprove).

Fried apples with fine sugar, gooseberry pie, honey cake, molasses pie, milk pudding and of course the usual range of cakes.

The usual range of cakes! Like cakes were *usual*!

Junebug's heart was skipping a jig in her chest. She'd found her wife!

I can keep a thriving kitchen garden and own my own cow and half a dozen chickens. These were gifted to me by my Granny Hopgood, who hoped a milk cow and some brooders might help my marriage chances.

Junebug could care less about another cow—she had her own to milk. And as for chickens, she had enough of those too. But *cakes!*

Lord, she'd done it. She'd found the needle in the haystack here. She'd best gather up the chokecherries this season, so the woman could bake up a pie as soon as she got here.

Junebug headed back inside to the desk and reached for her writing paper. It was only as she pulled her inkwell toward her that she remembered she had a problem.

Morgan.

Two problems.

Telling Morgan. And then introducing him to the woman—and not having her turn straight back around and run home.

He just wasn't an easy man to off-load. Listen to him out there, cursing a blue streak through the mellow afternoon. The man was too fractious by half. Junebug took note of some new words, planning to look them up in the dictionary, when she looked up *arrant*.

She'd been as honest as she could in the ad, because she sure didn't want to sell some poor unsuspecting woman a false bill of goods. These potential brides needed to know he was an ornery old cuss, stubborn as hell and not prone to niceties.

I think patience is the best virtue, don't you? Miss Epiphany Hopgood wrote, a little shyly, Junebug thought. Shyness wasn't ideal. *It's hard-won, but really the only thing that keeps harmony. I confess I have to wrestle hard with myself to practice it, but I win more often than not, and have trained myself to be a patient person.*

Well, that was good, wasn't it? Morgan would try the patience of a saint, so the woman would need a dose of patience. And the notion of wrestling was also helpful. It implied a warrior spirit, as Sour Eagle would say.

Over yonder, there was a great crashing and a bellow loud

enough to shake the oilcloth over the trading post windows. Then a whole bunch of new words. Absently, Junebug scrawled them down, so she wouldn't forget to look up what they meant.

I will caution you, Mr. McBride, I am not always an easy woman. But I will endeavor to do everything in my power to make you a house you'll be happy to come home to.

Junebug chewed on the tip of her fountain pen as she stared at the catalog, which she'd dropped on the counter. Forget happy to come home to, she wanted him to *stay put*.

Not an easy woman, huh?

Junebug listened to the invectives Morgan was shouting out in the meadow. You know, that might be just the thing. He wasn't an easy man, so why would he need an easy woman? A difficult woman with a dose of patience and a steady output of cakes might be just the thing.

For all of them.

Dear Miss Hopgood, Junebug wrote, coming to a firm decision, *I'm glad you answered my advertisement. Your letter was a breath of fresh air after the mail I've received from a slew of ninnyhammers. I appreciate your honest talk . . .*

Especially about the desserts . . .

. . . and I hope you took my plain speaking serious. I am about as difficult a man as you could find, so your patience will come in mighty handy.

Junebug found herself whistling as she filled two pages with Morgan's honest faults. And then another two with praises for her talk of pies.

This time she was sure the mail-order bride thing would work perfectly.

Outside, there was mayhem as the roof of the new house came down. But in here, everything was just dandy.

Two

Joshua, Nebraska

Epiphany Hopgood was resolved. This time she was going to get married, come hell or high water. She'd packed her things, organized train tickets for herself and Granny Colefax and rehearsed her speech to her parents in her head. She'd set her mind on marriage, and marriage was what she was going to get.

She was twenty-two (nearly twenty-three) years of age and fast running out of time. All of her sisters bar one had been safely, if not always happily, married off, and Pip was at risk of being stuck home forever, caring for her parents in their old age, like poor Esther Greenleaf. Holy crow, the last thing she wanted was to end up like Esther. The woman was like a mote of dust in her parents' house, floating about without weight or substance. Her youth had faded off into a dun-colored middle age, and she did nothing but cook and clean and do needlework for those sour old people who'd birthed her. Sometimes, when Pip went into town, she saw Esther sitting out on the Greenleafs' front porch, shucking corn or shelling peas, and she could just see the desperation in her, like river water roiling below the March ice. Pip felt the chill of it down her spine. It was like seeing a specter of your future self.

Pip imagined being left in the house alone with her parents, and it wasn't a happy imagining. Her brooding, melancholy, silent father, who sat in the parlor every evening, resembling nothing so much as the grandfather clock, and her mother . . . ugh, her *mother.* The very thought of living with them for the rest of her life made Pip feel like she was suffocating. Pip's youngest sister, Hope, had just turned sixteen and was starting to get attention, so Pip didn't have much time. Once Hope was gone, Pip would be the sacrificial daughter, for sure. She was nearly out of time, but also, unfortunately, nearly out of prospects.

Pip's hometown had stamped her with the stain of spinsterhood long ago. It was her own fault. She was too loud, too opinionated, too strong-willed, too tall, too active, too strong, too *everything.* Her first potential fiancé, Samuel Arcross, hadn't been shy in saying so either. The Arcrosses owned the farm next door to the Hopgoods, and Pip's and Samuel's parents had thought it was a good match. Samuel thought otherwise. The day Pip and her parents had expected him to propose, he'd gone to ground, leaving his parents to have an awkward conversation with Pip's father, wriggling out of all their promises. That had been one of the most humiliating days of Pip's life. She'd been sixteen and stupidly excited about the thought of marriage. Everything had seemed spring-fresh and sparkling, and the future was something to run toward, with her arms wide open, ready to hug the darn life out of it.

She'd learned a lot since then.

Pip remembered the swirling excitement as they waited for the Arcrosses to arrive. Pip's mother had scrubbed every last inch of the house and pulled out the good china plates, to best display Pip's prettily decorated honey cookies. Pip's mother and her older sister Naomi had also scrubbed Pip to within an inch of her life, making her squeal as they tried to tame the wild auburn tangle of her hair. Her mother had pinched Pip's cheeks so hard to get color into them that Pip had to restrain the urge to pinch her mother back. Pip had been crammed into a new pink dress, made special for the occasion of her engagement. She had loved that dress so much. At least, at first. It was a floor-length, grown-up affair, with puffy sleeves and a ruffle at the hem. Nothing too fancy, because Pip's mother didn't hold with fancy, but it was the best thing Pip had ever owned and she felt like a newly minted coin.

And then she'd gone downstairs, her mother and Naomi escorting her, fussing over her hair, which could never quite be contained, no matter how skin-pullingly tight they braided and pinned it, only to find her father arguing with the Arcrosses in the parlor. Pip had pulled up short before the closed door, startled by the sound of raised voices.

Thank heavens for small mercies the door had been closed, Pip thought afterward. Imagine if she'd barged in on them—imagine if *they* knew she'd heard everything they'd said about her. Imagine having to meet them in the street, or at church, all of them knowing that *she* knew what they thought of her and trying to pretend otherwise.

It would be too mortifying.

"You can't blame the boy for not wanting her," Mrs. Arcross had been snapping as Pip lurched to a halt outside the parlor. Pip could hear her clearly through the door. "She's no beauty, Timothy, and Samuel is a young man, full of oats."

Pip heard Naomi's indrawn breath behind her. Oh, the humiliation.

"You're backing out because of the way she looks?" Pip's father had sounded astonished.

Pip had been frozen in place. Sometimes she still dreamed about the parlor door, about the meannesses spoken behind it. She'd known the Arcrosses all her life. They'd known *her* all Sam's life. How could this be happening *today*, on the day she was spit-and-polished and waiting for him to propose? Holy crow, she looked the same today as she'd looked yesterday! Maybe even better, given the new dress and the braids.

"Now, Timothy, you know there was no firm agreement," Mr. Arcross growled. "It was just an idea between friends."

"It was more than an idea!" Pip's father had been hot under the collar, which was rare for him. "Where in tarnation is he? She's up there making herself nice for him and he has the gall to run off?"

"If she was just a touch plain, that would be one thing," Mr. Arcross interposed bluntly, "but it's more than that. The girl is beyond prettifying."

"Of course, she's not much to look at," Pip's very own father agreed, "but beauty is nothing to build a marriage on. Epiphany may be homely, but she's strong. Healthy. Perfectly capable of making a fine wife."

Homely? Pip had felt the color flare in her sorely pinched cheeks. She didn't feel at all like a newly minted coin anymore. She felt like a buck being passed.

"No one's disputing that the girl is healthy and strong, Timothy," Mr. Arcross grumbled. "Or that she's of good stock."

Now they were talking about her like she was a heifer. Pip's whole body felt like a pot of oil, roiling with heat. They didn't want her? *Samuel* didn't want her? Because of the way she looked?

Abruptly she felt big and clumsy in her pink dress.

"Healthy and strong is all good. But she's not feminine, Timothy. The boy feels he deserves a proper girl. Not a . . ." Mr. Arcross trailed off, leaving Pip imagining the worst. Not a what? What could be worse than being referred to as a homely heifer? And what did that mean, a *proper girl*?

Pip felt her mother at her back. *She* knew what it meant. She'd always known. Every time she scolded Pip for running instead of walking, or tried to compress her height with a stack of books on her head, or soaked her hands in paraffin to try to soften them;

every time she'd given Pip a lecture on manners and how to be a lady . . . she'd known. Pip had just never really believed her.

"I cain't say I blame him for begging off," Mr. Arcross confessed. "And if you were honest, Timothy, you wouldn't either. Now, no one is casting aspersions on the girl. We all know she's got a good heart." Mr. Arcross had shifted to trying to console Pip's father. "But when we made our plans, the kids were still young 'uns. No one could foresee how tall she'd get. Mercy, she's taller than Samuel! What man wants a woman taller than him?"

Pip heard her mother's dress rustle. Don't say anything, she begged her silently, remembering every time she'd refused to put the books on her head.

"Or stronger than him," Mrs. Arcross had added. "The girl looks like she could wrestle a bull and win. It's just not . . . what Samuel wants."

Damn Samuel Arcross. That stubby little man. How dare he. How dare he wait until she was trussed up in a new dress, her heart in her hands, before he decided he didn't want her. Pip had a mind to stalk right over to the Arcross farm and give him an earful. She wasn't a *proper girl*? Well, he sure as sugar wasn't a proper man.

It was a relief to grab hold of her shame and turn it into anger. Samuel Arcross might be good-looking, but he had less stuffing than a scarecrow.

"And he didn't know this until today?" Pip's father complained. "What am I supposed to tell her?"

"Tell her whatever you wish. Tell her he's not ready to get married yet. Or that he's in love with someone else."

"What has love got to do with it?" Pip's father sounded disgusted. "Marriage isn't about love. It's about practicalities."

"Well, the practicality is, without some loving urges, no marriage can be final, Timothy. You don't want the girl barren for life, do you?"

Pip felt like she'd been kicked. Samuel found her so repulsive that he didn't even think he could consummate the marriage?

That worm. How dare he tell his parents *that*. Pip had had enough. She elbowed her mother and sister aside and headed for the yard, pulling the painful pins from her hair as she went. Just wait till she got hold of that stuffingless scarecrow. She'd show him what a *proper girl* was, and then he'd think twice about telling people she wasn't one.

She got roughly halfway across the yard before it occurred to her that yelling at Samuel Arcross would only compound her humiliation. Right now, only her mother and Naomi knew that she'd heard those horrible things, and her mother would consider this a family stain, one that would need some serious bleaching. And they'd never be able to bleach it if she went storming over to the Arcrosses', screeching like a barn owl. Imagine the gossip that would follow. So, while it might have felt powerfully good to yell at Samuel Arcross, Pip hadn't. Because then she would have had to return to her mother's disappointment, which was as icy as a fall through a fishing hole into December waters. And to Naomi's hysteria over her own reputation being tarnished. And to her father's stolid grandfather-clock-like certainty that she was a burden to be borne.

Ultimately, it wasn't worth the trouble. Instead, she'd swerved and headed into the stable, straight to Sadie, her red mare, who never judged her. She'd buried her face in Sadie's neck, inhaling that comforting horse smell. She could feel Sadie's hot breath and hear her hooves shifting on the hard-packed earth floor. Sadie leaned into the hug. Pip gave her a pat.

"There's only one cure for it," she told the horse.

Sadie whickered.

What Pip needed was to saddle up and ride out, to get away from this claustrophobic house and into the bright sunshine. She needed to feel the wind and smell the green of growing things.

She needed Sadie to gallop full tilt down the straight dirt roads, until Pip felt like she was flying. Free.

But she couldn't. Because she was in the dumb dress, with its constraining skirt. She could hardly hike it up to her thighs, could she? And even if she could, she didn't fancy the chafing she'd suffer. Who'd be born a girl if they could help it? If she'd been born a boy, being tall would be a good thing, as would being strong. She could be as ugly as sin, and still find someone to marry, so long as she could provide for them. And she'd be wearing *pants*. She could ride whenever she liked.

Well, if she couldn't ride, she'd have to work off these nasty feelings another way. Pip had grabbed a shovel and set to mucking out the stable, feeling a sharp satisfaction as her new pink dress was splattered with the muck. She never wanted to wear the dumb dress again, not ever, and by mucking out the stables in it she made sure she never had to. Shovel by shovel, she worked off her rage, her hem growing black with dirt, and her bodice stained with sweat. Oh, it had felt good to get her heart rate up. And it gave her a sense of satisfaction to see the stables fall into order as she worked. Things went into their places. Calm descended. And before long she was counting herself lucky *not* to be hitched to Samuel Arcross and his shallow-witted family. It had been a providential escape, that's what it had been. She was better out of it.

Although deep down, packed away in the dark and out of sight, the shame of the day sat there, festering.

At the time Pip had thought that would be the most humiliating moment of her life. But then came others. The time her brothers had escorted her to a dance in the Salters' barn, and not a single man asked her to dance. Not even her wretched brothers. The time her father offered her hand to Jim Whitney—Jim Whitney, the widower with five kids, who was in desperate need of a wife— and he'd *refused*. Because even the desperate man wasn't *that* desperate.

The thing was, men in these parts wanted their women healthy and strong, but also girly as all get-out. They liked small hands and feet, and narrow shoulders, and delicate features. They liked a downcast gaze and a girlish giggle and a dash of coyness. None of which came naturally to Pip.

It got so she started thinking that there was something very wrong with her. When she went into town she grew too ashamed to meet people's eyes, knowing they all thought she was defective. Homely. *Unwomanly.*

And then came the horrid day when she was formally consigned to spinsterhood. Her parents simply gave up on her. They announced it at Sunday dinner, in front of the entire family. Which was their way. It was a horrid way, and Pip hated it. They were all crammed into the dining room, jammed elbow to elbow along her mother's long table. Every Sunday her brothers and sisters and their families came in various combinations, to eat modest servings of her mother's stingy meals. There was never enough to go round. Pip's mother didn't approve of waste, and she didn't approve of gluttony. Pip had taken to sneaking a slice of bread before dinner, just to keep her from being irritable with hunger. Sundays were hard enough without adding hunger-rage to the mix.

This particular Sunday, Naomi and her husband were in attendance, along with Pip's brother John and his wife, Ruth, and their children. The dining room could barely contain them all. Granny Hopgood and Granny Colefax were there, too, as they lived at the Hopgood farm, resentfully sharing a room upstairs. They didn't get along and were prone to not speaking. Mother claimed it was peaceful for everyone when they were spatting, because at least no one had to listen to them anymore.

Father sat at the head of the table, flanked by Mother and Granny Hopgood; Pip was sitting at the children's end, along with Hope and Granny Colefax. Hope, being sixteen, was unimpressed to be

still sitting with the children. Pip and Granny Colefax were resigned to it.

"Your father had a long conversation with Walter Millard this
morning," Pip's mother said, as she passed the bowl of peas down
the table.

Pip was barely listening. She didn't think her mother was speaking to her. What did Walter Millard have to do with her? He was
the old man who sat in the front pew at church; he had a farm farther west and kept himself to himself.

"And he has decided *not* to make an offer for Epiphany."

Pip felt every single head turn her way. She went hot and cold.

"Walter *Millard?*" she clarified. Surely she'd misheard. They
hadn't asked Walter Millard to take her. They couldn't have. He
was older than the Bible.

Pip's mother sighed, as only she could, putting real backbone
into it. Then she shook her head regretfully. "I'm afraid your father
and I feel that's the end of the matter. Mr. Millard was our final
option."

"Walter Millard turned her down?" Pip's brother John was disbelieving.

Pip wished she could crawl under the table and not come out
again until dinner was over.

"Surely he turned her down only because he's not in the market
for a wife?" Ruth suggested, trying to be kind. Ruth had the luxury
of being kind. She was five foot one, cute as a button and *married*.

"He says he can get a better wife through the *Matrimonial News*,"
Granny Hopgood blared. "Imagine." She was partially deaf and
prone to speaking at volume.

The peas reached Pip. She stared down at the sea of green globes
and imagined sitting on the front porch and popping them from
their shells, one by one, while her mother sat there sighing and
tutting, infinitely disappointed in her. For the rest of her life.

"Surely you haven't tried *every* man in the county," Naomi said, trying to be kinder than Ruth. "Pip's a great cook. There must be a man out there who values cooking?"

"It makes no sense to me why we can't find you a husband, Epiphany." There went her mother sighing again. Pip felt the December waters closing over her head.

Well, it certainly made no sense to Pip why she couldn't find a husband. She scowled down at the peas. No matter what they said, she couldn't really see that there was anything wrong with her. Meanwhile Samuel Arcross was an understuffed shirt, Jim Whitney was a long streak of misery and Walter Millard was as sapless as a cord of stovewood.

When Pip looked in the mirror, she was clearly missing what everyone else saw. She didn't think she was as bad as all that. Sure, she was tall, but she was well-formed. And sure, she was strong, but it meant she was firm in all the right places. Sure, she might not have silky neat hair, but her dark auburn waves were striking, especially against her skin, which didn't have a single freckle. Even Naomi had freckles. And sure, Pip didn't have delicate features, but she *liked* her features. She liked her wide mouth better than Naomi's pursed little rosebud mouth, and she liked her hazel eyes, which were the greenish gold of leaves on the turn at the end of summer, and she liked her strong arched brows.

Lately she'd been thinking that maybe the problem wasn't with *her*. Maybe the problem was with all these men.

Maybe she needed to find a different kind of man?

"There's not a single man in the county we haven't considered," Pip's father said, bending over his Sunday dinner. "There's no point in barking at a knot, so let's dismiss the matter."

He wasn't dismissing the matter, Pip thought sullenly; he was dismissing *her*.

"We can all be grateful Epiphany has a home with us," Pip's

mother said. "A home where she will always be welcome." She sounded almost as grim as Pip felt.

Pip stared into the bowl of peas, as though scrying the future in their green circles. All she could see was that she hated peas. And the hours it took to shell them.

"I never did like peas either," Granny Colefax said, taking the bowl from Pip and passing it along. "They're too smug."

As dinner progressed Pip felt the walls closing in on her. Every scrape of cutlery against the good dinner plates made her wince. The heavy smell of gravy turned her stomach. And the way the conversation kept returning to her unmarriageable state was an utter trial.

"Perhaps we can send Pip to Uncle Clem in Spiggot?" John suggested. "There's bound to be men in Spiggot."

"I think your sister has been through enough," Pip's mother said flatly, as she cut her food up into smaller and smaller pieces. "And if she hasn't, your father and I certainly have."

"Every family needs a girl at home," Granny Hopgood announced, practically yelling it down the table. "There's no shame in spinsterhood. My sister Frannie never married, and she was a blessing to my parents."

"Better you than me," Hope murmured to Pip, as she speared a pea with the tines of her fork.

Oh God.

"Excuse me, I'm not feeling well." Pip almost knocked her chair over in her haste to get up from the table. If she stayed here another moment, she was liable to faint dead away from the lack of air in this room. Or throw peas at everyone.

She was aware of the syrupy weight of pity in their gazes as they watched her go.

She plunged outside onto the front porch and gulped at the afternoon air, like a fish out of water. The cornfields stretched, green in every direction, the leaves making dry scratching sounds as the stalks clicked together in the breeze. The blue May sky was streaked with pale clouds. Pip grabbed hold of the porch rail and tried to calm herself.

Why did she feel like she was being buried alive?

She'd stood on this porch every day of her life, watching corn planted, grown and harvested. She'd watched the rain fall and the snow swirl. This was her home.

So why did she feel so out of place?

"You all right, girlie?" The screen door creaked as Granny Colefax emerged from the cool of the house to check on her. Granny held a hand up to shield her eyes from the brightness of the day.

No. No, Pip wasn't all right. She felt herself turning into Esther Greenleaf, no matter how she fought it. A living dust mote. But she couldn't say any of that. All she could say was, "Fine. I'm fine." She forced a smile. "It was just a bit close in there."

"It's always close." Granny Colefax joined her at the rail, her gaze sharp. "They ought to open the windows."

"Mother doesn't like the dust."

"Then she ought to get a canary, so we know when the air's running low."

The old lady barely reached Pip's shoulder; beside her, Pip felt like a big lump. Granny Colefax followed Pip's gaze and took in the cornfields. "Your grandfather loved these plains," she said thoughtfully. "Loved 'em more than he loved anything."

Pip wasn't in the mood to think about her grandfather now. He'd been a terse and intimidating man, rigid as a tent pole, prone to talking about agriculture in a rumbling monotone.

"Me, now, I hate the plains."

Pip was startled. She looked down to find Granny Colefax regarding the cornfield balefully.

"They're too flat." The old woman pursed her lips. "No matter where you look: flat. Straight roads for miles. Not a twist, not a turn. You can see past the darn horizon. What fun is that? Nothing can surprise you around here." Her brown eyes flicked up to Pip. They were sly. "Have you seen the view from my room?"

"Of course. It's the same as mine."

"Don't sass. No two views are the same," Granny Colefax said impatiently. "Come." Her surprisingly strong grip hooked around Pip's wrist, and she pulled her away from the rail.

"Granny," Pip protested. She didn't want to go back inside, and she didn't care a fig for the view from her grandmother's room. She didn't need to look to know what she'd see. Corn. As far as the eye could see.

But her strange old grandmother was unrelenting. Up the narrow stairs they went, and into the room at the side of the house that Granny Colefax shared with Granny Hopgood. Their room was stuffed full of furniture: the Colefax dresser was jammed hard against the Hopgood bureau; Granny Colefax's heavy oak writing desk hulked over Granny Hopgood's dainty china cabinet. Their whole lives were packed in there. Pip found it depressing.

Granny Hopgood's side was neat as a pin, thick with the smell of talcum powder and medicinal tonic; Granny Colefax's was an explosion of blankets and clothing, books and newspapers, and smelled like ginger cookies and stale coffee. Granny Hopgood's bed was made; Granny Colefax's was not.

Pip obediently went to the window and took in the view. Corn. Big cloud-streaked skies. And more corn. "I see," Pip lied. "You're right, it's completely different from this window than from mine."

"Oh, hush up, who cares about the view."

Granny was definitely losing her marbles. Either that, or she'd been at Granny Hopgood's tonics. They were higher proof than the Salter boys' moonshine.

"Here." Granny Colefax thrust a newspaper at her. "This is what I want you to look at, not corn. I could care less about corn. If peas are smug, corn is crass. I've had enough of rude vegetables."

She whacked Pip gently with the newspaper. "This is the answer to your problems."

Pip took it from her. The *Matrimonial News*. "You're not serious."

"I am." Granny Colefax was obdurate. "If Walter Millard can order himself up a wife, I figure a smart girl like you can easily find a husband."

Dear Lord, she *was* serious.

"Just don't let your mother see it. Not yet." Granny Colefax glanced over her shoulder at the open door. "You know what Verity's like. She can suck the life from an egg."

"I don't think that's a saying, Granny." Pip stared down at the newspaper. *A weekly journal devoted to the interests of Love, Courtship and Marriage.*

"If it's not, it should be, especially when it comes to your mother. That girl was born with a lemon in her mouth."

Pip squinted at the ads. They were in very small print, and there were many of them crammed on the page. *Bachelor (42) seeks spinster (under 40); German merchant looking for a respectable woman for the purpose of matrimony; Widower still in his prime hopes to find a female who doesn't mind children (7 of them).* There were miners and ranchers, cowboys and trappers, farmers and saloonkeepers; old men, young men; men of means and men looking to make their fortunes; men with land and men with nothing but hopes and dreams. Men from Idaho, Kansas, Texas, Minnesota, Montana. All of them looking for wives.

Pip felt her heart skip a beat. Her whole life she'd dreamed of being a wife. Mistress of her own house, with a man who came into her kitchen after a long day, warming the cold from his bones by her stove, staring at her with raw appreciation as she fed him, moaning with delight as she rubbed the trials of the day from his shoulders, like she saw Naomi do once to her husband.

She wanted to be useful. To be needed.

Was that too much to ask?

"Don't go writing to anyone without checking with me first," Granny Colefax ordered her. "You might be tall as a tree, but you're green as a sapling. I don't want you picking any malingerers or villains, you hear? You want a good, solid, respectable man. I don't hold with any of this poetry."

"Poetry?" Pip hadn't seen any poetry.

"Page four." Granny reached for a stack of newspapers next to her bed. "Here, there's all these too." She handed them over.

"Why do you have these?" Pip asked, her head spinning. Only moments ago she was facing a lifetime of spinsterhood, and now she had an armful of potential husbands.

"Why do you think? I was looking for a husband."

"*You* were looking for a husband?" Pip couldn't have been more surprised if Granny Colefax had announced she was going to be a dancing girl down at the saloon.

"What? You think I'm too old?" Granny fixed her with a briny look.

"*Yes.*" Honestly. She was a *grandmother.*

"See, you're green as a sapling," Granny grumbled. "You got no idea of a woman's needs. But you will, girlie, you will." She pushed Pip toward the door. "Go get those papers hidden somewhere in your room and let's get down before we miss dessert. I saw you making that cake and I'm not of a mind to miss it."

How many advertisements were there in that stack of papers, Pip wondered, once she and Granny had returned to the table. Hundreds? Thousands? There must be at least one in there who valued a nice wedge of angel food cake over a pretty face, she thought, as she watched her mother shave disappointing slices off the cake. She imagined a man alone would appreciate a woman who could cook.

How she managed to get through the rest of the meal, she didn't know. She hurried through the dishes and swept the kitchen fast as a dervish, and then locked herself in her room for an afternoon with the *Matrimonial News.*

Oh yes, she was resolved. She didn't need her parents to find her a husband. She was going to find one all on her own. And she was going to be as honest about herself as she could be, so his face didn't fall when he saw her. She was going to tell him she was tall and she was strong; that she wasn't a beauty. But she was also going to tell him what a fine wife she'd make. And somewhere beyond the cornfields there was a man who would agree with her.

Pip circled the ads that she liked, and Granny Colefax crossed them out. She said they were too glib, or too wordy, or that she didn't like butchers, or miners, or saloonkeepers. After a lot of arguing, they settled on one they agreed on. Mr. McBride from Montana.

"He's an odd duck," Granny Colefax admitted, "but an honest one. The last thing you want to do is fetch up in the wilderness to find you've been peddled lies. It's much better to know what you're getting into. Trust me. I had no idea what I was getting into when I said yes to your grandfather."

Mrs. Morgan McBride had a good ring to it. *Epiphany McBride, of Buck's Creek, Montana.* Oh yes, it sounded fine.

"They have mountains in Montana," Granny Colefax said with no small measure of satisfaction. "There's bound to be surprises in the mountains."

Granny had no idea how right she was. The mountains of Montana proved to be nothing *but* surprises.

Three

Morgan McBride's luck was turning. He could feel it. The past six years had been like something out of a nightmare. He'd come to Buck's Creek that fall six years ago only to check on Ma and the kids, planning a fleeting visit, a kiss on the cheek and a how-do-you-do. He'd been away on the trail for more than a year that time, and he knew Ma fretted over him. He'd come home for her, because it made her happy. He'd bought gifts for the family in Kansas City at the end of his last cattle drive: ribbons for the girls, a dictionary for Kit (and hadn't that been a nuisance to lug about), a hunting knife for Charlie, a pack of cards for Beau, new fiddle strings for Jonah; and for Ma he bought some fancy violet-scented water and a pot of almond face cream that promised youth and vitality. His ma had been a good-looking woman, and he knew she found the mountains a hard and spartan life.

Morgan had planned to blow in and bestow his gifts, holding his smile in place no matter what the old man said, and then blow back out again before winter could trap him there. But that wasn't how things panned out.

Instead, he'd got home just in time to catch Ma's last days.

A woeful, heartbreaking time that had been, Morgan thought as he brought a fistful of forget-me-nots and wild roses to his mother's grave on this sunny day six years later. From her graveside he could hear the rush of the creek, the clang of Kit's hammer striking iron in the forge and Junebug's chatter drifting over from the trading post. Today's Buck's Creek wasn't the place his mother had lived and died in. Morgan had worked hard to make it a better place. Because he'd failed her in so many other ways.

Today Buck's Creek held the family cabin and a forge as well as the rambling trading post; there was a stocked root cellar, a vegetable patch and a barn, a chicken coop and a cookhouse. And from where she rested under the chokecherry tree, Ma had a clear view of Kit and Maddy's brand-new house; from here Ma would be able to see her grandchildren born and raised. Morgan had given her that at least.

How she would have loved a house like Maddy's, he thought as he looked across the meadow at the two-story clapboard building. It was a simple timber-frame affair, but he was proud of it. Ma would have loved the fact that it had real glass in the windows instead of oilcloth; she would have loved the wood-burning stove they'd ordered all the way from Chicago, and the fancy brass bed with its real feather mattress. In Maddy's joy, Morgan had seen his mother. Ma would have run her hand over the new stove just like that, marveling that it was *hers*.

Ma had never had much of anything. Just a pack of kids and a life of trouble.

Morgan remembered the iron dread that had closed over him when he'd returned to Buck's Creek to find his mother on her pallet in the trading post, curled up with the sweating sickness. She'd been in a terrible state. And that *waste* of a man she'd married—Morgan refused to call him his father—had done nothing to ease her passage. He'd been too busy easing himself in a jug full of moonshine.

The look in her eyes when she'd seen Morgan walk in . . .

The hope. The relief. It had filled him with an airless terror; it had settled a coldness in his bones that he'd not shaken since. She'd looked like an animal caught in a trap . . . and she'd looked at *him* like he'd come to save her.

But what salvation did he offer? All he had was violet-water and face cream. Morgan had brushed her damp hair from her forehead and tried to keep his composure.

"You're home," she'd whispered.

Home. It wasn't a word he treasured.

And the home he'd returned to was even worse than the one he'd left. All the girls except for Junebug were gone, buried in a cluster under the chokecherry tree. It was a miracle Junebug was still alive and kicking, as she'd had the same sweating sickness that was now stealing their mother from them. After her illness, Junebug was like a rickety newborn colt, all elbows and skinny legs, her gray eyes giant in her hollow face. But even knocked down by illness, she sure could talk. She'd lit up when Morgan walked in, full of news about their trials and tribulations; she had no time for his ribbons and wanted to know why she couldn't have a hunting knife like Charlie. Morgan noticed she wouldn't look at Ma and, as she talked, she wrung her hands. The poor kid was tense with feeling.

Kit and Charlie had done a fair enough job of keeping the young ones alive, fishing and trapping the best they could, but they were all underfed and thin with looming grief. They'd eaten through the staples in the trading post, and no one had stocked for winter, which was close upon them.

"Where is he?" Morgan had demanded as soon as Ma had drifted off into a pained and fractious sleep.

They'd all known who he meant.

Kit and Charlie had shrugged, in that eerie synchronized way they had. They'd been lanky teens then. Watchful and not big talkers.

"He's off visiting," Junebug had told Morgan helpfully.

"That's what we tell her," Kit said as soon as Junebug was out of earshot.

"He's probably passed out down by the river," Charlie said, as though it was normal for your pa to be insensible in the tall grass while your ma was dying right in front of you. The whole lot of them were off-kilter from the wretchedness of it all.

They were all packed into the trading post, and it stank to high heaven of tanned hides and illness. And moonshine. Their pa had never got around to building that cabin he'd always promised; his family lived shoulder to shoulder with the sacks of sugar, piles of rank hides and his booze. Their pa was a man whose dreams came from a bottle, and then came to no good. Morgan had hunted through the trading post until he'd found the old man's moonshine still. It was a big heavy thing, but Morgan was strong. And he wasn't having his mother die inhaling the stink of that man's liquor. Morgan hauled the thing outside and upended it, letting the astringent liquor splash into the dirt. And then he'd smashed it to pieces.

"What are you doing?" Beau had followed him, horrified, leaning over the rail. He was white as a ghost at the thought of their father returning to find his liquor gone. "He'll go rabid when he sees!"

"Let him." Morgan hurled the pieces of the broken still into the creek. Morgan was younger, bigger and stronger than the old man. And he had enough anger in him for ten men. Let the old man come.

Most of those memories were sour ones. Morgan didn't want to wallow in them; he tried to shake free of them as he bent over his mother's grave. Years had tumbled by, like the creek water tumbling through the meadow. Time had passed and his mother wasn't suffering anymore, and none of them had to live in the trading post or put up with the old man. There was no more hunger, no more wretchedness. He'd done his duty.

"You always did have a soft spot for silly flowers," Morgan said gruffly to his ma, as he laid his modest bunch of wildflowers against the wonky cross on her grave. Time had silvered the wooden cross and smoothed the edges off her name. The leaves of the choke-cherry tree rustled above Morgan's head as he lowered himself to sit against its trunk. He sighed and stared out across the creek, which was tumbling by as always, throwing spangles of June sunshine back at the sky. "I guess you're wondering what I'm here for, since I'm not usually one for flowers. Probably makes you suspicious."

Sometimes he came to talk to her. It helped during the hard years, to feel like she was listening, like she understood. God knew he wasn't built for raising kids. He wasn't a patient man at the best of times. The boys had been hard enough, but then there was Junebug . . . and that kid had almost been the death of him, a dozen times over.

Ma had known what she was asking at the end there, Morgan thought, as he watched the breeze bend the meadow grass. She'd known she was asking him to give up his life on the trail, to surrender his youth, his freedom. But she'd also known that he wasn't built for this, and that he'd struggle. She'd not asked it of him lightly.

He cain't care for them, Morgan, and the twins ain't full-grown. Her voice had been whispery, like fall leaves rustling as they fell. *They need you.*

Her hand had touched his. It was like being touched by a spirit; she'd had no weight left to her.

Don't let me pass worrying about them. Please let me go in peace.

She wanted more of him than he wanted to give. But how could he refuse? What kind of man would he be?

A man like his father.

So that day the weight of the family had landed squarely on Morgan's shoulders. And what else could he do but shoulder it?

Absently, Morgan pulled the chickweed from her resting place. "I've come to talk." Morgan turned the chickweed over in his hand; the flowers were dainty white stars. Maybe he shouldn't pull it up. It was pretty, and she deserved pretty.

"Not just talk. I've come to ask permission, I suppose," Morgan admitted. He had a heavy feeling in his stomach, like he was letting her down. Even though he'd done his best. The kids were raised up—well, all but Junebug—and he wasn't needed no more. Not like he had been back then.

Morgan glanced over at the trading post. He could see Junebug out on the porch, jawing away with Sour Eagle and Thunderhead Bill, who'd set up camp for the summer. Nothing Morgan said would move them along faster than they wanted to move. It was plain irksome. But at least they kept Junebug occupied, and for that he was grateful. That girl could talk the hind leg off a mule.

"Vern Little Horse came by the trading post the other week," Morgan told his mother's wonky cross, running his thumb over the starry chickweed flowers. "He said my old trail boss Frank Ward is in Miles City, with the few cattle that survived the winter."

It had been a bad winter. Worst on memory—worse even than the winter after Ma died, when they'd been holed up in the trading post, without enough food. Just him and the kids. The old man had lit out by then, and Charlie had lit out after him. It had been a miserable, grieving winter, with them all heartbroken over Ma and worried sick about Charlie. Blizzard after blizzard had howled at the chinks in the palings, icing over their water pails, giving them chilblains and frostnip. The meadow had become a featureless white plain. Even if Morgan had been able to go after Charlie, how would he have been able to track him, with everything hidden by snow?

Morgan still dreamed about Charlie. They'd not heard from him since he'd left six years ago. He'd be a man now. Sometimes Morgan caught sight of Kit and his breath stopped. That's how

Charlie would look now. Maybe not so big, unless he'd taken up blacksmithing like Kit, but just as tall, just as square jawed, just as grown. Charlie had been feistier than Kit, more prone to a fight, less philosophical. Morgan wondered if he still was, or if things had happened to beat the fight out of him . . .

And there was that dark sinew of fear. Because if Charlie was alive, why hadn't he ever returned to them?

Hell. Morgan threw the chickweed aside. What was the point in thinking about the past? It was a no-good pastime, full of nothing but burrs and thorns. He wasn't here to think about Charlie and Pa and the mess of the past, he was here to talk to Ma about his old boss Frank Ward, and about hitting the trail again. He was here to talk about taking up where he left off . . . before he came back to this godforsaken mountain.

"Frank will finish fattening up his herd, and then ship the cattle off to Chicago by rail," Morgan told his mother, his gaze faraway as he pictured it. "After that he'll head down to Texas for next season. Vern says he's looking for cattle hands . . ." Morgan's mind drifted to Texas. The broad sweep of the land, the sagebrush and sky, the baking heat of summer . . .

In his day he'd worked the Chisholm Trail from Texas to Kansas, but things had changed. Now they ran cattle up from the Texas Panhandle to Montana, where they'd graze to get fat for market. The train took care of the herd after that.

This bitter winter had been a devastation, dead cattle everywhere, and some people were saying it was an end of the free range in Montana, but Morgan didn't believe it. He didn't *want* to believe it. The age of the cattle run seemed like it would last forever, under free blue skies and open plains.

"Junebug will be fine if I go," Morgan reassured his mother, the romance of the trail making his blood run faster. He had it planned. "Kit and Maddy are more than happy to watch out for Junebug— we built her a room in the big house. When I go, she can move in there, and Beau and Jonah can have the cabin to themselves. They're both full-grown and talking about heading off to one of the mines, or going prospecting with Purdy Joe, anyway."

Why did he feel so guilty? Morgan scowled at the trading post. Junebug would be *fine*. Hell, what did a young girl like Junebug need with an old cuss like him? Maddy was what she needed. A woman who could provide some mothering. Even if Junebug was powerfully determined not to be mothered.

Morgan scratched at his beard. "The thing is, Ma . . ." What was the thing?

He had a hard time putting it into words.

"The thing is, you said you didn't want to leave worrying, and that you needed my promise. Well . . . I promised. And now it's my turn. I want to go to Texas without worrying. Can you give me that much?"

The speckled light danced on the weathered cross as the choke-cherry leaves rippled in the June breeze. From the trading post, Junebug's honking laughter sounded. She laughed like a goose.

"Goddamn it, Ma. Six years! Six long, hard years. I did like I promised."

The cross was silent.

Morgan slumped against the tree trunk. The herbal smell of chickweed surrounded him, and Junebug's laughter took flight into the wide meadow.

"You look like a man at the wrong end of a bad day." Kit's voice broke into Morgan's thoughts.

Morgan hadn't noticed his brother coming down to the creek from the forge.

"What do you want?" That came out surlier than he meant it to. As usual.

"Nothing." Kit held his hands up defensively. "Just came to cool off after making all that cookware. Those miners buy it quicker than I can forge it."

Kit was flushed and sweaty from his work. Morgan didn't know how he could stand working in that forge. Morgan would have been ready for murder after spending the day in that sweatbox.

Kit stripped his boots and clothes off and threw himself into the creek.

Morgan swore as he was splattered with cold creek water.

"You should come in," Kit called, sweeping his arm through the water and dousing Morgan again. "It might cool you off."

"I ain't hot."

"You might not be hot, but you don't look too cool neither."

Kit had been irritatingly cheerful ever since he'd got hitched. Morgan scowled as he watched his younger brother swim blithely to the other shore. What idiot had named this a creek, he thought sourly. It was clearly a river. It was one more annoying thing about this place.

"So, what did she say?" Kit asked, once he'd returned to shore. He stood, waist-deep, and ran his hands through his wet dark hair.

"Who?"

Kit rolled his eyes. "Fine. Be ornery. You know who I mean."

Morgan glanced at the wonky cross, which was stubbornly silent. "She didn't say anything," Morgan snapped. "She's dead, remember? That's the whole problem."

Kit fixed him with that patient look he had, the one that no one enjoyed. "So, you've told her now. When are you going to tell Junebug?"

Morgan shifted restlessly.

"Morgan." Kit's inky gaze grew serious. "You have to tell her you're leaving."

"I don't see why," Morgan growled. "We all know how she'll take it."

Badly. Morgan braced at the thought of it. A displeased Junebug was like a raging hurricane. Something you had to hunker down and weather, but you couldn't head off.

"You can't leave without telling her." Kit was exasperated.

"I can do whatever the hell I like." Morgan stood. He didn't have to sit here and take this. He'd earned the right to do things his way. "Besides, she's going to pitch a fit whether I tell her or not."

"She sure is," Kit said flatly. "But it'll be a lot worse if you don't tell her."

"If I tell her she'll try and stop me." Morgan's stomach was doing that sour thing it did whenever he thought about leaving. His gaze went to Junebug, who was gesticulating wildly as she explained something to Thunderhead Bill.

"Without a doubt," Kit agreed.

"Well, hell. You ain't helping!"

"Junebug will cause trouble whether you stay or go," Kit sighed. "And you ain't going forever. You'll be back."

"Yeah." Of course he would. He'd bring gifts. No ribbons this time.

"And you can write to her, she'd like that. You know how she likes to write letters."

Morgan snorted, remembering the messes Junebug's letter writing had caused in the past. He watched her railing at Thunderhead Bill.

His heart pinching, he remembered what a bit of a thing she'd been when Ma died. He could still see her in the trading post that day he'd blown in, all worn from illness and worry. She'd had night terrors for years after, and only Morgan could soothe her.

What if she had night terrors while he was gone?

"Morgan?" Kit had emerged from the creek and was pulling on his clothes. He was watching Morgan carefully. "She'll be fine."

Morgan could imagine a thousand and one ways Junebug could come to harm. "What if she breaks her arm again?"

"Then we'll fix it—just like we did last time."

"What if she comes after me? Like Charlie went after *him*?"

"That's another reason why you need to tell her. So she won't go hunting after you."

Goddamn it. Morgan hated it when Kit was right.

He didn't *want* to tell her. Junebug was the one person in the world who always got the best of him. He glanced at the wonky cross. The only other person.

Morgan thought longingly of his uncomplicated life on the trail. When he was responsible for no one but himself and a herd of cows.

There went Junebug honking again, laughing fit to bust. As though she'd won already. Morgan straightened his shoulders and clenched his fists. Well, to hell with that. His luck was turning, goddamn it. He was *making* it turn.

"I'll do it now," he told Kit firmly. He strode to the trading post, resolved.

Halfway there he veered off.

"Morgan!" Kit called, peevish.

Morgan ignored him. He'd tell Junebug tomorrow. Or maybe the day after.

When he was sure he could hold his nerve.

Four

Pip was as high-strung as an unbroken filly as the train chugged and groaned and whistled its way up the mountains. At the last stop she'd changed into her good outfit, which she'd made herself. No pink this time, and no tilt at girliness. Pip had ordered from the Montgomery Ward catalog, mailing off for a pattern in the new, freer style and for a bolt of "juniper green" wool cloth. She wasn't looking for fancy, so she'd ignored the instructions for the trim and the oversized bustle. She'd have no need for frills and furbelows where she was going. The dress itself was simple and sheath-like, with a modest gathering where the bustle was supposed to be, and a tightly fitted waistcoat. It was a dress for a woman, not a girl, which suited her age and, let's face it, her looks.

To be honest, she wasn't the best seamstress in the world and the hem was a bit skew-whiff, one sleeve was longer than the other and the collar was bunched at the back of her neck, but who cared what she looked like. Morgan McBride wasn't marrying her for her looks.

You can't know how I dream of pie, he'd written in his last letter, and those words had been sweet as sorghum to Pip. *None of us are much for cooking and my poor little sister just about wears herself to the bone trying to feed us all.* Pip's heart had skipped a beat as she read his words. They were a perfect match: he needed a cook, and her cooking was her best asset. It was fate.

Pip had painstakingly copied out recipes from her mother's books into a brand-new ledger that she'd bought in town. She included three separate recipes for chocolate cake, and every kind of pie imaginable: fruit pies, meringue pies, custard and chiffon pies. She'd filled the ledger with desserts, and then went back into town for a couple more notebooks to hold the savory recipes.

Her mother had hovered, face pinched, pulsing with worry. She worried about Pip heading west, into the unknown; she worried that Mr. McBride would be a villain or a drunkard; she worried that he'd take one look at Pip and send her packing back to Nebraska. Pip wasn't bothered by her hovering and fretting; she felt like she'd been given a new lease on life. She was going on a train, away from here, into an unknown adventure. She was going somewhere where she was wanted, needed, to a home of her own, to a man who wanted her. Or at least wanted her pies.

Pip could settle for that.

In fact, she was overjoyed. She'd told Mr. McBride the stark truth about herself, and he *still* wanted her. She could feel the zing of it through every last inch of her. This was how Naomi must have felt when her husband had proposed. Desirable. Even if, in Pip's case, it was just that she was desirable for her baking skills. Even then, it was a good feeling. Pip walked taller and prouder, met people's eyes in town, sang louder in church, laughed often and filled her days packing her chest with pots and pans, ledgers of recipes, boxes of salt and spices. She, Epiphany Hopgood (soon to be McBride), was *wanted*. She invested in a new pair of boots, sewed her new dress and mended her winter coat. She was as busy as a squirrel getting ready for the winter.

And then finally the day arrived. Pip was bursting out of her skin with the thrill of it. It was a bright June day, fresh as a laundered sheet, with the sharp-as-sap smell of crops growing. Pip said her goodbyes, hugging and kissing each of her brothers and sisters, who had come to see her off and were clumped on the porch, flanking Mother, who was weepy and certain that Pip was headed for heartbreak. Pip should be feeling a pang at leaving home, she thought, but really she was just itching to get to the station. Her brother John was escorting her to Montana, and Granny Colefax was coming to act as her chaperone for a few weeks after he left. Just in case, they kept telling Pip. *You never know with men,* Mother said darkly. Pip had to restrain herself from snorting. As if anyone would take advantage of *her.* Wasn't that why she was in this mess in the first place? Because no man had the urge to touch her?

Pip waved gaily to the crowd on the porch as Father drove the buggy away from the house. John was driving behind, with Pip's trunks and the chicken coop piled in the tray. Tied to the back of his wagon was Pip's horse and her milk cow. Pip was proud she wasn't arriving on Mr. McBride's doorstep empty-handed. She was a woman of substance, and Mr. McBride would recognize her value, she was sure of it. The tips of the corn rippled gold from horizon to horizon as a haze of dust rose behind the buggy, clouding Pip's view of the house that had been her home.

The station in Joshua was a small clapboard building crouched under a cottonwood tree. They trundled up to the station just as Costa, the stationmaster, emerged, pulling his fob watch from his pocket and checking the time.

"You're early," he said amiably.

"Better early than late," Pip told him as he helped her down from the buggy. She would have died if she'd missed the train.

As she and Granny waited on the covered porch of the station house, Pip felt like the world had been brushed with a slick of magic. The cloud-speckled sky was robin's-egg blue, and the breeze carried the scent of cornflowers. Today was the first day of the rest of her life. Pip was trembling with excitement as the sound of the train came curling through the air. She held her carpetbag tight. She'd never once in her life been on a train; it was all a terrific novelty.

"It can't be good for your organs, traveling that fast," Granny Colefax observed, as the iron engine steamed toward them, but she sounded cheerful enough. In fact, she looked more sprightly than ever, all buttoned up in her good black dress, wearing the bonnet she only brought out for weddings, the one loaded with fat cloth cabbage roses.

The whistle sounded, earsplittingly loud.

Pip had to restrain herself from pitching in as Father and John hefted Pip's trunks into the baggage car and led her animals to the stock car. Helping would have settled her nerves. Her rooster, Jean-Marc, crowed in protest as John hauled his coop into the train car.

"Take care of yourself," her father said gruffly when it was her turn to board. He wasn't one for affection, but he managed an awkward one-armed hug. "Make sure you write and tell us about the wedding."

"Of course." Just try and stop her. Pip couldn't wipe the smile from her face at the thought of it. Holy crow, the *wedding. Her* wedding.

And then they were off. She and Granny took the window seats and left John to read his newspaper in the aisle. Children gathered by Joshua's station to watch the train leave; she gave them a wave. Down the street she could see Samuel Arcross hauling bags of flour from the mercantile and stacking them in his family's wagon. She'd never need to speak to him again, let alone force a smile at him, she thought with no small measure of satisfaction.

"Did you ever see so much corn?" Granny complained, as they pulled away from Joshua and the fields began to flash by in a blur of summer green and gold. "Or ever want to."

"There's a field of squash," Pip pointed out. She loved the rhythmic speed of the train; it felt like she was flying.

"Oh, squash." Granny was dismissive.

Pip pushed the window up and felt the buffeting of the wind, which smelled of oil and coal smoke.

"What do they grow in the mountains of Montana, John?" Granny demanded.

John looked up from his newspaper, surprised. "I don't rightly know, Gran. I'm not sure they grow anything. They're in cattle, I think?"

Granny Colefax made a satisfied noise and relaxed back on the bench, closing her eyes. "Tell me when the vegetables are gone."

The journey passed in a blur of fields and plains, big skies and long nights; they ate in half-dime lunchrooms by the stations; they changed trains in Council Bluffs, and again in Omaha, and then they were in Montana and, oh my, Mr. McBride's letters sure hadn't done it justice. The fields fell away, and in their place were rolling green valleys, streams and lakes as shiny as polished mirrors—and mountains the like of which Pip could never have imagined. At first they appeared on the horizon in purplish-blue smudges; then they became supine spines, like long sleeping lizards. But as the train chugged closer to the range, their sheer scale became apparent. Gray razor-backed ridges cut through thickly wooded slopes and the mountain tips seemed to pierce the deep blue sky itself.

"Would you look at that . . ." Granny Colefax was as fascinated as Pip was, her head almost sticking right out the open window. The cabbage roses on her bonnet were threatening to blow right off the brim in the blast of wind.

As they reached the foothills, the heady scent of pine came in with the smoky air and deep cool shadows fell across their faces. Pip had lived her life on the plains; this was a whole other world. It was like a forest in a fairy tale, Pip marveled. Mr. McBride said he lived in a place called Buck's Creek, in a high mountain meadow. Pip wondered if there were woods surrounding his meadow, and if they were as beautiful as this.

She loved every second of the journey, stiff back and sore neck, dirty sooty smoke and all, and she was almost sorry that it was drawing to a close. At their final stop before they reached the end of the line, Pip took the chance to clean herself up in the washroom and to change into the new juniper-green dress. And then she had to wrestle her hair. She clenched her teeth to keep from crying out as the brush caught in her tangles. The wind had wreaked havoc on her hair. Regretfully, she realized she'd have to close the window for the final leg of the journey, so she could arrive looking as decent as possible.

Morgan McBride might not be marrying her for her looks, but she was vain enough to want him to like the look of her, at least a little. She wasn't much good at hairstyles, so she brushed out the tangles and then managed a loose braid, which fell over one shoulder. It wasn't so bad. She'd bought a new hat for the occasion too. It was completely and utterly frivolous and would do nothing to keep the sun off her face. She'd bought it on impulse, when she saw an illustration of it in the catalog. Surely she deserved one fancy thing for her wedding. It sat high and tilted forward on her head, a silly little bit of straw, topped with a giant black velvet ribbon and a puff of white-speckled guinea fowl feathers. The whole thing was held in place by a couple of wickedly sharp hatpins. Before emerging from the washroom, she gave her cheeks a good hard pinch, just like her mother used to do, and hoped it gave her some color.

There was no mirror to check her appearance in, so she had to rely on Granny and John for an idea of how she was looking. She stepped out of the washroom and into the station lounge, carrying her carpetbag full of dirty clothes and feeling ludicrously nervous.

Their silence was horrifying. She felt their gazes sweep her head to toe. Some of the other passengers were looking her over, too, and she saw their eyebrows go up. Please let it be because she looked so much fancier than when she went into the washroom, and not because she looked like a kid dressing up in her mother's clothes . . . or worse . . .

"You scrub up real well," Granny assured her, breaking into a smile.

John swore under his breath. "Did Mother see you in that dress?"

Of course not. Mother had made her a perfectly hideous poplin thing to wear; it had a big fat apron skirt that made her hips look ten times bigger than they were. In pink, of course. Mother had a fixation on putting Pip in pink. Pip had scrunched it up and left it behind, hidden under the feedbox in the stable.

"She can't have approved of that dress." John seemed completely dismayed.

He was so annoying. "And why not? What's wrong with it?" Pip liked this dress, skew-whiff hem and all.

"Well . . . because . . . because you look . . ." He gestured at her helplessly.

"What?" Pip snapped. "Fat?" Sometimes having brothers was such a trial.

"No." He flushed. "Not fat." He shot Granny a panicked look. "You look . . . you know . . ."

"No," Pip said tightly, "I don't know." She put her hands on her hips. As if meeting your soon-to-be-husband wasn't nerve-racking enough, now she had to worry about her stupid dress too. And she *liked* this dress.

Pip remembered trying it on in front of the mirror in the hall at home. She'd looked *good*, she thought stubbornly. The deep arboreal shade of the cloth made her skin creamy against her bronze hair and gave her greenish eyes an extra clarity. The sheath suited her better than the silly fat bustles and apron-fronted dresses ever did; it showed that while she might be tall, she had a fine figure. Her legs were long, and her waist was accentuated by the curve of her upper hips before the skirt flared to the ground.

How come whenever she thought she looked good, other people didn't?

Pip tried to catch a glimpse of herself in the windowpane in the station lounge, but the glass was too sooty and dusty to cast a reflection.

"What your fool brother is trying to say," Granny Colefax reassured her, "is that you look womanly."

"A little too womanly, maybe," John suggested, turning scarlet.

Pip followed his gaze, which had dropped to her chest. "I'm buttoned up to the neck," she protested, her hands smoothing down the tightly fastened waistcoat.

"Yes, but . . ."

"Oh, hush, John." Granny Colefax flapped her hand at him. "That's enough. It's nothing Mr. McBride will complain about, now, is it?"

If possible, John went an even deeper shade of red, and then he turned tail and headed out to smoke his pipe, while they waited for the train to finish taking on water.

Pip felt the old ball of shame rolling around in her belly. It wasn't her fault she wasn't petite or slender. Could she help it if she wasn't a reed of a thing?

"I assume your mother gave you the talk before you left?" Granny asked thoughtfully as she watched Pip fuss with her dress.

"What talk?" Pip frowned at her skirts. "And why is looking womanly a bad thing? Isn't that how I'm supposed to look? Hasn't that been the problem all this time?"

Granny was thoughtful. "Well, you never wore that dress in Joshua, so I guess those fool men never realized."

"Realized what?" Pip was sick to death of them picking at her.

"What you've been hiding under those ugly pinafores your mother tied you up in. She might as well have dressed you in a tent."

Pip didn't have the patience for Granny's nonsense today. She was all in knots. What if Mr. McBride was as put off by her dress as John had been? Maybe she'd made a colossal mistake. Maybe she should have stuck to her usual style. Which was no style much at all. Oh God, should she have brought the poplin dress after all?

"Trust me, Epiphany, that husband of yours will love it," Granny Colefax said dryly, ushering her into their carriage.

As the train strained up the steep winding incline, Pip read through Morgan McBride's last letter. *My sister will meet you at the station in Bitterroot. I'd come myself but I can't leave Buck's Creek at the height of the trading season. We'll put you up at the hotel for a night or so. It's good to have a trial period, don't you think? To decide whether we're a good match.*

Not for the first time, Pip wondered how they were supposed to know if they were a good match if he wasn't even going to be there to meet her.

I trust Junebug to know if we'll fit or not—feel free to ask her anything you like, she'll be as honest as can be.

His little sister was going to decide whether he should marry her? And not *him*?

It was an odd arrangement, but then, Morgan McBride *was* a backwoodsman. And, as he'd written many times in his letters, he knew precious little about women. *They make as much sense to me as a woodpecker in a desert,* he'd written. So, she supposed it made some sense to trust the judging of a woman to his sister . . . even if she was only a girl.

If Junebug approves, she'll take you off your brother's hands and bring you up the mountain.

Pip glanced at John. She very much doubted he would hand her over without meeting the man she was supposed to marry. And he most certainly wasn't going to let her ride up the mountain with only a child for an escort. Not for the first time, Pip wished the mail between Nebraska and Montana wasn't so slow. She had a thousand questions for Morgan McBride, which she'd not been able to ask. Not least of all, why she couldn't head straight up the mountain and meet him as soon as she arrived. If he couldn't leave Buck's Creek, she was perfectly capable of coming to him.

What if Junebug approved, but when Pip got all the way up there, he took one look at her and decided he didn't want her after all? No matter how she turned it over, it wasn't a very good plan, to leave the judging of things to other people. Pip remembered the parlor door, and the Arcrosses doing Samuel's dirty work for him.

She and Morgan should decide these things for themselves.

And what if she got up there and she didn't like *him*?

It was a weaselly little thought, one that had crept into her head more often as they'd headed west. She'd been so all-fired determined to find a husband that she'd obsessed over whether he'd like *her*, but she hadn't given too much thought to whether she'd like him . . .

He said he was tall (which was good) and that he wasn't too hard on the eyes, *at least since I grew into my face* (whatever that meant). But it wasn't looks Pip was worried about (who was she to judge, when she knew how it felt to go through life homely?). What worried her was, what if she didn't *like* him? The way she suspected her mother didn't like her father . . . Mother had a way of turning away from Father that spoke more than words ever could. And for his part, Father treated Pip's mother like she was part of the furniture.

Pip didn't want that.

Pip wanted a man to sit in her kitchen with her, not alone in a parlor at the other end of the house; she wanted a man to converse with her over morning coffee, instead of heading out to the fields without so much as a good morning; a man who laughed and didn't gather dust; she wanted a man who . . . made her feel like she was just fine the way she was. He could be plain, he could be rough around the edges; heck, she'd even be all right with him being short, so long as he was kind, and honest, and . . . well, so long as he truly, genuinely *liked* her.

And maybe, with time, like could become something more . . .

Well, he hadn't been wrong about living in the middle of nowhere. Pip took a deep breath as she stepped from the train. The engine exhaled steam as it settled in front of Bitterroot's train station, which had the pretension of a clock, even though it was barely a smidge of a place at the end of the line. The stationmaster wore a shiny-buttoned uniform and blew his whistle proudly when it was time to disembark.

"Welcome to Bitterroot!" he bellowed as he opened the doors and helped the new arrivals down. "The gateway to silver country."

"It's definitely more of a gateway than an actual place," Granny sniffed as they took in the town.

The place was barely a clearing in the densely packed woods. Raw-framed timber buildings and canvas tents were dotted among towering pines. A stream tumbled through the center of the place, running right through the hard-packed dirt street. Pip took it all in, her heart in her mouth. It was definitely a long way from the cornfields of Nebraska.

The sprawl of it, the cool green shadowiness, the quiet that rose from the woods and stole the sharp edges off the sound of the train settling, all of it was so different from home. Above the trees, Pip could see mountains thrusting at the sky with rough purplish-gray rock fingers. As high as the train had climbed, there was still higher to go.

And up there somewhere was her new home . . .

Pip scoured the ramshackle town for a sight of the McBrides. She felt giddy with nerves. She wasn't a fainter, but if she had been, she might be fit to swoon, she was so excited. Where were they?

There was no one waiting for Pip on the "platform," which was more of a strip of dirt than a proper platform. The few people who'd arrived on the train with them had poured off and were in a commotion of collecting luggage and mining gear and animals from the cars at the back of the train.

The townspeople had paused their business to watch the new arrivals disembark. There was a knot of men at a wide-porched mercantile store, all leaning against the rail and having a gawk. Pip straightened her shoulders, determined to make a good first impression. Was one of those men Morgan McBride? Was he going to evaluate her from a distance? That's what she'd do if she were him. Pip surreptitiously darted glances at the cluster of men. They were a dusty bunch, in denims and flannel and battered hats. Most of them were chewing tobacco, which they spat in long brown streams right into the street.

Oh dear. They made the farmers back home seem positively prim.

But hopefully, for all their roughness, these men would treat her better than the prim little men back home ever had.

"Well, hey!" A voice cut through the afternoon. "Miss Hopgood?"

Pip snapped around, searching for the source of the call. She was skittery as a rabbit.

The only people she could see were a barefoot child in oversized coveralls and an old man in a dusty threadbare coat and a battered stovepipe hat. They were trotting down the dirt road; the kid was waving vigorously, and the old man was weaving, as though he had been at the bottle.

Oh no. Surely not. They made the men on the porch of the mercantile look positively respectable.

"You've got to be Miss Epiphany Hopgood from Nebraska," the kid called.

No. Pip's heart fell from her mouth to her toes as she watched the barefoot child barrel toward her, the old man following in her wake. Pip felt Granny and John freeze beside her. John swore under his breath, a word Pip had never heard before.

No, please no. This couldn't actually *be* the sister?

No. No way in all that was holy. This was simply a local kid who had been sent to fetch them to the hotel . . . Pip would reach the hotel and there would be Junebug McBride, a sweet young girl in gingham, just as Pip had been imagining. Junebug would be waiting on the porch, pink cheeked with excitement, and immediately Pip would lose this skittery panicky feeling, and the overwhelming dread that she'd made a terrible mistake.

"Well, you're a wily one, ain't you?" the barefoot kid said, coming to a halt, beaming from ear to ear as she took in Pip's dress. "You didn't mention that in your letters."

"I beg your pardon?" The blood was rushing in Pip's ears. *Look* at the child. Her dark hair was choppy, as though she'd taken the scissors to it herself, and her bare feet were so deeply ingrained with dirt that it seemed possible that she'd never washed in her life. Why wasn't she wearing shoes? Or a dress? She looked like a wildling.

"Why, you've got more curves than a ball of twine." The kid put her hands on her hips and surveyed Pip closely. "And that's a mighty fancy dress. Not the fanciest I've seen, or even worn, mind you, but still pretty darn nice. How do you get any work done in a dress like that?"

Granny Colefax interrupted. "Excuse me, but we've yet to be introduced."

Thank goodness for Granny Colefax, because a rush of vexatious fears had stolen Pip's capacity for speech.

What had she done? Coming all this way on the promise of a total stranger. She must have lost her wits. It was Mother's fault. If she hadn't been so free with her disappointment, Pip wouldn't be in this situation. Where *was* this? It wasn't even a town.

The men on the mercantile's porch took on an ominous cast.

Pip had dragged Granny and John to this wild mountain outpost, just because some man had written her a letter? Oh God. Just because *she'd* written some man a letter. Some man she'd picked from an *advertisement*.

A man who could be absolutely anybody.

Pip's blood turned icy as she took in the sozzled old man at the dirty kid's side. Just who had she agreed to marry? Dear God, it could be *him* for all she knew.

It took every ounce of Pip's strength to hold her nerve. If this *was* Junebug McBride (and please, please let it not be . . . please let Junebug be in pretty gingham on that hotel porch, with a clean face and a sweet disposition, and not standing here barefoot and in stained coveralls), if this *was* Junebug, then what on earth would her brother Morgan look like? If this was the state of her, what was the state of *him*? With no small measure of horror, Pip considered the old man who stood next to the barefoot wildling. The man had removed his hat out of a demonstration of politeness, but it hadn't helped matters at all. His gray hair stuck up in wild tufts and his whiskers were in dire need of barbering. He was clearly the worse for wear, and the red veins in his nose spoke to it being a regular state.

Please don't let him be Morgan McBride. Even the thought that he might be Morgan McBride's *father* was bad enough.

But if he *wasn't* Morgan McBride . . . Then, holy crow, Morgan McBride must be something awful indeed if he thought these two would make a better impression than he would . . .

"You'll have to forgive Junebug's manners, ma'am," the old man rumbled. "She was raised in the mountains, you know."

Junebug. Oh God, it *was* Junebug McBride. Pip felt light-headed. She could *smell* them. It was a musky smell, of bodies unwashed.

The old man held his hat in both hands, so it hid the missing buttons on his coat. He seemed a little bashful about his state. "She's not had the benefit of learning to behave proper-like."

"Oh, you hush," the kid—*Junebug!*—said, elbowing him. "You weren't raised no better."

"True enough. I was raised much worse," the old man agreed, although he said it amiably enough.

"Excuse me," John interrupted tersely. He was as displeased as Pip had ever seen him. His ears had turned red. "But you're not . . . I mean, you can't be . . ." He cleared his throat. "We're here to meet the McBrides."

"Well, spit, what do you think you've just done? I consider this met, don't you?" The kid looked him up and down cheerfully.

"It ain't met until you do the introducing bit," the old man reminded her.

"You're the McBrides?" John turned a baleful gaze on Pip. His ears were the color of ripe tomatoes. He was clearly scandalized by the state of these people. And who could blame him?

"Not all of the McBrides," Junebug corrected. She seemed to be enjoying herself immensely. Her gray eyes were sparkling, and her grin stretched from ear to ear. "We're just a taste of 'em. There are a whole pack more of them up the hill."

A whole pack. He'd mentioned brothers in his letters, but Pip had never considered . . . She'd pictured men like her own brothers. But now they were here . . . Pip took in the incongruity of John in this place, with his neat whiskers and good church suit. She compared him to the old man, with his wild hair and dusty coat and the thick black dirt rimming his fingernails, and to the slouching miners on the mercantile porch, and she swallowed hard.

What had she walked into? She'd assumed Morgan McBride was a man in his prime, not a scruffy old cuss. Her thoughts were whirling faster than she could grab hold of them. No, but he *must* be a man in his prime, Pip thought, steadying herself. After all, Junebug was young, and she was his sister. He couldn't be this old man. Then Pip remembered Old Man Millard back home and swallowed hard again.

Just because this old man was here didn't mean anything, she told herself sternly. Pip had to stop falling into these nervy thoughts and trust the truth of those letters. After all, truthfulness was Morgan McBride's watchword. He'd been blunt as blunt could be.

"I'm Junebug." The kid thrust her hand at John. She'd clearly decided he was the one who needed winning over. He looked at it distastefully but took it. Mother had drilled manners into them, and he wouldn't have had the capacity to refuse it, even though he clearly wanted to. Junebug shook his hand energetically. "I'm the potential groom's sister," she said brightly. "And this here is Bill. Don't mind him. He can put people off, but he's decent enough."

Bill. Pip almost sagged in relief. Thank goodness. He wasn't Morgan McBride. She felt Granny give her a reassuring pat on the arm.

"We're mighty pleased to meet you," Junebug chattered. "I assume you're the brother I've heard so much about." She was working John's hand like it was a water pump as she chattered her introductions.

Pip blinked. *The brother I've heard so much about?*

She'd heard so much about? Something the kid said earlier came back to Pip: *You're a wily one, ain't you? You didn't mention that in your letters.*

She'd read Pip's letters? Pip flushed. She hadn't thought Morgan McBride would share her letters with anyone. She'd been frank about herself in those letters; she'd exposed herself, revealed her shortcomings. Holy crow, she'd told him about the whole humiliation of the Samuel Arcross affair . . .

Pip didn't fancy Morgan showing his family her private business. "He let you read my letters?" she said tersely.

Junebug gave her a startled look. She cocked her head. Pip could practically see the thoughts flicking through her head, like fish darting through a swift-moving stream. "We're a very close family," she said, wide-eyed with innocence. "And Morgan trusts my opinion."

The old man coughed.

"He said in his letters that you'd know if we were well suited . . ." Pip still found it hard to believe, looking at the state of her.

The kid's gaze was frank as she met Pip's. "Yeah." She grinned. "He'd be an idiot not to. If there's one thing I can do, it's spot a quality woman at fifty paces."

Pip almost laughed at that. This was absurd. "Can you, now?" she said. "Just like judging a cow, is it?"

Junebug shrugged. "Yeah. Only harder. With a cow you don't have to worry it'll be improvident with money, or indolent in the cookhouse."

She certainly had a vocabulary and a half for a wildling.

"I've known an indolent cow or two in my time," the old man disagreed.

"Not in no cookhouse though." Junebug seemed to have more to say on the matter but stopped herself. "You're getting me off track, Bill. This ain't the time to be arguing over cows."

"Enough from you, child," Granny Colefax said firmly. "It's time to let your elders sort this mess out." Granny trained her disapproval on the old man, who took a nervous step backward.

"What mess?" The kid was taken aback. "Everything's happening just as it ought, as far as I can see. We came to meet a Miss Epiphany Hopgood from Nebraska, for the purposes of matrimony, and here she is."

"Where's your brother?" John demanded. The red stain had spread from his ears to his whole face. "I want to know where the man who propositioned my sister is. This is untenable."

"We all seem to be getting off on the wrong foot," Junebug said, frowning. "It's possible there's a disparity between how they do things in Nebraska and what happens here."

"We mean no disrespect," the old man murmured to Granny Colefax. He still had his hat in his hands and was giving Granny a bashful look.

"For the love of God, Bill, stop talking!" Junebug snapped. "You've got them all in knots."

"It ain't me, you quarrelsome sprout. It's you what's got them knotted. You ain't got the manners God gave a beaver." Bill's bashfulness evaporated the minute he addressed Junebug. He sounded like a schoolmaster on a rampage. "You got to sweet-talk a young woman, not go comparing her to a ball of twine."

Now it was Junebug's ears turning red. "Don't you be talking about manners, Bill. People who live on porches got no business throwing stones at glass houses. And calling her a ball of twine was a compliment. I *was* sweet-talking her."

This insanity was getting well out of hand. "Enough," Pip said sternly. Her head was spinning with the talk of beavers and porches. What did she mean he lived on a *porch*?

But Junebug and her drunken companion didn't seem of a mind to listen to her, even though they were drawing an audience. The men gathered at the mercantile were laughing. Some first impression she was making in this town, Pip thought in dismay.

She turned to John, who was equally appalled. Granny, on the other hand, seemed to be taking it in her stride. Enjoying it, even.

"You're not staying with these people," John said quietly to Pip, his voice acid with disapproval.

Pip's stomach sank. No. It didn't seem possible that she would be. And yet, she didn't want to go back to Mother with her tail between her legs either.

"This is the last time I do you a favor, you whelp." Bill and Junebug were still at it. Bill had jammed his hat back on his head and was waving a finger, like a politician throwing his weight into a stump speech.

"What's a whelp? I don't like your tone of voice, so I don't rightly reckon I like what you're calling me neither."

"Enough!" Pip felt like grabbing them both by the ears. She felt the shame of it, being part of a scene in public, with the stationmaster and all of Bitterroot watching their display. "Let's retire some-where private to sort this out, shall we?" She turned to John. "We'll need the baggage and the animals, before the train sets off again," she reminded him.

"I hardly think we need any such thing, when we're plainly leaving when the train does," he told her shortly.

"Leaving!" Junebug was outraged. "What do you mean, leav-ing? You only just got here. What kind of shenanigans are these?" Her ire was redirected at John. "What did you come here for, if you were just going to turn around and leave again? You ain't even met my brother, how do you know you wouldn't like him?"

"Just a hunch," John said dryly.

Pip took a deep breath to stop from shouting at them all. The last thing they needed in this situation was more shouting. It was all happening too fast, and in a hurricane of chaos. Order was needed, and quickly.

"Hush," Pip said, channeling her mother's icy politeness. "We're at the weary end of an arduous journey and the last thing we need is you railing at us, child."

Junebug took sore offense at being called a child, Pip could see. But she wasn't taking any more of her nonsense. "My brother and I just need a quiet word," she said swiftly, before Junebug could launch into a rejoinder. Pip took John by the arm and yanked him back toward the train, where they stood in its shadow, both tense and discombobulated.

"So, this is how introductions normally progress in Montana, is it?" she heard Granny Colefax muse to the McBrides.

"It's more of a Buck's Creek thing than a Montana one," Bill was telling her as Pip gathered her thoughts. "Even Bitterroot folk are given to better than this."

"I don't know why I brought you, if you're just going to cast aspersions," Junebug griped.

Pip turned her back on them. "Now, John," she said softly, giving his name the inflection Mother used. He winced. "Obviously, none of this is as we expected." Pip was feeling peppery with shame. Why couldn't finding a husband be simple, like it was for other girls? She was a nice person. A good person. What had she done to deserve this?

"Those people are animals." John was flustered. She could see how the responsibility of the situation was chafing on him. He'd thought this would be a short jaunt, a break from everyday life, a bit of fun, and now here he was with Pip's fate in his hand—a fate Mother and Father wanted resolved. She could see him resigning himself to taking her home, bringing her up the drive, as Mother watched them approach . . . with that *look* on her face.

Pip pressed her lips together. She cleared her throat. "They're mountain people, not town people," she said tightly. "Maybe we should adjust our expectations. It doesn't mean they're not decent folk."

"You can't honestly think to go ahead with it?" John was genuinely shocked.

As well he could be, going home to his cute-as-a-button wife.

"I'm not doing anything yet," Pip told him sharply. Truth be told, she didn't have the measure of her mind yet. Not one bit. "But it's been a long journey, and this is all a surprise; it would be nice to find the peace of the hotel, in order to freshen up and gather our wits."

"The train won't wait." He was looking at her like she had two heads.

"There will be another train if I decide to leave."

He was obstinate. "No. You're being ridiculous. This is completely unworkable."

"What do you mean, no?" Pip was well out of patience. All her hopes were crashing down around her. "This isn't your future we're talking about here, John, it's *mine*."

"I know you're desperate, Pip, but honestly!"

Desperate. Pip felt like she'd been slapped.

"I thought it was ridiculous when Mother told me about this whole mail-order marriage scheme, but . . ." John gestured at Junebug and her drunk companion. "This is beyond the pale!"

Pip lifted her chin and clenched her jaw. *"Desperate?"* She felt like she might choke on the word as she spoke it. Her own face was turning red now; she could feel it stinging, as though she'd suffered sunburn. How dare he be so . . . so . . . *honest.* What if she went around being honest about him? How would he like it if she said he was narrow and unexciting and *bland*?

"Surely not even you want to live in a hut in the hills, with people like this!" John snapped. "You'll end up barefoot and pregnant and surrounded by heathens."

Surely not even you . . .

Pip had to resist the urge to snatch her boots off and throw them at her brother's head. She'd rather go barefoot than speak to him for another moment.

She left him to his vile honesty and stalked toward the stationmaster, who had been watching the whole drama, along with the rest of the town. "Excuse me, sir, would you please help me get my belongings from the train?"

The stationmaster grinned and dropped his whistle, where it hung from its silver chain, glinting merrily in the sunshine. "You're staying, then, miss? That's good. I know she don't make the best first impression, but you'll find our Junebug's a secret treasure. Even if she can't tell time to save her life."

Pip blinked. "Oh." My, these people were frank.

"There ain't no one who can chew the fat like Junebug. The whole afternoon can pass before you've even got past your how-do-you-dos." He seemed to think that was high praise.

"Epiphany!" John snapped at her like she was a dog he was calling to heel.

"Let's get you sorted," the stationmaster suggested, ignoring her brother. "Do you need help getting things over to the hotel? I assume that's where you're headed, since there's nowhere else to stay in these parts. At least not for a lady."

"Hey, Bascomb, don't you go putting her back on that train!" Junebug came stomping over as the stationmaster led her to the baggage car. "Look, Miss Nebraska, I didn't mean no offense." She thrust herself between Pip and the train. "My brother Kit says I've been raised by wolves, and he should know, since he helped raise me."

Pip held up her hand. "Please," she begged. "It's been a very long journey and I have a splitting headache. No more yelling."

"I ain't yelling!"

"She ain't going nowhere, Junebug, so there's no need to be so het up." The stationmaster grunted as he hauled himself into the car to retrieve Pip's luggage.

"She ain't?" For the first time since Pip had met her, Junebug seemed lost for words. "You ain't?"

"The only place I'm going for now is to the hotel. There is actually a hotel, with a booking for us, I presume?" Pip asked primly.

Junebug lit up. "Well, hell, that's great news! You know, I was always afeared you'd turn back around when you saw this place, that's why I . . . I mean, that's why I told Morgan he should be blunt and truthful with you."

Truthful. Pip almost rolled her eyes. If he'd been truthful, she would have been expecting a barefoot wildling and not a sweet gingham-clad sister.

"I don't rightly know what all the fuss is about. You must have been expecting me to meet you, not him." The kid seemed genuinely puzzled by Pip's reaction.

"Sort of," Pip hedged. She didn't want to hurt the child's feelings by telling her what a shock she was. "He did say his sister would greet me."

"And here I am," Junebug said happily.

"Here you are," John agreed sourly. "But where is your brother?"

"Oh, he's up the hill at home. He'll be along once I've got the measure of her."

"Will he, now?" John was heating up again. "And when do we get *his* measure?"

Junebug blinked. "You want his measure? But it's all in the advertisement. There ain't much more than that. He's reliable in that way."

"Stop," Pip begged them. "Wait until we're at the hotel. I've had enough of making a spectacle of myself for one day."

"Are we staying after all?" Granny Colefax joined them. "Oh good, I'm not ready to go back yet. I want to see more of this place. But first, Epiphany, where are your manners? You need to introduce us all properly."

The day could only get better from here, Pip reassured herself as names were exchanged.

"Are you staying too?" Junebug asked Granny Colefax curiously. "I didn't know about you. Do you cook?" But before Granny could answer, Junebug spied all Pip's baggage. "Well, all that luggage speaks of serious intentions, even if you're feeling skittish." She sounded much happier.

"How are you getting all that baggage to the hotel?" Bill asked suspiciously. He took a step back, clearly not of a mind to help.

"Oh, that ain't a problem." Junebug stuck her fingers in her mouth and let out a head-splitting whistle. "Hey, boys!" she called to the men gathered on the porch of the mercantile. "Help a lady out, won't you?"

"You ain't no lady, Junebug," one of them hollered, and they all laughed.

"Not me, you half-wit. Her." Junebug pointed at Pip.

"What's in it for us?" another yelled.

"You get to meet her," Junebug said, putting her hands on her hips. "And she's a right looker! See the curves on her!"

Pip wished she could disappear. The mortification. Those men could very well see what she looked like and she didn't take kindly to Junebug poking fun at her appearance.

But to her astonishment, the men came filing over to lend a hand, and as they tipped their hats and said "howdy, ma'am," their eyes roamed her body in shocking ways. Pip had never experienced such lasciviousness. This place was a scandal.

"Don't none of you get ideas—she's spoken for," Junebug told them happily, as they loaded up and trudged off to the hotel.

"Epiphany," John insisted, seeming to still believe he had a say in anything that was happening, "don't you even think about following them."

Pip shot him a scathing look. "I'm hardly going to let them take my belongings and *not* follow them," she told him, keeping her voice even and icy. "Now, be a good brother and fetch the animals, won't you?" Pip kept her head raised as she strode up the dirt street. She wasn't desperate, she thought fiercely. She just had limited choices. And anyone who judged her for that could go and be damned.

Five

Morgan was only going along with Junebug's nonsense because he felt so wretchedly guilty. Guilty enough to let her boss him into scrubbing up, shaving off his beard and putting on his good shirt. Just to go into Bitterroot, for the love of God. What did anyone in Bitterroot care what he looked like?

She'd come home from Bitterroot the other day babbling about cakes and cookies and all sorts of nonsense. Morgan knew how she felt about cakes, but this was a new level of frenzy, even for Junebug. She was on a mission to drag them all down the hill to sample *the best food you'll eat in your whole entire life*. Junebug had always been one to gild the lily.

"What the hell is a high tea, anyway?" Jonah complained. He'd been made to clean up, too, and was out of sorts. His dark hair was still damp from Junebug's aggressive combing and fussing. She'd been in a right state all day.

"A high tea is something cultured people do, you ignoramus," Junebug scolded. She was trussed up in one of the new dresses Maddy had made for her over the winter, which Junebug had steadfastly refused to wear until today. For some reason, today was the day she gave up her coveralls and crammed herself into "girl clothes," as she called them. The daft ideas that kid got in her head. It was the Bellevue, for Pete's sake, in *Bitterroot*. It wasn't like they were headed to some grand hotel in London or New York, like in one of Kit's books. Junebug was at the Bellevue every week, gossiping up a storm. Why'd she need to wear a dress to do it today? And why did *he* have to suffer the tedium of shaving when he'd only grow the beard straight back again afterward?

Junebug was fussing with her collar. She kept jamming her fingers down it, as though it was suffocating her. Morgan had been glad to see the dress Maddy made was a prim and girlish pale yellow cotton thing, buttoned right up to the chin. He still had nightmares about the first time he'd seen Junebug in a dress, looking too grown-up and womanly for her own good. Or his. There'd be time enough for the nightmare of Junebug attracting men in the years to come. For now, she could stay looking like the kid she still was.

Morgan had to admit that even in the prissy cotton dress she looked too grown up for his comfort. Maddy had gone and pinned up Junebug's shaggy chin-length hair, which showed off her square jaw and high cheekbones. The kid was a looker, there was no doubt about it. And there was also no doubt about the fact that it was ruining Morgan's whole day. How could he leave her here, prey to who only knew what kind of man? What in hell would all those miners in Bitterroot make of Junebug in a dress? Morgan wasn't looking forward to finding out.

The McBrides were headed down the hill for an afternoon out as a family—possibly their first one ever—because Junebug had got it into her head that they had to go to high tea at the Bellevue Hotel. She'd hounded them until they'd agreed, and none of them were a match for a truly determined Junebug. And now here they were, scrubbed to within an inch of their lives, crammed into the wagon, riding more than four hours downhill for a cup of tea and a slice of cake. It was absurd.

"There's these sandwiches with the crusts cut off," Junebug said excitedly, leaning over the buckboard of the wagon, wedging herself between Maddy and Kit so she could call over to Morgan, who had refused to ride in the wagon. He might have agreed to go along with this fool escapade, but he was riding his own horse. He was too old to be crammed into the tray of the wagon with the boys and Junebug. He also wanted the freedom to leave whenever he got the urge. He didn't rightly see the appeal of a sandwich without its crust and figured he might want to escape.

"Sandwiches don't seem like food cultured people would eat," Jonah needled Junebug. She'd been gasbagging all day about them needing to act cultured.

"These are cultured sandwiches," Junebug said furiously, "not like them old slabs of stale bread and greasy bacon things you make."

Morgan's stomach pinched. He wouldn't complain about one of Jonah's greasy bacon sandwiches right now. All he'd had today so far was Junebug's watery oatmeal, which had been half-cold and completely miserable.

"These sandwiches have *cucumber* in them," Junebug told them proudly, like she was making them herself. "Like in that book Kit read us, about that heiress who married the wrong man and came to no good. She had cucumber sandwiches at that garden party, remember? At the manor where she met ruination."

"I'm not sure you're selling the virtues of cucumber sandwiches particularly well," Maddy observed, holding a hand to her head to keep her hat in place as the wagon rocked down the hill.

"Cucumber!" Morgan couldn't help himself. The thought of a crustless cucumber sandwich was too depressing. "Cucumber ain't real food."

"It ain't, huh? So, why do you make me grow them, then?" Junebug shot him a disgruntled look. "I spend half my life picking caterpillars out of the cucumbers. If they ain't food, why cain't I

leave them to the insects? Besides, there ain't *only* cucumber sandwiches, there's also chicken salad."

"Chicken ain't a salad," Beau disagreed. He was wearing his new
black derby hat that he'd ordered from a catalog in Minneapolis; it
had a tall crown and a rolled brim, and he was proud as a peacock
in it. Morgan noted sourly that Junebug hadn't had to push Beau
too hard to spruce up for town. Beau had discovered the pleasures
of women and was often as not prettifying himself and sneaking
down to Bitterroot instead of doing his chores. There were precious few women in Bitterroot, but what few there were had fallen
head over heels for his pretty face and glib charm. He was bound
for trouble, Morgan thought. He'd have some girl in the family
way; and Morgan wasn't raising any more kids, so Beau would be
on his own with any mess he made on that front.

"What would you know about what's salad and what ain't?"
Junebug sniped. "You ain't never eaten chicken salad in your life."
Junebug looked ready to push Beau out the back of the wagon.
Hard.

"Well, neither have you," Beau said, adjusting his derby to a
rakish angle.

Junebug had gone red in the face. Morgan almost felt sorry for
her. Here she was, excited, trying to get them to enjoy the day, and
all they gave her was grief.

For all her vinegar, she was just a kid. One who deserved a few
feminine treats, like a yellow cotton dress, and a pretentious high
tea at a backwoods hotel.

"I'm amazed Rigby is still doing his high tea," Maddy broke in,
trying to head off a full-blown McBride brawl, "given how much
Mrs. Champion hates doing them. And with Willabelle gone, I
don't imagine there's much call for them anymore."

"It ain't Mrs. Champion who's doing it," Junebug griped. "I told
you, there's someone new in the kitchen of the Bellevue today."

"New?" Beau perked up.

"You never listen to me! This ain't Rigby's usual yellow cake and burned coffee affair." Junebug was at her wit's end with them. "This is *fancy*."

"So you said," Morgan sighed. His mind wandered back to Buck's Creek. He was doubting the wisdom of leaving Sour Eagle, Thunderhead Bill and Roy in charge of the trading post. He bet Roy was helping himself to the chewing tobacco. Maybe Morgan should have stayed back himself; he could have taken the opportunity to get his saddlebags sorted and his gear in order, while his fractious family were all gone. He only had a couple of days before he headed out, and there was still a lot to organize.

"What are you looking like that for?" Junebug demanded.

"Looking like what?" Morgan didn't appreciate being dragged out of his thoughts. "What am I looking like?"

"Like someone shot your dog."

That ain't how he was looking. Besides, he didn't have a dog. He scowled at her. If he was looking like anything, it was like a man on the edge of freedom. It was so close he could smell it.

"You of all people should appreciate good food!" Junebug scolded him. "Spit, you're always bitching about my cooking."

"Watch your language." Maddy swatted her on the arm. "Remember, you're a lady."

Beau and Jonah hooted at that. Junebug gave them a rude gesture over her shoulder and Maddy swatted her again.

"Making sandwiches ain't cooking," Morgan sighed. He wished she'd stop talking about food; he sure was hungry. He'd give his right arm for a plate of beef and beans and a hunk of fresh corn bread. Soon he'd be on the trail and there'd be a cook who'd hand him a plateful of happiness every night. He remembered Early Parsons, who used to run the chuck wagon on the old trips. Early wasn't fancy, but he sure could do a good plate of beans.

"It ain't just sandwiches, I told you." Junebug glared at him.

"Why do you have to be so all-fired negative all the time! Try and open yourself up to an adventure or two, why don't you!"

Morgan noticed Kit suppressing a smile. He didn't appreciate it. He was plenty open to adventure. He was damn well headed off on one soon. Very soon. In fact, it couldn't come soon enough.

"I don't consider afternoon tea an adventure," he growled. This tea thing was shaping up to be a trial, through and through. Morgan could only imagine what would happen once they were crammed inside Rigby's dining room, where, Junebug had informed them, there would be linen and china teacups and an expectation of manners. McBrides and manners didn't mix well.

"You don't consider it an adventure . . ." Junebug's ire was pricked. "That's only because you have all the imagination of a mule. How can it not be an adventure when there are four different kinds of *cake*," she declared.

Morgan rolled his eyes. "Which four?"

"I don't know yet, but I'd bet my hat one's chocolate." Junebug was leaning so far forward she was practically on the bench between Maddy and Kit. Her eyes were shining.

"You ain't got no hat to bet," Beau observed. "Shame, because it would cover up the fact that you ain't got any hair."

"Oh, shut up," Junebug said, "I do, too, got hair. Enough for Maddy to torture me with all these pins."

"Who's this new cook at the Bellevue?" Poor Maddy was still desperately trying to head off the fighting. She hadn't been around quite long enough to learn that nothing could stop McBrides from fighting, Morgan thought with a sigh. It was one reason he longed for the quiet of the trail.

"She just arrived on the train from Nebraska," Junebug said. Ignoring the obstacle of her skirts, she climbed over the buckboard to wriggle between Kit and Maddy, so she could talk more directly across to Morgan, who rode alongside.

Morgan's heart just about jumped out his mouth when she pitched forward as she climbed. She would have gone headfirst under the horses if Kit hadn't caught her. Goddamn, that kid took years off his life. What if she'd been trampled?

Kit met his gaze and tried to look reassuring, but Morgan could see he was shaken too. Hell.

Kit gave an imperceptible shake of his head. He'd said they'd manage fine without Morgan a thousand times, but Morgan didn't believe him.

"She bring a husband with her, this cook from Nebraska?" Beau asked curiously.

"She ain't for the likes of you," Junebug snapped.

"Why not? She old?"

Junebug ignored him. "Her name's Epiphany Hopgood," she told Morgan, Maddy and Kit. "Ain't that a name and a half?"

Morgan wasn't really listening. He'd gone back to fretting about leaving Junebug and the trading post.

"Mrs. Champion says she's the best cook Bitterroot has ever seen," Junebug was chattering.

"That wouldn't be hard," Kit said mildly.

"I reckon we're in for a treat today," Junebug insisted. "And you all better mind your manners, because I don't want her thinking we're animals."

Animals.

That changed Morgan's line of thought. He'd take the geldings with him when he left, and then he'd pick up a third animal in Miles City. The buckskin and the roan were good solid mounts; he'd need reliability on the trail, and they were young and healthy and strong. They'd do well. Morgan ran through the logistics of the journey. He needed to stop fretting about Bug, he told himself sternly. Kit had promised to look after her. And she would be *fine*. And Morgan would find a third horse in Miles City, and he'd ride south, and he would be fine too.

"Morgan!" Junebug snapped.

He snapped out of his thoughts, feeling the familiar flush of guilt. Sometimes it felt like she could read his mind. Like she knew exactly what he was up to.

"Ain't you got no curiosity about her?" Junebug demanded.

"About who?" Morgan was genuinely at a loss.

She fixed him with a look that was equal parts disappointment and fury. "Epiphany Hopgood!"

"Who?"

The words that came streaming out of his sister were ample proof that she wasn't a lady, no matter how prissy a dress Maddy put her into.

Morgan wasn't built for high teas. He was too big and clumsy for the whole affair. The chair beneath him was narrow and so short he had to stretch his legs straight out under the table; the china teacup was dwarfed by his hands, to the point that he could barely fit his finger through the handle; and he just felt like a bull elk set loose in a fancy parlor. He was sure he was going to break something.

Rigby had decked out his dining room like he was expecting royalty. The linens were snowy white and starched stiff, there were fresh flowers bursting from vases on every table and the whole place smelled of baking. Rigby himself had slicked his hair back and waxed his mustache and looked like a character who'd stepped out of one of Kit's books.

"How come we're the only ones here?" Morgan asked uncomfortably. "And why cain't we all sit together?" He was at a table by the window with Junebug. Kit and Maddy had their own table on the other side of the room, and Beau and Jonah had been relegated to a corner.

"Because there ain't a table big enough." Junebug was playing fancy, putting some of Maddy's lady lessons to use. She unfurled a white linen napkin and laid it daintily across her lap and she had a strange hoity-toity expression on her face, her lips pursed like she was about to whistle. She sure had some queer ideas about what ladies must look like.

"We can join a few tables together," Morgan suggested, glancing around. It would be less stiff if they were all sitting together.

"No, we cain't," Junebug snapped. "It ain't civilized."

"Since when?"

"Since you got invited to high tea, that's when. Now hush up and behave."

She was loving this. Morgan almost laughed as she sat ramrod straight, prim as a schoolmarm.

"This ain't my first high tea, you know," he told her.

She snorted, which ruined her poise.

"It ain't." Resigned to the ordeal, Morgan rested his elbows on the table. "I went to a teahouse in Abilene."

Junebug was dubious.

"It was the front room of a little house right on Main Street," Morgan told her. "Down from the saloon, run by a widow named Dumphries." Oh, that widow . . .

"Why'd you go there?" Junebug cocked her head and narrowed her eyes.

Maybe this wasn't the right story to tell . . . Morgan cleared his throat, as he remembered the very hospitable widow.

"You ain't the tea type," Junebug said, "so it must have been for the food."

Definitely not the right story to tell. Hell, talking to girls was hard. "Yeah. It was for the food." Morgan gestured for Rigby. "You got something stronger than tea?" he asked.

"Morgan!" Junebug scowled. "That ain't in the spirit of things." She turned her scowl on Rigby. "Don't you dare bring him anything but tea or coffee."

Rigby glanced nervously back and forth between them. "I ain't of a mind to refuse a paying customer, Junebug."

"Morgan," Junebug wailed.

Morgan felt the guilt licking at him. If he was going to be abandoning her in a couple of days, the least he could do was give her a pleasant day before he left. He forced a smile. "Fine. I'll have coffee, Rigby."

"Why don't you try the tea?" Junebug suggested brightly. "It's a high *tea*, you know."

He knew because she wouldn't shut up about it. Morgan didn't like tea, but he gave in, to keep her happy. Rigby brought the teacups to the table, the china clattering in his hands and the tea splashing into the saucers.

"Ain't you supposed to pour it at the table?" Morgan asked.

Junebug kicked him under the table.

"What?"

"It ain't good manners."

Junebug had been hung up on manners all day. It was laughable, given the usual state of her. She just about rapped his knuckles when he reached for the sugar cubes with his fingers, rather than using the silly little tongs. And she watched him like a hawk when he bit into his first sandwich. It made a man awkward, being watched like that. The fussy little sandwiches arrived on one of Rigby's chipped plates, a fan of narrow fingers that seemed more for looking at than being eaten. The bread was white and soft; it was a bit like eating air.

"What do you think?" Junebug asked breathlessly. She was on the edge of her seat.

"I think it's not much for all the fuss," he admitted, shrugging. "It's barely a mouthful." He could fit the whole finger in his mouth in one bite. The cucumber was all right, he guessed, but it was cucumber.

Junebug frowned. She picked up one of the cucumber sandwiches and looked at it balefully. "It's probably the wrong place to start," she muttered. "Rigby! We need something more substantial."

"It ain't time for cake yet," Rigby told her.

"It don't have to be cake. See if there's some sandwiches with a bit more heft to them, will you? What about chicken salad? Or ham? Weren't there going to be ham sandwiches?"

"Don't fuss, Junebug," Morgan sighed. "I'll eat what I'm given." He took a sip of the tea and grimaced. He never would understand why people liked the stuff. It tasted like old grass clippings soaked in water. "Wait, Rigby! Get me a coffee while you're at it." He pushed the tea away. "I tried," he apologized to Junebug.

She was looking tense. Her fingers were pleating the skirt of the tablecloth and she was wriggling in her chair like she had fleas.

"Will you relax if I eat another one?" he asked, picking up one of the cucumber and white bread slivers, tossing it down in one bite. "See? I'm enjoying myself."

Another plate of sandwiches arrived, this time on different bread, but still in finger slices.

"The pale brown one is chicken salad on some kind of bread I forget, and the darker one is ham on rye," Rigby told them.

Morgan was more interested in the tin mug of hot coffee. It sure smelled good. He was used to Junebug's tarry brew, which he drank black and unsweetened, even though it was strong enough to fell a horse. In comparison to Junebug's sludge, the first mouthful of this coffee was a shock to the system. It was *good*. So good he almost let out a moan. Hell. Who knew coffee could taste that good? It was smooth, with an aftertaste of raw sugar and something else he couldn't put his finger on.

"It's something, ain't it?" Rigby marveled. "I've put away a whole pot of it myself already today. It goes down a treat with some of the carrot cake."

"Carrot cake?" Morgan didn't fancy the sound of that. Who made a cake out of vegetables?

Junebug didn't fancy the sound of it, either, judging by the way she leapt on it. "No one asked for no carrot cake," she snapped. "Honestly. Where's the chocolate?"

"You want the cake now? You ain't touched your sandwiches yet and you explicitly told me—"

"Hush up and bring the cake," Junebug said shortly. She slumped back in her chair.

Morgan took in her mule-face. "What's up with you, Bug? I thought you were looking forward to this."

"I am. I was. But you ain't enjoying it." She glared at him. "You were supposed to enjoy it."

Morgan almost laughed. Why on earth would she think a mountain man like him would like a high tea with linen and baby-sized sandwiches? "I'm enjoying it more than Beau and Jonah, at least," he pointed out.

The two younger McBride men were in the process of having Rigby top up their coffee with slugs of whiskey.

If looks could kill, Junebug would be up on charges. "I tell people we're not animals, and then they go act like 'em," she muttered. "What will people think, them drinking in the middle of the day . . ."

"Who cares what people think?" Morgan asked. "It's only old Rigby, and he's too busy pouring himself a shot to be judging anyone."

She was descending into one of her moods, Morgan saw. It gave him an uncomfortable curdled feeling in his stomach. He didn't like to see her upset.

"What's not to like about coming and eating fancy food?" She frowned. "Look, Maddy's enjoying it."

Maddy might be, but Kit clearly wasn't. If Morgan was too big for the room and the china cups, Kit was like a man crammed into a child's dollhouse.

"I guess I'm more of a beefsteak kind of man," Morgan said,

trying to jolly her out of her sulk. "Give me a beer or a shot of whiskey and a cut of beef cooked on an open fire and I'm happy."

"No, you ain't," Junebug scoffed. "We do that all the time and you're never happy."

"A *well-cooked* cut of beef," he amended, cradling the coffee in both hands. It smelled as good as it tasted. He kept ducking his head to inhale the perfume of it. He'd have to ask Rigby where he got the beans from.

"My beef is well cooked!" Junebug was irate at his aspersions on her cooking.

"It's cooked well-done," Morgan disagreed, "which is no way to treat a good steak." He picked up one of the ham sandwiches. The coffee was reminding him how hungry he was. God, he wished Junebug could cook. At least the ham sandwich was a sight better than the cucumber one. It was thick with creamy salted butter and a good shave of ham, and something else Morgan hadn't tasted in a long while. Mustard. He took another one.

"I brought you the carrot cake as well as the chocolate," Rigby said, arriving with the cakes and throwing a rebellious glance at Junebug. "You might not think carrots would make a cake, but you'd be wrong. I'll top up your coffee."

Morgan looked down at the plate in front of him, which was piled with cake, and laughed. "I can see why you wanted to come." Junebug's greatest love was cake, and these were two of the fattest slices he'd ever seen. Both of them were in three layers, with cream puffing out in whipped white glory.

Look at her. Her whole face was shining with glee. It did his heart good to see it.

Today, he thought, as he watched her take a fork to the cake. I'll tell her today. Just as soon as she's full and content from the sugar.

Morgan tentatively took his fork to the pale orange carrot cake. He was guessing it was the cream Rigby enjoyed, because how the hell did you make carrots into a cake? His fork came away in a soft sigh of crumb and cream. Despite his misgivings, he found himself melting into his chair at the first bite. Hell. Morgan wasn't normally one for sweets, but a cake like this didn't come along every day. The cream, or whatever it was, was tangy, and the scattering of crushed walnuts on top gave a satisfying crunchiness to the whole thing. But the cake itself was the high point. It was fluffy and dewy, and Rigby hadn't been wrong: coupled with the coffee it was an experience and a half.

"You're onto a winner with this cook, Rigby," he said, when the hotelier came back to refill his mug. By then, Morgan had polished off the chocolate cake, too, which had been darkly bittersweet. Junebug had cream on her face and chocolate stains on the sleeve of her new dress. "I don't think anything has shut Junebug up for more than a minute in her whole life until now. We'll have to get the recipe."

"You like it?" Junebug hooted. "I knew you would. Rigby, go give Morgan's compliments to the chef! Tell her he's hooked!" She looked quite literally like the cat that got the cream.

Morgan felt himself exhale at the sight of her grin. Look at her. She was fine. Better than fine. She was happy. Here in town, surrounded by family, with cake and cream and silly teacups full of grass clippings.

He'd done it, he thought, feeling a relief so intense it made him weak. He'd brung her up. And here she was. *Happy.*

Now was the time to tell her. Because now, for the first time, Morgan felt like she'd be just fine, whether he was here or not. All she needed was cake.

Six

"Well, he's a looker," Granny Colefax had exclaimed when the Mc-Brides had arrived for high tea at the hotel.

"How do you know which one he is?" Pip had taken up a post at the window of her hotel room to watch for the McBrides, a good hour before they were due to arrive. It had been a long hard morning and she was frazzled and stressed. She'd been up since well before dawn baking the cakes Junebug had asked for, but all she could think about was the impending meeting.

"The route to a man's heart is through his stomach," Junebug had insisted to Pip. "I read that once and I reckon it's true. It'd be true for me. If I met a man who could bake, I'd marry him in a heartbeat."

Junebug had been back to sample Pip's cooking more than once, bringing not just Thunderhead Bill but two other trappers down from the mountain with her. The trappers sat obediently at the kitchen table, sampling the pies and cakes and cookies and biscuits.

They were a motley bunch. Thunderhead Bill had made an effort to improve on his first impression; he'd had his hair barbered and his whiskers trimmed, and his clothes were fresher, smelling of the creek water he laundered them in. His companions consisted of a squirrelly man named Roy, who insisted on keeping his rifle on him, even in the kitchen, and a tall solemn Crow Indian named Sour Eagle.

"You're only here by my good grace," Junebug reminded them imperiously, "and if you so much as stick a toe out of line, you ain't getting any cake." She took an equally dark view of Pip and Granny talking to the trappers. "They don't have anything to tell you that I cain't. Don't talk to Roy in particular. He don't speak a lick of sense."

"Junebug's very particular about how this should go," Sour Eagle told Granny Colefax placidly. He seemed completely unruffled by the girl's dictatorial nature. "She's got her heart set on things working out."

"Not a peep, Sour Eagle," Junebug ordered, riled. "The only thing I want from you is an opinion on her cooking."

Each time Junebug arrived at the hotel, Pip's heart was in her throat, thinking *he'd* come finally to meet her. But it was never Morgan McBride. It was just Junebug and her trappers, asking for some new kind of pie or cake or pastry. The kid sat in the hotel kitchen, watching Pip like a hawk as she made piecrust, peppering her with questions while Mrs. Champion, the housekeeper, and Ellen, the maid, eavesdropped mercilessly.

Eventually Pip refused to humor her anymore. "Surely you've seen and eaten enough," she said. "You've got enough information on my cooking to make up your mind." Or rather to make up *Morgan's* mind. She couldn't believe the man hadn't deigned to come and meet her yet. Wasn't he curious? It was a concern, and there was no doubt about it.

"Oh, I've made up my mind," Junebug said. "I'm keeping you." She'd spoken with her mouth full of wild strawberry pie. Junebug had hauled the foraged berries down to Bitterroot herself earlier in the week. "I've just got to get him to taste this pie, or one of them cakes, before he can make up his own mind. Don't worry," she assured Pip, "it's just a formality. Morgan likes his food. One bite of your baking and he'll be sold."

"He wants me to bake for him before he decides? He could have come down any day this week." Pip gestured at the table full of samples she'd been forced to cook.

"You read the ad. Bad cooks need not apply. He'll be here. We just need to do it proper-like." Junebug held out her plate for another hunk of pie.

So here Pip was, tasked with making high tea for the entire McBride family.

Pip had lobbied for a hearty family dinner instead of a fussy tea; she would have relished a chance to fry up chicken, or slow cook a joint of beef. Of course she would have followed it up with a dessert or two, but she confessed to being taken aback that desserts were all he really wanted to try. She had a sweet tooth herself but couldn't subsist on dessert alone. And high tea? It was completely incongruous in a place as rough-and-tumble as Bitterroot. What kind of mountain man only wanted to eat cake?

It had been Mrs. Champion's suggestion to throw in a few sandwiches, at the very least. "You'll send them all into a frenzy of sugar," she warned Junebug, when she saw the menu the kid had drafted. Junebug had commandeered the hotel for the event, and she'd sworn the hotel staff to secrecy about the high tea.

"It ain't for anyone but us," she insisted. "I don't want one of them miners getting a taste of this pie and stealing her off me."

Pip was surprised Rigby and Mrs. Champion hadn't asked more questions. But they seemed to take Junebug entirely in stride.

"Morgan is the private sort," Junebug insisted whenever anyone so much as raised an eyebrow at her demands. "Why, if he thought he was a figure of gossip, he'd be ungovernable in his displeasure."

Pip had experience of being a figure of gossip, so she supposed she understood, but she was nervy. Something wasn't right. *Every-thing* wasn't right. This wasn't how marriages were made . . .

But maybe she just wasn't used to the way things were done on the frontier. All the rules and strictures that Pip had taken for granted her whole life were barely present here in Bitterroot. No one was at all scandalized that Junebug McBride traipsed around town barefoot, bold as brass. In fact, they all seemed rather fond of her and her wildling ways. Things were just . . . odd. The place was full of people who would have been out of place anywhere else. John was continually appalled. Men roamed drunk down the main street in the middle of the morning, there was a fight over a mining pick on the porch of the mercantile and a man was almost shot over it, the buildings were so new you could see the gleam of the nail heads in the sun and there was a brashness to every exchange that was utterly disconcerting. The day after the almost shooting, John had threatened to bundle Pip onto the first train home.

"This is no place for my sister!" he was prone to exclaiming. Pip wondered how he would feel about it if she *wasn't* his sister.

Fortunately, Junebug had a gift for managing people, and John was no exception. Junebug could see the inertia of sitting around the hotel was wearing on Pip's brother, she said. It gave him too much time to think. She organized for one of the local prospectors take him out hunting for silver in the mountains—a scheme Pip didn't believe John would take to. But she'd underestimated Junebug.

"It don't do to be cooped up in town all the time," Junebug had told John cheerfully, as she handed him his hat and all but strong-armed him out the door. "You need fresh air. And who knows, maybe you'll find silver and return a rich man."

"I don't—"

"Have any equipment?" Junebug cut him off. "Don't worry, Purdy Joe will sort you out."

Junebug had returned to the hotel kitchen, to eat cakes and lick out batter bowls, while John went traipsing around the woods. "He looked like he could use some fun, and Purdy Joe will show him a good time. Everyone likes Purd," she told Pip.

It turned out Junebug had read John right. A day out in the open air did him a world of good. He'd talked of nothing but prospecting since. Pip had even seen him perusing the shelves of the mercantile, evaluating mining tools.

"Men need things to do, or they cause trouble," Junebug told Pip sagely. "Trust me, I know a lot about men. I live with enough of them."

Pip had an idea that Junebug might also need things to do . . . She devoted far too much time to meddling in other people's lives. Including Pip's.

The McBrides' high tea plan was unnecessarily complicated, and a lot of pressure. And it was costly. Pip paid the bill for the provisions for the high tea gingerly, aware that she had few reserves to draw on. What if she wasted all this money for nothing? John wasn't shy about voicing all of her deepest fears aloud, either, which only served to make Pip more stressed. On the day of the high tea, Pip took a leaf out of Junebug's book and sent John off for a walk, because he was making her anxious with his doomsaying. He refused to go, even when she threatened him. In the end, he only left because she got teary; like every man she knew, he couldn't stand a woman crying "at him." Honestly, he all but ran from the room, rather than soothe her. From the window of her hotel room, Pip could see her brother loitering down the street, waiting to get a glimpse of Morgan McBride.

He stuck out like a sore thumb.

Well, it was only what Morgan McBride deserved. If he'd had the decency to greet her when she arrived and to meet her family, like a proper man would, they wouldn't have to gawk like this. Pip herself felt like she was a prize pig, about to be judged at the fair. She didn't see why he shouldn't feel the same way.

Pip would never give John the satisfaction of knowing it, but she agreed with every qualm that he had about Morgan McBride. What the heck was wrong with the man that he couldn't just quietly meet her, one-on-one, to see if they suited? Why did she have to perform for him? And why did everyone have to *watch* the first time they set eyes on one another, and bear witness to his judgment of her?

At least her mother wasn't here. That was one bright spot. Although maybe this would have gone better if Mother *had* been here. Mother probably would have dragged Pip straight up the mountain on the first day, demanding to see Morgan McBride, and this ordeal would be resolved already. Mother never would have held with a child such as Junebug having power over Pip's fate. She would have wanted a direct accounting of the man Pip was hitching herself to. Not that Mother's standards were that high, Pip thought dryly, remembering Old Man Millard.

At least all reports about Morgan McBride were favorable. More than favorable. Pip, John and Granny had been discreetly ferreting out information, and the folks of Bitterroot were not skimpy in their warmth toward the McBrides; they thought particularly highly of Morgan. The Langers at the mercantile praised his prompt payment of accounts, Abner at the saloon said he drank enough to be sociable but not enough to be classed as a regular drinker, Purdy Joe called him "a stand-up guy" and Mrs. Champion, the hotel housekeeper, sang his praises to the sky. John had been like a bloodhound, sniffing even into business that wasn't his own. Holy crow, he'd gone asking after Morgan McBride at the cathouse!

"He's not a frequenter," John said when he returned, satisfied, blushing from nose to toe at even having to mention it. He liked to pretend such places didn't exist around Pip, but it was hard to ignore the place, given that the cathouse was right over the road from the hotel. Pip even had a view of it from her room. The lights burned at all hours of the night over there, and the miners were noisy drunk as they came and went. But Morgan McBride was not one of them.

"He's respectable," Rigby, the hotelier, said of him. "Bit of a one for glowering, but you can't hold that against a man. And not much of a talker. But then maybe he just can't get a word in edgewise with Junebug around."

Mrs. Champion confirmed that Morgan McBride had taken on the raising of Junebug and his brothers after his mother died, and that he'd done so with fortitude. So far, he matched up to the description of himself he'd given in his letters. Although, the people of Bitterroot thought a lot more highly of him than he did of himself. He'd been hard on himself in his letters. That spoke of either humility or a low sense of self-worth. Either way, he sounded a long way from Pip's worst fears, which had been stoked on her arrival by Junebug and Thunderhead Bill.

But for all the questions Pip and John had asked, no one had mentioned Morgan McBride's looks. Except to say he was tall. Well, *big* was the word they used. Pip counted that in his favor too. She wasn't a small woman, so a big man was preferable to a small one. But not one of them—not even Mrs. Champion, who seemed to adore him—said he was *beautiful*.

Pip's stomach was churning as she watched the McBrides' wagon rattle to a stop outside the hotel. She was a wreck by that point. She'd barely slept the night before and couldn't settle her nerves. She'd had nightmares about the stupid high tea, about collapsing cakes and burned pies and a long, abject train journey home to Mother.

But as the McBride wagon hove into view, Pip realized she hadn't known what nerves were until now. She felt sick with expectation.

And then she saw the McBrides up close . . . and it was worse than any nightmare.

Granny gave a long low whistle. "Well, he's a looker," she said appreciatively.

"How do you know which one he is?" Pip wasn't appreciative. She was *appalled*.

"It doesn't matter which one he is," Granny Colefax observed. "They're *all* lookers."

There were three men in the wagon, one driving and two in the tray, and a fourth riding alongside on a big bay horse. They were all big. Unusually so. And, holy heck, they were good-looking. *Too* good-looking. Pip couldn't take it all in. They were overwhelming.

As was their sister, Pip thought in shock, noticing Junebug sitting next to the driver. There was no trace of the wildling in coveralls now. Junebug was glowing in a lemon drop–yellow dress, her short shaggy dark hair tamed into a pretty hairstyle, with curls framing her square-jawed face. If *this* girl had met Pip at the train station, she wouldn't have harbored a single fear! This young miss wouldn't have been out of place at a barn dance back in Joshua.

But there were no men like *these* back at the barn dances in Nebraska, Pip thought witlessly.

The four men in the street below were built for this rough-hewn town. They were large and strapping and bronzed, with the bulk and gait of men who worked their bodies hard. Next to the McBrides, the men of Joshua seemed like boys. It was impossible to have a straight thought when you were confronted by such men . . .

The one driving the wagon was the biggest of them, a complete mountain of a man. It was a wonder the horses could pull the wagon with him in it. He had a close-trimmed black beard and a slow calm manner. The two McBrides in the back of the wagon were leaner and younger, both clean-shaven. One was still boyish, with his hair slicked down, and he was awkward in his good shirt; the other . . . oh, *he* was trouble, Pip thought. He was handsome as the devil himself, and he knew it. His clothes were fancier than the others and she took note of how he brushed off his coat before he jumped from the back of the wagon. That one cared to make a fine impression.

Then there was the fourth. He was a solid brooding presence at the edge of the group. Not as big as the mountainous man at the reins of the wagon, but pretty darn close; he was tall, with shoulders wider than a doorway and long muscular legs. He was easy in the saddle, she noticed; he and the horse moved like they were of the same mind. His hat shielded his face from Pip's view, but she had no doubt he'd be as masculine as the rest of them.

Junebug had glanced up and caught Pip at the window, staring. She'd grinned and surreptitiously raised a finger in the direction of the man on the horse. Pip swallowed hard.

Morgan McBride. That was him. Finally. After all the letters, and the long journey; after all this baking and worrying and imagining the very best and the very worst: here he was. Pip found she was holding her breath as he dismounted and hitched his horse to the rail.

Then he took his hat off and squinted up at the hotel.

Pip jumped back from the window as though she'd been burned. No.

No, there'd been some terrible mistake. That couldn't be Morgan McBride.

She crept back to the window and stole another look. Dear God. *Look at him.*

Granny let out another low whistle. "Well, my girl, you've sure fallen into the clover patch. I haven't seen a man that fine in all my days, and I've lived a lot of them."

Fine didn't do him justice, Pip thought stupidly. Her body felt as though it had turned to butter and was melting, like she'd been thrown into a hot skillet.

Morgan McBride was . . . there weren't even words for it. He had a mop of dark hair, which tumbled over his high forehead in wild swirls; his jaw was strong and square and his nose straight. His lips were perfectly sculpted, the lower one pouty in its fullness. He simply oozed masculinity. Pip's gaze traced his wide chest and long legs, taking in the size of his hands, the sun-kissed caramel of his skin against his ice-white shirt, the serious cast of his thick eyebrows.

"There must be a mistake." Pip struggled to get the words out. She felt her face turn red. He wasn't for the likes of her. He wasn't even for the likes of Naomi. This man deserved some kind of goddess in human form . . . not plain and unmarriageable Epiphany Hopgood from Nebraska.

"There's no mistake, not judging by the way that kid keeps pointing at him. She has all the subtlety of a sledgehammer." Granny cackled. "Imagine setting that girl loose back home with your mother. Verity wouldn't know what hit her."

Pip couldn't tear her gaze away from Morgan McBride. Her heart was cantering and her palms sweating as she watched him. He moved with tightly packed grace. Good Lord. She'd become a bit weak. Maybe she was getting sick. Maybe the exhaustion of the trip had caught up with her. Maybe . . .

Oh. Look at that. Pip pressed her hand to her heart, as though she could catch hold of it as it exploded into a gallop. Morgan McBride reached up to help a woman down from the wagon—that must be Kit's wife, Maddy, the one Junebug said couldn't cook—and as he did his white shirt stretched tight over his shoulders. Shoulders that tapered down to a long waist, and . . . oh Lord, he was firm in those tight black pants . . .

"You might want to sit down before you fall down," Granny suggested dryly.

"There must be a mistake," Pip insisted, a touch wildly. She couldn't go down and meet that man. He'd take one look at her and split his sides laughing. She wasn't for the likes of him.

Down below, Junebug was grinning like a well-fed house cat.

Pip pulled back. She felt like someone had played a horrible trick on her. How could she go down there? How in all that was holy could she bear witness to his disappointment? She'd seen the same dismay so many times on so many men's faces: the startlement at her height, the ripple of distaste, that final expression that settled in once a man had taken stock of her. Overly polite and reserved, trying hard not to hurt her feelings, not wanting to cause either of them too much shame and embarrassment. In the worst cases, there was amusement hiding behind the manners. *How could anyone think I'd marry that . . .*

"Epiphany," Granny Colefax said sternly. "You sit down on that bed and put your head between your legs. Don't you go fainting on me, I ain't got the strength to get you up again if you keel over. Not with the size of you."

Pip ignored her. She wasn't going to faint.

She caught sight of her reflection in the small mirror on the wall and flushed. Abruptly she felt ridiculous in her new dress. What was she playing at? He wanted a cook. He'd made that clear as day in the advertisement and in all the letters. He'd shown no interest in getting a look at her—all he cared about was whether she could bake or not. Holy crow, he wasn't even meeting her *now*. He wanted to eat her cooking first. Junebug had made that perfectly clear: Pip was to stay in the kitchen until after the tea; only once he'd eaten her food would Junebug bring her out. He was marrying her for the practicalities of getting a cook and a housekeeper, not for love. Her looks didn't enter into it.

"What are you doing?" Granny demanded as Pip started unbuttoning.

"I can't cook in this," Pip said tightly, "it'll get ruined."

"There's hardly much to do—you've already done all the baking!"

Pip kept unbuttoning. She'd wear her usual clothing, one of those plain and sensible dresses her mother had made, and an apron. She wouldn't humiliate herself by pretending to be other than she was. A big, homely girl who could cook. They'd spoken plain in their letters and there was no point in doing otherwise now. This was an exchange, not a love match.

"You can't meet him looking like that," Granny protested as Pip wrestled herself into one of her mother's ugly dresses. It was a shapeless sack of a thing, sprigged with pastel flowers that did nothing for Pip's complexion.

But she *could* meet him like this. And she would. She was plain old Pip Hopgood and she wasn't too proud to know it.

Pip made a whole series of resolutions as she worked in the kitchen, sending out plates of sandwiches and tarts and cakes. She wasn't going to make the same mistakes she'd made in Joshua. This time she would be a perfect lady. She would control herself. She would walk, not run; she would keep her voice quiet and respectful. She would make up for her height and her wide shoulders and her overwhelming *too-muchness* by being mature, poised, thoughtful. Morgan McBride was the best-looking man she'd ever seen in her life, and he was bound to be disappointed in her, but she would work hard to alleviate that disappointment. He was looking for a woman to run his house, and she would be that woman. She would bring calm and care to his life.

Pip watched the plates come back empty from the dining room, feeling more confident. She was comfortable in the kitchen, feeding people. There was no need to look pretty for the cookstove. And if he liked her cooking, then they'd be getting off on the right foot, wouldn't they?

Morgan McBride wasn't so keen on the cucumber sandwiches, according to Mr. Rigby, but Pip didn't hold that against him. She wouldn't have eaten them either. Junebug had a firm idea that if sandwiches were on the menu, they should be cucumber ones, because of some book she'd read once. "They ate them at a garden party, and cut the crusts off, and everyone nibbled on them, declaring them *a sheer delight*," Junebug had chattered happily. "I never thought anyone could find anything delightful about a cucumber, but then, I ain't never put one in a sandwich before."

After many afternoons watching Junebug sampling cakes and designing the menu for the high tea, Pip had suspected this whole idea was Junebug's, and not her brother's. And now that she'd seen him, Pip didn't think Morgan McBride looked like the high tea sort of man at all. But he was clearly a man who valued his little sister. Junebug had been so set on the cucumber sandwiches, just like the ones from that book, that she'd even provided the cucumbers from her own patch. Some of them were more than a little nibbled by the caterpillars, but Junebug insisted they were salvageable. If this sugar-laden high tea *was* Junebug's idea, and not Morgan McBride's, Pip supposed it spoke well of him that he wanted to make his sister happy by going along with it. Maybe he'd wanted Junebug to meet Pip first not because he trusted Junebug's opinion of women better than his own but because it was important to him that Junebug like his wife. Maybe the need for a good baker was simply to please Junebug . . . the girl sure did like desserts. Maybe Morgan McBride needed a woman to help raise the girl. From what Pip had seen, she certainly needed some raising.

If it mattered to Morgan McBride that Junebug like his wife, and he was using this high tea as a way to win Junebug over to the idea of him getting hitched . . . well, Pip decided, that was to his credit. It showed a softness of heart that was encouraging.

Theories and speculations were swirling around Pip's head, and by the time Rigby came swinging into the kitchen, loose and ruddy from a couple of swigs of whiskey with the younger McBrides, Pip was feeling quite besotted with her idea of Morgan McBride, the loving older brother.

"I was told to tell you that Morgan is hooked!" Rigby crowed.

Pip felt the floor drop out from under her.

It was happening. She'd been approved of.

"Take your apron off," Granny Colefax fussed. "And take a minute to freshen yourself up before you head in there."

Pip wasn't going to do any such thing. She was going in there dusty with flour and pink from the hot kitchen. This was the woman he'd ordered, and this was the woman he was getting. *This* was the woman who had won his sister over. Determined, her vulnerability and self-doubt packed deep inside, out of sight, Pip gathered herself for the big meeting. She headed for the dining room.

But before she got there, all hell erupted.

Pip froze at the sound of crashing plates and smashing teacups. Over the top of it all was an ungodly shrieking. Startled, Pip looked to Rigby and Mrs. Champion for an explanation. But they seemed as flummoxed as she was.

What on earth was happening?

Pip dashed in, her heart pounding, only to find Junebug in a demonic rage. She was hurling plates at Morgan McBride, who was standing patiently, arms crossed over his face to protect it from shards. The girl was upending the entire dining room—and he was just letting it happen.

"What is this?" Pip gasped.

"Hey! You'll pay for those!" Rigby was right behind her. "I ain't made of plates, you know!"

Why weren't any of the other McBrides stopping the hellcat? Pip's gaze darted around the room. The two younger ones had stood up, looking vaguely surprised, but they weren't rushing to help. Maddy McBride had also leapt to her feet, stricken, but her husband had tight hold of her wrist, preventing her from flying to Morgan McBride's aid.

But why wasn't *he* stopping Junebug? Pip stared wide-eyed at Morgan McBride, who simply stood there, letting the plates shatter against him. He was roughly ten times bigger than Junebug. He could have stopped her with barely an effort.

Junebug herself was inarticulate with fury. She kept shrieking, but Pip couldn't make out the words. The kid hurled the milk jug and it hit her brother squarely in the groin, sending milk flying across the walls.

"Goddamn it, Junebug!" he bellowed.

Pip had had enough. "Junebug McBride!" she snapped. "You put that mug down this instant!" The wretched girl had snatched up one of the tin coffee mugs and was winding up to pelt her brother with it, full force. "What kind of beastly child are you to behave like this!"

Junebug froze, shooting Pip a startled look, as though she'd forgotten who she was. Then she wound up again. "You'd be throwing mugs, too, if you'd heard what I just heard!"

The mug clanged off Morgan McBride's elbow and he swore.

When Junebug snatched up a teacup, Pip took her firmly in hand. "No!" She pulled Junebug away from the table and stood between her and her brother. "Stop." Pip's heart was running wild. This was insanity!

Junebug was breathing heavily, her gaze fixed on her older brother. She looked like she genuinely wanted to murder him, but Pip could also see the slick shine of tears in her eyes.

Pip prepared herself for the worst. Things were clearly not going to plan. But she was resolved. She'd come here to get married, and she wasn't going to give up easily. He'd asked for a good cook, and she was a good cook. Junebug loved her baking. So, what had gone wrong?

Had he seen her at the hotel window when he arrived?

It wasn't her fault he was ridiculously good-looking and she wasn't. She'd told the bald truth about her looks in her letters, so he had no excuse for rejecting her on that front. And he'd certainly not been forthcoming about his own pretty face, she thought wildly.

Pip turned to Morgan McBride just as he lowered his arms from his face. Holy crow, she wished he'd put them back up. Up close he was twice as lethal as he'd been at a distance. For a start there were those *eyes*. They were a disconcerting shade of gray, like a late winter sky, with just a hint of the blue warmth to come in spring. You'd think gray would be a hard color, she thought witlessly, but the gray of his eyes was soft, hazy. Like an April mist.

"How can you do this to *her*?" Junebug screeched.

Pip flinched. Lord, the girl was loud. It was possible she'd just burst something in Pip's ear, she was at such volume.

Morgan McBride was looking guilty. Damn it. He'd definitely decided to reject her. Pip was only glad John wasn't here. He would quite happily whisk her off to the train station before she'd had a chance to salvage the situation.

"Her?" Morgan frowned and met Pip's gaze.

Pip felt it all the way to her toes. It was like leaning too close to the fire. She felt singed.

"Epiphany Hopgood," Junebug yelled. *"Her!"* She jabbed a finger at Pip.

"The cook?" Morgan gave Pip a bewildered look.

Pip abruptly wished she'd worn the juniper-green dress after all. He was so *tall*. And he smelled like the woods. When he spoke, dimples winked in his cheeks and the combination of his hard masculinity with those winking dimples was head-spinning.

"Yes, the cook!" Junebug was screeching like a parrot. "You've ruined everything!"

"I'm sorry," Morgan said. He took a deep breath. His face was hardening into a mask. He had the capacity to be a very intimidating man, Pip thought, not least because of the size of him. He was a good head taller than her—something Pip didn't think she'd ever experienced before. Her brothers were her height or a bit taller, but none of them loomed over her like this. He made her feel practically dainty, which was not a sensation she was overly familiar with. "It was a fine high tea," he told Pip awkwardly. "I'm sorry Junebug ruined it."

"Me!" Junebug sounded on the verge of hysterics. *"I ruined it?"*

She let loose a string of invectives so filthy that Pip didn't even know the meaning of half of them.

"Now, Junebug . . ." Morgan sighed. His attention was solely on his sister again. It gave Pip a chance to regain her composure. She could feel her ears burning. She must look like a tomato, she was blushing so hard.

"Don't you 'now, Junebug' me!"

"Excuse me." Pip cut her off. "But this isn't quite how I imagined this was going to go." She prepared herself for the worst. "I don't quite understand. Rigby said you liked the food?" She ignored Junebug and addressed herself to Morgan McBride. She was proud that she kept her voice steady. She was keeping to her resolution; she was a lady, and she would act that way. Besides, she didn't want him to know how he affected her. Although she was sure he had some idea, given that she was bright red, and also because, with a face like that, he probably had women fainting all over him.

Morgan shot her an irritated look. Somehow it only made him look more deadly handsome. It made that lower lip extra pouty. "This ain't about your food," he said shortly. "This is family business."

"She *is* family business, you blockhead!" Junebug wailed, sweeping the cups and plates from the table with one violent push. The china smashed. Coffee splashed. "Why do you have to be such an infernal idiot!" And then Junebug called him the filthiest names Pip had ever heard. These ones she knew. "I got no mind to speak to you again! Not ever! You hear me? You're as good as dead to me!" Junebug smashed one more plate for good measure and was off. Pip heard her burst into tears just before the front door slammed behind her, hard enough to rattle the windows in their frames.

Morgan McBride looked like someone had just shot him through the heart.

Pip was trying to make sense of what she'd witnessed. Clearly it had gone badly, but she wasn't quite sure why. He hadn't even *met* her when Junebug started throwing plates.

She could see that Morgan McBride was shaken. A whole parade of emotions marched across his face; Pip could see that part of him wanted to run after Junebug, while another part of him was dismayed, and yet another was locked up and stubborn.

He didn't go after her. He took a deep, shaky breath and then he knelt and started picking up the broken plates.

"She'll come round, Morgan," Kit McBride rumbled. He'd not even stood up from where he sat at the table. He pulled his wife closer and gave her a soothing pat. Poor Maddy McBride was looking close to tears. Pip could understand why. This was all very jarring.

What did he mean, "she'll come round"? Come round to *what*? Pip was utterly discombobulated. "Um . . ." She wished she were alone with him. How on earth could she ask what was wrong with her, in front of all these strangers? Pip reminded herself that even though Morgan McBride was more handsome than expected, he was still the man she'd been writing to. The one who'd written honestly and sometimes kindly. Not knowing what else to do, Pip sank to the floor and joined Morgan in picking up the pieces of the hotel's dinner set. There was the small clink of the shards as they gathered them. "I'm not quite sure what the problem is . . ." she admitted nervously, her voice barely a whisper.

Morgan McBride didn't answer. He was radiating dark feelings. He didn't seem to really register that she was there.

"You're paying for this!" Rigby moaned behind her. "Look at the state of the place!"

"Here, Rigby, have a whiskey, it helps with Junebug-related problems." One of the younger McBrides passed him the bottle.

"Don't talk to me about Junebug-related problems. I never have anything but! You got any idea what a fuss she made about this high tea? I ain't done nothing but get ready for this all week. And what the hell did that mean, she *is* family business?" Rigby demanded, gesturing with the bottle at Pip.

There was a long, charged silence.

A *very* long, *very* charged silence.

Pip looked up to find them all staring at her.

"Oh no," Maddy McBride protested. "She wouldn't . . ."

Pip turned, at a loss. The younger ones had gone ashy pale. What was happening? Morgan McBride was frozen, a jagged shard of plate in his hand. He was staring at her, his gray eyes wide and shocked.

"She wouldn't do it again . . ." Maddy said breathlessly.

"She wouldn't do *what* again?" There was an exclamatory pop as Rigby pulled the cork from the whiskey bottle.

Morgan McBride looked like he'd been kicked by a horse. Hard. "No," he breathed. "No, she wouldn't." He took in Pip's floury hands and clothes. "No . . ."

Pip had a horrible sinking feeling. Much worse than the feeling she'd had that day outside the parlor door. "I beg your pardon . . ." she said carefully, "but would you mind telling me what . . ." She trailed off, losing her nerve. She had a feeling she didn't want to know what was happening. Whatever it was, it wasn't good.

"You didn't answer an ad by any chance, did you, lady?" one of the younger McBrides asked dryly.

"Beau!" Kit McBride snapped. "You and Jonah get out of here this minute. Go and find your sister. And Rigby, you just get out. This is for family only."

Pip heard them leaving as though from a great distance. She was too hypnotized by Morgan McBride to pay attention to the rest of them. He seemed in a state of shock. He couldn't stop staring at her, and the look on his face was that of a man who'd seen a ghost. They were both still crouched on the floor, surrounded by smashed crockery.

"Did you?" he asked finally, in a strained voice. "Did you answer an ad?"

And in an instant, she knew. A swirl of images: Junebug licking batter off a wooden spoon; Junebug planning this bizarre high tea; Junebug complaining about how hard it was looking after so many brothers; Junebug and Thunderhead Bill meeting her at the station . . . *You didn't mention that in your letters.* The letters! Pip flushed. She remembered Granny telling her how valuable an honest man was, and that this one was honest to a fault.

But maybe those letters hadn't been honest at all . . .

"Did you?" he demanded. He sounded chilled.

Oh my God. He hadn't placed the ad. He hadn't ordered a wife. It was plain as day on his face. He wasn't here to meet a wife; he hadn't even known that she existed. To him, she was a bolt from the blue, and not a welcome one, by the look of him.

Not sure she could trust herself to speak, Pip nodded jerkily.

Morgan McBride looked like he wanted to throw something. But everything was already smashed.

Seven

"I'll reimburse you your train ticket and you can go back to your family."

Well, Pip could certainly see where Junebug got her bossiness from. Morgan McBride had done nothing but give orders since that scene in the dining room. He'd told Kit and Maddy to round up the younger ones and head up the hill, then he'd given instructions for how they were to deal with Junebug—they were to leave the disciplining to him. He'd paid Rigby for the damage inflicted on the hotel dining room and invited Mrs. Champion and Ellen to clean it up; and then he'd addressed Pip. Like she was on his to-do list and needed ticking off.

For the sake of privacy for what was sure to be an awkward and embarrassing conversation, Morgan had herded Pip to the front parlor of the hotel, which was just a cramped room with a battered velvet chaise and a couple of rocking chairs. It looked straight out onto the street, where they had a clear view of Junebug being bundled into the wagon. The girl was rigid and white-faced with fury. She'd ripped all her hairpins out and her shaggy mop was a wild corona around her head. She'd also removed her shoes and stock-

ings and was aggressively barefoot again. Pip noted that she refused to look at any of her brothers, or even to speak to them. She
sat herself at the rear of the wagon and glared mutinously out at
the street.

Morgan seemed equally white-faced and furious. He seethed.

Pip watched him carefully, aware that she didn't know him, or
what he was capable of. He'd been nothing but coldly polite to her
so far, but he was a big man, and an unknown quantity—especially
now that she knew it wasn't he who had written the letters.

"I imagine this is a shock to you," he said tightly as they watched
the McBride wagon trundle away.

The word *shock* didn't really begin to cover it. It was a bitter pill,
a defeat, a blow, an upset. A goddamn calamity. Pip could only imagine going back to Joshua after *this*. Imagine what John would say,
and what he'd tell Mother. "I knew it was a disaster in the making,"
Mother would sigh, and she'd give Pip that look. The one that made
Pip want to scream. "But you always have a place here, with us . . ."

By the time Morgan McBride got through his litany of orders
(which included telling Pip not to bother writing home before she
left, as she'd be there before any letter could arrive) and had announced with magnanimity that he would organize her train ticket
home again, Pip had played out the whole horrid homecoming in
her head. The long ride up the drive, through the cornfields; the
family waiting on the porch, their faces folded into lines of perfect
Christian charity; the dusty ticking of the grandfather clock in the
parlor; the days and months and years ahead . . .

And she wasn't doing it.

"I don't think that will be necessary," she said slowly. Her mind
was whirring. She remembered copying out all those recipes, one
by painstaking one, while Mother stood reading over her shoulder; she remembered ordering that silly hat from the mail-order
catalog and hiding it so no one would give her a pitying look; she
remembered lying awake into the night, imagining being mistress

of her own house. And she remembered seeing Samuel Arcross loading sacks into the back of his wagon as the train pulled away from Nebraska. She'd been thrilled to see the back of him. And she wasn't about to chug back into town and have to force a smile for Samuel dang Arcross, while everyone gossiped about how even when she answered an advertisement for a *bullheaded backwoodsman* she couldn't get a husband.

Morgan McBride was impatient. "It's fine. It's the least I can do."

He was just going through the formalities, Pip realized. He wanted to get rid of her, as quickly and efficiently as possible, so he was going to buy her a ticket, bundle her onto a train and get on with his life. But if she got on that train her life might as well be over.

He didn't seem to register the sheer oppositeness of their experiences in this moment. He may not have ordered a wife, but she'd sure as heck planned to be one. It didn't change his life one jot to send her home again, but it meant everything to Pip.

She was just about to speak when he cut her off.

"The thing is," he said, staring blindly out at the street, "she thinks she won last time. That's the mistake we made." A muscle twitched in his jaw. "I got lulled into a false sense of security," he mused, "and never saw the trap she was setting."

Trap? Hold on . . . was *she* the trap in this scenario? Pip opened her mouth to protest . . . but he talked right on over her.

"She needs schooling," he said, mostly to the street outside, "something to keep her occupied and out of trouble."

Pip didn't doubt it. But she also didn't see why *she* should bear the brunt of Junebug's troublemaking. "I've come a long way, Mr. McBride," Pip said, persevering even though he kept talking over her. She raised her voice to be heard. "In good faith, no less."

"It wasn't easy for her, growing up with only us boys."

Oh my God, he was annoying. He just kept talking like she

wasn't even part of the conversation. He wasn't even *looking* at her. He was just giving a gosh-darn monologue to the window!

"But it's time that she learned."

Pip had a lot to say about who needed to learn what—but none of these McBrides seemed interested in hearing it! She felt like she'd been stampeded by a herd of cows.

And it didn't improve. Somehow Morgan McBride got through an entire apology without once apologizing, and then he was leaving! Pip rushed after him, trying to grab hold of him, but it was like trying to catch a storm.

"Hey!" she yelled as he swung into his saddle.

But he didn't listen. At all. It was unbelievable.

The man rode off, even as she was shouting his name. It was like he couldn't even hear her. She'd been dismissed and forgotten, even as she stood here.

And then she saw John appear from the saloon down the road and groaned. Look at him, like a groundhog popping its head out of its hole. He jammed his hat on his head and trotted down the road. "Where's McBride going?" John asked breathlessly as he arrived. "He didn't want you?"

Goddamn it. Pip felt like pushing him off the hotel porch. Why did he immediately think she'd been rejected?

"Don't be silly," she said tightly, not sure what she was thinking, even as she spoke. Something in her had pulled loose. "Of course he wanted me. He placed an ad for a wife, didn't he?" As the words came out of her, she felt a surge of something she couldn't quite name. Something powerful and downright disobedient.

"Oh, thank goodness." John just about melted with relief. Like someone had plucked the bones right out of his body. "When I saw him, I got worried."

"Did you?" Pip crossed her arms and regarded him archly. "And why would that be?"

John had the good sense not to run headfirst into that one, but Pip knew exactly what he was thinking. *He's not for the likes of you.*

Well, John hadn't met him. Once you met him, you sure got an idea of why he wasn't married. The man had the personality of sandpaper.

A secretly gumptious woman with a mind of her own and a bit of backbone is required for wifely duties. Pip snorted as the words of the advertisement came back to her. No wonder this wife needed some gumption and backbone. That man was as overbearing as they came. He was despotic, peremptory and insensible to others. He certainly needed a wife who could hold her own.

Must be able to soothe a fractious temper, the ad had said.

Junebug's ad . . . That poor kid! Imagine living with him!

No wonder the kid had thrown all that porcelain back there. What else could you do with a man who wouldn't even listen to you? Pip's mind raced as she remembered all the letters, which she now realized were written by Junebug. There had been a lot in there about Morgan McBride's *poor little sister.* Who was tasked with tending to that bullheaded nightmare of a man . . .

No wonder Junebug wanted a wife for him. She must be desperate for some protection. An image of him standing patiently, arms protecting his face as Junebug slung teacups at him, flickered. Maybe she was being unfair. Maybe Junebug protected herself just fine. Even though he was a perfect brute.

A bullheaded backwoodsman.

Well. Pip couldn't say she hadn't known what she was getting into. After all, it had been in the letters . . . the temper, the high-handedness, the inability to listen . . . She really had no right to be shocked. It was just that reading about it and experiencing it first-hand were two different things. And it was different when she thought *he* was writing those things about *himself.* It showed a measure of self-awareness. But the man who'd just stampeded over Pip in the parlor had no self-awareness at all. Not even a jot of it!

"So, he's happy to go ahead?" John broke into Pip's thoughts. He still sounded disbelieving.

"He is," Pip said abruptly. She felt like she was leaping off a cliff and into thin air. What was she saying? Morgan McBride had made it perfectly clear that he wasn't happy to do any such thing . . .

But Pip had come here to get married, and she was darn well going to get married. She'd entered into this agreement in good faith, and she'd see it honored, come hell or high water. So yes, Morgan McBride would be happy to go ahead. He just didn't know it yet. Epiphany Hopgood might not be pretty, or dainty, or desirable, but she was nothing if not *gumptious*. And she was going to make Morgan McBride a happy husband, whether he wanted it or not.

She'd made the right decision. Pip was reassured by the way everything clicked into place. She hadn't even needed to buy John a train ticket—Morgan McBride had taken care of that for her. Admittedly, he'd planned for Pip to use the ticket, which was what Mr. Bascomb told her when he arrived at the hotel, waving it, but some things were just not meant to be. Not for Morgan McBride anyway.

"Morgan stopped at the station on his way out." Mr. Bascomb had given her a sympathetic look as he handed her the ticket. "I guess things didn't go to plan . . . ?"

It was a ticket for the late afternoon train. *Today's* late afternoon train. Holy crow, that man didn't waste any time, did he? Pip felt a lick of anger. And the darker, more familiar stirrings of rejection.

But *this* time she wasn't about to accept rejection. Why should she? She hadn't done anything to deserve it. And this time the stars were aligned in Pip's favor, because Morgan McBride had bought only *one* ticket. He hadn't known about her brother John or her

Granny Colefax. Because he hadn't asked her a single question or listened to a word she'd said. The minute Pip saw that ticket, she knew exactly what to do with it.

"Oh, that's not for me," Pip told Mr. Bascomb with forced lightness. "That's for my brother John. He's heading home. My granny is staying on to chaperone me."

It turned out Pip was a natural-born liar. And a believable one, to boot. She was learning more about herself every day.

"I can't leave before you're married!" John protested, and loudly, when she handed him the ticket, announcing that Morgan McBride had approved of her, and he was happy to fund John's journey home.

"Of course you can leave before I'm married," she said cheerfully, as she packed John's bag for him. She'd learned a thing or two from Junebug. Keep talking, keep moving and don't listen to protests. "You've talked to everyone in town—you know Morgan McBride is a stand-up guy. And you've seen him now—"

"From a distance," John objected.

"Which is enough to know there isn't anything wrong with him. Isn't that right, Granny?" Pip turned to Granny Colefax for support. She was sure her granny would be up for the adventure of staying. She certainly showed no signs of wanting to go home.

"Wrong with him?" Granny hooted. "That McBride man is righter than spring rain!"

"Why does he want me gone so fast?" John asked, suspicious. "Why not let me witness the wedding?"

"This afternoon's train is the last train for days," Pip invented swiftly. Who knew she had such a capacity for fabricating? "He doesn't want to keep you from home a moment longer than necessary."

"You could get married *now*." John was being wretchedly difficult. "Before the train."

"Don't rush the girl," Granny scolded. She handed Pip John's shaving kit from the bureau, to be packed. "You haven't got a clue how it feels to be a young woman on the cusp of wedding," she told him. "A girl gets skittery. If she wants to take another day, then who are you to stop her?"

"Besides, there's no time! The train leaves soon." Pip glanced out the window. The train was already at the station. She'd deliberately waited to hand him the ticket until the last minute. She didn't want him to have time to bolster his arguments.

"But I should *be* here," John insisted. "It's inappropriate to leave you before you're wed! What would Mother say!"

"Tell her you saw the wedding," Pip suggested. "Then she won't say anything."

"Lie?" John gasped, as though she'd suggested he murder someone. "To *Mother*?"

"It's not a lie," Pip assured him, checking the room for anything she'd missed. "It's just a deferred truth." She handed him his bag and his hat. "I am getting married, after all."

"And I'm here," Granny reminded him. She was playing along with vigor. Pip knew she'd heard every word that had been said in that dining room; God knew, the McBrides weren't quiet people. Granny seemed to dread returning to Joshua even more than Pip did, and was bending over backward to help Pip get rid of John. "It's not like you're leaving her on her own."

"You?" John gave their diminutive grandmother a disbelieving once-over. "What good are you against a den full of wild mountain men?"

"A den full of wild mountain men," Pip scoffed. "You saw them! They're perfectly respectable." It was a good thing he hadn't seen the shattered plates in the dining room, Pip thought, or he never would have bought that line.

"Don't fret," Granny Colefax soothed John as she took his arm and pulled him to the door. "I brought my derringer."

Pip was shocked. "You have a gun?"

"Of course. Surely you don't think I'm dumb enough to brave the frontier without a gun?" Granny Colefax tutted.

"Did *you* bring a gun?" Pip asked John. She'd taken him by the other arm and was hurrying him through the hotel.

"No." John resisted their pull.

"So, how could you possibly protect me any better than Granny can?"

"Epiphany." He'd adopted a tone.

She didn't like it. "Yes, Jonathan?"

"It's not right." He grabbed the banister of the hotel staircase and refused to budge.

"No, of course it's not," Pip snapped. "What's *right* would be if I'd married Samuel Arcross half a dozen years ago! What's *right* would be me established in my own household already. *Nothing* about this is right, John! Nothing! Do you think I want to be here, marrying some man I'd not met until today?"

John blinked. He had no rejoinder to that.

"But I'm here. And I'm finally about to be married. So why can't you be happy for me?"

"I am . . ." he protested. He was blinking rapidly, in that way he had when he lost track of the argument. And she could always make him lose track. John was many things, but quick on his feet wasn't one of them.

"Oh, thank you, John!" This was a technique she'd also learned from Junebug. Act like people agreed with you, even when they clearly didn't. She threw herself at him and gave him a smacking kiss on the cheek. "I can't tell you how happy it makes me, that you agree."

"I what?"

But Pip and Granny had him down the street and on the train before he quite realized he'd lost the argument.

"You give that sweet little wife of yours a hug for me, now, you hear?" Pip told him as she pushed him through the carriage door.

"And all those lovely nieces and nephews of mine—tell them I'll write."

"But . . ."

The screech of the train whistle cut him off.

"Bye, John!"

"You're a lot craftier than I ever gave you credit for, my girl," Granny said as they waved him off. Pip could see his bewildered face through the window.

Pip tried to look innocent, but she could see that Granny Colefax wasn't buying it.

"Seeing you manage him gives me hope that you might be able to manage that McBride man too," Granny mused. The pale steam of the engine puffed above the trees as the sound of the train receded. "But you'll have your work cut out for you. For starters, how are you going to get him to the altar?"

"I don't see that that will be a problem," Pip lied, even though she knew perfectly well Granny was aware of the full extent of her predicament, "given he advertised for me in the first place. That's why I'm here, remember?"

Granny snorted. "Don't think you can manage *me*, girl. I got more years on you, and a heck of a lot more experience. I heard all that yelling and plate smashing. You're about as far from wanted as it's possible to be."

Pip's spine stiffened. "He may not want me yet, but he will," she promised.

Granny Colefax eyed her, brown gaze glinting. "And how are you planning on achieving that?"

Pip had no idea.

Granny laughed. "No need to worry," she said, looping her arm through Pip's. "I'm wily enough for the both of us. And I've got plenty of tricks up my sleeve. The first one involves that new dress of yours."

Pip frowned.

"Those letters may have said he didn't care about the way you looked . . . but he didn't write those letters, did he?" Granny Colefax sounded sly.

"You were eavesdropping," Pip accused.

"It ain't eavesdropping when people are yelling loud enough to wake the dead," Granny sniffed. "Now, stop interrupting. I reckon if we pair that dress of yours with your cooking skills, why, we're in with a fighting chance."

Pip didn't think her dress was *that* nice. The hem was absurdly uneven. "We?"

"We," Granny said firmly. "And if you catch him and keep him, I reckon you'll need me to stay for longer than three weeks."

"Oh, you do?" Pip surrendered to the old woman's strong pull.

"I've taken a shine to these mountains. They're a darn sight more interesting than corn."

"*If* I can catch him . . ." Pip felt the full import of what she was doing hit her. She must have lost her mind.

"And keep him," Granny reminded her. "Catching a man is often as easy as wearing that gown of yours. Keeping him . . . well, that's a whole other matter . . ."

Pip wasn't optimistic about either.

But she was powerful determined to try.

Eight

Morgan couldn't believe it when he saw the wagon rattle out of the woods and into the meadow. It was that damn *wife* Junebug had ordered up for him, the one who was supposed to be gone already. He'd organized it, damn it. He'd bought the train ticket. What in hell was she doing here when the train had left yesterday? There was no mistaking her, even from a distance. She was unlike any woman Morgan had seen in his life; taller than most men, she looked strong enough to wield his ax without breaking a sweat. And then there was that hair, rusty red and blazing like fall leaves. There was no other woman like her in these parts—he was definitely in no doubt about who was driving that wagon.

"Junebug!" he roared. This was it. He didn't care how much Kit and Maddy defended her, she was going to boarding school. He had the name of a place in Chicago, and he had no compunction about packing her off. Not anymore. She needed discipline. From women, not from the likes of him; she needed that Upcott Academy for Girls, whose advertisement promised to turn her into a perfect lady.

"Junebug cain't hear you," Thunderhead Bill scolded Morgan,

from where he lay dozing in the sun on the porch. He was reclining in the rocker, with his feet up on the railing. "The only person who can hear you is me," he grumbled, "and I ain't pleased about it. I was having a mighty fine dream about a chorus girl I once met in Butte. Junebug's off hauling coal for the forge, remember? You've got her choking on soot, and that girl is sour as a toothless beaver, son."

"I ain't your son," Morgan reminded him shortly.

"Shame too. If you were mine, I would have taught you some manners. Who goes around waking an old man from his dreams?"

Morgan reached over and pushed Thunderhead Bill's boots off the porch rail. "Make yourself useful and go get my sister."

"She ain't likely to come."

"She will if you tell her we got company." Morgan jerked his head at the oncoming wagon and then stomped off to meet it.

His temper was running hot. Goddamn Junebug and her meddling. He couldn't wait to get out of this place, and away from her scheming ways. Morgan couldn't hear anything but his blood pounding in his ears as he ran through the litany of reasons why he was glad that this was his last day in Buck's Creek. And most of those reasons were named Junebug.

Pull in your horns, he counseled himself as he felt his temper getting the best of him. *It ain't this woman's fault.* Only, why the hell was she here and not on the train? He'd *told* her. If he was in the market for a wife—which he wasn't—he sure as hell didn't want a stubborn one. He already had one female who didn't listen to him. He didn't need two.

"Stop right there!" he ordered as he plowed through the meadow grass. The sparrows startled and rose into the air at the crack of his voice.

Obediently, the wagon rattled to a halt, all the way across the meadow. Morgan grunted. He was hot and bothered by the time he reached her. The noonday sun was pounding down on him, and he was sweaty and ten times more irritable than he'd been when he'd set off to meet her. He squinted up at her. He had to crick his neck to do it, she was that tall sitting up there.

She wasn't alone, either, he saw. She had an older woman with her, decked out in black like a crow, perched ramrod straight on the wagon bench. And then he saw the tray of the wagon, with all its luggage, and the chicken coop, and the horse and cow tethered to the back of it. What the *hell*?

"What are you doing here?" he barked, although he knew. And he wasn't having it. He didn't want a wife, and he'd been as clear as clear could be about that fact. He couldn't believe the nerve of her, not listening to him.

She was shocked by his manner. He could tell by the way her mouth fell open. He scowled. Well, he had no time or patience for niceties, and he didn't care to placate some woman he'd not invited. She was a damn *intruder*.

"How did you even get here?" he demanded. All the impotent rage he felt at Junebug was swirling around in him like the creek current after the snow melted.

"We borrowed Mr. Rigby's wagon," she said. Her initial shock had transitioned into a faint frown.

"I can see that. I mean, how did you get up the hill?" Were they mad, to go headlong up the hill, through the woods, on their own?

"We followed the track," she said, like he was simple.

He swore. Wasn't that just like a female. "You came up here all alone? You got any idea what could have happened to you barreling up here?"

"We had a map," the old lady told him. She was just as calm as the redhead as she held up a sheet of paper. "The hotelier drew it for us."

"You could have got lost," Morgan railed, disregarding her. This was just the kind of reckless behavior he was sick of from Junebug. "It ain't safe roaming the woods. You could have got set on by a bear, or worse."

"What's worse than a bear?" The redhead seemed surprised. But at least she had the good sense to glance over her shoulder, alarmed.

He swore. "You sound like my sister. There's plenty worse than a bear! You ever met a miner who ain't seen a woman for months?" Morgan struggled to get hold of himself. He felt like a kid throwing a tantrum. It was only exacerbated by her coolness. Where did she get the nerve, driving into his home and acting like she had a right to be here?

"No. I can't say that I have," she admitted.

She looked different, he thought abruptly. She hadn't looked like this yesterday. Yesterday she'd been wearing . . . what? He couldn't remember. But it sure hadn't been this. Morgan's gaze drifted as he took in the form-fitting gown. Or rather, the form fitted by the gown. Hell, that was a lot of woman . . .

His gaze was stuck on her chest, he realized.

He flushed and tore it away. "Have what?" He couldn't remember what they were talking about. It was because of that damn dress. How was a man to think straight when a woman's chest was all on display like that? Even though she was buttoned up to the chin, she looked more naked than not. It was just the . . . size of her. The woman was all dips and curves. Especially in the front.

"Met a miner who hasn't seen a woman for months," she reminded him.

The woman was talking nonsense; he couldn't follow it.

"Are you going to stand here yelling at us for much longer?" the old lady inquired. "Because it's been a long journey and we wouldn't mind hitching up and resting a spell."

Over his dead body. "No."

"No, you're not going to stand here yelling? Oh good. Come on, Pip, off we go."

Morgan grabbed the horse's bridle. They weren't going anywhere. He felt all turned around—like he was arguing with Junebug.

"Would you like to ride with us?" the redhead asked. "You look a bit peaky."

"You're not staying," he growled.

She cocked her head and pursed her lips. "Possibly not. But I think we need to talk before anything is decided."

"We did talk. Yesterday." The woman was impossible. "And we agreed—"

"*We* didn't talk," she said primly. "*You* talked. And I never agreed to anything."

Morgan felt like she'd just hit him over the head with a mallet. That was just a flat-out lie. He had a clear memory of leaving that hotel with a firm agreement. She was Junebug's doing, not his; he didn't want her; she was going back to her people. The end.

"Pip, love, why don't you get down from the wagon and have a good talk with Mr. McBride. I'll ride on. The animals need watering, and it looks like he might be a while."

It didn't matter how Morgan protested, neither of these stubborn females would listen to him. Somehow the old woman was driving the wagon on to the trading post, and he was stuck here in the meadow grass with this obstinate redhead.

Up close she was even more disconcerting. She was as tall as he remembered, but everything else was discombobulating. It was that dress. It was a deep green sheath that clung to every corseted inch of her. Yesterday he thought she'd been solid, today she was . . . Goddamn distracting, that's what she was.

"I just want to say my piece, Mr. McBride," she said. She met his gaze frankly, without coyness. Her eyes were tawny green and gold, like the sun flickering between summer leaves.

"Why?" Morgan didn't see what there was to talk about. He didn't want a wife. She *knew* he didn't want a wife. So, what was there to discuss?

"Because I haven't said it yet." There was a snap to her now. "You didn't let me get a word in edgewise yesterday."

"That ain't true." But even as he said the words, he knew it might be true. He was prone to talking more than listening—Junebug and his brothers were always telling him so. He racked his brains to think through their conversation. For the life of him, he couldn't remember what she'd said.

He didn't remember much of her at all, if he was honest. She'd been aproned and floury, with a pile of red hair pinned up on her head. That was about it. He remembered being absurdly irked that Junebug had ordered Kit a pretty wife but had settled on a plain one for him. Even though he wasn't taking her, pretty or plain, or blue in the face, so looks didn't matter one bit. But it still irked him.

But now that she was standing here in broad daylight, Morgan saw that she wasn't plain at all. He'd clearly been too angry with Junebug yesterday to pay attention to this woman properly. Not to her words, or to her looks. Because she was the flat-out opposite of plain. She was as striking as all get-out. There were those gold-lit eyes, the rusty red hair, the expressive mouth and that *figure*. That figure was the stuff dreams were made of. That sack of an apron yesterday had done her no favors at all.

Not that it mattered, he reminded himself, since he didn't want her.

"It won't hurt you to listen to me," the redhead told him. There was a startling mix of irritation, amusement and sympathy in her voice.

Morgan tried to remember her name. Junebug had said it a million times in the wagon ride down the hill to that ludicrous high tea. Something "good"? Morgan wondered if it was ruder to admit he couldn't remember her name, or ruder to continue not knowing it . . .

Did it matter, since he wasn't going to know her after today?

Hopgood! Her name was Hopgood. Something Hopgood.

"Are you listening to me?" The gold lights disappeared from her eyes, and they became a brooding dark green. "You're not listening. *Again*."

Morgan didn't need this. It was his last day here; he had a lot to do. "How long will this take?" he asked abruptly.

There was a whistle from across the meadow and Morgan turned to see his whole family standing on the damn porch of the trading post, watching him and the redhead. Junebug was whistling and holding up the coffeepot. She waggled it, clearly curious to know if they wanted coffee. Morgan swore. What did she think this was? Another high tea? She better not think that him talking to this woman out here in the meadow changed anything, because it didn't. Junebug was working in Kit's forge until the minute he packed her off to that ladies' academy.

"The advertisement said you had a surfeit of family," the redhead, Miss Hopgood, observed dryly. "I guess your sister didn't lie about that."

"What else did the advertisement say?" Morgan hated to think. Junebug hadn't told him a word about it. Not that he'd asked; he'd been too busy shouting at her to let her explain. What was there to explain anyway? They all knew what she'd done, because she'd done it before. "Do I snore and have all my own teeth?" Morgan snapped. That was what Junebug had said about poor Kit when she'd put out an ad for his wife. The fact that it was true was beside the point.

"*Wanted: Wife for a bullheaded backwoodsman . . .*"

To Morgan's astonishment, the woman reeled off the entire ad from memory. He was unsettled, both by the fact that she knew it by heart and by Junebug's ridiculous wording. *Has it in him to make you laugh—mostly not on purpose?* What the hell did that mean? *Will mend your boots and give you unwanted advice?*

"And you *answered* that stupid thing?" Morgan was horrified.

Miss Hopgood flushed. "I liked your honesty."

"Not mine," he reminded her tersely.

"No," she admitted. Then she fixed him with that disconcertingly direct gaze again. "What would you have said about yourself?"

Well, that was a question and a half.

"Bad-tempered man, not looking for a wife under any circumstances," he snapped. But he immediately regretted it when she flinched. His anger subsided as suddenly as it had erupted, as it always did, leaving him feeling exposed and embarrassed. The heat drained from him, and his blood slowed. He was taking his frustration out on the wrong person. What had this poor woman done, other than answer an advertisement? This was Junebug's fault, not hers. Junebug was the one he should be railing at. This woman was as much a victim as he was.

"You might as well come and have coffee while you're here," he said gruffly. "You'll want to be leaving soon though. You don't want to be out on the trail in the dark."

"You're not worried about the bears and woman-starved miners anymore?" she asked archly.

Morgan scowled. Of course he was still worried, but she wasn't his responsibility to worry over, damn it. And this wasn't how his day was supposed to go. This was his last day. He'd wanted it to be . . . ah hell, he didn't know what he wanted it to be. Something other than this, at least.

It had proven to be a heaviness, leaving Buck's Creek. Heavier than Morgan had imagined it would be. Not that he wasn't looking forward to leaving—he was. It was just that there were so many ghosts in Buck's Creek, and it was hard leaving them to their meadow. He'd been out of sorts even before this unwanted bride had invaded.

"Wait!" she protested as he walked off. "Where are you going? I haven't finished talking!"

Morgan didn't think he could take more talking. The last twenty-four hours had shredded his nerves to hell and back. He'd talked himself blue in the face all night long. Ah, he hated fighting with Junebug. It made him feel like he'd rolled in poison ivy. But this time tomorrow he'd be away from her, out on the trail to Miles City, just him and his horses. No sisters, no unwanted brides, no talking, no listening. He'd be free.

"I have more to say," the redhead said firmly, dragging his mind back to the meadow. For the first time, Morgan noticed that she had her fists clenched in the folds of her skirt. Maybe she wasn't as cool and collected as she seemed. That made him feel a little better, for some reason.

"You can't say it over coffee?" He gestured at the trading post.

"Not in front of all those people." She seemed horrified by the idea.

"How about on the walk there? How long is it going to take?" He pinched the bridge of his nose. Why did everything have to be so *hard*? Why did *people* have to make things so hard?

"It will take as long as it takes. Can't you just let me say it?" she snapped. She definitely wasn't cool and composed now. Something about her irritation made her even more striking. It was the color in her cheeks, maybe; it made her look . . . well, aroused. The way her chest heaved too. Hell.

He pulled his gaze back up to her face. "Fine. Say it."

She took a deep breath. "I want you to marry me."

Morgan was startled into a laugh. "You what?"

"I want you to marry me," she repeated, more firmly.

"No." He considered her. She didn't seem to be joking. "Of course not."

"Why 'of course not'?" She lifted her chin.

"Because I didn't place the ad."

"I know. But you're not married, are you?"

"No."

"So, there's no reason you *can't* marry me?"

No reason except that Morgan was *happy* not to be married. He'd already told her that, yesterday.

"I answered that ad because *I* want to get married," she said patiently.

Obviously. He didn't understand why she was telling him this. Did she think he was simple? He *knew* she'd answered the ad because she wanted to get married. But *he* didn't. It wasn't his ad.

Maybe *she* was simple?

No. Her gaze was too sharp for that.

Morgan felt a bit flustered under her stare. She was looking at him like he was a recalcitrant child. He didn't like it.

"I answered that advertisement in good faith," she said.

She'd said the words *good faith* before. This whole good faith business seemed to mean a lot to her. He guessed he understood that. Junebug had gone and ruined his good faith, too—more than once. It was an upset, and no mistake.

Her gaze was still a solemn green. "I left my family and came all the way across the country for this," she told him. She sounded calm, but those fists were still bunched tight. So tight her knuckles had turned white.

"Is this about money?" he hazarded. "Because I told you I'd reimburse you for the ticket out here."

Her breath caught in astonishment. Or outrage. Some kind of strength of feeling. He wished it hadn't, because it made her chest hitch, and now he was back to looking at her breasts. Like he was a fool boy who'd never caught sight of a woman before. Although to be fair, he'd never caught sight of *this much* woman in his life before. She sure was something. He couldn't help but have thoughts of unwrapping her . . .

Hell, that was like taking a straight hit of moonshine.

"You're not *listening*!"

And now that magnificent chest was heaving wildly. Morgan's heart just about stopped at the thought that she might pop a button.

"Look me in the eye and tell me that you're listening to me," she ordered.

Morgan flushed. It was mortifying to be caught staring. Again. He dragged his gaze back up to her green eyes. The gold lights were back, but this time they were crackling like sparks off an anvil. She was riled.

It did fine things for her.

"I'm listening," he promised, hoping it was a promise he could keep. He'd do his best. Junebug had outdone herself this time, he thought stupidly. Maddy was a sweet girl and all, but she wasn't . . . this.

"I accepted a proposal of marriage, Mr. McBride," she told him. "And I mean to be married."

Morgan frowned.

"Given the circumstances, I think it would be gentlemanly of you to honor the agreement. After all, I've come all this way."

Morgan was gobsmacked. She wasn't serious? After he'd explained it all to her? More than once! And she had the nerve to tell him that *he* wasn't listening. "You think it would be gentlemanly for me to marry you?" he repeated.

The daft woman actually seemed relieved. She nodded, looking like he'd agreed to something. Which he hadn't.

"Well, it may have escaped your notice—Miss Hopgood, is it?—but I'm not a gentleman."

"It has not escaped my notice," she said patiently. "But I had hoped you'd rise to the occasion."

Was she being suggestive? His gaze dropped back to her chest. Because he *was* rising to the occasion, and he didn't appreciate it.

"You're not married, and I'm not married," she sighed, her chest swelling and falling. "And I've come all this way. Surely we can at least get to know each other? Maybe you'll discover I have hidden charms."

She had too many charms already; Morgan didn't want to learn about any more. "I'm only saving you the trouble of a deferred rejection," he told her. "Sure, you can stay; sure, we can get to know each other. But it won't change anything." He was being rhetorical. He thought that was plenty clear. Only apparently it wasn't.

"Oh, thank you!" A smile lit her face.

Goddamn it. Morgan felt like she'd socked him one. What was *that*? She smiled and her whole face transformed. She went from striking to something else entirely. Goddamn gorgeous was what she was. It was like witchcraft. He was so distracted that he didn't listen to a word she said. Which was a problem, as somehow she'd got the wrong end of the stick and thought she was *staying*.

"*I'm* not even staying!" Morgan railed at Kit as he watched Maddy lead the redhead and her grandmother into the new house.

"Oh yes, you are," Kit objected. "You're not heading out in the morning and leaving *me* to explain it to her."

"I'll explain it to her," Beau volunteered magnanimously.

It didn't escape Morgan's notice that his younger brother had changed into his good shirt. It also hadn't escaped his notice that Beau had been ogling the redhead. That they'd *all* been ogling the redhead, even those mangy old trappers.

"You ain't explaining anything," Morgan growled. "You keep away from her."

"Why? It ain't like you want her." Beau grinned and straightened his collar.

"A woman like that'll get you into trouble, you runt," Morgan warned. "You got no experience with women, especially a woman like this."

"I've got experience!" Beau protested. "More experience than you've had in a good long while."

"Experience at what?" Junebug popped up, like a beaver out of its dam. She was perky again. All trace of her colossal tantrum and ensuing sulk had evaporated. In fact, the kid looked downright chipper.

Morgan had half a mind to pitch her in the creek.

"None of your business," Kit told her shortly. He gave Morgan a warning look.

"Is this about Beau visiting the cathouse? Because I know all about that," she scoffed.

Morgan cuffed Beau upside the head. "Why in hell are you telling her about that!"

"I didn't tell her anything," Beau yelped. "You know Junebug, she sticks her nose in places it don't belong."

"Better my nose gets stuck places than your—"

"Junebug!" Morgan was outraged. "You ain't got an ounce of ladylike in you!"

She rolled her eyes. "Of course you yell at *me*. I ain't the one visiting cathouses, but *I'm* the one you yell at."

"Maybe he won't need to visit the cathouse anymore," Jonah suggested slyly. "Now that we've got ourselves an unhitched woman on the premises."

Morgan and Junebug erupted at the same time.

"She ain't for the likes of you!" Junebug yelled at Beau.

"You treat her with respect," Morgan bellowed. "She's a guest in our house."

"My house," Kit corrected. "And the lot of you would do well to remember it. So long as she's under my roof, she's *my* guest and you'll have me to deal with if you do wrong by her." He fixed Beau with a dark look. Kit was the biggest of them, and the only one never bested in a wrestling match, so there was no doubt they'd listen.

"Was it the curves?" Junebug asked curiously, once Beau and Jonah had slunk off, and Kit had headed off to help unload the wagon.

Morgan scowled at her. "Don't go getting ideas. She ain't staying." He headed for the cabin he shared with the boys and Junebug.

"She's not, huh? How come she's unloading all them trunks,

then?" Junebug followed along after. She was as stubborn as a mayfly.

"She's only staying one night," Morgan growled. He still didn't know how that had happened. But it didn't matter. He'd humor the woman for the day and then inform her in the morning that he still didn't want a wife. For the hundredth time. And then he'd leave, just like he'd planned. Her staying changed nothing.

"A lot can happen in one night," Junebug said with relish. "Just ask Becky Sharp."

"Becky who?" He regretted asking, as Junebug launched enthusiastically into a potted summary of some book Kit had read her. Morgan had perfected the art of not listening to Junebug's endless chatter, which was a blessing now, as she'd got up a good head of steam. Morgan didn't appreciate her blitheness. She was supposed to be suffering his punishment for her misdeeds, and yet here she was, grinning from ear to ear and counting her unhatched (and never going to hatch) chickens. Junebug seemed under the misapprehension that just because the redhead was here, she was winning. Well, she had another thing coming.

Because Morgan McBride wasn't getting married. And that was that.

Nine

"I hope you don't mind sharing a bed," Maddy McBride apologized, opening the door to the room Pip and Granny would be occupying.

Like the rest of the house, the room was simple, but welcoming. The timber walls were whitewashed, and a big sash window flooded the room with light. And the window looked out onto a view that made Pip's heart stumble. Buck's Creek was about the prettiest place you could imagine. The meadow grass was lusciously green and threaded with wildflowers in blues and golds, with the odd pop of cheery red. Along the creek there were thickets of purple iris, and a single chokecherry tree curved over the bank, its boughs garlanded with bunches of black-red berries. The creek itself was a tumble of clear water, wide as a river and rilled with white foam as it swirled over slick rocks. The meadow was fringed by thick woods, and above it all the mountain peaks rose into the heartbreakingly blue sky. This was about as far from the plains and cornfields of Nebraska as Pip could imagine.

"This room was supposed to be for Junebug," Maddy said, smoothing the patchwork coverlet on the brass bed as she passed it on her way to the window. She slid the sash open, and the sweet smell of meadow grass and creek water danced in. "But she refuses to leave the cabin. She says it's done her well enough for all these years and she's got no call to be leaving it now." Maddy pulled a face. "We thought she might be tempted by a proper bed and a feather mattress, but she lasted half of the first night and then went back to her loft in the cabin. I don't know if it's the cabin or Morgan she can't bear to part with."

Pip was grateful for Maddy McBride. She was a gentle blue-eyed woman, with a lilting Irish accent and a calm manner; it was like finding a bluebell amid the brambles. Her presence was soothing; she lacked the fractiousness of the rest of the McBrides. This place had too many overwhelming men in it by half, Pip thought, and she was still reeling from her conversation with Morgan in the meadow.

He was simply impossible. The man had a complete and total inability to listen. He just plowed through her like she was a snowbank. *Bad-tempered man, not looking for a wife under any circumstances,* he'd growled. But bad-tempered didn't even begin to cover it. The man was choleric in the extreme.

But also confoundingly unguarded. There was something about the way he chafed under conversation that tugged at her. There was a vague air of panic to him, she thought, remembering the way he pinched the bridge of his nose, and fidgeted, his dark hair falling restlessly over his forehead. His gray eyes were turbulent. There were moments when he looked like a boy, burdened by things he couldn't quite bear.

For all his bluster, Pip didn't find him frightening. She should, she thought. He was enormous and powerful, and a stranger, capable of God knew what. But he didn't radiate violence. Just vexation, really, and a quite petty crossness. It was almost amusing how vexed he was by everything. Like a sour old tomcat, grumpy about being disturbed, when all he wanted was to snooze in the sun.

There was something about those dimples and the way they flickered in his cheeks that made Pip feel safe. Which was ridiculous. What did dimples have to do with anything? But her gut told her he was harmless. And Pip could understand his irritation too. Imagine having an unexpected wife foisted on you! Pip was an unwelcome and shocking imposition.

But she didn't have to stay an imposition, did she? And he looked like a man who could use some burdens eased, as Granny would say.

"Men need us," Granny had told Pip as they rattled their way up the hill to Buck's Creek. It was a long journey and there was plenty of time for talking. "Without a woman, a man turns sour," she said sagely. "Like bad milk."

Well, Morgan McBride was plenty sour, that was for sure.

"What you need to do is sweeten them," Granny advised. "Give them a reason to smile. Ease their burdens, show them the fun side of life."

Pip thought that over. She remembered her dour father, and the way he and her mother barely crossed paths. He sure needed sweetening. But then, to be fair, so did Mother.

"Who sweetens us?" Pip asked curiously. She wondered if there was such a thing as mutual sweetening in a marriage.

"Honey, if you're lucky, you'll get better than sweetening." Granny had been exuberant in her reply. "If you're lucky, you'll get a hit of spice!"

Pip had made the mistake of asking what she meant by spice, and the reply was downright scandalous. But also very thought-provoking . . .

"How long have you and the big one been married?" Granny Colefax asked Maddy McBride now as she showed them the bedroom in the big house. Granny had wasted no time in sitting on the bed and bouncing, to test the comfort of the mattress.

"We got married last winter," Maddy said, flushing happily.

"And we only built the house this spring. You can probably still smell the cut timber and paint."

"You answered an advertisement too?" Pip had been dying of curiosity since that moment in the dining room when Maddy herself had blurted, *She wouldn't do it again . . .*

"Not quite." Maddy turned even pinker. "You might need a decent pot of tea to hear that story. If you want to freshen up, I'll get the water on." As soon as Kit had deposited their baggage (which filled up most of the room), he and Maddy left them with a washbasin and fresh towels and promised to have the tea ready when they came down.

They were delightful, Pip thought. The whole place was delightful, like something out of a dream. She took in the room, with its simple furniture and the good woodsy smells drifting in from the outdoors. This was exactly the kind of house she'd want, she thought, reaching out to touch the simple, blue-patterned calico curtains, which sighed inward in the breeze. Everything was calm and homely and peaceful. There was none of the buttoned-up strangulation of her mother's house back in Joshua.

Through the window, Pip could see Morgan McBride striding through the meadow toward a small log cabin that sat farther up the creek, close to the tree line of the woods. Junebug was trotting along beside him and, even from this distance, Pip could hear the chatter of her voice, even though she couldn't quite make out the words. Junebug had obviously lost her fury at Morgan. There was no trace of the plate-hurling harpy today. But even though Junebug was cheerful as a sunny day, Morgan McBride had his head down, like a horse riding into a punishing headwind. He perpetually looked like he was living the hardest day of his life, Pip thought. There was no lightness to him.

"You're going to need to talk to that girl," Granny Colefax mused, splashing the wash water from the pitcher into the basin as soon as they were alone.

"Of course. We'll go down to tea in a minute," Pip said absently as she watched Morgan disappear into the log cabin, followed closely by Junebug. She wondered what it was like in there, where he lived. It was far more modest than this brand-new two-story house; it was hard to believe three of those big men were crammed in there. Plus Junebug.

"Not Maddy. The other one." Granny set to scrubbing their travels off herself. "Junebug. She's the one who ordered you up, so as far as I can see she's the best ally we have."

"Are you sure?" Pip was dubious. "She didn't do a very good job convincing him to wed back down in Bitterroot." Pip wasn't too surprised her own forthrightness hadn't worked in the meadow just now either. But she'd had to try. Granny's plans were dubious at best, and Pip had hoped he'd listen to an honest pitch. It had been a long shot, she thought with a sigh. Given his inability to listen.

"Junebug's just a sprout. You can do the convincing, but she can give us some helpful information. There's got to be a way around him. And she lives with him, doesn't she? She'll be a gold mine." Granny laughed. "Or a silver mine, given this is silver country."

Pip supposed that was true enough. And she needed as much information as she could get. This wasn't going to be easy. Because while she'd managed to get herself lodged here in Buck's Creek for now, she still wasn't sure how to win him over, let alone get him to marry her. He was firm as firm could be that he wasn't in the market for a wife.

And if he changed his mind, what was to say he'd want *her*? He might be a grumpy cuss, but he was still the best-looking man that Pip had ever seen. If he wanted a wife, he could get one all too easily, one as pretty as Kit's wife, Maddy, or even prettier.

What did Pip have to offer? Her cooking? That seemed a paltry trade. Plenty of women could cook.

Although, according to Granny, Pip also had something else to offer . . .

"Girl, men are simple creatures," Granny had instructed as they'd lurched up the steep incline through the woods. "You show them a bit of leg, or some of that bust of yours, and they'll eat out of the palm of your hand."

Pip had been equal parts shocked and intrigued.

"Why do you think any man wants to get married?" Granny asked, shaking her head at Pip's innocence.

"For companionship," Pip had hazarded. "For a helpmate? For children?"

"For a bedmate, more like," Granny snorted. "Children are just a consequence."

Pip had never heard such crudeness from her grandmother, or from any woman she knew. Or from any man, either, for that matter. It was . . . surprisingly refreshing.

"You want to seduce the man, my girl," Granny told her baldly. "I'm not suggesting anything immoral," she assured Pip, when Pip protested. "A little flirting, that's all. A little charming. Displaying the assets. That kind of thing."

"You're forgetting my lack of assets," Pip had reminded her nervously. "I'm not the kind of woman men are charmed by."

"I'm not forgetting anything." Granny had grinned, looking like a fox facing an open chicken coop. "You know your problem? You had Verity for a mother, and you grew up in a place that thought too much about sin and not enough about pleasure. Epiphany, I have spent my whole life feeling like I was walking backwards, and I got no mind to watch you feel that way too. Not everyone is like your mother and those balled-up croakers back home. Some people will look at you and see you front-on, not backwards. And they'll celebrate all the things your mother despaired of. Because you, my girl, surely do have assets. Substantial ones."

Not for the first time, Pip wondered how her mother had come from this woman. Granny Colefax had always been a little too fresh for Joshua; too forthright, too undisciplined, *too much*. But now that she was out here on the frontier, she somehow seemed just the right size.

"You, Epiphany, are a woman who makes a man think of pleasure," Granny Colefax told her with relish. "And that scared the hell out of your mother."

Pip crossed her arms and scowled. "Stop poking fun." She remembered Samuel Arcross and all the men at those barn dances who wouldn't ask her for a single dance. Pleasure, her foot. She was a woman who made men think of running a mile.

Granny gave her an arch look. "You can't judge anything based on Joshua, not when you were dressing in tents and looking like a haystack. Now that you've liberated yourself from your mother's toggery, you pay attention. See where those McBride men look when they're talking to you."

"I don't appreciate this," Pip said tightly. "You got no call making fun like this when you *know* how I've borne the brunt of my looks."

Granny gave a sharp barking laugh. "Honey, your tides have turned." She gestured at the window. "You're in a place with a dearth of women, and you are the womanliest woman these men will have seen in their entire lives. Or are ever likely to see again, in my opinion. Now, those narrow-minded, thin-spirited, pleasureless people back home have no idea about the set of a man's needs, let alone a woman's. They've spent their whole lives squashing them. You think these McBrides look squashed?" She grinned her foxy grin. "These men are just what a girl like you needs. And *you* are going to drive them daft."

If anyone was daft, it was Pip's granny, she thought, taking her own turn at the washbowl. She unbuttoned the collar of her dress to scrub the trail dirt from her neck.

"Leave your collar open," Granny instructed when Pip was done. "And take that waistcoat off."

"I can't, it's part of the dress."

"You need more clothes. Next time, you let me make them. Your mother dressed you in too many sacks; she's got you thinking you deserved them." Granny's nimble fingers undid the buttons of Pip's gown, all the way to the V of the waistcoat.

"That's not decent," Pip protested.

"Sure it is. It's a hot day. Here, I'll do mine too. Does that make you feel better?" Granny unbuttoned her own gown at the collar. "And while we're at it, let's really let our hair down."

She meant literally, Pip realized, as Granny Colefax tugged the hairpins from her own silver-streaked rusty hair. Pip had never seen Granny with her hair down before. It tumbled down in thick waves, framing her face and making her look startlingly younger. But maybe it was Montana making her look younger. Her cheeks were pink, and her brown eyes hadn't stopped sparkling since she'd stepped off the train.

"My hair looks better up," Pip told Granny. And it was the truth. Pip's hair was too undisciplined by half.

"Stuff and nonsense." Granny was having none of it.

Pip yelped as Granny yanked a pin from Pip's head. "I'll do it!" If Granny kept yanking, she'd pull most of Pip's hair out with the pins. "What's gotten into you?"

"You need a quick education in men," Granny told her, as she fussed through their baggage for a hairbrush. "They like long hair, and they like to see skin. Not too much, not yet—you want to tease him with just a hint."

Pip caught her reflection in the small oval mirror hanging on the wall. She highly doubted Granny was right. Her auburn hair was a scraggly corona; not quite curly and not quite straight, it was a bushy nightmare. And her open collar revealed the plump crease of her cleavage, which just made her look fleshy. Experience had taught her that men liked willowy girls, like Naomi. Right now, Pip looked like nothing so much as a slattern.

She gave a startled screech as Granny attacked her with the hairbrush. "That hurts!"

"Fine, you do it. But do it properly. One hundred strokes at a minimum."

"I think you've lost your mind," Pip muttered.

"You need to trust me, Epiphany," Granny scolded as she pulled a small glass bottle from her carpetbag. "Aha!" She opened it and took a sniff.

Even from across the room Pip could smell it. "What is that?"

"Scent!"

Scent? Pip's mother had always told her that only loose women wore scent. "No," she said firmly. "I want to be a wife, not a loose woman."

"In an ideal world, you get to be a bit of both," Granny laughed, dabbing the scent on her own wrists.

"Where did you even get that?"

"I ordered it from a catalog. It's French."

"How could you afford French perfume?"

"It's not from France," she tutted, "I'm not made of money. It's from Canada."

"You smell like a bordello."

"I smell like musk and roses," Granny disagreed.

She certainly didn't smell like any rose Pip had ever met. "I think I'm just fine smelling of soap, thank you." Maddy McBride's soap smelled of lemon oil and pine, and Pip vastly preferred it to Granny's heavy odor.

"You've certainly got a head of hair on you," Granny observed, once Pip had brushed out her tangles. "You get that from me." She took the brush and set to work on her own hair.

"Why are you prettying yourself up so much?" Pip asked, pricked. "And why the scent?"

"I told you back in Nebraska. I'm on the hunt."

Pip's mouth dropped. She hadn't thought about the fact that the stack of *Matrimonial News* editions had belonged to Granny since they'd answered the ad. Somehow, she'd forgotten that Granny had been searching them for a man.

"These men are a little young for you, aren't they?" Pip said, shocked.

"Don't be ridiculous. A couple of those trappers have half a dozen years on me at least."

"You want to marry one of those trappers?" Pip was twice as shocked. Those mountain men made the McBrides look positively cultured.

"Who said anything about marriage? Those trappers ain't the marrying kind. Now, come along. That tea will be ready." Granny gave her own wrist an appreciative sniff as she opened the door.

Pip didn't know whether to laugh or cry. Her granny had clearly lost her final marbles. And now that she was away from Joshua, she seemed to have lost all her morals too!

Pip looked at herself in the mirror. Her fingers moved to her buttons. She couldn't go out like this, she thought, as she heard Granny all but dancing down the stairs. But then she remembered Samuel Arcross loading flour sacks into the back of his wagon, and Mother standing on the porch, her handkerchief clasped to her mouth; she remembered Esther Greenleaf shucking peas; and she had a sudden bright memory of Morgan McBride's gaze dropping to her chest as she tried to talk to him. She'd thought he just didn't want to meet her eye . . . But maybe there'd been something else at play?

Pip left the buttons undone.

What did she have to lose?

"You're a flat-out revelation," Junebug said, when Pip found her. The girl was in the cookhouse, red-faced and cursing up a storm.

The day was waning, and Pip hadn't seen Morgan McBride since she'd first arrived in Buck's Creek, which was hours ago now. The small cookhouse was perched right on the bank of the creek, its narrow iron chimney puffing hectic clouds of woodsmoke into the summer sky. Pip had heard Junebug swearing all the way from the porch of the big house, when she'd stepped out to use the outhouse. She'd slipped out while Granny continued to pump Maddy McBride for information. They were on their third pot of tea, but Pip was starting to feel waterlogged. She was also tense from waiting. Where had all the McBride men gone? She was here to win Morgan over to the idea of marriage, but how could she do that when he wasn't even here? She'd thought to try to find at least one McBride after visiting the outhouse, and that was when she'd heard Junebug cursing a blue streak. The sound of her voice carried across the still meadow. Pip headed down to the outbuilding, sure of what she'd find before she even got there. No matter who had written them, those letters had made it clear enough how much Junebug hated cooking.

The kid was infinitely glad to see her. Her entire face lit up when Pip appeared in the doorway. "You're not just a revelation, lady, you're a straight-out goddamn *epiphany*." Junebug laughed at her own joke, and then she dropped the knife she was holding with a clatter. "Was I ever glad to see you riding into Buck's Creek in old Rigby's wagon! Your timing was perfect. You never said you were this wily in your letters." Junebug was as wriggly as a puppy. "But here you are, looking like that, and getting under his skin like a tick!"

The girl was back in her coveralls, her feet bare and her hair newly chopped into an even shorter and more ragged halo. She had a bucket full of fish beside her and was doing a terrible job of scaling and filleting them, by the looks of it.

"You should really be doing that outside," Pip suggested. "It's a messy job."

"Ain't it just!" Junebug rubbed her filthy hand down the front of her coveralls. "But forget the dumb fish, I want to know why you're here!"

"You know very well why I'm here," Pip said. She stood in the doorframe, blocking Junebug's exit. She had a thing or two to say to this meddling girl. "I'm here, if you remember, to marry your brother. It is, after all, the whole reason I left Nebraska and came all this way."

Junebug hooted. "I *knew* I liked you!"

"You may like me," Pip said dryly, "but your brother sure doesn't. In fact, until yesterday, he didn't know I existed. Did he?"

"Well, he certainly knows now!" Junebug was gleeful. "You should see him, stomping about, acting like a storm cloud."

"And that's a good thing?" Pip felt like grabbing the kid by the coverall straps and shaking her. Pip was stranded up here in the mountains because of her, stuck between a rock called Morgan McBride and a hard place called her mother. And was the kid apologetic? Remorseful? Even sympathetic? No!

"Of course it's a good thing!" Junebug cocked her head. "This isn't my first rodeo, you know."

"So I just heard," Pip said dryly. "From Maddy."

The kid didn't even have the good grace to pretend chagrin. "I know when a man's hot and bothered," she crowed, "and Morgan is as hot and bothered as they come."

"Because he's furious!" Pip felt powerfully sorry for Morgan McBride right now. Imagine having to wrangle Junebug every day. No one deserved being blindsided by an unordered bride. "He has every right to be furious."

"Sure he does," Junebug agreed amiably. "But he'll get over it. Kit did."

Pip didn't even know where to begin with that one.

"Look, you've met him. He's impossible." Junebug was rock sure of herself; she didn't seem to harbor a single doubt about what she'd done. "He has no idea what's good for him, and one day he'll thank me."

Was it possible that she was completely insensible to morality? Pip thought. She was flabbergasted by the kid's lack of contrition. Junebug had lied and connived to get not one but *two* poor women stranded in the wilderness. With men who didn't want them. Didn't she see how dangerous that was?

If she didn't, Pip would be happy to tell her.

"Will this take long?" Junebug asked, when Pip launched into her tirade. "Because Morgan told me I had to have dinner ready and there's a lot of you people to cook for now." She used her fingers to add them up. "Eleven, including Sour Eagle and the rest on the porch. That's a lot of fish to fillet, and I still haven't raided the vegetable patch or built a cookfire. This stove ain't big enough for all these fish and Maddy won't let me use her kitchen at the big house. She's got a notion that I'll burn her house down."

"You could have got me killed!" Pip refused to be sidetracked. The kid needed to learn.

"That's a yes, it will take a long time, then." Junebug sighed and picked up the knife. "Fair enough. If you've got to do something, you might as well do it properly. And I admire that in a person. You go ahead with your speechifying, just don't mind me if I keep working while you rail at me."

Not listening must be a family trait, Pip realized, dumbstruck by the brazenness of it. They didn't even *pretend* to listen. She was quite aware that her words were washing over Junebug like a tide flowing in and then straight back out again. And the kid was positively destroying all that lovely fresh fish.

"You're using the wrong knife," Pip said tersely. She hunted the cookhouse for a better one. "Here." And then she went back to scolding her for her duplicitous letter writing.

"All I can see," Junebug interrupted, as she wiped the sweat from her forehead with her forearm, "is that you're nearabout perfect

for him. You like yelling at me just as much as he does." She fixed
Pip with a calculating gray stare, one that was enough like her
brother's to be disconcerting. "But I'll bear it, if it means I can get
some help in this damn cookhouse."

"You need it," Pip said acidly, "given the way you're ruining
those fine fish."

"They ain't fine one bit. They're full of bones. If I leave the
bones in, the boys give me hell. But filleting them gives me con-
niptions."

"Of course it does, because you're doing it all wrong." Pip shook
her head. "Honestly, what a way to destroy the best meat."

"If you've got so many ideas about it, why don't you fillet them?"
Junebug asked mulishly.

"I'll show you how, then you can do it."

"I don't *want* to do it," the obstinate kid grumbled. But she
stepped aside and handed Pip the knife.

Pip looked down at her juniper-green dress. "Do you have an
apron?"

The kid looked at her like she'd asked for a lace parasol.

Pip sighed. "How about a tablecloth? Anything I can cover myself with?"

"Give me a minute." Junebug pushed past Pip and left the cookhouse.

Pip hoped she'd come back, because she wasn't planning on
filleting all these fish on her own. They were mighty pretty fish,
she observed, turning one over; it was silvery, with a luminescent
shimmer of color down the side. It was plump and just begging to
be baked.

"Here!" When Junebug came back she was brandishing a blue
and white flannel shirt. "It's an old one of Morgan's, he won't mind."

It was huge. Pip wasn't a small woman, but she swam in it. His
shoulders were twice as wide as hers.

"You reckon it'll do up across your bust?" Junebug asked curiously. "You sure got a set on you!"

"Junebug!" Pip turned scarlet. "Ladies don't talk about other people's bodies."

"Mine ain't anywhere near that big, but I reckon I still got some growing to do." Unperturbed, Junebug was staring down at her own chest, which seemed perfectly flat in those coveralls.

Pip kept her head down as she buttoned the shirt over her breasts. Honestly. The child might as well have been raised in a cathouse, the way she spoke. She needed a firm hand.

Morgan's old shirt was soft from years of wear. Pip dipped her head sideways, catching an intoxicating scent. The perfume of him, a fresh woodsy smell, was embedded in the cloth.

"I hope it don't stink too bad," Junebug commiserated. "It's clean, but he sure can get a stink up when he's working. I should know, I have to wash his clothes."

"It's fine." Pip cleared her throat and rolled the sleeves up. "Come on, now, there's a lot of fish here, and the day's wasting."

With neat, precise movements, Pip showed Junebug how to scale the fish without ruining the skin. Then she neatly flicked the knife, removing the bits she didn't want and butterflying it. The whole process took less than a minute.

"You know your way around a fish," Junebug said appreciatively.

"We have a lot of fish in Nebraska." Pip handed Junebug the knife. "Your turn." She watched as the girl attacked the next one. She was a quick study, Pip would say that for her.

"You also have a lot of corn, by the sounds of it," Junebug noted. "You talked about a lot of corn recipes in your letters."

"My father grows corn." Pip paused. "So do my brothers, and my brothers-in-law." And just about everyone she knew. Absently, she reached out and showed Junebug where she was going wrong with the deboning. "Here, it should be one smooth movement."

"That ain't hard at all!" Junebug was astonished.

Pip laughed. And then she remembered that she was supposed to be scolding the kid. She squashed her laughter and returned to her topic of Junebug luring unsuspecting brides into the wilds.

"I grow a bit of corn." Junebug cut her off like she wasn't even talking. "I grow a bit of everything. None of it well. What kind of corn thing would you make to go with this fish?" she asked curiously.

"I'd keep it simple and toss the cobs in butter and salt." Pip caught herself. "Stop distracting me."

"Can you show me how?" Junebug fixed Pip with her large gray eyes. All of a sudden, she looked like nothing so much as a begging puppy. "No one ever taught me to cook, not properly. That's one reason I wanted *you*."

The kid was as transparent as a rain puddle. But Pip still felt her heart tugging. "What about your mother?"

"Oh, she's dead." Junebug said it so matter-of-factly that she might as well have been talking about the weather. "She's out there under the chokecherry tree with all my sisters. It's just me and the boys. Or it was until Maddy came. And, don't get me wrong, Maddy has many fine qualities, but all she knows how to cook is mashed potatoes. And I don't even grow many potatoes."

"Keep filleting," Pip told her, gesturing at the fish. Pip had read Morgan McBride's—correction, *Junebug* McBride's—letters so many times that she had them memorized. There'd been a lot in those letters about needing a cook. But maybe Junebug needed more than a cook. Maybe she needed some mothering too. Maybe she needed someone to *teach her* how to cook. "If I teach you how to bake these fish . . ." Pip paused. "What kind are they?"

"Rainbow trout." Junebug's head had snapped up at the suggestion of a bargain. She was like a bird of prey, Pip thought. A falcon, about to swoop at a field mouse. Well, Pip wasn't a mouse. The girl could learn that the hard way.

"If I teach you to bake these rainbow trout, with a nice side of corn and greens, will you tell me everything I need to know about your brother?" Pip asked.

"I already did," Junebug said, disgruntled. "It's all in the letters."

"No, it isn't." Pip rolled her eyes. "That man didn't write any letters, *you* did. I want to know what Junebug McBride thinks of Morgan, not what Junebug-pretending-to-be-Morgan thinks."

Junebug got a cagey look about her. "And why do you want to know?"

"Because I want him to marry me," Pip said bluntly. "And I need to know how to make that happen."

Junebug grinned. "You still want to marry him, even after you've met him?"

Pip remembered the misty gray of Morgan's gaze, and the way he frowned all the time; she remembered the width and solidity of him, the flicker of dimples. The scent of him enveloped her from the shirt she was wearing. "Yes," she said, trying to keep her voice even. "Even after I've met him."

"Lady, you've got a deal!"

Ten

It was only one night. Morgan repeated the phrase to himself like a prayer as he packed his saddlebags for the morning. The woman was only here for one night; and so was he. And at least the redhead was keeping Junebug well occupied, because Morgan didn't have the stomach for dealing with his sister today. Her reaction down at the hotel had nearabout ripped the heart out of him. And then there'd been the tears and tantrums and cold silence when they got home. Morgan felt like he'd been through battle, and he didn't have it in him to suffer her enraged and grief-stricken face as he packed.

If you thought about it, the Hopgood woman's timing was perfect. It would distract Junebug, Morgan told himself as he checked his saddle and tack, waterproofed his boots, double-checked his provisions and filled his canteens with water. He wanted to get off early the next morning. Miles City was a long haul away. This way Junebug would be happily occupied and not tangling herself up over his abandonment, as she called it.

Morgan had seen Junebug and the redhead from a distance several times as he went about his business, but he refused to care about what they were up to. Let Junebug marry the woman, if she wanted another wife so bad. He did pause when he saw the woman was wearing a flannel shirt over her dress. *His* flannel shirt. But that was just natural curiosity. It wasn't like he was staring at her for any other reason, except that a man cared to know who was wearing his shirt. Especially when he hadn't given her permission to wear it.

At least she'd covered herself up. That was another favor she'd done him. Not that he was getting close enough to look at her.

Damn it. Why did he keep circling back to thinking about her? It was like a tic.

It was to be expected, he supposed, when a bride turned up out of the blue at you. It was plain unnatural and disturbing to have a potential wife thrust at you, like a gift you were supposed to be grateful for. Of course he was thinking about her under the circumstances. It was too odd not to think about.

He was also antsy about leaving, he knew. His thoughts kept snagging on things that could go wrong while he was away. What if the boys didn't clean out the chimneys properly? The log cabin could go up like a tinderbox. What if they didn't stock the root cellar properly and there was a heavy blizzard? What if some lowlifes came up the trail and thought the trading post was soft pickings? What if . . . Ah, there were too many what-ifs.

He had to stop it.

He'd done what he could. He'd overstocked the root cellar and told Jonah to clear out the chimneys regularly; he'd oiled the rifle and made sure it was under the counter at the trading post; he'd ordered up feed for the animals and even told Kit to give the horses a fresh shoeing. They were as prepared as he could make them for every eventuality. He couldn't do more . . .

"Guess this is going to be a goodbye dinner, then?" Kit observed in his usual placid way, when Morgan picked his spurs up from the forge. Kit had fixed them up for him, as they'd not been worn for a good long spell. "You ain't changed your mind?" He'd paused at the anvil, a mass of muscle; Morgan's little brother, who'd long outgrown him.

"And why would I change my mind?" Morgan was nonplussed. "When do I ever change my mind?"

"Next to never," Kit sighed as Morgan took the spurs and left.

"Are you sure you don't want to wait another day or so?" Jonah prodded when Morgan went to the barn to prepare his horses. The kid was forking hay from the loft but paused to watch Morgan work.

"And why would I do that?" Morgan chafed under his brother's stare.

"I don't know," Jonah said slowly. "Maybe because we've got guests?"

"They're leaving tomorrow too," Morgan reminded him shortly.

Of all his brothers, only Beau didn't push him on staying, and that was only because the damn fool was too busy preening. He was in the cabin, trying to give himself a close shave.

"You'd be better off doing that outside, where you can see properly," Morgan snapped at him. The cabin was dim. And too small for the both of them, given the way Beau had spread out his washbowl and toweling.

"Can I have your bed when you go?" Beau ignored his jibe, carefully scraping the razor over his chiseled jaw. "I'm mighty sick of sharing that bunk with Jonah." Beau examined his handiwork in Morgan's small shaving mirror, which he'd helped himself to without asking.

It irked Morgan how vain his little brother was. Even more irksome was that his vanity was so well deserved. The kid was too good-looking by half, just like their father had been. It was only going to bring him trouble. "What in the hell are you prettying yourself up for?" In Morgan's experience, pretty men grew glib and useless. The kid would do better to concentrate on developing a skill or two, rather than priding himself on a face he'd had no part in creating.

"What do you think?" Beau shot him a wink. "It ain't often we have a beautiful woman here for supper."

"She ain't beautiful." He only said it to be contrary, but it was kind of true. Beauty wasn't the right word for that woman. She was too . . . something. Hell. He didn't need a word for it; it didn't have anything to do with him.

"Have you gone blind?" Beau's words pricked him. "Have you seen the figure on that woman? Hell. She'd give a saint palpitations."

"What would you know about saints?" Morgan threw his red flannel shirt into his bag. That Hopgood woman better have the good sense to stay away from Beau.

"I know *nothing* about saintliness." Beau laughed. "And I got no desire to ever learn. But I figure you probably don't go to heaven having thoughts about a woman like that, let alone acting on them."

"Don't you go falling into Junebug's trap." Morgan bunched his long underwear angrily into a ball. "I don't want to get a letter saying you've up and married this woman," he complained. "The last thing we want is to reward Junebug for this, or she'll be ordering up a whole passel of wives."

"Who's talking marriage!" Beau was flat-out appalled. "I got no plans to marry anyone. I just want to have a little fun."

"She ain't the fun type," Morgan growled. The look on Beau's pretty face was infuriating. He was always so smug.

"Well, there's only one way to find out, ain't there?" Beau grinned at him and wiped the soap from his face.

Just one night, Morgan reminded himself, as he stole his shaving mirror back and packed it. Just one. This was the one and only time he'd have to suffer through Beau flirting with Epiphany Hopgood, or to watch Junebug knot herself up trying to get Morgan to marry the woman. Just a few measly hours. It was worth it, to get away cleanly in the morning. Without plates thrown or, God forbid, weeping.

Morgan stepped out of the cabin just as the sun was slipping behind the western mountains. The katydids were starting up in the shadows of the woods and the light was bluing with the early shades of nightfall. Morgan could see Junebug and the redhead building a cookfire in the meadow. Goddamn it. The poor woman had no idea.

"Junebug!" he yelled, his voice cracking across the meadow, sending crickets leaping. "Those are your chores, not hers!"

"You sure are set on scaring her off, ain't you?" Beau drawled, stepping from the cabin behind Morgan. "Suits me." He clapped Morgan on the back. "I'll go sort this for you."

Morgan scowled as Beau swaggered his way down to the cookfire, which was now crackling away merrily. Above, the birds were wheeling home across the lavender sky. He took a deep breath and gathered himself. *Only one night.*

His very last one.

The falling evening took on an unexpected sharpness. Buck's Creek was spread before him: the grasses rippling, the creek catching the last of the peachy daylight, golden lamplight glowing up at the big house and down at the trading post. The air was filled with the scent of pine resin and the spicy sweet smell of the night-scented wildflowers—gillyflower, his mother had called them, even though they weren't actually gillyflowers. They grew in long wands of purple and violet and white, their throats pale green or yellow, their scent heady on summer nights. He should have planted some on her grave long ago, he thought suddenly, fiercely. She would have liked that.

He saw Kit leaving the forge and heading over to the big house, and Jonah emerging from the barn. Down at the trading post the trappers were stirring from the porch and drifting to the cookfire. The smoke rose in a silvery tendril above the leaping flames.

Home.

The thought came unbidden, and unwanted.

His gaze drifted to the wonky cross under the chokecherry tree. He'd done his part. *Here they all are, Ma, safe and grown.* It gave him an unexpected slug of heat in his chest, like he'd swallowed a hot coal. It was pride. He was proud to have raised them up, he realized. They each had their flaws but, all in all, he'd done a good job. Ma would have been proud of him . . .

Down in the meadow Junebug was flinging wood onto the fire with dangerous abandon, laughing like a goose. He felt a keen affection for her now that he was going. It was a sharp feeling, like slicing your finger on a newly sharpened hunting knife. The ladies' academy could wait, he decided spontaneously. Let her be a kid a while longer. He'd just get Kit to take away her pen and ink and ban her from the post office. That should sort her for a while. And since no one was marrying her mail-order wife this time, she'd learn her lesson. The mistake last time had been Kit taking a shine to Maddy.

"Hey," Jonah said as he reached the cabin. He frowned as he took in Morgan's expression. "You all right?"

"Fine," Morgan assured him. He even smiled. He was right as rain.

Jonah had reached his height, Morgan realized for the first time. He was still skinny, but his shoulders were much bigger than Beau's and his hands were huge. He was going to be a big man, like Kit. But his gray eyes were like Ma's and Junebug's, only a little darker maybe. He was a good kid. Morgan wasn't sure if he'd ever told Jonah that; he should probably tell him before he left. Just in case anything happened . . .

"I'm going to clean up for our guests," Jonah told him. "Did Beau leave any water, or do I have to fetch some from the creek?"

"I'll go," Morgan volunteered gruffly. He gave the kid an awkward pat as he collected the pail and headed down to the creek. He was aware of Jonah's mild shock at his gesture. Couldn't a man give his brother some affection? They all treated him like he was some kind of ogre. Hell, of course he was being affectionate. He was saying goodbye.

Now, there was a thought with some flight to it. Morgan could just about taste the dusty trail and see the wide sea of cattle spreading in front of him. His heart skipped a beat. He felt himself easing. But he was also flooded with surprising nostalgia—for a place he never thought he'd miss. How many times had he hauled water, just like this, as the golden day faded behind the mountain range? Cool air rose from the whispering water, and he could hear the frogs gearing up for their evening sing-along. There was the splash of beavers farther upstream, and the sound of an owl deep in the woods.

Tomorrow night, it would be the same, but he wouldn't be here to hear it. The creek would tumble on by while Beau or Jonah hauled the water instead of him. It gave him an unsteady feeling and he didn't like it. He'd been desperate to get out of Buck's Creek for as long as he could remember, and now here he was on the cusp if it, and he was . . . what? Getting cold feet?

No. It was just that he'd got into the habit of the place, that was all. He'd been carrying his brothers and Junebug for so long that the thought of putting them down made his arms feel empty. He'd get used to the change. He'd form new habits. Morgan stared at the fractured rush of the dark creek, and for a moment he felt more scared than he had since Ma died. It was an airless feeling, like he couldn't breathe. What if he didn't exist anymore outside of Buck's Creek? He'd been parent and guardian and caretaker and keeper for so long . . . Who was he, without it?

He heard laughter from the cookfire and jerked. Hell. What was wrong with him?

He forced himself to scoop the pail into the rushing water, just as the last pink rays of sunset faded from behind the mountains.

This was his last night, he told himself firmly, and he was going to enjoy it. He owed it to himself, and to Junebug and the boys, and he owed it to Ma. Tonight wasn't just an ending; it was a beginning. *His.* It wasn't a wake or a trial. Tonight was a goddamn celebration.

As he took the pail back to the cabin, Morgan decided he was going to clean up too. But not for their guests—for himself. He was still young. Buck's Creek had stolen six years from him, but it wasn't stealing any more. He had a whole unmapped life ahead of him and it was going to be *good*.

Half an hour later, when Morgan stepped into the shivering circle of firelight, Beau scowled at him. Morgan winked, a parody of the wink Beau had shot him earlier. Let the kid sweat. Morgan might not be as pretty as Beau, but he scrubbed up all right, at least well enough to give Beau some stiff competition with the ladies. Definitely well enough for the women of Kansas and Texas, he remembered, feeling a burst of good cheer.

He'd carried a barrel of beer down the meadow to the cookfire. It weighed a ton, and he was glad to settle it beside one of the logs they kept circled around the semipermanent cookfire.

"Stop showing off," Beau muttered. "Jonah could have helped you with that."

"I don't need Jonah's help. Besides, Jonah had to carry the mugs."

Jonah ambled into the flickering circle of light with his fiddle and bow and a pail full of tin mugs.

There was no sign of the redhead, Morgan noted. Or of Junebug. But he could see a lantern bobbing in the indigo shadows of the vegetable patch, so he assumed that was them. The redhead's grandmother was here at the cookfire, although she didn't look so grandmotherly anymore. She was perched on a log, with Thunderhead Bill on one side and Sour Eagle on the other, her hair flowing over her shoulders, her stiff-necked gown unbuttoned, and if Morgan wasn't mistaken, she was partaking of Bill's particularly vile moonshine.

"Here, give the poor woman a beer before she blinds herself," Morgan told Beau. He snagged a mug off Jonah and filled it. "Tip that swill she's drinking out. I'm always scared Bill will kill someone with that stuff."

"You're wearing your good shirt," Beau observed. He didn't sound pleased.

"And looking mighty fine," Kit said, looming out of the darkness, with a basket in one hand and a bottle of whiskey in the other. "You shave again? I thought you only shaved once a year."

"I had to compete with Beau. Let me guess, you've brought some kind of potatoes?" Morgan peered into Kit's basket.

Kit grinned. "At least they're good potatoes. Not like before Maddy came, when Junebug served them up black on the outside and hard as a rock within."

"So long as Maddy's cooking them, Kit will eat potatoes for the rest of his life and not complain once," Jonah laughed. He'd cocked his fiddle under his chin and was tuning up.

Kit didn't disagree.

That was one McBride that Morgan didn't have qualms about leaving, he thought with satisfaction, as he filled mugs and passed them out. Kit was neatly settled. He didn't need Morgan at all anymore.

Morgan quietly stole Thunderhead Bill's bottle of moonshine when he handed him a beer. The stuff was too dangerous. Surreptitiously, Morgan stepped out of the firelight and poured the moonshine into the meadow grass. The astringent smell brought back unwelcome memories of his old man. Morgan had no desire to think about him tonight. He pushed the memories away.

As he poured himself a beer, he caught sight of Junebug dashing down from the big house, her arms full of Maddy's soda bread. Maddy was following behind, carrying blankets. Even in summer it got cold at night, up here in the mountains, and a blanket or two didn't go astray as the evening wore on.

Morgan frowned as Junebug galloped closer, as it occurred to him that she hadn't been in the vegetable patch after all, and that everyone else was accounted for . . . except the redhead. Morgan turned to see the lantern still bobbing about among the vegetables. "Where's the woman?" he growled at Junebug, although he knew the answer.

"Epiphany Hopgood, you mean?" Junebug sounded mighty pleased he was asking after her. "She's over in the vegetable patch. She said she needed something to stuff the fish with. Did you know that we should have been stuffing fish all these years? Ain't that a revelation?"

"Junebug!" Morgan could have throttled her. The woman was a guest, and here Junebug had her off in the darkness, trying to find something salvageable in the miserable excuse of a kitchen garden.

"What?" She gave him one of those wide-eyed looks that was all fake innocence. "You don't like fish?"

"You got no call to be working her like a servant when she's a guest!" Honestly. The kid was allergic to work. "You go get her."

"*You* go get her." Junebug stuck her tongue out at him. "I got things to do." She was off and running again, this time to the cookhouse.

Morgan swore.

"What's wrong now?" Maddy asked as she reached him.

"Junebug's got the woman in the vegetable patch." He pointed at the lamp flickering in the darkness. "Go get her, will you?"

Maddy rolled her eyes. "She won't bite you, Morgan. She seems like a perfectly nice lady."

"I don't want to give her ideas," he said defensively.

Maddy laughed. "You won't. Everyone is perfectly clear on your position."

Damn women. Morgan had yet to meet an amenable one—at least in these parts. From memory, the women over in Kansas were plenty amenable. And the Texans were friendly as all get-out. Maybe it was just something about Buck's Creek.

Yet another thing he wouldn't miss.

"Don't tell me you're scared of her," Maddy teased. Then she took pity on him. "I'll get Beau," she offered. "He'll be happy to go."

"No." Morgan was appalled at the thought of Beau being left alone with the woman in the dark. "I'll go," he grumbled, heading off through the meadow.

Moths fluttered dusty white from the long grasses as he strode to Junebug's ill-kept vegetable garden. "Miss Hopgood? You lost in there?" he called.

He heard a rustling. The lamp was low down, half-obscured by the sad bunches of greens. Junebug never remembered to water them enough in summer. At least caterpillar season was over, he thought with a sigh, as he batted a clumsy moth away.

"Oh!" The redhead appeared, lit from below by the lantern. "Morgan!"

They were on first-name terms? He didn't like that. She needed to be disabused of any notions of intimacy.

"Miss Hopgood," he said firmly. "Junebug needs to be tarred for making you do her work for her."

She was taken aback. "She's not making me do anything," she protested. "I volunteered to show her how to cook the fish."

"That's what you think," he sighed. "Come on out and I'll get her to finish this off."

"She's busy cooking up the corn." The woman dismissed him and crouched back down among the vegetables. "Do you know where the herbs are?"

"What herbs?"

Up she came again, looking all startled. "What do you mean, 'what herbs'? You must have herbs! Parsley? Sage? Chives?"

Morgan didn't see that there was any *must* about it. "What you see is what we got," he warned her, "and as you can see, it ain't much. Junebug ain't much of a gardener, or much of anything else for that matter."

"Well, she's certainly good at fishing," the redhead observed tartly, "judging by how many fish I just filleted."

"*You* just filleted . . ." he drawled. So much for not doing Junebug's chores for her.

"*We* just filleted," she amended. She gave the greens at her feet a hopeless look. "You really have no herbs . . . ?"

He took pity on her. He didn't know why, maybe he was just in a generous mood because it was his last night. "Does nodding on-ion count as an herb? 'Cause we got plenty of that in the woods. Kit and I throw it into the pot sometimes to add some flavor. God knows we don't get much flavor around here."

The redhead cocked her head, thinking it over. Her hair was down, he noticed. It fell down her back in messy waves, dark in the scarce lamplight. She was still in his shirt, and it was stained all to hell and back. With fish guts, by the stink of it. He made a note to remind Junebug to wash it in the morning.

Then he remembered he wouldn't be here.

Oh well, it was an old shirt—he wouldn't need it. He had to travel light anyway.

"Nodding onion," the redhead mused, still thinking about herbs. "Yes, that would work." She gave the woods a nervous look. "Is it safe?"

"We don't have to go far in—the stuff grows everywhere at the edge of the meadow. You stay here." He bent to scoop up her lan-tern, but her hand snatched out and stopped him, her fingers dig-ging into his arm.

"You're not leaving me here in the dark," she yelped.

"The moon's coming up," he pointed out, nodding at the fat yellow moon rising over the woods. "It's plenty bright enough for you to gather your greens."

"You're not leaving me," she repeated, more firmly.

She was scared, he realized, amused. "Don't they have darkness where you're from?" he asked, prying her fingers off him. "Where *are* you from?" He didn't know the slightest thing about her, he realized, except that she baked cakes and had a grandmother who was partial to moonshine. And that she'd come here to marry a man she'd never met.

What kind of woman did that?

"I'm from Nebraska, and we have plenty of darkness, thank you." She composed herself, brushing her hair out of her face. "We just don't have woods. Or bears."

"I reckon we're safe enough from the bears," he reassured her. He held the lamp up and headed for the meadow edge. He could hear her hurrying to keep up. "I've been to Nebraska," he told her conversationally, mostly to keep her mind off the bears. He could hear her gasp when critters dashed out of their way in the long grass. She was skittery as all get-out. "Well, not so much *to* Nebraska as *through* Nebraska. Which part are you from?"

An owl swooped low overhead, chasing a muskrat, and Epiphany Hopgood leapt a mile. Her hands clawed at him again.

"I'll let you know when to panic, lady," he said, trying to sound soothing. Soothing wasn't natural to him; it came out just vaguely less surly. He covered her hand with his, meaning to just give her a pat, but it was a colossal mistake. It was like shoving his hand into the sparks of a fire. He jolted away. She'd been warm and velvety soft. And now he was too aware of how close she was. Even though she smelled of fish, being near her was too pleasant by half.

He'd been too long without a woman, he thought dryly. That would need remedying. But not now, and certainly not with this little trap Junebug had set for him. Morgan was well practiced in pushing his wants and needs down; it was no trouble to do it now, he counseled himself. "Here," he said, as the soft shimmer of the lamplight caught a cluster of late-flowering nodding onion. The flowers were pale starbursts in the night. Morgan crouched and pulled up a clump. "How many do you want?"

"A lot. There's a lot of fish," she said, a bit fretfully.

"All of them. Got it." He handed the bunches up to her as he unearthed the bulbs.

"I only need the stalks," she protested. But she took them, holding out the front of her shirt—*his* shirt—to form a makeshift basket to carry the haul.

There was a moment of quiet, with just the sound of him pulling up plants and the rustlings of the meadow and woods.

"There are so many creatures about," the redhead said, still sounding nervy. "I mean, the cornfields back home are full of mice and groundhogs, and there are bats at night, but compared to this . . . I see what you mean about not traveling through the woods alone."

Morgan was amused. "Yeah, you might get bit by a squirrel."

"You're the one who told me about the bears," she protested. "*You're* the one who said I might be eaten."

"Not eaten. Just mauled. The bears in these parts are pretty well-fed, and I reckon they'd rather go fishing than eat you."

"That makes me feel so much better," she said wryly.

"If you do come across a bear, the trick is not to run." He grinned as she inched closer to him. "Make a lot of noise."

"They don't like noise?"

"Who knows? I've never tested it—but that's what the trappers always told us." He'd exhausted the patch of nodding onion, and to her obvious relief, they headed back to the vegetable garden. Only to find the hares were feasting on the mustard greens she needed. As the lantern light hit the row, they scattered in a flicker of white tails.

"See? It's the hares that you need to watch, more than the bears," he told her. "Nothing scary about a rabbit. Unless you're a vegetable, anyways."

The redhead bent over to gather what remained of the mustard greens and chard. Morgan wished she wouldn't. Her skirt was tight around her hips and outlined her derriere, which was the plumpest, most touchable rear end he'd had the pleasure of seeing for years. Maybe ever. God, the woman had curves.

"Come on," he said curtly. He'd only come over here to stop her doing Junebug's chores and now here he was, doing them too. He ended up carrying the greens for the woman all the way to the cookhouse, where Junebug was gleefully preparing corn.

"Don't let the cobs go cold once you've cooked them," Epiphany Hopgood instructed. "You cover the pot as soon as you're done. And don't be stingy with the salt. Or the butter."

"You know you're going to have to churn more of that butter if you use it all, though," Morgan warned his sister, who was as covered in fish remains as the redhead was. Scales glittered on her arms, like she was turning into a fish herself. And, somehow, she even had them in her hair.

"If I'm stingy with things, it's his fault," Junebug told Epiphany, sanctimonious as all hell. She hefted the pot. "I'll take this out to the fire. Morgan can help you stuff them fish."

Junebug was gone in a snap. She had a goddamn talent for that.

"You're teaching her to do this, huh?" he said dryly. "I can see she's going to be learning a lot about stuffing fish from out there by the fire."

"Can you clear off the table?" The redhead was single-mindedly focused on supper.

"Look, Epiphany," he said, preparing to educate her on the finer points of Junebug management even as he cleared off the table so she could drop her shirtful of nodding onion onto it.

"It's Pip," the redhead corrected him. "Only my mother calls me Epiphany."

Pip. Huh. It sure suited her a lot better than Epiphany did.

"Can you please pass me the tray of fish?" She held her hand out.

Somehow Morgan found himself passing it. And then, he didn't know how, he found himself stuffing fish with nodding onion and wrapping them in parcels of mustard greens. The woman was just about as good as Junebug was at coercing people into chores, he thought begrudgingly as he fiddled with tying leaves around the stuffed trout.

But unlike Junebug, Pip Hopgood somehow did it without him minding.

In fact, he quite enjoyed it. The cramped cookhouse was intimate by lamplight, and humid from the hot stove and boiling water. The steamy peace and the quiet task were irenic. While his family were loud and abrasive, the redhead worked calmly. She was oddly soothing. They stood opposite one another at the table, bent over the fussy task. Now and then she reached out to correct his folds or tighten his leafy envelope.

"Ideally I'd use more herbs," she said.

She cared a lot about dressing a fish, he thought, as he watched her long white fingers work. He noted that they were hands that showed a history of labor: short nails and calluses. But elegant for all of that.

"You're not just good at cakes, then?" He was only making conversation. But the woman lit up. Like someone had struck a match inside of her.

"Oh no! And I need you to know that the high tea was Junebug's idea."

"I figured," he said dryly.

"I wanted to cook you a joint of beef. I can slow roast a shoulder of beef to perfection." And then she waxed lyrical about it.

Morgan wished she wouldn't, because he was hungry as hell, and it made him feel like beef and there wasn't any beef, there was just all these little fish, and he doubted they'd fill him up like beef would.

"You like cooking, huh?" he grunted.

"It's what I'm best at." She was proud as punch.

She was a looker, and she could cook. So why in hell was she answering ads for a husband in a damn newspaper? Surely a woman like her had her pick of men?

It bothered Morgan like a burr as he carried the tray of wrapped fish to the cookfire for her. What was *wrong* with her?

Eleven

It was the drinking that did it.

It had started off innocently enough. They'd had a couple of beers while Pip taught Junebug how to form a bank of coals, in order to bake all those fish parcels. And then they'd had a couple more beers over supper, which was better than Morgan had expected.

Hell, that wasn't even halfway fair. Epiphany Hopgood's cooking was the best he'd ever tasted. So good he'd eaten about half a dozen trout. They didn't seem to have any bones—how did she do that? One of the things that had always put Morgan off fish was all the lethal little bones sticking his mouth like it was a pincushion. That and the fact that when Junebug cooked them they went all rubbery. These trout weren't rubbery; they were flaky, white and juicy as could be, and the nodding onion gave them a zing. Add in salty buttered corn, coupled with Maddy's creamy mash, and Morgan was happier than a pig in mud. Pip Hopgood even managed to get mustard greens to taste good.

After supper, Morgan slouched by the fire, his belly stretched full, listening to Jonah warm up on the fiddle and watching the

sparks drift into the starry heavens. He figured this was about as
fine a way to end his Buck's Creek purgatory as he could imagine.
Everyone was in a good mood, there was no sniping or bickering
and no one needed wrestling into line. This was how he wanted
to leave, he thought contentedly, with everyone perfectly happy.

That was about when he told the boys to go get another barrel
of beer from the root cellar. By then everyone was merry. Except
for Junebug, who he'd packed off to wash the dishes. Pip tried to
help her, but Morgan wouldn't let her. "You've done enough chores
for her already!" he scolded. It was about then that he realized he
might have had too much to drink, because he'd grabbed her hand
and yanked her down onto the log beside him.

He'd forgotten he shouldn't touch her. Sparks went spitting
through him at the feel of her hand in his. He dropped it like a hot
coal.

"Pip, you should take that horrid shirt off," her grandmother
called over. "It's filthy!" The old lady was up tapping her feet to
Jonah's fiddle and was clearly also a few drinks down. She pulled
Thunderhead Bill up and demanded that he dance with her.

"I'm sorry about your shirt," Pip apologized to Morgan, looking down at the state of it. "Junebug said you didn't have any aprons
and that this was the best she could do. I only have the one nice
dress and I didn't want to ruin it."

He waved the apology away. Or he tried to. His hand kind of
lost momentum when she started unbuttoning the shirt.

Skin. He could see skin. There shouldn't be skin . . .

As she shrugged out of his flannel, he saw that the neck of her
dress was unbuttoned underneath it. Her skin was pale and creamy,
and there were plump curves and valleys. One very mesmerizing
valley in particular, right between the swell of her breasts. Morgan
felt the urge to run his finger along it.

He was drunk. Or not drunk enough. One or the other.

He tore his gaze away and wished Beau would hurry up pouring out the beer from the new barrel. He drank deep when his fresh mugful arrived. Jonah had lit into "Arkansas Traveler" and Pip's grandmother and Thunderhead Bill were dancing up a storm.

"You want to dance, Miss Hopgood?" Beau asked, all polite like a citified gentleman.

Miss Hopgood looked startled. "Me?" She had the flannel shirt off now and damnation if she wasn't a sight to behold. Her hair tumbled over one shoulder, brassy in the firelight, curving over her ample breast. Morgan had an invasive image of how she might look naked, with just that brassy hair to cover her.

Good. She'd look good. He had no doubt about it.

"Yeah, you," Beau said, and Morgan winced at how practiced he already seemed with women. He'd perfected a look that was meltingly seductive.

"No." Morgan stood up and pushed Beau out of the way. "She don't want to dance with you, Romeo." God, the boy would end up at the wrong end of a shotgun one day. He had no idea of the consequences of things.

"That's right," Junebug interjected, having clearly abandoned her dishwashing chores to come racing back at the sound of the fiddle. "She wants to dance with Morgan, not you. You ain't tall enough for her."

"I'm as tall as she is."

"But Morgan's taller. So, he wins. But I'll dance with you." She grabbed Beau's hand and hauled him off.

Morgan was cornered. Somehow trying to save Pip Hopgood from Beau had led to him being left at her mercy. She was standing in front of him expectantly. This wasn't good. Not least because from this angle he had a clear view down the open neck of her shirt. And it was about the finest view he'd ever seen.

"I'm not a great dancer," she warned him. "No one has ever asked me to dance except for my sisters. And I had to take the gentleman's part."

Morgan didn't want to dance with her. Not when touching her gave him sparky feelings.

"I can't say I know this one . . ." She bit her lip.

And that didn't help, either, because it only drew his attention to her mouth. It was a pretty gorgeous mouth. Expressive as all get-out. Infinitely kissable.

He told himself that he'd only dance with her so he wouldn't kiss her. It was a distraction, wasn't it? Although possibly the wrong kind, because taking her hands was an overwhelming sensation. He was just drunk, he reassured himself, and happy to be leaving Buck's Creek on a good note. Was it wrong to be happy? There was no doubt the feel of Pip Hopgood in his arms was a happy feeling. Ah, why was he fighting it so hard? She was a good-looking woman—he could enjoy that for one night, couldn't he? Didn't he deserve that? Sure he did. Dancing with a woman didn't mean you had to marry her. And who could resist dancing to Jonah's fiddle? That boy could light up the night.

Morgan had danced with women plenty of times in his youth, but he'd never had the pleasure of dancing with a woman who was so close to him in height before. It was a revelation. She fit into his arms like she'd been made for them, and her long legs matched him step for step.

"You might not have danced much, but you're sure good at it," he told her when the song came to an end. He was struggling to catch his breath.

She smiled at him, and he felt all kinds of warm, like he'd stumbled right into the fire.

Too much beer.

And now Kit was breaking out the whiskey. This was becoming a proper going-away party. Morgan brushed away the thought that more drink might lead him into trouble.

"Play something slow," Sour Eagle suggested, stepping between Pip's grandmother and Thunderhead Bill, claiming his turn with her. The older woman was a resounding success with those two. Old Roy was watching morosely, obviously feeling more than a little left out. Junebug told him to stop looking like a toothless old hound dog and dragged him up to dance with her, which left goddamn Beau free to come angling for a dance with the redhead again. Morgan wasn't having a bar of that.

As Jonah slipped into a yearning rendition of "Bonny Eloise," Morgan took Pip back in his arms before Beau could reach her. Beau glared at him. The moon had risen high overhead, flooding the meadow with shimmery light. The moths were pale clouds above the grasses, and the soft summer breeze was spicy with the wildflowers. Not-gillyflowers. Ma would have loved this, them all out here, together. Faintly, Morgan could hear Junebug chastising Roy for treading on her toes, but he couldn't quite focus on the words. It might have been the drink's fault, or it might have been the fault of the woman in his arms, but he had the feeling of slipping his harness. And it felt just fine.

"Your brother sure can play a fiddle," Pip Hopgood said, close enough to his ear that he could feel the warm swirl of her breath on his skin.

Morgan shivered. It wasn't cold, but here he was, shivering like it was bitterest November. "*Now* he can," he said, trying to focus. "But you should have been here the winter he taught himself to play." Morgan was distracted by the way her hair swayed when she moved; it caressed his hand, which rested on the small of her back. The tips of his fingers brushed the slight swell of her rear end. Damnation, that was some fitted skirt she was wearing.

Is that what women were wearing off the mountain now? If that was the case, he couldn't wait to get to Miles City to see. Although he doubted if any of the women in Miles City could fill out a gown like Epiphany Hopgood could. That skirt must sheathe the longest legs, given her height. He wondered what they'd look like out of the skirt . . .

"He taught *himself*?" She turned her head to watch Jonah, impressed.

Morgan got a waft of her scent. It was confounding. He could tell by the lemony fragrance that it was just Maddy's soft soap, but it smelled a hell of a lot better on Pip than it did on him, or anyone else in Buck's Creek. He wondered if she smelled like that all over . . .

"How did he teach himself?" she asked curiously.

How could she expect him to think about Jonah and his stupid fiddle when she was warm against him like this? Morgan struggled to assemble his thoughts, assailed by lemony scents and the feel of her under his palm. "Ah . . ." Jonah's fiddling, that's what they were talking about. "Our old man left the fiddle behind, and Jonah found it one winter, when he was bored to tears being locked up in the cabin. He taught himself by scratching out cat-strangling noises for eight hours a day." Morgan winced at the memory. That sound had been so nerve-shredding awful that he and Kit used to slog through the snow to hide out in the barn, just to get away from it. But even in the barn, sometimes the snapping wind carried the screech of the fiddle their way. "All through the depths of winter, while we were trapped in the cabin with him, he played the damn thing," Morgan told Pip, remembering how irritable it made him, "until we threatened to pitch him into a snowdrift. But by the spring thaw the cats sounded pained instead of strangled. And then, somehow, he got good."

"My mother taught me the piano," she confessed, "but I never got out of the cat-strangling phase." She shot a glance up at him through her eyelashes. It made his head swim.

This is what happened when you got stranded on a mountaintop for years without women, he realized. The minute you saw one, you went daft. How else to explain the slowed-down thud of his heart or the dryness of his mouth?

"That's enough hogging her," Beau snapped the minute the last note of "Bonny Eloise" shivered into silence. He swooped in and pulled Epiphany Hopgood away from Morgan. It happened too swiftly for him to react. One moment Morgan was holding her, and the next he wasn't. He was just standing there while Beau wheeled away, the redhead spinning in his arms, as Jonah kicked up with a roof-raiser.

Morgan scowled to see Pip Hopgood laughing at something his peacock of a little brother had said to her.

"You like her." Junebug sidled up to him, smug as could be. "I can tell."

Morgan grunted and poured himself a double shot of whiskey.

"She's a looker, ain't she? That's a bonus. It weren't what I advertised for, but it's a boon, given you're more into looks than I thought you'd be."

Morgan wasn't going to snap at her. Not on his last night. He wanted to though. "Why on earth wouldn't I want a good-looking woman?" Morgan strove to keep his voice even. "*If* I were wanting a woman, which I'm not."

"You're always on at Beau for being vain. And you never give the cathouse girls the eye, like the others do."

Morgan really had to squash his response to that. What in hell were those boys doing, staring at whores, with Junebug right there?

"But Pip's better looking than any of the girls at the cathouse," Junebug continued. "You ever seen a chest that monumental on a woman before?"

"Damn it, Junebug!" He couldn't contain himself at that one. "You've been raised better than to talk like that!"

"Have I?" She looked surprised. "I thought chest was a nice way to say it. It's a sight better than the other words I know for it. How *should* I say it, if I can't say chest?"

"You shouldn't say it at all!" He glowered at her. "You don't comment on a woman like that. Or a man. Or anyone!"

"Well, I'd hardly comment on a man, would I? They don't have—"

Morgan cut her off before she could finish her sentence. He had a feeling she was about to air one of the words he wished she didn't know. "Junebug, you're too old for this kind of talk. Act like a lady."

She got that mulish look that pricked him sore. "And how would I know what a lady acts like?"

"Do you hear Maddy talking like this?"

"Maddy is a maid, not a lady," Junebug reminded him. She was darkening.

He didn't want her nonsense on his last day. He threw her a bone, just to shut her up. "Leaving aside any discussion of her looks, Pip seems a nice enough sort. And she's a damn fine cook."

Junebug eased. Good. He wanted to enjoy tonight.

"You like her! I knew it." The kid beamed.

Morgan had to resist arguing.

What did it matter if he liked her or not? He'd never see Pip Hopgood again after tonight. Let Junebug congratulate herself— she'd work out eventually that no matter how good a cook or how chesty . . . ah hell, now Morgan was thinking thoughts he shouldn't be thinking. His gaze locked on to Pip, who was still dancing with Beau. Hellfire, Junebug wasn't wrong. As Pip danced, her breasts danced, too, jiggling in ways that made Morgan hurt.

"And ain't she a good cook!" Junebug was chattering. "That worked out better than expected too!"

Morgan felt his blood slow as he watched Pip Hopgood dance. Sparks rose from the fire behind her, forming a glittering veil.

"Although she makes too many dirty dishes when she cooks," Junebug complained. "We'll have to cure her of that."

Morgan dragged his attention back to his sister, who was also staring at Pip.

"She can learn some one-pot meals, 'cause I ain't washing that many dishes every night." Junebug was firm.

"You ain't washing that many dishes now," Morgan observed.

"They'll keep till tomorrow." She was blithe. And lazy as a house cat, as Kit was prone to complaining.

"They might keep," Morgan said. "But she won't. You don't get to keep her, Bug. She's going home tomorrow." He poked her nose with his finger.

"Sure she is." Junebug clearly didn't believe him.

Morgan sighed. He might as well argue with the wind as try to convince Junebug of something.

"Stop being so briny and come dance with me." Junebug tugged at him. "I ain't seen you dance in years. You don't look as bad at it as I remember."

"Oh no?" Morgan finished his whiskey in one swallow and put the mug down. "You don't think I'm so bad at it?" He hauled her off her feet. Junebug squealed fit to wake the dead as he whirled her around, feet flying. "How about now?"

Her goose laugh honked as he tucked her sideways under his arm. "Morgan!" She held on for dear life, honking away.

Morgan laughed. "You got the daffiest laugh I ever heard." It *had* been a long time since he'd danced, he realized. And the last time he'd danced with Bug she'd been just a slip of a thing. They'd had some good times out in this meadow, on those nights when she was feeling sad and small. He'd always been able to jolly her into a smile. He could still remember the feel of her skinny little body in his arms.

Tonight he hefted her upright and adopted a formal pose, like they were waltzing, only she was dangling half a foot above the ground. She stuck her nose in the air like a fancy lady and grinned. As impossible as she was, he was going to miss her. Maybe even because of her impossibleness. Of all of them, Junebug was the most like him. It wasn't something he liked to admit, because she drove him crazy with her bullheadedness, but it was something he was absurdly proud of. She had enough grit for ten men. And she was indefatigable, no matter what she did—even if it was avoiding doing the dishes, or ordering up these damn mail-order brides no one wanted.

He would get her the best writing paper money could buy when he was out on his travels. And a new pen. Maybe even a set of pens. And he'd write to her every chance he got—because she loved receiving mail. He'd send her newspapers from every town he passed through, so she could pore over them the way she did, excited to read about towns she'd never visit and people she'd never know.

It did his heart good to see her shining with joy as he waltzed her around the cookfire. He didn't dance with anyone else for the rest of the night. It was a good excuse to keep well clear of Epiphany Hopgood and all those sparky feelings. And once Jonah had wrapped up the fiddling, Morgan sat beside Junebug by the fire, his arm hooked around her shoulders. It was their last night together, and he was going to miss her something fierce.

But maybe that was just the whiskey talking.

His brothers sipped whiskey and swapped tales, as they'd done on countless nights, through countless seasons. Morgan felt himself come over sentimental as the moon crested, beginning its westward slide. Morning was coming, and with it, his time to depart. It made him a touch maudlin.

"Remember the year we built the cabin? The *first* cabin?" He gave Junebug a squeeze and passed the bottle to Kit, who snorted at the memory.

"Who could forget?" Beau moaned. He was perched next to Pip, who sat directly opposite Morgan, across the mellowed cookfire. Her hair caught the light like polished brass. Hell, she was striking; Morgan could look at her all night. The flickering gold firelight illuminated the strong lines of her face, filigreeing that expressive mouth; she looked like a statue of a goddess cast in bronze, like Morgan had seen in a saloon once in Kansas.

"Oh, I haven't heard this story!" Maddy unfurled a blanket around herself and Kit.

The boys all groaned.

"That first cabin was the bane of my existence," Morgan sighed. "We had no idea what we were doing." He watched as Beau offered Pip a blanket, to wrap around her shoulders. It was sad to cover up all that glory . . .

Sour Eagle and Thunderhead Bill were fussing over Pip's grandmother, making Beau look positively stingy in his attentions to Pip. The older woman let one of them wrap a blanket around her shoulders and the other drape one over her knees. They were acting like a pair of green suitors. Roy, much younger than the pair of them, was the odd man out. He'd slumped off by himself and was shooting them sour looks.

Morgan shook his head. They were all desperate for women up here. Junebug could do a roaring trade ordering up wives, if she'd just do it consentingly. It was her underhanded approach that caused all the trouble, and the fact that she kept ordering wives for men who had no call for them. She ought to order some women up for Bill and Sour Eagle. He rested a hand on his sister's shaggy head and ruffled her hair, amused. What kind of kid went and placed an ad for a wife, just like she was ordering up a sack of flour or a new cook pot? Only Junebug. It was lucky she ordered brides one at a time, he guessed. Imagine if she'd ordered four of them at once! He laughed, realizing he could imagine it all too well.

Now that he was close to riding out, he could see the funny side of it.

Junebug looked up at him and frowned. "Why are you being so nice?"

Morgan still had his hand on her head; he turned her head away from him and back to the fire. "Don't look a gift horse in the mouth, Bug."

"I never understood that expression," she griped, shaking his hand off her head. "What the hell is a gift horse?"

"Your pony is a gift horse," Morgan told her, "I paid for him and gave him to you. So, trust me, you know very well what a gift horse is."

"I didn't want a pony, I wanted a horse. A big one, like Kit's."

"And there you go. You also understand looking a gift horse in the mouth."

"Gift pony," she reminded him.

Morgan grinned as he accepted yet another splash of whiskey from his brother.

That was the splash too far. Afterward, he was sure of it.

Across the fire, Beau pressed Pip Hopgood into accepting a mugful of it too. That was also a big part of the problem. Without the whiskey, she wouldn't have compromised herself the way she did. And he certainly wouldn't have kissed her. At least not more than once. And without the whiskey he certainly wouldn't have almost bedded her by the creek . . .

Twelve

Pip couldn't leave the dishes undone. It wasn't right. She'd never be able to sleep thinking about the tower of pots and plates that Junebug had left on the banks of the creek. Pip had been raised to leave no job left undone. Her mother insisted on coming down in the morning to a spotless kitchen, and while a creek bank wasn't a kitchen, dirty dishes were dirty dishes just the same.

Junebug had readily abandoned her after-dinner chores in favor of dancing, and Pip couldn't blame her for that. She'd enjoyed the dancing, too, and the two of them had worked hard to cook for the crowd, so why shouldn't they enjoy a dance? After a long happy night, Junebug had fallen asleep by the fire, her head against Morgan's chest, his arm wrapped around her, dirty dishes the furthest thing from her mind. Pip felt a crazy envy seeing her cradled against Morgan; it looked like a wonderful place to be.

The man was a constant surprise. His gruffness certainly hid a tender heart. He'd been kind to her in the garden, and patient as he learned to wrap the rainbow trout in greens. And the way he'd danced with Junebug was something to see. Junebug had dangled from his arms, her feet knocking against his knees as he skipped her about like she weighed nothing at all. He hadn't removed his arm from around her shoulders afterward, as they sat companionably by the fire after the dancing. He was fatherly, in the best possible way. There was no trace of the man she'd met down in Bitterroot, the one who blew right over her like a hurricane. That Morgan McBride was bombastic and had a complete inability to listen. This Morgan McBride was attentive and . . . well, sweet. Pip was mesmerized by the way he nudged Junebug awake, pushing her mop of hair off her face and telling her to get to bed. Pip had almost expected him to carry the girl like she was a small child, but he'd merely pulled Junebug to her feet and led her up the meadow to the log cabin. Pip had watched them go, feeling keenly bittersweet at the sight of them. She'd never had anyone treat her as lovingly as Morgan McBride treated his little sister. Her father had certainly never danced with her, or even put his arm around her. Pip remembered the way Morgan had stood there in the dining room of the hotel, patiently absorbing the impact of all those shattering plates and teacups that Junebug had thrown. For such a seemingly cantankerous man he hadn't shown much temper then. He was a riddle, Pip thought with a sigh, as he and Junebug disappeared into the night.

Pip had enjoyed a truly wonderful night with the McBrides. The loose and relaxed way they dined around the campfire, plates balanced on their laps, was a far cry from the stuffiness of Pip's parents' dining room. There were no napkins, no passing of porcelain bowls around the table under Mother's watchful eye; no clock ticking minutes off on the mantel; no scrape of cutlery against plates in the stultifying, conversationless silence. Instead, the McBrides tossed chunks of soda bread to one another, wiped their hands on their trousers, splashed beer and whiskey into tin mugs, helped themselves to seconds and thirds and talked over the top of one another at volume. They were boisterous, jocular, convivial.

Pip loved it, all of it, even the smell. The scent of woodsmoke was familiar, but underneath Pip inhaled that heady perfume of pine and meadow grass, creek water and night-scented flowers. If there was a heaven, it would smell like Buck's Creek. And the sky was so clear above that Pip felt like she could just about float away into it. It was a luscious deep purple, blazing with millions of stars. Why would anyone ever subject themselves to a suffocating dining room when you could eat out here, surrounded by all this glory?

"I thought he'd be a much tougher nut to crack than this," Granny said, stopping to talk to Pip before she headed off to bed. "You did yourself proud tonight."

Yes, she had. Pip glowed at the praise. "The fish worked out so much better than I'd hoped. Luckily for me, as I've never cooked it on a campfire before!"

"The fish," Granny scoffed. "Forget the fish. I was talking about the way you handled those men. Particularly *him*. Trust me, honey, that man is on the hook and ready to be hauled in." She leaned in close and dropped her voice to a conspiratorial whisper. "Now, if you can just get him to kiss you, he'll be well and truly landed." She glanced over her shoulder impishly. "And if he doesn't, you kiss him. It doesn't matter how the kissing comes about, one kiss and that boy is done for."

Granny Colefax was more than a touch tipsy from all the drink. So was Pip. She'd never taken a drink before in her life, and the splash or two of spirits had gone straight to her head. Without it, she might have been more shocked by her grandmother's suggestion.

Pip had also never been kissed in her life. And she doubted she would be now.

The younger McBrides were zesty from the drinking, laughing and whooping it up. They had a game going where they kept stealing each other's mugs. Pip wasn't half so energetic. With each sip of the whiskey, she'd felt like she was sliding into a bubble, drifting into the air. She was loose-limbed and easy with herself, in a way she didn't ever remember being before. She relaxed, watching the lazy snap of the fire, listening to the McBrides joke and bicker.

The evening had started wrapping up when Morgan ushered Junebug off to bed and Kit escorted Granny Colefax up to the big house. Pip said she'd be along soon. She wanted to help Maddy gather up the empty mugs and strewn blankets. In truth, Pip didn't want the night to end.

"I'm sure you're used to better than this campout," Maddy apologized, as she gathered the blankets. She paused over the trappers, who were stretching themselves out by the fire. She sighed and then redistributed the blankets over them.

"No, I had a lovely time," Pip assured her.

"We're going for a swim," Beau called over. "You pretty ladies wouldn't care to join us, would you?" He gave an exaggerated wink.

"Oh, get on with you," Maddy scolded him. "You're not fit to be swimming. You're stocious, the both of you."

"I don't know what that means, but I'm determined to take stiff offense at it," Beau teased her. "Just like my brother," he told Pip. "You've probably noticed by now that Morgan takes offense at everything."

"Don't mind him," Maddy said as they watched the two youngest McBrides head up the creek, disappearing into the darkness. "He's a wild lad, but sweet for all that."

They heard more whooping and then an almighty splash.

"They're mad." Maddy shook her head. "I don't mind a dip in the bright of the day, with the sunshine to warm you, but at this hour the creek is too cold for the likes of me."

They heard Beau laughing and splashing. Jonah's voice drifted on the night air, but they couldn't make out his words.

Beau would have set the girls back home in Joshua aflutter, Pip thought, with his pretty face and his shameless flirting. But back in Joshua he wouldn't have looked twice at Pip, not if there were other young women about. He was only paying court to her because she was the only game in town.

His brother, on the other hand . . .

While Beau was like a cat toying with a mouse, Morgan McBride looked at her like he was hungry enough to pounce. Pip had never had a man look at her like that. She'd never even seen a man look at *someone else* like that. He made her feel downright naked. And while you'd think that would be an uncomfortable way to feel, it strangely wasn't. Instead, it was . . . invigorating. Like splashing yourself with cold water and feeling your skin zing with the sensation of it. Back home it would cause a scandal if a man went around staring like that.

But nothing here was like home, including *her*. She felt like a different person. Imagine if Mother could see her now. Pip had men asking her to dance, men waiting on her, men treating her like she was the most desirable woman they'd ever seen. And looking at her like they could devour her whole. She shivered, remembering Morgan's gaze across the campfire. He was hypnotic. And she was more than happy to be hypnotized.

"I'm heading up now, are you coming?" Maddy asked. She was giving Pip a wistful look that Pip couldn't quite read.

If this worked out, Pip would soon be married, she realized, feeling the happy shock of it. She and Maddy would be sisters. She would be a member of this sprawling, rambunctious family.

Not one person here had given her a pitying look, or viewed her with distaste; in fact, they all rather seemed to like her. Even Morgan McBride, who had certainly not been keen on her staying when she first arrived this morning . . .

It seemed too good to be true. But if it kept going this well, she *would* be married—after all this time!—and not just married but married to the most incredibly beautiful man. One who had built a successful home high in the mountains—a place Pip would love to call home too. It was too perfect. She imagined moving into the little cabin up the meadow, cooking down here by the creek through the summer, watching the woods blaze in full autumnal glory through the fall, cozying up indoors in winter as the snows set in . . .

She felt a warm glow, just imagining it.

Nothing had ever worked out this well for her before.

And she wasn't going to ruin it by leaving a pile of unwashed dishes. When Maddy headed up to bed, she stayed behind. She felt safe enough, with the trappers bedded down by the banked fire, and the younger McBrides splashing about up the creek. She could see lantern light in the windows of the big house and up at the cabin; there were people should she need to scream for help. Although she doubted any bears would head this way, given all the noise Beau and Jonah were kicking up.

It wouldn't take a minute to wash up, and she also needed some time alone. A lot had happened since she'd arrived in Buck's Creek, and she hadn't had a moment to think it through. Like that dance, for example. What did it *mean*? Morgan McBride had been so overbearing and insensitive yesterday, and again in the meadow this morning, but tonight . . . Tonight he'd held her close, his big hand covering the small of her back, giving her the queerest feelings. He'd glowered every time Beau claimed her for a dance and stared at her with an intensity that made her head spin. She felt turned around by the attention.

On her way down to the creek, she passed the open door of the cookhouse and groaned. They'd left it in complete disarray. She winced. She supposed she'd have to clean that up too. But look at the state of it! Pip ruefully looked down at her new juniper-green dress, which was rumpled but still clean, except for the dusty hem. She wasn't dressed for a scrubbing of the order needed for that cookhouse. Morgan's flannel shirt was back by the campfire . . . but to be honest, it wasn't going to help much, given the amount of work that was needed in there. If she set to cleaning the place, she'd ruin her new dress . . .

But she couldn't leave the place in such a state; it went against the grain. Pip glanced back at the campfire. The trappers were all asleep . . . she could hear snoring. She bit her lip. It wasn't like she'd be naked . . . She had the flannel shirt . . .

Maybe it was the whiskey that made her reckless, or maybe it was just the pressure of a job left undone, but Pip decided to strip off her dress and set to cleaning the cookhouse clad in nothing but her underwear and Morgan McBride's blue flannel shirt, which stank to high heaven from the fish she'd prepared earlier.

She carefully hung her dress on the door of the cookhouse and buttoned the flannel shirt up to the chin. It came down to her thighs, and she was wearing a full petticoat underneath, so she was decent enough if anyone stumbled across her. Pip blocked out her mother's voice in her head, which set to railing at her about her loose morality. It was *fine*. She was alone, and even if she was only in her petticoat, it was a substantial petticoat. Besides, Mother wasn't here. Pip rolled up the sleeves of the flannel shirt and set to work.

It took a lot longer than she expected, as the cookhouse seemed not to have been cleaned in a good long while. She threw the dirty knives and utensils in a bucket, to take down to the creek for a scrubbing. She had to fetch water several times, and she really had to put her back into scrubbing the table, which had fish scales and mustard greens stuck to it. But by the time she was done, the place was spotless and smelled like lye rather than fish and nodding onion. The lye soap wasn't very good—she'd have to make a batch for them sometime, she thought as she headed down to the creek to finally do the dishes, holding the lantern aloft, hoping she didn't step in any holes or burrows and do herself an injury. The grass was thick and pillowy as it sloped down to the creek.

The younger McBrides had clearly finished their swim while she'd been scrubbing the cookhouse, because she couldn't hear them splashing or talking anymore. All she could hear was the bubble and dash of the water tumbling by, and the uneven sawing sound of Thunderhead Bill snoring. A soft breeze sighed through the chokecherry tree, which leaned from the bank of the creek out over the water. She could see the cluster of wooden crosses beneath it, one tall, the others small. Her heart pinched to see them. She remembered Junebug saying that was where their mother was buried. Pip wondered what she'd been like, the woman who had mothered all of these strapping McBrides. And what it must have been like for Morgan to step into her shoes once she was gone. It couldn't have been easy.

It was quite a contortion trying to wash the dishes in the rushing creek, Pip found, as she bent to her task. There was no easy shore to kneel on, as the curve of the grassy bank was sharp. But she managed. And even if it was as uncomfortable as all get-out, it was an experience she'd never had before, washing dishes in a mountain stream. Another adventure, she thought, as the moonlight chased the rippling creek like silvery fish darting through her fingers.

"Ah hell."

The voice behind her almost sent her skidding into the water in surprise. It was Morgan McBride, and he didn't seem pleased to see her. Pip could only imagine how she looked, awkwardly dangling over the creek, petticoated, back in his filthy old shirt, stinking of lye now as well as fish.

"What are you doing?" he demanded. The feeble lamplight barely reached him, and his face was shadowy and unreadable. He was just a hulking big silhouette against the moonlit meadow.

Pip was painfully aware of her state of undress as she crouched by the creek. Her petticoat seemed to shine as white as sugar frosting in the moonlight. She felt her skin prickling, aware that it was late and that they were alone. It wasn't proper. Especially given that earlier he'd looked at her like he wanted to . . . what? Kiss her?

Pip's heart jumped. Her mother always said men weren't to be trusted—but she'd been talking to Naomi, not to Pip.

Trying to appear composed, Pip brandished a dirty plate in his direction. "I'm doing the dishes."

He swore under his breath. "The dishes? Seriously? You're *still* doing her chores for her?"

Pip blinked as he joined her on the bank. He hunkered down until they were eye level and then, gently, he tugged the plate out of her hand.

"No dishes," he told her. "You're a guest, not a servant."

But this was what she was here for. To cook and to clean; to make life easier for them all.

"Junebug can do them in the morning," he said, putting the plate down on the pile.

"No," she protested. Oh, he smelled like whiskey and woodsmoke now, as well as pine; it was intoxicating. "Honestly," she said, struggling to focus, "they're halfway done already. And if you leave them all night, they'll be the devil to wash. It's best to do it before things congeal." Pip picked up the plate again. "Please, I won't be able to sleep, knowing these are sitting here, undone."

He was clearly displeased. It did quite heart-stopping things to the hard angles of his face. His lips were full and sulky. Dear Lord, he was temptation made flesh, she thought.

"Fine," he sighed. "I'll do them. You can take the lamp up to the big house. I'll be fine by moonlight."

"No!" She was supposed to be showing him what a good wife she'd make, not sleeping while he did chores.

His eyebrows rose in surprise. "You like dishes that much?"

She almost laughed at that. She *hated* dishes. With a passion. Holy crow, when she thought of the years and years of dishes she'd done after family dinners . . . "No one likes dishes," she told him, exasperated. "In fact, most of the time I wish I could smash them to bits instead of washing them, the way Junebug was throwing them around back at the hotel. But they need to be done, and I'd rather do them now than dread doing them tomorrow."

The dimples flickered in his cheeks. Pip's stomach did a strange floaty turn.

"I'm happy to do it, really," she insisted. "You go off to bed. This won't take long." She tripped on the word *bed*. Silly. But it conjured up images . . .

"We'll do it together," he corrected her. He liked correcting people, she'd noticed. "I'll wash, you dry." He rolled up his sleeves. She rather wished he wouldn't, as she took in the lengths of velvety muscle it revealed.

He knew his way around a scrubbing brush, Pip noted, after they'd got through the plates and he took the brush to the pots. She could hear the steady rhythm of his breath as he worked. It was a peaceful sound.

"You seem more relaxed tonight than you did this morning," she observed mildly. Her heart was skipping along madly. Maybe, given the way he'd looked at her earlier, he was thinking about keeping her? Maybe now was a good time to talk about it?

He grinned as he handed her the scrubbed pot. "I guess a day makes a lot of difference."

Pip almost dropped the pot. "It does?" she asked breathlessly.

His dimples came to life, deep grooves in his stubbled cheeks. "It sure does. And I have a feeling tomorrow is going to be even better."

Pip regretted those slugs of whiskey now, as her head was spinning. "You do . . . ?"

He grinned and, oh my, it was something to behold. He looked wolfish, dark hair tumbling over his eyes, teeth white against those sultry lips. "I sure do," he said. He had a deep rumble of a voice; it passed through her like an earth tremor.

Pip grinned back, feeling a wave of euphoria. Granny had been right. Out of Joshua, she had value. Even to a man like *this*. "I look forward to tomorrow, then," she said.

A shadow crossed his face. Pip supposed a man didn't like to back down; he'd been fervent about not marrying her, and publicly so. It probably pricked his pride to have to swallow his words. Well, she wouldn't be one to rub it in; she'd take care to be gracious.

Maybe it was best *not* to talk about it right now, given that she was enjoying his company and didn't want to dampen the mood.

"Miss Hopgood," he said abruptly. The mood was definitely dampened, given that he was now scowling down at the cook pot.

"Pip," she insisted. "It seems silly to stand on formalities, given the circumstances."

"What circumstances?" Now he'd turned the scowl on her.

Oh dear. He was reverting back to his grumpy self. She shouldn't remind him that he was capitulating, she decided. He liked to be right, that much was clear. "The circumstances of me doing your dishes in my underwear," she blurted, and then immediately wished she hadn't. She felt herself turning beet red. What was she doing, drawing attention to it? She cursed herself. Why couldn't she be poised, like other women were?

At her words, his gaze immediately swept her, and that intensity blazed again, even as the scowl blackened. "Why *aren't* you clothed?"

"I *am* clothed," she squawked, although she wasn't. Not really. "I'm in your shirt," she said, a touch desperately. But that didn't seem to help. Now he was staring at the shirt, specifically where it buttoned over her breasts. "I didn't want to ruin my dress," she blathered. Oh heavens. He was looking at her like he was going to eat her again.

"But you were fine to ruin my shirt?"

Pip was all upside down and turned around. Was he angry? Or

was he teasing? Flirting even? Was that amusement? Or something else? She couldn't tell. He really was the most confounding man.

"I can take it off, if you want," she volunteered hastily, without thinking. Oh no. She shouldn't be allowed to speak. She couldn't say anything without it sounding . . . suggestive.

He froze. The air grew charged, the way it did on the plains when there was a tornado brewing. Now Morgan McBride was staring at her with an expression she didn't recognize. It was a strangely lazy look, sleepy eyed, but also like he was somehow coiled, all his energy barely leashed. She heard his breath grow uneven, heavier.

Pip had lived through enough tornadoes to know they were dangerous, and this sure felt dangerous . . . She was only inches away from him, without her dress on, and he was looking at her like he wanted to—Pip wasn't sure what he wanted to do, but she was sure it wasn't proper.

Not proper, but possibly very nice, she thought stupidly. She could feel every inch of her skin tingling in response to his gaze, as a slow pulse uncurled in her belly.

He felt it, too, she could see he did. "You'll take it off?" he repeated slowly.

Oh, that did something to her. His voice was husky, rough like sandpaper.

Pip should be panicking—a nice girl would panic in this moment; a nice girl would get to her feet right this instant and go running for the safety of the big house.

Pip realized that maybe she wasn't a nice girl.

And maybe she didn't want to be one. Not if these were the feelings you could have, when a man looked at you like that, and asked you to take your shirt (*his* shirt) off.

If you can just get him to kiss you, he'll be well and truly landed, Granny had whispered. Was that what he wanted? To kiss her? Pip's gaze dropped to his lips. They were parted and his breath was coming hard. Oh Lord, she was quivering like a leaf in a gale. If she didn't do something soon, she was liable to be blown away.

"You did get it plenty dirty," he said, his voice still sandpapery rough.

"Sorry," she breathed. She felt mesmerized, like a mouse staring at a snake.

"And it smells pretty bad." His gaze had dropped to her chest again. Pip felt it all the way through her, and low down, much lower than where he was looking. He sounded drugged, but she *felt* drugged.

What would it feel like to kiss him?

Pip felt a savage longing to find out. She wanted to be the kind of girl a man kissed. He said tomorrow would be better than today. Well, it was tomorrow, wasn't it? The moon had sunk low, and everyone else was sleeping . . .

If he doesn't, you kiss him . . . Granny had said.

Oh my goodness. *She* could kiss *him*. It was a revelation.

But was she brave enough? Probably not while she was wearing this stinking shirt, she thought helplessly. It was covered in scales and blood and stank to the heavens. If she kissed him while she was wearing it, she might knock him out with the stench. Or he'd associate her with fish stink from now until kingdom come. The problem was, the impulse to kiss him only grew the longer they crouched here, staring at each other.

But underneath the shirt, she was only in her underthings . . .

It *was* dark . . . how much could he see by hazy lamplight? Oh Lord. She wanted it so bad. She was shivering with how much she wanted it. But he didn't move. He just stayed there, frozen, staring at her like she was a conjuration. All of that leashed energy simply pulsed between them, growing by the minute.

He wanted her. She could feel it. It must be the stinking shirt keeping him away . . . otherwise, why wasn't he doing anything?

Trembling, Pip's fingers moved of their own accord to the buttons of the shirt. Once she'd undone one, her courage rose. "You're right," she managed to say, her voice threaded with tension, even to her own ears. "This thing is repellent." And she didn't want to repel; she wanted to attract. She started at the bottom of the shirt, fumbling. Her heart was pounding so loud that she felt it could wake the dead.

A soft noise escaped him as the buttons slid open.

He was disbelieving. But there was also something more. Something so primal it made her stomach clench.

Pip's nipples hardened. The feel of her linen chemise rubbing against them made her restless. Her breasts felt heavy, swollen against the padded press of her corsetry. *They like to see skin,* Granny had said, *not too much, just a hint.*

Was this too much? Pip wondered, as she peeled off the flannel shirt. She felt painfully, exhilaratingly exposed. She clenched, waiting for him to laugh, or to flinch. She couldn't help but hear the Arcrosses in her head: *If she was just a touch plain, that would be one thing, but the girl is beyond prettifying.* Pip knew she didn't look like other girls. She might be called handsome maybe, in a pinch, but not pretty. There was too much of her for prettiness. Pip braced for the expression of distaste to fall across Morgan's face as she revealed just how much of her there was.

But the distaste never came. Morgan McBride might as well have been a statue. He couldn't take his gaze from her as she dropped the shirt to the grass. She felt sinuous under his stare, like she was submerging in warm water. Unless she was completely mistaken, he was looking at her with . . . *awe.*

Pip glanced down at herself, trying to see what he saw.

Her petticoat pooled around her, a froth of white in the velvety night. The softly padded corset smoothed over her flaring hips and cut into the more than generous swell of her breasts, which were full and straining at her chemise. Her nipples were large and dark as they jutted against the whisper-thin linen. There was more lamplight than she'd hoped. She blushed, feeling a tingle wash all the way down her spine. If he was going to reject her over her looks, now was the time he would do it.

In the breathlessly long moment, Pip could hear the orchestra of frogs along the creek, tuning up for the midnight show. This was the riskiest, most shocking thing she'd ever done. She shivered. It felt *good*.

He still wasn't moving. She'd exposed herself to him in the most unladylike and scandalous fashion imaginable, just to get out of that stinking shirt so he could kiss her, and he still wasn't kissing her.

If he doesn't, you kiss him.

She'd been *this* brave, she thought. She'd come all the way to Montana, on the promise of a stranger (best not to think about how flawed that promise had been), and now she was here in her not-much-at-alls, exposed to his judgment . . .

But if she'd been this brave, she could be even braver.

Before she could lose her nerve, Pip lunged.

He wasn't expecting it, and she'd been so anxious that she'd thrown all her weight into the kiss, which sent him flying. It was possibly the most humiliating thing that had ever happened to Pip—and that was saying something, given her humiliating history with men.

She made contact with his lips, but for barely less than a heartbeat. Her momentum carried them both over the bank and headlong into the creek. There was an almighty splash as they landed. It was only the cold that kept Pip from screeching. The water was so icy that it stole the breath from her lungs. She broke the surface and scrambled to keep her head above water. Oh God. What had she done? Her sodden petticoat was a weight, pulling her down to the creek bed. She felt a wild moment of panic as she went under.

Then a pair of hands grabbed her and hauled her toward shore.

She spluttered as she swallowed water. "Pip!" He was at her back, and he had an arm around her waist, holding her up. "You can stand. We're by the bank."

Pip straightened, gingerly searching for the creek bed with her booted feet. There. Oh, thank goodness. She felt like a total fool. "I'm sorry," she said miserably.

"Don't be." His voice was strangled. He was still behind her, with his arm around her waist. She could feel his muscular forearm pushing at the undersides of her breasts. She wiped creek water from her face and looked up at him. He was transfixed. Pip followed his gaze back down to her breasts, which were above water. And, holy crow, her chemise was transparent after the soaking. *Completely* transparent.

Pip yelped, wrenching free of his grip and ducking back under the water. The current slapped at her face. She heard Morgan McBride exhale shakily.

"You kissed me," he said numbly.

"Hardly." Pip spat out a mouthful of arctic water. "I *tried* to kiss you. It didn't end well."

He gave a startled laugh. And then he sank down into the water until they were almost nose to nose. "Do you want to try again?"

Pip could feel his knees brush hers underwater. His face was a silhouette in the darkness, but she could hear the tinge of humor in his voice.

"I'm game if you are." He was so close she could feel him. She could smell the whiskey on his breath. His hands settled on her waist and pulled her so close that her nipples brushed his chest. She shivered.

He leaned in and his lips brushed hers, featherlight.

And oh my, oh heavens, oh my *goodness*. Oh, *such* goodness.

He kissed her gently, teasingly. Pip was glad he had his hands on her waist, because she'd lost all strength and was in serious danger of being swept away by the current. His lips were slick from the creek, but warm. So warm. Pip melted into him. *This was how a kiss felt?* She'd known it would be good, she just hadn't imagined how good.

Tentatively, feeling clumsy, she kissed him back. He moaned against her mouth, which made her insides shiver. His hand ran up her back until it was hot on her neck. Pip startled as she felt his tongue slide against her lips. The hand on her waist pulled her hard against him, squashing her breasts against a muscular expanse of chest. This time it was Pip's turn to moan and, as her lips opened, his tongue slid inside.

It was a thousand times more head-swimmingly intoxicating than the whiskey. Pip eased her arms around his neck, holding on for dear life as his tongue teased her senseless. Oh God, the feel of him rubbing against her. His long legs tangled with hers as his hand slid from her waist, over her hips, to her behind. She made a small noise of protest, but relaxed when he stopped. His hand was light against her derriere, unmoving. Shockingly pleasant.

The kiss deepened. Pip opened for him, surrendering completely to the sensations. She was aching. She felt like she was climbing him as she tried to get closer. Her hands clawed around his shoulders, and she hooked her leg around his hip. Instinctively, she wanted more.

"Hold on, sweetheart," he moaned, pulling away. His fingers tightened around her buttocks and, oh heavens, it made her wild. She didn't want to hold on, so she kissed him again. He tried to pull back, but only for an instant; when she licked at his lower lip, he gave up and kissed her back. Pip followed his lead and ran her hands down his back, exploring his body by feel, without thought. The man felt like he was made of rock.

He tasted like beer and whiskey and fresh air. His mouth was hot.

Pip was so mindless with the pleasure of it that she didn't notice where his hands were wandering until they found her breasts. She just about jumped out of her skin at the feel of his fingers against her. His wide palms covered her, squeezing gently. Pip felt a surge between her legs, an intensity of pleasure that was shockingly good. She could feel herself growing slick, and the rub of her pantalettes was exquisite torture. He backed her toward the bank, rising from the water and bringing her with him. Pip felt the grass against her back as the water dropped to her waist.

"God, woman, you're the best thing I've ever seen," he sighed as he broke the kiss and stared down at her. Pip was aware of her breasts straining at the soaked linen. His thumb traced her swollen nipple through the wet cloth, and she groaned. His big hands squeezed, and she tilted her head back, enjoying the strength of the sensation. More. She just wanted more. Of everything.

And then Morgan McBride lowered his head and kissed her cleavage. His tongue traced the valley between her breasts and Pip thought nothing could feel better than this. At least she did until his tongue flicked across one nipple, and then the other. He pressed her into the bank and Pip arched her back, wanting *more*. As his mouth closed over her nipple, giving it a long suck through the wet cloth, she let loose a low moan. As he sucked, his hand ran over her behind, lifting her hips toward his. She felt him hard against her. As he rubbed, the friction sent sparks cascading through her.

"Morgan," she gasped, her hands clawing into his wet hair as he nipped her with his teeth. "Dear God, Morgan . . ." She felt like she was crawling out of her skin at the sheer explosive pleasure of it.

"Pip!" Maddy's voice broke the spell. "Pip! Oh, Kit, I'll never forgive myself if something's happened to her. I should have brought her back with me."

Pip and Morgan wrenched apart, both breathing hard.

"Don't fret yet," Kit's rumble sounded from close by the cookhouse. "I'm sure she's here somewhere." He whistled. "She's certainly been busy—I don't reckon the cookhouse has ever been this clean."

Morgan cursed softly.

"Pip!" Maddy still sounded worried.

Pip was painfully aware of her state of undress. Her breasts were completely visible through her wet chemise. She ducked under the water again, unable to look away from Morgan, who was staring at her in some kind of shock. He glanced toward the voices. "Tell them you were cleaning up, and then decided to get the muck off you as well," he whispered, backing away. "I'll swim upstream, so they don't see me."

Pip's heart was skittering like a wild rabbit as she watched him retreat. She still felt drugged. Her face burned from his stubble. She wrapped her arms around herself under the water as she watched him go.

She felt like someone had ripped a curtain open, revealing a whole new world.

And she wanted more.

Thirteen

Junebug couldn't believe it. The goddamn yellow-bellied two-faced *blockhead*. If stubborn had a face to it, it would be Morgan's.

She'd known something was wrong the minute she woke up. The cabin felt different, all hushed up and empty. Usually the boys woke her, complaining about how she hadn't got the coffee on, or asking why she hadn't set to fixing breakfast. On a regular day, by the time she got down the ladder from her tiny loft, they'd be heading out the door, calling orders for bacon or beans or oats over their shoulders.

But not this morning. This morning she woke up to complete silence. It was still early, the dawn not even quite broke, but the cabin was empty already. And yet, she couldn't hear any voices outside either. McBride men weren't known for their quietude, so immediately Junebug was on edge. But not on edge enough, apparently—because the fact that Morgan was gone came as a rude shock. Once she'd scrambled down the ladder from her loft, she stood in the doorway to his bedroom, taking in the way it had been stripped bare.

He was gone.

His clothes were gone, his saddlebags were gone, his goddamn shaving kit was gone.

That bastard had lit out on her. How *dare* he!

Damn it, it was her own fault for getting complacent. She'd seen him kissing Pip Hopgood and had thought it was a done deal. Goddamn him. He didn't have the sense God gave a goose. He clearly liked Miss Nebraska—more than liked her, given the way he'd been ogling her, and dancing with her, and loving her food, and goddamn well *kissing her*. But here he was, barreling on, as though nothing had happened.

Junebug had slunk down to the creek as soon as Morgan had left the cabin the night before. She'd made a good show of snoring it up, so he thought she was asleep. And then she'd gone haring off through the grass after him. And spit, was she glad she had! If Kit and Maddy had been smitten with each other, these two were *smote*. They could barely be around each other without striking off sparks. It did a girl good to see her judgment come to rights. Those idiot brothers of hers should put a little more trust in her, because every decision she made on their behalf had so far worked out better than even she had predicted. She had a knack for this wife-finding business.

Junebug had hung around the creek long enough the night before to watch them bicker, fall in the creek and get to kissing. She'd left her hiding place pretty quick after they got to moaning and pawing each other. It turned her stomach to no end. But good for them, she'd thought happily, as she skedaddled back to the cabin. So long as she didn't have to watch it, they could go hard.

By the time she'd got back, Beau and Jonah were back from their stupid swim, so Junebug had to go in through her loft window, which was no mean feat in the darkness, as it required hauling herself up a young larch, whose boughs were nowhere near strong enough to hold her. The branches had a way of bouncing and bending under her weight, which made it a devil to climb. But she could hardly go waltzing in and out the front door, not when Beau and Jonah were right there. She'd flopped through her window, huffing, feeling like she'd stolen the moon plumb from the sky. Everything had gone so well!

Only now it had turned to crap.

When had Morgan left? Why hadn't she heard him? Their cabin was small as all hell. She'd heard him coming in, sopping wet, long after Beau and Jonah had passed out in their bunks. She'd been dozing happily as she listened with half an ear to him shucking off his wet clothes down in his room. She'd thought the fact that he'd been kissing and pawing Pip meant that he was convinced, so Junebug had been hazily dreaming of all the cakes Pip Hopgood was going to make her in the coming months. Not to mention the dishes she was going to wash afterward . . .

Junebug should have known better. Since when had Morgan ever done anything the easy way?

This also explained his uncharacteristic good cheer last night, Junebug thought sourly, as she took in the empty hooks on the wall of his small bedroom. There were still two beds, from when Kit had bunked in here too. Junebug sat on Kit's old bed and glowered at Morgan's, which, she realized, hadn't been slept in. That bastard. He'd gone all out charming her last night, not because he was actually enjoying her company, but because he was trying to lull her into complacency, so he could go and *leave her.*

This was the day he'd said he'd leave, and this was the day he'd gone. How bloody Morgan, through and through. If he said he was doing something, he went and did it, even if it went against all his best interests. And his interests were plainly in Epiphany Hopgood. Morgan wasn't that good at deception. He liked the woman. He just didn't *like* that he liked the woman. Because he was an idiot.

Junebug gathered her thoughts. He must have left as soon as he'd got back from the creek last night; she'd assumed all the noise was him taking care of his wet clothes. But maybe it had been him hauling his bags out to the barn . . . Damn it. She'd thought he was hanging his clothes on the line. She'd got tricked.

She swore. She should never have relaxed her guard.

Junebug headed for the stable through the pink dawn light, in order to confirm her suspicions, but they were confirmed before she even got there, by the way Jonah caught sight of her and turned on his heel, headed away from her as fast as he could go without breaking into a run. He was avoiding her. And heading for the big house, which meant he was calling in reinforcements to deal with her.

Damn them all! They *knew*?

Of course they knew, she thought grimly, as she stepped into the stable and saw that his horses were gone. His horses, his saddle, his tack, his saddlebags. All of it: gone. Junebug kicked at a pile of hay. This was the worst thing that he'd ever done by far. He'd gone and left her, and he hadn't even said goodbye!

Worse, the rest of those blockheads had aided him in this foul mendacity. It made her madder than a hornet. Well, he (and they) had another thing coming, she thought grimly. No one lied to Junebug McBride, *no one*. And no one damn well left her. Especially not him.

Junebug considered her options. By the time she left the stable, she had a pretty clear idea of how to proceed.

Junebug liked a plan, and this was a good one.

She schooled her face into an expression of heartbreak and dejection and forced herself to walk slump shouldered up to the big house. This had to be played carefully, she thought. And hell, it was going to be hard not to tell them all what she thought of them. In detail. She might even need the dictionary to do it justice. And throw a plate or two.

Junebug took a deep breath before she stepped into the big house. Here she went.

Her brothers and Maddy were all in the kitchen, clumped

around the table, clutching coffee mugs in white-knuckled hands. They looked at her like she was a cougar come prowling in. As well they might, she thought savagely. But she kept her dejection in place. They had to think she was defeated, or this wouldn't work.

"He's gone," she said miserably. And to be honest, the misery wasn't completely feigned. Under her rage there was a horrible sick shivery feeling. If she gave in to it, she thought she might throw up. Or cry. And she wasn't crying around these blockheads.

Maddy rose from her chair. "Oh, pet."

Junebug tensed as her sister-in-law hugged her. The traitor. She'd known and she hadn't said anything. But still, the way Maddy stroked her back was oddly comforting; Junebug thought she could probably enjoy the comfort without forgiving her.

The boys were looking guilty as all hell. Of all of them, only Kit could meet her eye. And he was giving her a look of such compassion it made her want to belt him one.

"You knew he was leaving, Bug," Kit rumbled.

It took all of Junebug's willpower not to let him have it. "I thought he might have changed his mind," she managed to spit out, "given yesterday . . ."

Kit's compassion turned to pity, and that boiled her blood so badly she had to bury her face in Maddy's shoulder just to hide her expression, which she was sure was murderous in the extreme.

"He didn't want a wife, Junebug."

Goddamn it, she hated when Kit spoke to her like *she* was the idiot.

"He made that more than clear." He took a sip of his coffee.

Junebug hoped he choked on it. She took a deep breath, reminding herself that she was supposed to be dejected, not baneful.

"Has he told *her*?" Junebug asked, her voice muffled by Maddy's dress. She couldn't quite get the bane out of her face yet. She was rigid with fury. Luckily Maddy took it for some other kind of strength of feeling, and made soothing noises.

There was silence at her question. Junebug looked up in time to see her brothers exchanging panicked looks.

"We were about to flip a coin," Maddy sighed, "to see who had to do the deed."

Junebug straightened. Oh good. "I'll do it," she volunteered.

They stared at her in shock.

Junebug strove to make her voice sound as small and contrite as possible. "It's my fault she's in this mess. I should be the one to tell her."

Kit gave her a suspicious look, which she didn't appreciate. Like *he* could make judgments about people, given the way he'd played along with Morgan's goddamn deceiving ways. Kit was a falsifier of the first order in his own right. He didn't get to be suspicious of *her*.

"It's best if it comes from me," Junebug said, congratulating herself on sounding meek, as she pulled away from Maddy and headed for the stairs. She could feel the relief coming off her stupid family in waves. Cowards. Her foot on the first step, Junebug paused and turned, as though a thought had just occurred to her. "I guess you might want to get her wagon ready," she said, trying to sound defeated. "I'm sure she'll want to leave straight after this. I would, if I were her. I'll escort them down the mountain, with Sour Eagle and Bill. It's the least I can do after this debacle." Debacle was a good word; Junebug had been wanting to use it for a while.

Kit nodded. "Good idea, Bug."

He had no idea how good, and he wouldn't realize how good it was until she didn't come home this evening, she thought with no small measure of satisfaction.

"I suppose Morgan is well on his way to Miles City by now," she sighed. She tried to look like she was going to cry and to her surprise found tears right there waiting for her. They welled up. Her throat felt like she'd swallowed a potato whole, and it had lodged in there.

Her brothers flinched at the tears, as they always did. Good. It kept them from looking at her dead-on.

"Given he's riding, I reckon he's got a fair piece ahead of him," Kit said. "It'll take him a good few days to get there."

So, he *was* headed to Miles City. Junebug had figured—even though Morgan had never been kind enough to share his plan in detail—but she was mighty pleased to have it confirmed.

"I told him to take the train." Beau shook his head. "But you know Morgan, he's allergic to good sense."

The train. Hellfire, why hadn't Junebug thought of the train? Spit, she could beat him there! She'd just have to find a way to mislead this bunch of idiots, so they didn't catch up to her before she caught up to Morgan. It shouldn't be hard. With old Bascomb's help down at the train station, she was sure she could hoodwink them into thinking she'd hopped a train somewhere else. Maybe all the way to Nebraska with Pip . . . or maybe to somewhere that had a circus. Her brothers knew how much she wanted to see a circus. They'd believe that. Especially given how heartbroke she was over Morgan's abscondment, and how much she'd need cheering up. Ha. They didn't stand a chance.

"I'd best get this over with," she told her brothers, her mind racing as she turned and dashed up the stairs.

"Good luck," Jonah called after her.

She didn't need luck. Junebug formed a mental list of everything she needed to do before they set off. She felt a lick of energy. This was going to be fun. How often did she get to go off adventuring? Never! This was one of those once-in-a-lifetime opportunities, this was, and she was going to make the most of it. She'd even get to go on a train, like she'd always wanted!

She barged into the bedroom that was supposed to be hers. She didn't really care for it. It was too wide-open and exposed; she couldn't stomach sleeping in the middle of the room like that, in a tall bed. Junebug much preferred her pallet in her loft; no one could sneak up on her in there.

"Rise and shine," she announced as she pulled Maddy's fancy

curtains aside and let the pink sunrise flood the room with rosy light.

Epiphany Hopgood and her grandmother were all bundled up under that heavy quilt Maddy had made for Junebug. Junebug didn't care for that either. She had her own quilt, one her mother had made her when she was just a tadpole. Sometimes, if Junebug burrowed into it just right, it released a phantom scent of Ma. It was a good smell and one Junebug had no intention of giving up.

"We've got a problem," Junebug announced, putting her hands on her hips and staring down at Pip, who was blinking like a vole pulled up out of its burrow. She was still in bed, her red hair all braided up, her face puffy from sleep.

Pip struggled to sit up, keeping the quilt pulled up to her chin. "Good morning," she said, blinking as she tried to absorb Junebug's presence.

Her grandmother wasn't quite so sanguine. "You're a trouble-some child, you know that?" the old woman said, glaring at Junebug. "You need some good old-fashioned discipline. Who wakes up guests so rudely?"

Junebug hadn't the time nor the inclination to argue the point, so she just continued as though Pip's granny hadn't spoken. "He's gone."

Pip frowned. "Who's gone?"

Junebug could see it was all a bit too much for her on first wak-ing. But in Junebug's opinion it was best not to beat about the bush. "Morgan," she said firmly. "He's gone."

The color went from Pip Hopgood like she'd been bled dry. For a minute Junebug thought she might swoon. Probably best she was still in bed. "What do you mean, he's gone?" she asked, her voice cracking.

"Gone where?" Pip's grandmother demanded.

"Miles City," Junebug told them. "He thinks he's going to be a cowboy again."

Pip seemed stunned.

"What are you talking about, girl?" Pip's granny was out of bed, wrapping a shawl around herself and fixing Junebug with a hard stare.

Junebug told them, but she kept it brief. "He's been looking to escape for years," she said. "That's why I ordered you up. I thought he might want to stay if he had a wife. Men do that. That's why they call wives 'the old ball and chain,' ain't it? Or at least so Thunderhead Bill says."

Pip's granny snorted. "Typical men, getting it backwards. If anyone's chained in a marriage, it's the wife."

Junebug quite agreed with her. She had no interest in wifing. Which was exactly why she'd ordered up the wife in the first place—to take over from her.

"He's gone . . ." Pip's voice failed her. She stared into space, looking like she'd seen a ghost. If only. Junebug had looked for ghosts for years, to no avail. "Gone . . . ?" Epiphany Hopgood seemed to be broken. She was still sitting there, her fat red braid falling over her shoulder, her mouth making gasping shapes, like a fish fresh pulled from the creek. "But he'll be back?" Her big tawny eyes met Junebug's and there was a sharpness in there that was good to see.

"Not under his own steam." Junebug felt a fresh burst of rage at him. "That man has a burr under his saddle about chasing cows across the country. It sounds like a trial to me. Who wants to babysit a bunch of dumb cows?"

"But he kissed me!" Pip blurted. Her eyes were wide with horror.

Junebug thought that was an interesting way to look at it. As far as she could see, Pip had done as much kissing as Morgan had.

"He kissed you?" Pip's granny snapped around like a bird of prey. Junebug made a note of it. That was a wily one. She might come in useful.

At least the blood was coming back to Pip now. And all in a rush, by the looks of it. Her whole face was rosier than the daybreak.

"Why didn't you say anything!" Pip's grandmother demanded. "All you said was you had a wash in the creek . . ." She trailed off. "With him?" she hazarded. She was looking at Pip as though she was meeting her for the first time.

Pip scrambled from the bed, her flannel nightgown flaring around her.

"Epiphany!" Her grandmother followed her as she snatched her dress off the hook on the back of the door. "You tell me right this minute what happened!"

"I can tell you," Junebug volunteered, watching as Pip's expression grew mulish. She didn't have time for all this hectoring and resisting. They had a train to catch. "They fell in the creek from the force of kissing, and then they pawed at each other. I ain't never been so glad to see something, and yet so repelled, in all my born days."

"Well, I never," Pip's granny said. But she didn't sound upset. In fact, if anything, she seemed cheered.

"You were watching us!" Pip accused. She had a look of complete and utter mortification. Consternation, even.

"I left after he laid hands on you," Junebug assured her. "I didn't want that abhorrence seared on my memory."

"The man has compromised you," Pip's granny declared excitedly. "And we have a witness! He has to marry you now."

Pip looked at her like she'd lost her mind. "He's not here," she reminded her grandmother. "He ran off." She made a startled noise. "I think I'm going to be sick." And then she was, right in the washbowl.

Junebug was astonished. She'd been feeling a touch sick over Morgan leaving herself. But Pip had just met him—what did she have to feel sick about?

Junebug opened the window to let fresh air in.

"Don't you fret, my girl," Pip's granny soothed her, as she pulled her braid out of the way and patted her while she was ill. "We'll make this right. You're not the first girl to have a shotgun wedding and you won't be the last."

"I don't reckon you'll need a shotgun, not given the way they were at each other," Junebug snorted. "I reckon we just need to throw her in his path, and he'll come around. He won't be able to help himself."

Pip's grandmother gave her a sharp look. "And how do we do that, given he's not here?"

Junebug grinned. "Easy. We go to him."

The old woman pursed her lips. "Tell me what you've got up your sleeve."

Junebug did. Including the bit about lying to her brothers. That bit was perhaps the most important. The last thing they wanted was those three lumps making trouble; this was going to be a challenge enough as it was.

Especially given that Epiphany Hopgood was surprisingly not of a mind to be cooperative.

"Didn't you like all that kissing?" Junebug asked curiously. Because she sure had seemed to.

"I am not begging the man to marry me." Pip proved to be stubborn as all hell. Maybe as stubborn as Morgan could be, which was saying something.

"We're not begging him, we're forcing him," her grandmother said.

That was the exact wrong thing to say. Junebug knew it even as the words came out of the older woman's mouth. She'd read Pip's letters and knew enough about her past to know that her pride was pretty tattered. She was too proud to be foisted on a man. Plainly. But Junebug wasn't interested in any foisting.

"We ain't forcing him," Junebug interrupted fiercely. "Firstly, because Morgan cain't be forced to do *anything*. He's immovable, like the damn mountains. Secondly, because sugar catches more flies than vinegar, lady."

Pip turned her back on both of them and began dressing. But Pip's grandmother looked interested.

"Morgan's just an idiot," Junebug told them patiently. "He's like the creek at the end of winter, when the thaw's coming: all iced up on the surface, but seething underneath."

Pip stopped dead at that and turned to stare at Junebug. "I wrote that. In my letters . . ."

"Yeah, you did," Junebug told her. "You were writing about some woman who likes to shuck peas."

"She doesn't," Pip said numbly. "She doesn't like shucking peas. She hates it. That's what I meant about the river. She looks composed, but underneath she's screaming."

Whatever. Junebug pressed on. "That's Morgan," she told Pip, and she meant it. "He's screaming too. He's been screaming since he got saddled with the lot of us. He don't really want to be a cowboy—he just wants to stop screaming. But he's too stupid to realize it. He thinks he can go out on the trail, chasing cows, and he'll suddenly feel better. But he won't. Because he's still all iced up." Hell. As she said the words aloud, Junebug had a revelation. Morgan wasn't angry at all. He was sad. And maybe scared. She remembered that horrible time when Ma was sick, when Morgan first came home. She remembered how he'd clenched up at the look of their ma on her pallet, coughing fit to shake the rafters. He'd not really unclenched since. Except maybe when he was kissing and pawing at Epiphany Hopgood in that creek last night . . .

Pip had stopped dressing and was listening. Junebug had a gift for convincing people like that. It was a skill she was proud of.

Junebug relaxed into her speechifying. She liked a good speech. "He ain't never really grieved our ma." Spit, that big old potato was back, quite out of the blue. It lodged in her throat and her eyes were prickling. "I don't s'pose any of us did." That had been a god-awful time and Junebug chose not to think on it much. Morgan was the same. They just pushed the burdensome feelings down and let them get covered in ice. Only, Junebug thought, they were still down there, tumbling away, waiting for a snap thaw. She knew he felt these things, because she and Morgan were the same. And she loved him more than anyone. She knew him better than any-one. The big old stubborn idiot.

"I reckon he'll get out there on the trail," Junebug predicted, "away from Buck's Creek, and the whole weight of it will come crash-ing down on him. And once he's felt all those thawed messed-up feelings, he'll come to himself. And it will work out for all of us."

"So why don't you just let him go?" Pip asked huskily. "If you think he'll come to his senses on his own, why don't you just let him try it?"

Junebug scowled. Over her dead body! Because just the thought of Morgan being gone, well, it opened up a great big sucking hole right through the middle of her. And she might just disappear into that hole and never come out again. Thawing old grief was one thing; losing the one person who kept you safe was another.

"It might take years," Pip's grandmother said sourly. "Your grand-father never came back when he went."

"Grandpa never went anywhere." Pip seemed annoyed at the interruption.

She had some fire to her, Junebug thought with satisfaction. Just what her stupid brother needed.

"Not in body," Pip's grandmother complained. "But he took off in spirit and stayed that way."

"Junebug." Pip fixed Junebug with a troubled look. "I'm not go-ing after him."

Junebug rolled her eyes. Of course she was. Spit, why did peo-ple need to be talked into things all the time? Why couldn't they just do the sensible thing on their own? "Sure you are," she said. "Now get packing."

"No." Pip returned to buttoning her dress.

Junebug resented having to waste time and energy convincing her. They were probably going to miss today's train if they took much longer. And Junebug wasn't riding all the way to Miles City, not if she could catch the train instead. "Look, I know you're used to those Nebraska men, who treated you cold. But that ain't Morgan. He's stupid, but not that stupid." Junebug saw Pip flinch, but she plowed on. "He *likes* you."

"Clearly not," Pip said sharply. "Clearly, he was so appalled by me last night that he had to leave the state."

"He ain't leaving the state. Miles City is still in Montana."

Pip threw her a spicy look at that.

"And he weren't appalled. Not one bit. From what I saw, he was having the time of his life." Junebug could see exactly what was happening here. Pip was falling into her own big sucking hole. One that told her she wasn't good enough. Junebug made a note to stay well away from Nebraska men. They must be some pieces of work. "This ain't about you. This is about him."

"I'm not doing it."

Oh, she was a prideful one. How annoying. Still, Junebug had time to work on her; it was a long way down the mountain.

"You get packed," she said in her gentlest manner. "The boys are getting your wagon ready. They think we're just escorting you down to Bitterroot, so you can arrange your way home."

"Which is exactly what's happening," Pip said firmly.

It wasn't. But if thinking so got her down the mountain, then all well and good.

Fourteen

Pip couldn't believe the nerve of them. They'd tricked her.

Although Junebug insisted it wasn't a trick at all, as there *was* a train that left Miles City for Nebraska. "This *is* your way home," the infuriating kid said as she stood grinning on the platform in Bitterroot. "And it's not like you've got much choice, as the next train due in here is going plumb in the opposite direction to where you want to go."

They were at the station and ready to board before Pip learned that Junebug and Granny had bought tickets to Miles City, the very place where *that man* was headed. That man she never wanted to see again in her life.

"I'll wait here in Bitterroot," Pip said stubbornly. "There will be a train to Nebraska in good time."

"And how will you pay for that? We just spent the last of our money on these tickets," Granny said cheerfully. She and Junebug were as thick as thieves. Junebug was even calling her by her given name, which seemed impertinent in the extreme, although Granny didn't seem to mind. The two of them had grated on Pip all the way down the hill. Only Sour Eagle seemed to be on Pip's side.

"Leave the man be," he said disapprovingly, as Junebug hatched her insane plans. "He's not going to like this."

Pip thought that was an understatement if she'd ever heard one. Morgan McBride had *left town* after kissing her. If that didn't speak plainly about his feelings, she didn't know what did. "Forget *him*," she'd snapped. "*I* don't like this."

She wouldn't marry the man if he was the last man on earth, not after this. So, they could forget their plans. Pip took a deep breath and silently counted to ten to quench her fury, as she stared at the tickets in Granny's hand. Why were there more than two of them? Pip had a sinking feeling the trappers were coming with them. What was this, a farce?

"Sell them back," she instructed tersely. "We only need two tickets—to Nebraska. Sell those back and use the money to buy the new ones."

"Oh, you can't sell them back, miss," Bascomb, the roostery stationmaster, said cheerfully. He was still in the grandiose ticket window of the tiny station house, his hat at a jaunty angle. "It's against company policy."

"There you go, it's against company policy." Junebug snatched her ticket from Granny and peered at the clock. "How long till the train gets here, Bascomb?"

"Now, Junebug, how many times have I told you, the big hand—"

"I don't want to hear it, Bascomb. Just tell me."

Pip's headache throbbed as she listened to them argue. "Why are those men coming with us?" she asked Granny grimly, although she suspected she knew the answer.

"Well, we can't go unescorted, can we?" Granny all but batted her eyelashes at the trappers. "After all, the frontier is a dangerous place. And these kind gentlemen have agreed to escort me. Ah, us," she corrected.

"Not me," Roy disagreed, looking shifty. "I got no desire to see Miles City."

"Roy's a wanted man in Miles City," Thunderhead Bill rumbled, "on account of a bad hand of cards."

"Possibly more than one," Roy said glumly.

"Our Roy will stay here and throw the McBride boys off the scent," Bill continued.

"Please don't," Pip pleaded. She couldn't imagine that would go well.

"Stop interfering with my trappers," Junebug cut in. "Roy will tell the boys exactly what I told him to tell the boys, or I won't give him that letter from the yeller-haired lady he's been writing to."

"It's a crime to withhold mail," Roy grumbled.

"Not when it's addressed to you, and that letter is addressed to me, Roy, given as how I'm the one writing to her on your behalf. You don't got a legal leg to stand on, so don't go threatening me."

Roy scowled, impotent.

Sour Eagle just stood there disapprovingly. Pip couldn't believe he was going along with this daft endeavor. But he couldn't seem to let Granny go off alone with Thunderhead Bill. Honestly. There were other women here in Bitterroot. Although, Pip supposed, they might not be interested in a couple of mangy old trappers. Not like Granny, who was flirting shamelessly with them.

"Did we pay for *all* these tickets?" Pip asked furiously. They had so few resources, and Nebraska was a long way away.

"They'll pay us back." Granny swatted away her concern.

Pip just wanted the whole ordeal to be over. She couldn't believe how high her expectations had been when she'd arrived in this wretched town a week ago. *Only* a week ago. What an eternity it seemed. She felt like she'd been dragged downhill through the mud since then. She just wanted to get home and pretend none of this had ever happened. She'd even withstand Mother's smugness at being right, for the chance to hole up in her old bedroom to lick her wounds in private.

Pip's stomach roiled at the memory of Morgan McBride back-

ing away from her in the creek last night. She'd thought he was
feeling the same way she was—intoxicated. But he'd obviously been
feeling very differently. Or at least intoxicated for very different
reasons. She'd been drunk on him, and he'd just had too much
whiskey. In the stark light of day, Pip felt only crushing humiliation, as she remembered climbing him, and sliding her tongue
into his mouth . . . Today she felt disastrously sure she'd forced
herself on him . . .

But then she remembered him sinking down into the water,
nose to nose with her, murmuring, *Do you want to try again?* She
tingled just at the memory of his voice, which had been soft and
teasing. He had not been an unwilling participant, darn it. Unbidden, she felt the phantom pressure of his hands closing over her
breasts, and her nipples tightened.

Damn him. How dare he toy with her like that?

He must have known that she wasn't the kind of woman practiced with men. Look at her, for heaven's sake! Pip caught her reflection in the station window. She was taller than Roy even, and
broader in the shoulder. Did Morgan McBride think he could take
advantage of her because of her looks?

All last night's confidence had evaporated, and Pip was back to
feeling lumpish and unattractive. Only worse than ever.

Oh God, and now she had to go home to Mother . . . Maybe it
was a blessing in disguise that they were taking the long way home.
Although she didn't plan to tarry in Miles City; she was catching
the first train out of there, so she didn't run the risk of seeing Morgan McBride. She never wanted to see him again in her lifetime.

She should never, ever have trusted Granny to buy those damn
tickets. After a long wait in Butte to change trains, they arrived in
Miles City in the early morning to find it wasn't much of a city at
all. In fact, the sign read "Miles Town." The place was nothing but

a raw sprawl of ramshackle timber buildings in the dirt, and most of those buildings seemed to be saloons.

"Huh. So, this is what a cow town looks like," Junebug said as they stepped from the train onto a boarded platform. "Ain't much, is it?"

No, it certainly wasn't. It was barely a place at all.

"It ain't all this dusty," Thunderhead Bill reassured them. He was fond of holding forth and was clearly ready to do so again on Miles City. Or rather Miles *Town*. "Down that way is the Tongue River," Thunderhead Bill said with a grand gesture of his arm. "It's almost pretty down that way."

Pip noted he used the word *almost*. And the Tongue? That didn't sound appealing in the slightest. "I'm buying us tickets for the next train home." Pip headed for the ticket window, and then she remembered that Granny still had her purse from back in Bitterroot. "How much money do we have left?" she asked anxiously, holding her hand out for the purse.

Granny puckered her lips. "Enough for a cup of coffee," she said, trying to sound bright. "Couldn't everyone use a coffee after that journey? I can never sleep on trains."

Oh God. No. No, no, no.

Pip turned to the trappers. "Could we please ask you to reimburse us for the cost of your tickets here?" she asked politely.

Sour Eagle and Thunderhead Bill exchanged a glance.

"Coffee does sound good . . ." Thunderhead Bill rumbled, scratching at his whiskers.

"Please . . ." Holy crow, she might cry. Pip felt the tears coming. Surely they had the money?

"They don't have a cent to their names," Junebug told her, returning from the far end of the platform just in time to catch Pip's horror. "But don't worry, providence will step in. It always does."

Pip could have pushed her off the platform.

"We don't have the money, but we can get it," Sour Eagle assured her. "As soon as the saloons open for business."

Pip frowned. What on earth did that mean?

"Sour Eagle plays a mean hand of cards," Junebug told her cheerfully. "As soon as he gets a seat somewhere, he'll get your money for you."

"Are you serious?" Pip exploded. Those deceitful rodents! The lot of them. "Are you telling me that we're stranded here in this wild place, without a cent to our names? And we're reliant on Sour Eagle's *luck*?"

Sour Eagle was put out by that. "Luck has nothing to do with it."

"We have a cent." Granny was equally put out. "I told you, we have enough for coffee."

Pip tried to stay calm as she considered her options. Her trunks and her animals were being unloaded from the train—she could see them now. Maybe she could sell something? Not Sadie, her horse; she loved her horse. But maybe the chickens? Someone around here must want some laying hens? This looked like a place in need of eggs . . .

"Come on," she snapped, gathering her skirts and heading for the station. It took her an age to convince the stationmaster to let her store her belongings in the station house; in the end she had to leave Thunderhead Bill behind to watch it all, which he was vociferously against, but they needed Sour Eagle to earn some money and Pip wasn't leaving Junebug or Granny unattended in a place like this.

"Oh, hush your whining," Junebug told him sternly, when Thunderhead Bill complained that he was being abandoned. "Martha will come back with some coffee for you, won't you, Martha?"

Pip clenched her teeth at their amiability. None of them seemed to realize what a fix they were in.

Granny gave Thunderhead Bill a coy smile. "I'll even put extra sugar in it."

"Men are strange creatures, ain't they?" Junebug sighed, falling into step with Pip as they headed off the platform and into the town. "You can get them to do anything, so long as there's some form of sugar involved."

"I think I could get *you* to do anything, so long as there was actual sugar involved," Pip countered sharply. Oh, when she thought of all those cakes she'd baked back in Bitterroot! She was such an imbecile. John had been right. She *had* been desperate. So desperate she'd let herself be used by them all.

Pip slowed her pace as they reached the main street. Oh God. On one side of the dirt road there was a saloon, a dance hall, another saloon, a mercantile, yet another saloon and a bordello; on the other side there was a boardinghouse, a saloon, a farrier, another dance hall and then a final saloon that promised "Best Girls!"

This was where Morgan McBride ran to, after kissing her? This was preferable to marrying her in the idyll of Buck's Creek? Her mother was right. Pip was completely unweddable.

"There are a lot of people sleeping in the street," Junebug observed blithely, taking in the bodies slumped in doorways.

"I don't think they're sleeping," Pip said grimly. They were passed out cold. Pip supposed they'd been there all night.

"There's a place that advertises coffee," Granny called out. She had an arm looped through Sour Eagle's and seemed undaunted by the seediness of the place.

They'd just stepped onto the boarded sidewalk in front of the coffeehouse when a small fluffy dog came exploding out of the doorway, yapping up a storm. It positioned itself in front of them, barking like it was giving a fire-and-brimstone sermon. Pip would have been worried, if it hadn't been so small and ridiculous looking. And if its tail hadn't been wagging so happily.

"Beast!" Junebug exclaimed. "What are you doing here!" She

scooped the puffball up and it growled happily. She caught Pip's astonishment. "This is my old dog," she told her. "Kind of."

"Kind of?"

"Merle! Don't you go running off again!" A woman exploded from the same doorway, a canary-yellow blare of satin and feathers. She stopped dead at the sight of them. She seemed as astonished to see Junebug as Junebug had been to see the dog. "Oh. It's you."

Pip had never seen a woman like her. She was like a combustion of millinery. And pretty as a china doll.

"Hey, Willabelle." Junebug grinned ear to ear. She turned to Pip. "See, I told you providence would step in."

"Give me my dog back."

If this Willabelle was providential, she didn't look too pleased to see them.

Junebug tried to hand the dog over to her, but the dog wasn't having it. He growled and bared his teeth at the canary-yellow woman, who gave a long-suffering sigh.

"Fine. You bring him in."

Junebug peered at the building the woman and dog had emerged from. "Is this your place?"

It was a dining hall. There was a big white card in the window that read "Cook Wanted," next to the sign that advertised coffee for five cents.

"It is," Willabelle said primly, "for now." She swept back inside.

Pip followed Junebug and the dog in, and Granny and Sour Eagle brought up the rear. The place was as basic as Pip had expected, but at least it was cleanish (except for the ubiquitous dust). The floor was bare boards, the walls were unpainted and the chairs and tables were new pine so fresh it looked like it might give you splinters.

"It's . . . nice," Junebug said, looking around. The dog was lolling in her arms, his pink tongue hanging sideways as he panted. "I don't imagine you decorated the place though. It don't seem your style."

"No," Willabelle agreed, her nose wrinkling. "It's awful. I won it off a man named Smockley, or Hockley, or something-ley."

"You won it? Playing poker?" Junebug lit up at that.

"Sort of . . ." Willabelle was evasive.

Pip cleared her throat. "We might trouble you for a coffee," she said, not sure she wanted to know how the woman had won the place, given the state of this town.

"It's ten cents for coffee," Willabelle said brightly, heading to the door at the back of the room, where Pip assumed the kitchen was.

"It says five in the window," Pip called after her. Ten cents for a coffee! That was obscene.

"Price has gone up," Willabelle called back sharply. "Coffee is scarce in these parts."

"Can we afford it at that price?" Pip asked her grandmother archly.

"We can share . . . ?"

Pip glared at her. This was unbearable. Where were they going to sleep tonight if Sour Eagle didn't win at cards? Out in the streets, with all the drunks?

Willabelle's coffee smelled downright terrible too. Pip was actually glad she only had to take a sip or two of it. Willabelle leaned against the counter and watched them discontentedly as they passed the cup back and forth. She seemed like a most incongruous person for Junebug to know. But maybe they were friendly enough to throw themselves on the woman's mercy? Maybe she could put them up for the night? After all, she was bound to be sympathetic, given that she was also a woman alone in a rough town.

"How do you know her?" Pip whispered.

"I was her wife," Willabelle said, not even pretending that she wasn't eavesdropping.

Pip looked at Junebug, astonished. *This* was the first wife?

When Maddy had said the first wife Junebug had ordered was inappropriate, this wasn't quite what Pip had imagined. She took in Willabelle's yellow silk gown, with its enormous bustle, and the feather bobbing from her blowsy blond curls. She couldn't begin to imagine the woman in Buck's Creek. Although . . . she couldn't imagine her here, either, and yet here she was.

"Almost," Junebug corrected, disgusted. "Luckily Kit took a shine to Maddy instead."

"Shame. I could use Madeleine here." Willabelle pouted.

"I don't really know why you're here," Junebug said, eyeing her. "This don't seem like your kind of place."

"It's not." Willabelle scowled. "I hate it here. I got stranded."

Oh God. Pip had a vision of herself still here in a month's time, just as stranded as Willabelle was.

"No money, huh?" Junebug pulled at the dog's ears, and he made an appreciative noise.

"I'm just trying to scrape together enough to get the hell out of here." She pursed her rosebud lips. "You sure you don't want another coffee?"

"No." All four of them said it at once. Even if they weren't out of money, it was mighty bad coffee.

"Shouldn't you be busy at this time of day?" Pip glanced out at the street. "I would think all those men will be hungry when they wake up."

Willabelle made a disgusted noise. "They will be. And they used to come here. But they stopped." She glared at the empty tables. "It's that wretched Stockley's fault. He refused to work here anymore once he lost the place. How am I supposed to run a dining hall without a cook! I do my best, but do any of them appreciate it? No!"

"Pip can cook," Junebug said triumphantly. "See, providence!" she told Pip. "If this ain't providence, I don't know what is. We're out of money, she needs a cook, you can cook . . ."

"I don't want to cook," Pip hissed at her.

"So, you'd rather sleep on the street?" Junebug asked in wide-eyed innocence. The whelp.

"You said Sour Eagle would have the money," Pip reminded her.

"I will." Sour Eagle's chair scraped on the floorboards as he stood, his pride wounded. "What time do the saloons open?"

"Oh, they don't rightly ever close around here," Willabelle sighed. "Between the soldiers from the fort, the cowhands, the mule skinners and what have you, there's always someone looking for a drink."

Sour Eagle grunted and headed for the door.

"I'll come with you," Granny Colefax insisted, finishing their meager cup of coffee with one pained gulp. "For luck."

That cheered Sour Eagle to no end.

"Granny!" Pip gasped. "You can't go to a saloon!"

"Sure I can."

"I'm sure they don't let women in." Pip glanced at Willabelle, who shrugged.

"There's always whores in there," the blonde said. "They count as women, don't they?"

"How come you haven't earned your way out of here whoring?" Junebug asked Willabelle curiously as Pip watched her grandmother and Sour Eagle leave.

Pip had a horrible feeling that things were deteriorating, too rapidly for her to get a handle on.

"I ain't no whore, you little cat." Willabelle's accent slipped. For a moment she sounded just as backwoodsy as Junebug did.

"You wouldn't be looking to buy some good laying hens, would you?" Pip asked her, feeling a surge of complete desperation. She didn't want to stay in this place a moment longer than she had to. "I'm sure you go through a lot of eggs in an establishment like this."

"You'd think so, wouldn't you?" Willabelle was sour. "But like I said, I don't have much custom at the moment. And unless you want to buy something to go with that one cup of coffee, I'm not liable to be able to afford to eat this week myself, let alone go buying hens."

"She needs a cook," Junebug reminded Pip helpfully.

Goddamn it. "How would she even pay a cook?" Pip snapped. "You heard her, she doesn't have any money."

"Wait." Willabelle straightened up. "Was she serious about you cooking?"

"And why wouldn't I be?" Junebug asked indignantly. "I ain't no liar."

Willabelle gave an unladylike snort. "You're the very picture of a liar, luring me out here with those letters and all that talk of a *wealth of land.*"

"That's true! Kit has land!"

Willabelle rolled her eyes. "Because of you I'm stuck in this stupid place."

"You're the one who lied," Junebug railed at her. "You went and ran off with that miner back in Bitterroot, and then that cowboy after Maddy married Kit. If you want to blame anyone for landing you in this place, blame the cowboy! Whatever happened to him, anyway?"

"Stop," Pip ordered. "Enough. There is no point in rehashing old gripes."

They didn't listen. They both plainly liked a gripe.

"He took off on a cattle drive, the fiend," Willabelle complained.

"I guess that is what cowboys do."

"What are you doing here, anyway?" Willabelle asked. "How come you're not in Balls Creek?"

"Buck's Creek."

"Same thing."

Pip couldn't stay here. She'd go mad. "How much do you pay? For a cook?" she blurted. Dear God, she needed to get out of here somehow. Maybe she could do a day, and then leave?

"Eight dollars a month." Willabelle was quick to answer.

That seemed very low. Pip did the math. That was less than twenty-eight cents a day. She wasn't buying a train ticket for that. She wasn't even buying a train ticket in a month at that price. And then there was Granny to consider. Not to mention getting Junebug home again. Pip swore.

Junebug was impressed. "I didn't know you knew words like that!"

Pip hoped like hell that Sour Eagle was as good at cards as he thought he was. But she couldn't pin all her hopes on that—and she had the kid to consider. She couldn't have the girl homeless. Where were they going to sleep tonight, if Sour Eagle didn't make any money?

"I'll cook for you, in exchange for room and board for all of us," Pip said, quickly, before she could change her mind. "But only until we scrape together the money for train fares." Which, God willing, would be by tomorrow, if Sour Eagle did as he promised. But at least they'd have a roof over their heads for tonight.

Willabelle clapped her hands. "It's a deal," she squealed. "How good a cook are you?" she asked.

"She's the best," Junebug told her. "You ain't eaten until you've eaten Pip's food."

Willabelle sparkled like the sun off polished glass. "We'd best put the prices up, then!"

Fifteen

Morgan was travel-weary by the time he dragged into Miles City. He was out of practice. It had taken him a day longer than he'd expected to get there, and he was saddle-sore and ready for a beer and a bath.

He hadn't seen a soul on the trail, just clumps of wary goats, who lowered their horns at him and fixed him with baleful stares. He should have made better time than he did: the weather was pristine, with long blue sunny days and sharp clear nights; there was game to cook fresh on the campfire, and summer grass to pillow his sleep. But he couldn't ease into it. It was too quiet. All he heard was the sound of his horses, hooves drumming, breath snorting; the blithe and carefree call of birds; and the gentle tease of the wind in the trees. The world stretched out at his feet, every day unscripted. It was everything he'd dreamed of. Hell, it was perfect.

Only it wasn't, damn it. It was *oppressive*. The lack of other McBrides left a wide-open whistling silence that threatened to untether him. All these goddamn *thoughts* rushed in. Memories. None of them wanted. Ma's face; Ma's cough; the shriek of winter winds down the mountain, nipping them all bloodless and blue; Charlie gone in the night; Junebug grieving so hard he felt it like someone was tearing strips of his skin clean away. Ma before she was ever sick, careworn, standing by the creek in her apron, watching him go the last time he'd lit out for Texas. She'd had that sad patient look, the beaten-down one, the one that said she hoped for nothing more from life except an easier day than the one before. She hadn't wanted Morgan to go. Had begged him not to with those defeated eyes. She needed him, in ways that weren't fair, because her waste of a husband wasn't fit for anything but the moonshine. Morgan had always been a substitute adult, there to lend an ear and a shoulder. When he went, what did she have? Children, that was all. Mouths to feed. Too many of them to keep alive.

He'd left her to her fate. Her and those kids, the ones who'd ended up under the chokecherry tree with her, most of all.

But how could he have stayed? If he'd stayed, the old man would have killed him. Or Morgan would have killed the old man. Things had grown too tense.

No, not tense. Tense didn't do it justice. Things had been *desperate*.

That brought more memories, deeper ones, the ones he refused to think on. Only now they wouldn't stay refused; they came flooding in through the long silent nights on the trail, when all he had to listen to was the soft sizzling of the banked campfire and the hooting of the owls.

In the depths of the night, Morgan felt small and powerless again, *impotent*. He flinched at the memory of fists thudding against flesh, of the cold shocking pain of the belt buckle, of the reek of the old man's breath. But worse, much worse, was the memory of fists thudding against flesh that wasn't his. Memories of huddling under his blanket at night, frozen, unable to do more than listen to the beatings the old man inflicted on her, even when she was hard bellied with his next child.

Morgan *hated* Buck's Creek. He hated everything about the dirty patch of ground the old man had pitched their threadbare tents on. He hated the isolation; the lack of people to run to; the weight of his mother when he helped her up, her arm like a harness around his neck. And more than anything he hated the weak, quivery, yellow-bellied feeling he got, even now that he was full-grown and ten times stronger than the old man had ever been, whenever he remembered.

Morgan McBride was scared fit to die, out here with his memories. The night was full of jagged shadows, each one loud with the past.

When it got too bad, he sat up in his bedroll and stoked the fire and waited for the shell-pink dawn. He watched it come, urgently calling up better memories. He'd seen the ocean once, in Texas. It was a hell of a long way from Abilene, but he and the boys had gone on a ride down to Galveston, to spend some money and have some fun before the next cattle drive. *That* was a memory worth having, he thought, as he fed the fire to keep the last of the night at bay. He remembered the wealth of Galveston, the women with their round shoulders and twangy voices, the salty smell of the air. He remembered the jangly, spangly light reflected off the water. He remembered swimming in the sea with the boys and thinking how much his brothers would love splashing about, and how his ma would love the cascade of pretty shells lying in drifts on the shore. He'd sifted through them, slipping a few into his saddlebags to take home to her: fan-shaped peachy pink shells no bigger than his thumbnail, curved and glossy speckled curls and long tightly spiraled spears the shade of the sand. As he'd gathered them, he'd felt a weight settle on his chest, like someone had dropped an anvil right over his lungs and was crushing the air out of him. She was back there with the old man, while he was splashing it up in Texas, looking to soothe his conscience with *shells*.

Goddamn it. Did every memory have to lead back there? Wouldn't he *ever* be free?

He scowled at the campfire. All these years later, with Ma long gone and Pa long run off, with the kids grown, and he *still* wasn't free.

Morgan needed a memory that didn't involve Ma, or the old man, or any of the stinking old pain. He needed something fresh and clean and honest. As honest as that Pip Hopgood woman, the plainest-speaking, most honest person he'd ever met.

I want you to marry me, she'd said straight to his face in the meadow, on the day she'd fetched up in Buck's Creek. There was no beating about the bush, no looking to him to rescue her, no half-truths or flat-out lies. She just looked him dead in the eye like an equal and spoke her mind plain. It was goddamn refreshing.

Morgan felt himself easing as the old days were replaced by more recent memories, and the fire snapped cheerily, just as the cookfire had the night she cooked fish on it. That had been some mighty good fish. Morgan's stomach rumbled at the memory, even though he'd had himself a big helping of hare for dinner; breakfast was still a long way off. He wouldn't mind some of that fish for breakfast. And some of that coffee she'd made at the hotel.

He sure felt bad about running off on her. She hadn't deserved it. She'd never done anything but treat him fair.

Morgan grinned as he remembered the way she'd lunged for a kiss, knocking him ass over elbow into the creek. Forget speaking her mind, the woman acted her mind too. Ah, she was too good for the likes of him. She deserved a man who was . . . what? Not a wanderer, that's what was what. She deserved someone who'd stay put with her and build a life and raise some kids. And Morgan McBride had raised more than enough kids for one lifetime. Staying put was too much like entrapment. He didn't want it.

But she did. She'd come all the way to the mountains of Montana for it. Epiphany Hopgood wanted all the things he was running from, and she'd have no trouble finding them. Men would queue up to marry her and give her everything she deserved.

The thought was a burr.

Morgan imagined she'd head home to her people in Nebraska. She was probably already on the train home, buttoned up in that distracting green dress, headed for some churchgoing merchant or farmer, who'd count his lucky stars at snagging such a high-quality woman. Morgan imagined she'd have a wedding with all her folks padding out the pews, her ma weeping into her handkerchief with joy and Pip herself bursting with happiness as some fresh-faced midwesterner said his *I do*s and then kissed her.

Morgan scowled.

Although, if she'd come out here in the first place, maybe there weren't no marriageable men in her neck of the woods? Maybe those fresh-faced huskers weren't enough for a woman like Pip. Maybe she needed a man made of stronger stuff. Maybe she'd stay on and marry someone in Montana.

That butcher Hicks kept making noises about finding a wife. Morgan had a sudden vision of Pip Hopgood as a butcher's wife, with a pack of well-fed kids hanging on to her skirts. Hicks was doing a roaring business and would no doubt build her a big old house, where she'd be queen of her own castle. Morgan thought she'd like that. He bet it would be a homely, well-run castle, too, the kind of place that welcomed you in to warm yourself by the stove while she chattered at you. Morgan could see her, floury from baking, with Junebug coming to pester her for treats when she made her weekly rounds. And Morgan would just be some passing bit of gossip, nothing but a distant memory. Some man she'd come out to marry, who'd let her down. Just like he let everyone down.

But he bet she damn well wouldn't forget his kiss. Morgan

scowled, not liking the tenor of his imaginings. Theirs wasn't the kind of kiss that came along every day. Hell, he hadn't had a kiss like it in his entire life. And he didn't care how far in the past it was, it would never be a distant memory for him. He bet it would stay a fire in his blood every time he thought on it. And he bet it would for her, too, butcher's wife or not.

Ah hell, now he was out of sorts again. What was *wrong* with him?

Whatever it was, it only got worse as the trail wore on, and by the time he scuffed into Miles City he was sore and surly. It was late in the day and the sunlight fell in thick dusty wedges, the shadows long on the ground. The animal smell of cows was heavy in the air.

Morgan had not been to Miles City before. He'd been out of the trade for such a long time, and things had changed since his day. When he was running herds, he ran them across from Texas to Kansas. Now the herds were driven up here to Montana from Texas and free ranged, before being shipped off by rail to Chicago. The fort-cum-cowtown was sprawled in a valley by the Tongue River in Cheyenne country and was rough as rough could be.

Morgan might not have been here before, but he had been to dozens of towns just like it. It was like slipping back into an old pair of boots, he told himself as he eased down the main drag toward the livery. Prices were high, just like they were in all these places, but he could afford it after so many years of running a successful trading post. Although he still winced as he paid for the stabling of his horses. His horses should be eating better than he did for that price.

The boardinghouse was no better. He probably could have saved a buck by going to the bunkhouse farther up the road, but he didn't fancy bunking in with a rabble of drunks. He'd grown soft, he thought ruefully, as he paid for a private room and a bath.

"I don't suppose you know a man named Frank Ward?" he asked the guy at the front desk of the boardinghouse.

"Sure, I know Frank. Sending his herd off east tomorrow, I hear. He'll be out rounding them up right now, but you can probably find him at the Silver Dollar tomorrow night, drinking to a job well done."

Morgan grunted. It looked like he'd arrived just in time. Another day or more and he might have missed Frank altogether. "Thanks," he said, leaving a tip. "You wouldn't be able to suggest somewhere that serves half-decent food, would you?" Morgan was ravenous. He'd forgotten how hungry a day in the saddle could make you, and persistent memories of Pip's cooking didn't help matters. What tortured him most was that somewhere out there she was cooking right now, and he'd never know what it was, let alone be able to eat it. Given the magic she worked on cakes and fish, he could only dream of what she could do with a beefsteak.

Damn it, why couldn't he shake thinking about her?

The boardinghouse keeper laughed. "There's only one place in town anyone's going this week, and that's the old Trentham dining room. You might have to queue to get in though."

"The food's that good?" Morgan was surprised. These towns never had good eats.

"Definitely try the corn bread," the man told him sagely. "It's the best I've ever had."

Morgan was partial to a good corn bread, and he hadn't had it in years. Junebug's was inedible, so they'd banned her from cooking it. "Thanks." He headed up to his room to drop off his saddlebags. He threw them down and sat on the bed with a groan. The room was tiny and hot, and the bed was hard, but he wasn't complaining. He flopped backward. He was so tired, he could just stay here. But if he didn't get bathed and fed before he faded completely, he'd end up still here in the morning, still dirty and even hungrier than he was now.

Moving like a stiff old man, he pulled a fresh shirt and his shaving kit from his bags and headed down to the bathhouse in back of the building. There were four tin baths set up in the rickety shed in the yard, and water bubbling on the stove. Morgan was relieved to see there wasn't a queue—it was too early in the day, he supposed. He flipped the boy working the stove a coin and ordered up a fresh bath. Then he stripped off his shirt and lathered up his shaving soap. He'd grow his beard out on the trail proper, but he wanted to look decent when he met Frank to apply for the job. Morgan made short work of his whiskers and was in the bath the minute it was full. He groaned in pleasure as the hot water loosened his muscles. Hell, he was sore.

"The girls at the Silk Stocking are good at getting the trail kinks out," the kid at the stove told him. "Or so I'm told."

Morgan bet they were, but he wasn't looking for that kind of night. He grunted and rested his head on the back of the tin tub, closing his eyes, hoping the kid would take the hint and shut up. Oh God, this felt good. Morgan let his mind drift. But as usual since he'd left Buck's Creek, it drifted in one direction only, back to that creek and the redhead, in all her petticoated glory. Morgan tensed at the memory. Wet hair; the way the water slicked her skin; the heavy weight of her breasts in his hands; the taste of her . . .

His eyes snapped open, and he sat up. No. He wasn't having those thoughts while he was here, naked in a public bathhouse.

Only he seemed to have those thoughts *everywhere*. They were downright intrusive. He'd thought the long days of hard riding would drive her out of his head, but they did the opposite. They gave him too much time to think, and his thoughts were willful at best, torturous at worst. If he wasn't oppressed by memories of Ma and the old man, he was chased by the temptations of Pip Hopgood. Damn it, he didn't need, or want, any of them. He was a man comfortable *alone*. Happy *alone*. Looking forward to a free and easy future *alone*.

"It costs extra, mister, if you want to sit there," the kid told him. "There's other people needing the bath."

Morgan considered the empty bathhouse and gave him a sour look. Everything had an extra cost, didn't it? Including kissing redheads. And he was paying for it.

But he could hardly get out of the bath now, given how het up he was by thoughts of the woman.

"I'll pay the extra," he growled. And then he set to thinking about anything else but Epiphany Hopgood. Which was proving to be nearabout impossible. If he'd finished what he'd started that night, maybe he wouldn't still be haunted by her, he thought irritably. Maybe it was just because he'd left that creek frustrated as hell, and he was *still* frustrated.

"The girls at the Silk Stocking might fix your mood too," the kid suggested dryly, and Morgan realized he'd been scowling at the far wall.

"Does you shutting up cost extra too?" Morgan snapped. He didn't need a whore. No whore could scratch the itch he had, because none of them would be *her*. No one was her. He'd never seen another woman like her. She was the uniquest woman he'd ever met. And it wasn't just about her looks. Hell, there were good-looking women in every state and territory. It was more than her curves, or her green eyes, or even the way she felt and tasted. It was . . . He couldn't put it into words. It was just something about the way she was in the world. On her own two feet. Reaching out for him, not to have him hold her up, but just because she wanted to touch him. It was her forthright nature, and her strength, and her sharp gaze, and her laugh, and her close attention to everything, even folding a fish in a mustard leaf. Pip Hopgood was all in, no matter what she was doing, whether it was scrubbing a pot or kissing him senseless. And Morgan thought it looked like a damn fine way to be.

Damn it. Why couldn't he stop thinking about her?

"Frank?" Morgan was astonished to see his old trail boss in the queue at the dining hall. But maybe he shouldn't have been, because half the town seemed to be lined up out here.

"Morgan McBride?" Frank Ward lit up to see him. "Goddamn, you're the last man I expected to see."

Morgan frowned. "I am? Didn't Vern Little Horse tell you I might come?"

"No, cain't say as he did. But Vern's been a bit absent-minded since he showed up a couple of days ago. The man is soft in the head for the woman at this place." Frank jerked his head at the dining hall. "He can barely even remember his own name."

Frank hadn't changed a bit, Morgan thought, more than a little surprised. He was lanky and ropy with muscle, his skin the color and texture of tree bark. He was even chewing on a cheroot stub, the way he had back in the day. It was a shock, because Morgan sure as hell didn't feel the same. He felt like a different person. Surely other people should have changed, too, given all the time that had passed?

"You here for a job, then?" Frank grinned at him around the cheroot. "Because that would make my day. It's been a hell of a year. Cain't tell you how many beeves we lost this winter."

"Yeah, it was a brutal one, weren't it." Morgan had spent the blizzardy winter holed up in the cabin—and then later in the trading post with those annoying trappers, after Kit and Maddy had married and had taken over his bedroom. That had been when he determined to build them a house as soon as spring hit. "And yes, I'm here for a job," he told Frank, pushing away memories of Buck's Creek.

"You got it." Frank held out his hand to shake. "Want to join me for dinner to seal the deal?"

The men behind protested loudly when Morgan cut in. Frank swore at them good-naturedly.

"Ain't you supposed to be shipping out your herd tomorrow?" Morgan asked, curious as to why Frank was here and not out with the herd.

"I am. I just thought I'd come into town to eat. The boys weren't too pleased about being left behind, but I figure it's the trail boss's prerogative." He grinned at Morgan. "Trust me, when you taste the food here, you'll understand. And the view's nice, too, if you know what I mean." He winked.

Morgan felt his stomach sink when they stepped into the dining hall. Hell, he knew the woman at the counter. It was that nightmare of a woman Junebug had ordered up, the wife she'd picked for Kit: Maddy's mistress, the blowsy beauty with the heart of burned-up coal. Willabelle Lascalles was on her usual showy display, Morgan noted with distaste, queening it at the counter, counting a fistful of cash. Vern sure had bad taste in women, if this was the woman he was besotted with. Although, Morgan had to admit, Willabelle wasn't so bad when you first met her, when you were blinded by her charms. But those charms wore off mighty quick.

Morgan would have turned around and left on the spot if Frank hadn't been there. He wondered what the hell Willabelle was doing in this place and if there was any way he could avoid talking to her.

"The guy at the boardinghouse said this was Trentham's place?" Morgan asked Frank as they inched closer to the counter. "Is the blonde up there married to him, by any chance?" That would save him having to fight off her advances. God, he'd had a tiresome time of it once Kit was hitched, and the Lascalles woman had refused to leave. Thank God that cowboy had come through and caught her eye.

"Nah. She got the deed off Trentham one night over at the Seven Stars. Old Trentham left town not long after."

They slid in front of Willabelle, and Morgan braced himself.

"Trentham, that was his name!" Willabelle exclaimed as she overheard them. "Thanks, Frank. I couldn't remember it for the life of me." She turned around and called through the hatch toward the kitchen. "The man who lost this place to me: his name was Trentham! I told you I'd remember it."

"Trentham isn't at all like Smockley, or Hockley, or something-ley," a woman's voice snapped back from behind the serving hatch. She sounded disgusted. And harried. Morgan guessed she was too busy cooking for the crowd to be bothered with Willabelle's nonsense.

"Same thing." Willabelle shrugged. "A Trentham by any other name."

"Willabelle?" Morgan figured he might as well get it over with.

The parrot looked up from her fistful of money and her eyes widened. "Well, look who the cat dragged in!" She didn't appear pleased to see him. "There aren't any tables free," she said shortly. "You'll have to leave."

Well. That was about as far from flirtation as it was possible to get.

"There's a table right there," Frank protested. He dropped his cash on the counter. Morgan could see that Willabelle was torn between wanting to kick him out and wanting to take the money. Morgan was astounded by her about-face—the last time he'd seen her she'd given him an aggressive kiss farewell. One he hadn't been quick enough to dodge.

Frank took advantage of Willabelle's lingering look at the cash to push Morgan toward the table. Willabelle gave Morgan the evil eye as she took the money, but she let them sit down. Morgan shook his head. She'd always been a trial. Just like that horrible dog of hers, the one that liked to bite his ankles and growl at him. He hadn't missed either Willabelle or the dog. Although Junebug had been mad as hell when the dog had gone. She'd railed at Morgan that they should go after the woman and get the dog back. Junebug considered the animal hers, even though it wasn't.

Hell. Best not to think about Junebug. Every time he did, he got an attack of the guilts. "What's best to order?" he asked Frank, shaking off thoughts of Junebug and Buck's Creek. He focused on the rowdy dining room instead. There didn't seem to be any staff, just Willabelle alternating between taking money at the counter and running food from the kitchen hatch.

"Oh, you don't get to order." Frank took his cheroot out of his mouth and tucked it into the pocket of his shirt. "They just bring you whatever they've cooked today. And coffee. That's it." He leaned back in his chair. "But, trust me, whatever they're serving will be good."

It turned out they were serving beef and beans, and corn bread slathered in butter. Willabelle dropped it unceremoniously in front of them. "Eat quick, there's a queue," she said, no friendlier even after taking their money. "I don't want you taking up a table longer than you have to."

Morgan bit his tongue. The woman was a piece of work. He couldn't believe he'd once been attracted to her. It had only been because he hadn't seen a woman in an age though. Not like with the redhead . . .

Damn it. He wasn't thinking about her. He *wasn't*.

The food helped take his mind off her. It was amazing. So good, he and Frank ordered up seconds. Willabelle only complied because they tipped. The coffee was good too. As good as . . . No. He wasn't thinking about her.

"You don't like the eats?" Frank was frowning at him.

"What?" Morgan realized his thoughts had him looking sour as hell. "Of course I like it. It's the best food I've ever had."

"How come you look like someone shot your horse, then?"

Morgan sighed and stabbed at the beans with his fork. "It ain't nothing to do with the food."

Frank leaned his elbows on the table and talked through a mouth full of beef. "It's a woman, then."

Morgan scowled. No, it wasn't.

It *wasn't*.

"Well, the trail will fix that," Frank assured him. "It always does. I cain't tell you how many broken hearts I've mended on the trail. All of them mine."

Morgan's heart wasn't broken. Not one bit. His heart wasn't engaged at all. But the rest of him sure was. There was no denying it; just the thought of her had him hot. And he wasn't damn well even thinking of her. He was hot just *not thinking* of her.

"Poor old Vern Little Horse will be in your boat, too, pining over that woman." Frank jabbed his knife kitchenward. "You know the fool actually wants me to ask her to come with us?"

"Hell no!" Morgan was horrified. Willabelle Lascalles would be a nightmare on the trail.

Frank grinned. "I told him women got no place on the trail—but you know, I eat her cooking and I get sore tempted. Imagine eating this every night." He smacked his lips. "And you ain't even seen her yet. She's got more to recommend her than just her cooking." He sniggered.

"Cooking?" Morgan caught up. "Oh, you don't mean Willabelle."

"No. Although she's got plenty to recommend her too." He eyed Willabelle appreciatively.

"Well, so long as it ain't Willabelle, I wouldn't be averse to a woman, not if she can cook like this."

"I doubt old Early would be pleased if I sacked him in favor of a lady cook," Frank said as he wiped his plate clean with the last hunk of corn bread.

"Early Parsons is still with you?" Morgan was again surprised. It was jarring how much everything was the same. "Who else is still with you?"

"Oh, most of the crew. Joe and Rico. Glad Pierce. Vern, obviously. Petey Wallis ain't. He went and got married to some girl down in Kansas, and Lyle stayed behind in Texas this time. Had another sprout and his wife screamed blue murder about him heading out and leaving her alone with all those kids."

Morgan shook his head. It looked like maybe he could step right back into his old life, like nothing had ever happened. So why didn't he feel easier about it?

"You're done." Willabelle whipped their plates away the moment they'd finished the last bean. "Out you go, I've got people waiting."

"Our compliments to the cook," Frank told her placidly, rising from his chair.

"Tell her it was something," Morgan agreed.

Willabelle seemed to take strange offense to that. "Don't you go thinking about my cook," she told him darkly.

"You reckon she's heard word that Vern's keen to steal her away?" Morgan asked as they left, bewildered by Willabelle's behavior.

"Probably, the way that fool has been mooning over the woman." Frank clapped him on the back. "Come on, I'll buy you a drink." He tipped his hat at Willabelle on his way out. "We'll be back in the morning for breakfast, after we've seen the herd off," he called to her.

"If she'll let us back in," Morgan said dryly.

"Oh, she'll let us in. That woman likes a dollar too much to turn us away." Frank stopped dead as they stepped outside, when he caught sight of the man at the head of the line. He swore. "Goddamn it, Vern! You're supposed to be with the herd!"

Morgan guessed Vern had it bad for this cook. He felt sorry for him. It was hell on earth not being able to get a woman out of your head.

Sixteen

"Willabelle, you scheming witch!" Junebug came hooking through the kitchen door, as enraged as Pip had ever seen her. Plate-throwing angry, in fact. "Why didn't you tell us that Morgan was in town!" The dog barked. It was at her heels, as always.

Morgan was in town? Pip dropped the pot she was holding, and water splashed everywhere. Luckily it was cold and not boiling, or she would have scalded them all.

"Morgan's here?" It was Pip's worst nightmare come to life. She hadn't wanted to still be in this wretched town when he arrived. They were supposed to have left days ago!

But Sour Eagle was now in debt, and Thunderhead Bill was gambling hard just to keep him out of trouble with the brutes he was in debt to. It had got so bad that last night Granny had hit the card tables, too, ignoring all of Pip's protests. Junebug had offered to help, but Pip categorically drew the line at that. The kid was not going into any of those hellhole saloons, and she certainly wasn't gambling! Pip wished they'd *all* stop gambling. They were just digging the hole deeper.

Pip was slaving away in Willabelle's kitchen, for no pay, just to give them a roof over their heads at night. In order to try to salvage the situation, Pip had forced Willabelle to hire Junebug as a dishwasher and kitchen hand, much to Junebug's intense displeasure. The two of them sweated day in, day out, for Junebug's measly pay, as Willabelle refused to pay eight dollars a month for a dishwasher. She said six dollars was plenty generous, given it was an unskilled job. Pip was at her wit's end. She'd sold her hens, but no one wanted her cow—the town was overrun with cows. She had held out against selling Sadie, her horse, but they were a long way short of train fare. And now here was Morgan McBride, the one man she didn't want to see. And the one man who could probably get them out of this mess, she thought with a groan.

"Morgan's in town?" Willabelle was wide-eyed with dramatic astonishment.

"Cut the crap, witch." Junebug advanced on her.

"Junebug!" Pip scolded, as she fetched the mop to clean up the mess she'd made. "Watch your language."

"What? She *is* a witch. She knew he was here, and she didn't tell us!"

"That's not the word I meant, and you know it." Pip was tense and out of patience. Morgan was here. And with a sinking stomach, she knew that she'd have to ask him for a handout. That or stay here indefinitely, working for this selfish woman, for no pay. Pip imagined the conversation, standing before him, *begging.* Ugh. But it was that or sell Sadie, and that was too heartbreaking to consider. She loved that horse.

"You know perfectly well he's in town," Junebug railed. She'd backed Willabelle up against the meat safe. "Because he ate here last night."

"What?" Pip's hands clenched around the mop handle. "He what?"

He'd been in the dining hall? Had he seen her? Pip felt the all too familiar burn of shame. She bet he had. When the hatch was open you could see into the kitchen. She could only imagine what he'd thought when he saw her . . .

He'd run all this way to get away from her, and here she was. Had he thought she was chasing him? Pip felt sick. One look at her, in this old dress and this stained apron, with her hair a barely tamed frizz, and he would have been horrified that he'd ever kissed her. He would have run a mile—again. And he would have considered her a desperate lump, a wallflower who went hounding men who didn't want her.

"He ate here last night!" Junebug growled again. The dog growled, too, offering Junebug support. That animal had no love for his mistress.

"He did?" Willabelle pursed her lips. "I think I would have seen him if he had," she said dismissively.

"You did see him, you cow."

"Junebug! Would you please mind your language!" Pip was fretful with anxiety. How was this happening? Things just kept going from bad to worse. What if he'd left town after seeing her? When she needed help, fearfully so.

But, also . . . what if he *hadn't* gone . . . what if she had to face him?

Both outcomes were awful.

"Cows ain't bad," Junebug scoffed, "and I ain't apologizing for calling her one. Although you ain't a nice cow, Willabelle. You're one of them mean ones, the kind that kicks you when you try to milk them."

"Why would I lie, you horrid child?" Willabelle asked imperiously, sidestepping Junebug and heading for the dining room. "And if I'm a cow, I'm a blue-ribbon thoroughbred, not a milker."

Junebug followed her, trailing the dog. Pip could hear them arguing through the hatch.

"You lied because you don't want to lose your damn cook," Junebug snapped. "Pip's making you money hand over fist, and you're lying through your teeth just to keep us stranded here. You know Morgan would get us out of here."

"It's my establishment making the money, I think you'll find, not Pip," Willabelle disagreed.

Pip leaned her forehead against the wall beside the open hatch. The street outside was just turning rosy with the first touch of morning. It only served to illuminate the squalor.

"Your establishment is making money off the back of her cooking." Junebug was determined to argue with the woman. Pip didn't know why she bothered. Willabelle was shameless—and not liable to care about the finer points of any argument. But Junebug forged on. "And you hate the idea that Morgan will take her away from you!"

Pip winced. As if Morgan cared to take Pip away from anyone.

Junebug was extremely put out. "And then he'll probably pack us off on the first train out of here."

She could only hope. Pip took a deep shaky breath. She hated needing him like this. How could she cling to any pride, when she needed him?

"But that ain't happening," Junebug said. "We're staying."

Pip bumped her head on a cabinet as she jerked at Junebug's words. Over Pip's dead body, they were staying. She had only one reason to tolerate Morgan McBride, and that was to get a ticket out of here.

"Unless he leaves," Junebug amended. "Then we're leaving too. I'm going to be on that man like a burr on a shaggy dog."

Merle barked.

"Pip," Junebug ordered. "Go and change into a different dress. You look a fright. I don't want you scaring him off."

"There's no time," Willabelle said as she straightened the battered tin cutlery on a table. "The morning rush will be here soon."

"Not until after the cows get shipped off," Junebug disagreed.

"She has to get the breakfast on." Willabelle clicked her fingers at Pip and gestured at the kitchen.

"*She* doesn't have to do anything," Pip said stiffly, feeling the urge to close the hatch on the both of them. She was sick of them talking about her like she wasn't even here. "And if you don't start talking straight, I won't be making anything."

Willabelle pursed her lips, and her eyes narrowed as she considered Pip. She must have decided Pip was serious, because she capitulated. "Fine. He was here. With Frank Ward. They ate two helpings and left a decent tip."

"Did he see me?" Pip blurted.

Willabelle cocked her head. "See you? No." Her stare was calculating. "Why?"

Pip's cheeks burned.

"Ah," Willabelle said slowly. She sized Pip up. "You weren't at Buck's Creek or Bitterroot when I was there. Remind me how you know the McBrides, again?"

Pip had dreaded that question. She'd counted herself fortunate that Willabelle had been too self-focused to ask it until now.

"Never you mind," Junebug interrupted.

But Willabelle clearly had enough experience with Junebug to draw an accurate conclusion. "Again? You did it again?"

Junebug scowled.

"And with her?" Willabelle looked Pip up and down. Her perfect little nose wrinkled.

Pip felt a blast of rage at the disbelief in her expression. She straightened her shoulders. "Yes, with me."

"And *Morgan* needs a wife?" Willabelle's hand went to her golden curls thoughtfully. She straightened a hairpin.

"Not you!" Junebug snapped. "Besides, you hate Buck's Creek."

"Well, he doesn't seem to be in Buck's Creek anymore, does he?"

"He doesn't like you," Junebug said shortly. "None of us do."

Willabelle was unflapped. "You seem to like my money just fine. And my spare room."

Pip had a feeling their bickering could have gone on, if the cattle hadn't arrived on the main street. The cutlery began to rattle, then the lamps, then the windows in their frames. Then came the river of cows, kicking up a huge cloud of red dust into the early morning air. As the sun speared over the buildings, the dust glittered, a haze that blocked out the sky. The sound was deafening.

"Go get changed, Pip," Junebug said firmly. "Morgan's coming to breakfast, and I don't want him seeing you like that."

Pip flushed. She wasn't in the mood to be bossed around. Especially by Junebug McBride, who'd given her nothing but trouble since the day they'd met. "What does it matter how he sees me?" she said tightly. Good dress or bad dress, hair up or down, stinking of fish or fresh from the creek, none of it *mattered*. He didn't want her.

Willabelle laughed. "Oh, this will be fun." She gave Pip a pitying look. "You do know men care about the way a woman looks? Not just the way she cooks."

Pip could have hit her with the mop. Of course she knew. Her whole life had been one long hard lesson in that fact. "I have no interest in what Morgan McBride thinks of me," she said through gritted teeth. It wasn't true, but she wanted it to be true. Wanted it so much that she was determined to make it so.

"Well, I do care," Junebug complained. "So go get changed."

"No." Pip closed the hatch with a snap. She would have an honest conversation with Morgan McBride when she saw him, and she would get herself and Granny home to Nebraska, and the rest of them back to Buck's Creek. And she would pay Morgan McBride back every single cent of the money she'd borrow, even if it took her the rest of her life. She refused to be in that man's debt one moment longer than she had to be.

———

"You're not looking to marry him, then?" Willabelle asked curiously half an hour later, as she leaned through the serving hatch to watch Pip pull a tray of biscuits from the oven. They were five minutes away from the dining hall opening and Pip was sweating already. The cramped kitchen was like a furnace.

Willabelle had changed into another dress, Pip noticed sourly. This one was a rosy pink and covered with shiny beads, which swayed and clicked as she moved. And she'd done her hair even fancier than usual. Pip didn't like the implication.

"No," Pip said shortly. "I'm not." Not anymore.

"I don't blame you. He's a grumpy one, isn't he? You know the one I'd pick if it were me?"

"Beau." Pip didn't even have to think about it.

Willabelle was surprised. "Gawd no. I'd go for the young one. That Beau would be a handful. I like my men easy to manage."

Pip wished the woman would get back to her business and leave her alone.

"You know, I've been thinking on our arrangement . . ." Willabelle's blue eyes were trying to seem guileless but looked just the opposite. "Given the state of business this week, I think I can afford to pay you a wage, as well as the room and board . . ." She gave Pip an encouraging smile. "What do you say? Seven dollars a month?"

Pip couldn't believe the nerve of the woman. "You originally said eight."

"You drive a hard bargain, but: agreed. I'll pay you eight."

She was shameless. Pip shook her head, upending the biscuits onto the cooling rack. "I have no desire to stay in this place." And eight dollars would get her nowhere. She'd be here for months at that wage.

"Fine. Ten!" Willabelle pouted when her offer was met with

silence. Her beads clicked as she huffed. Then she seemed to get bored with haggling. "Ugh. Look. You don't want to talk to Morgan, that much is clear. What if I spot you a ticket home—on the condition you stay one month and earn me some money? I want to get myself to San Francisco."

Pip paused. The thought of not having to beg Morgan for money was appealing. But she didn't want to stay here a whole month. "One week. And I need a ticket for my grandmother too."

"Now you're just taking advantage." Willabelle didn't say no though. "Two weeks?" she offered.

Pip hated working in this kitchen—it was cramped and sweaty and the hours were backbreaking. But she also hated the idea of asking for money from Morgan McBride. Maybe she could stick it out for two weeks . . .

"I'll think about it."

Willabelle beamed. "You do that, honey. Why, you'll be home after only fourteen little days."

Junebug came into the kitchen just in time to see Willabelle's sunny smile. "Why's she so happy?" she asked suspiciously.

"Because she's about to open for business and there's a queue." Pip wasn't about to tell Junebug about Willabelle's offer. The kid would pitch a fit. "Get the water warming. There's about to be a heck of a lot of dishes to do."

"What time do you reckon Morgan will be here?" Junebug ignored her and peered into the dining room through the serving hatch. Willabelle was just opening the door. Pip heard her sneeze at the dust, which was still hanging in the air like a fog.

"How do you even know he's coming?" Pip asked tersely. She felt her stomach clench hard. He may have skipped town if he'd seen her the night before.

"Your granny told me."

"What?" Granny hadn't come in until long after Pip was asleep, and she'd still been in her narrow bed when Pip got up for the breakfast shift this morning. "When did you talk to Granny?" She froze, suspicious to the core.

"I'd best get the water on." Junebug moved out of arm's reach.

"Junebug!" Pip was furious. She had a feeling she knew exactly when Junebug had spoken to Granny.

"You said I should get the water on, so I'm doing it." She was all innocence. The little wretch.

Pip closed her eyes and counted to ten. She and Junebug had fought heatedly the night before, because Junebug had wanted to go to the Cow Poke saloon to see how Granny was doing at cards. Pip had absolutely, categorically banned her from going.

Which meant, Pip thought grimly, that she'd probably gone. It wouldn't have been hard to sneak out while Pip slept, given that Pip was so exhausted after her sixteen-hour days that she slept like the dead. The kid had no understanding of the dangers she risked with her fool behavior.

"You went to the saloon," Pip accused her.

"Ask me no questions and I'll tell you no lies." Junebug blithely went about her chores.

"Please tell me Granny won, at least . . ." Pip knew she hadn't. If she had, they would have woken her up.

"Ask me no questions—"

Pip cut her off with a string of epithets she'd learned from listening to these cowboys all day. "How did Granny know that Morgan was in town?" she demanded.

"She saw him."

Pip's heart stopped. "She saw him . . ."

"At the saloon."

He'd been at the saloon? Oh, there was no way he was still in Miles City if he'd caught sight of Granny and the trappers.

"Did he see her?" Pip asked.

"Nah," Junebug said happily, "Martha said he was too busy

drinking with his buddies to bother with the card tables. She and Sour Eagle saw him at the bar, but he didn't see them back."

Pip had walked past the Cow Poke saloon on her way to fetch her belongings from the train station that first day. It made the cathouse back in Bitterroot look positively tame. There were barely clothed women slouched on the porch, draped in gaping wrappers, their garters visible, their corsets in gaudy colors. The stink of stale beer came rolling out of the place when the door opened. Right next door to the saloon was the bordello, which made the saloon pale in comparison. If the girls at the Cow Poke were barely clothed, the girls at the Silk Stocking weren't clothed at all. Pip had seen them at the windows, their breasts bare.

She didn't like the idea of Morgan McBride in those places . . . let alone Junebug.

"He was just drinking?" Pip hated herself for asking. It burst out of her, and she wished she could take it back.

"Apparently so. I didn't see him myself. He was gone by the time I got there." Junebug realized she'd incriminated herself and shut up quick smart.

Pip shook the wooden spoon at her, too furious to speak.

"I've got a table of four and a table of six that have just come in," Willabelle called through the hatch, and Pip was denied the chance to scold Junebug properly. "All of them want the big breakfast."

"I'll talk to you after service," Pip promised, making it sound like a threat.

The breakfast trade started slow enough to keep on top of, because a lot of the cowhands were still driving cattle to the station. It gave Pip's nerves a chance to sprout. Oh God, he might actually show up. The floor trembled underfoot and the pots rattled every time a new herd was driven down the street to the station. She wondered if he was down there. As she fried a mountain of bacon, she heard the train arrive down the street, announcing itself with a cheery whistle. Soon, she promised herself, soon it would be her who was boarding a train out of here. If she could just survive seeing Morgan again.

Eventually trade picked up and she got so busy cracking eggs and sliding crispy bacon onto plates that she forgot about Morgan McBride. Even though she'd been expecting it, it was an absurd shock to hear Junebug squawk, "He's here!"

Pip couldn't help herself. She dropped the serving fork with a clatter and peered through the hatch. She tried to keep to the side, so she wouldn't be visible from the dining room. Junebug was doing the same thing, on the other side.

Oh God, there he was. Somehow, he looked even better than she remembered. She'd forgotten the size of him. He filled the doorway as he came through it, his shoulders like a slab of granite. His saddlebags were slung over one shoulder, falling down that broad chest. He took off his hat as he stepped through the door, and tapped it against his long thigh to shake out the dust. His hair was a tumble of darkness, his jaw stubbled and square. He had a blue bandanna tied around his neck, which only served to draw attention to the V of caramel-colored skin revealed by his unbuttoned collar.

"He looks pretty miserable, don't you think?" Junebug said, with no small measure of satisfaction.

No, Pip didn't think. In fact, Pip thought he looked perfectly content as he ambled up to the counter. She ducked out of view and hissed at Junebug to do the same.

"He looks peaky about the eyes," Junebug whispered. "I reckon he's not sleeping."

Pip rolled her eyes. He was probably just tired from the trail. He looked the same as always to Pip—maybe even better.

"Well, good morning, Morgan McBride, you're looking chipper today," Willabelle chirped. She was playing it up because she knew they were eavesdropping.

Pip heard him grunt. He was still a big one for grunting, then.

"You want the regular breakfast, or the big breakfast?" Willabelle asked coyly. "I figure you for a big one, myself."

"That whore," Junebug hissed.

Pip threw a biscuit at her. "Language!" she mouthed.

"What's the difference?" Morgan rumbled.

Oh, Pip had forgotten that voice. Deep and sandpapery. With the impact of an earth tremor.

"One's bigger than the other." Willabelle was playing the coquette. "You fancy them big?"

Junebug wasn't wrong, though, Pip thought sourly. Willabelle was being a touch whorish.

"You do look hungry," Willabelle purred.

"I'll take the big one." Morgan didn't rise to the bait, judging by the tone of his voice. But then he kept talking and Pip's heart dropped to the floor. "You're sweeter than you were last night," he said dryly.

Pip and Junebug exchanged stunned looks. Last night?

"Well, last night I didn't know your intentions, did I?" Willabelle teased.

"Right, that's it." Junebug grabbed Pip by the arm and hauled her toward the back stairs. "You cain't let her get away with this."

"Get off me." Pip wrenched her arm away. She felt hot and cold and sick to her stomach. Morgan and Willabelle. It made perfect sense. Willabelle was as pretty as a china doll. Just the kind of woman who should be with a man that fine.

"You go make yourself decent, damn it." Junebug kicked the wall. "I ain't giving up without a fight!"

"This isn't about you," Pip told her fiercely. She was so tired of standing in the shadows of women like Willabelle and her sister Naomi. And she was so tired of these *men*. "This is about *me*. And I'm not fighting for a man who doesn't want me!"

"Don't you be a blockhead too!" Junebug raged. "I got enough blockheads in my life without adding another one to the mix. Of course he wants you—you saw him back in Buck's Creek. He cain't take his eyes off you. Even a kid as green as me can see that."

Pip was poisonous with feeling. She wasn't setting herself up for humiliation again. Her head was full of visions of Morgan and Willabelle. His mouth on hers. His hands on her body. They made sense together.

"At least wash your damn face and put on a clean dress and take some goddamn pride in yourself!" Junebug threw her hands up. "Why do you insist on staying down when people stomp on you!"

Pip felt like she'd been slapped. "I don't!"

"Well, what in hell do you think you're doing?" Junebug demanded. "That idiot brother of mine treated you badly! Terribly! And you're skulking around with your tail between your legs, all eaten up with shame! Goddamn, woman. If anyone should be ashamed, it's him! Get some backbone. Put on a pretty dress, shove that chest of yours in his face and show him what he's missing. You make him regret it, you hear me! Ain't that what you want?"

Junebug's words were an assault. Pip felt them piercing her like a bristle of arrows, hitting right in the heart of her deepest bruises, bull's-eye after bull's-eye.

"I have to cook breakfast," she said numbly.

"Oh, screw breakfast. Those boys'll wait for their bacon. Where else are they going to go?" Junebug gestured at the stairs. "Come on. I reckon you and Willabelle have close enough measurements and she owes you."

It dawned on Pip what Junebug meant. "I am not stealing her clothes." But part of her wanted to take everything from Willabelle. How was it fair that she got him, just for being born pretty?

"Don't worry, I've done it before," Junebug said. "But hurry up."

Pip felt like she was being swept away by a strong current. No matter which way she swam, she felt farther and farther from the shore. And Junebug's voice kept ringing in her ears: *Get some backbone.* She had backbone, damn it. Her mother and everyone back home thought she had *too much* backbone. So, which was it? Too much, or not enough? No matter what she did, it was never good enough.

Her problem wasn't backbone, it was clarity.

Her problem was that she didn't know *what* she wanted. She'd thought she wanted a husband . . . so she could be like all the girls she'd grown up with. She wanted to be everything they told her a successful woman was. But then she'd met Morgan McBride. And the man had sent her head, her heart, her spirit and her entire body into a spin. He'd lit up the whole world, like the sun breaking through the clouds—and all with a single kiss. But he'd also rejected her—more than once. The thought of marrying anyone else seemed impossible, the thought of marrying him unworkable.

So, what did Pip want?

If anyone should be ashamed, it's him, Junebug had said.

What Pip wanted was to believe it; not just say it, but really, deeply believe it. She wanted to show her mother, and Samuel Arcross and his parents, and Old Man Millard, and Morgan Mc-bloody-Bride that she was worth more than they thought she was. She wanted to show *herself* that.

Upstairs, she could hear Junebug throwing open the door to their room.

"Get up!" the kid was hollering.

Pip ran up the stairs to find Junebug yanking the covers off Granny, who was sacked out in the narrow bed in the corner of their shared room. Then Junebug kicked the trappers, who were on their blankets on the floor in the hallway outside. "You three get down there and finish cooking for the breakfast shift. We got things to do."

The three of them were sleepy and resistive, but no match for Junebug. "Martha, you cain't tell me you don't know how to scramble an egg, after raising all those kids. And Bill, you can scrub a pot as well as I can." She threw their shoes at them. "Off you go, Sour Eagle, or I'm telling those gamblers you owe where you're at." She kept railing at them as she disappeared down the hall into Willabelle's room. Pip hurried after her.

As Pip stepped into Willabelle's room, she caught her reflection in a tall mirror. She *was* a fright. The apron and the dress were covered in bacon grease and flour, and her hair was a bird's nest.

No more. She *would* take pride in herself, she thought fiercely. Because if she didn't do it, no one would.

"What color goes with red hair, Nebraska?" Junebug demanded, as she threw open Willabelle's closet.

No one except for Junebug, Pip amended. Junebug took pride in her, more pride than she took in herself. For some reason, the kid believed in Pip. Even when Pip had trouble believing in herself. And Junebug was many things, but a fool wasn't one of them.

"Hey! What color?" Junebug snapped her fingers.

"Not pink," Pip said sharply. "And nothing pretty, nothing sweet." Pip was done with being sweet. "I like bold," she decided. "Something you can't ignore."

"Now you're talking."

Seventeen

Morgan had filled two pages of a letter to Junebug by the time Frank and Vern and the boys turned up for breakfast. He'd been so absorbed that he hadn't even noticed that his breakfast had failed to arrive. He hadn't even had coffee. But he *had* managed to describe his journey in extreme detail on the thin writing paper. He wondered if Epiphany Hopgood would still be in Buck's Creek when his letter arrived, and whether Junebug would read it aloud, so she could hear what he'd been up to . . .

He'd taken care to use his best hand, just in case she picked it up. And maybe he'd included that bit about not being able to sleep on the off chance that she wasn't sleeping either. Because every time he closed his eyes, he was back in that damn creek.

"Well, the beeves are off and we're free men until we get to Texas," Frank crowed, as he pulled up a chair.

"Not me," Vern Little Horse said. He towered over their table, his hat in his hand. "I ain't going to Texas, not unless she comes with me."

Morgan packed up his letter. "She who?" he said absently.

"The cook I told you about last night," Frank said, rolling his eyes.

The other boys pulled up another table and joined it to Morgan's. There were a dozen of them crammed around tables that could optimistically seat four. Morgan winced as Brent Dinkel's elbow jabbed him in the ribs. Most of them still stank of last night's liquor.

"She ain't just a cook," Vern objected. "She's the best-looking woman in Montana." His hand sketched a curvy figure in the air and the boys hooted.

"Is she?" Morgan didn't believe it. As far as he was concerned, there was a better one back in Buck's Creek. One with rusty hair and gold-green eyes and a mobile mouth . . . Damn it all to hell. "Willabelle, where's the goddamn coffee?" he snapped. "I been waiting here an age."

"Don't blame me, my wretched cook ran off midservice." Willabelle was sour as she dropped a stack of tin mugs on the table and then started pouring from a coffeepot.

"Ran off!" Vern went white as a sheet.

"Don't throw a tantrum, you big lummox, I got someone else to finish the cooking." Willabelle handed him a mug of coffee.

Morgan winced at the hectic noise of them all. Was he actually missing the relative quiet of Buck's Creek? Or at least the hectic noise that belonged only to his kin? It was something he'd never thought he'd say. But miss it he did. Miles City was rambunctious in the extreme, at all hours of the day and night. There was drinking and whoring, gambling and fighting. And it was ugly as sin out there, the street all dusty and full of cow shit. He felt like he'd never scrub the dirt off himself. He missed the mountain air, and the sound of Kit's hammer on the anvil; he missed the comfort of his own bed, and the sound of Jonah's damn fiddle. When did he become this person? he thought sourly.

Where was the romance of the trail that he'd dreamed of? Where was the sense of freedom, and possibility? Back in that damn creek, that's where they were. Goddamn it, who knew a woman could light the sky on fire like that? Light everything on fire. Including him.

It was ridiculous. He'd known her for two days. Which meant he didn't really know her at all. So why was he all tangled up in thinking about her? He'd find what he was looking for on the way down to Texas, he reassured himself, as he bent to pack his letter-writing gear back in his saddlebag, which was slumped at his feet. Frank was right. The trail would sort him out. He'd get rid of this angsty feeling and these persistent thoughts of—

"Epiphany!"

Morgan jerked, slamming his head against the underside of the table. He swore. That hurt like hell. Gingerly he rose, rubbing his head, sure he'd imagined her name. But as soon as he sat up, he swore again.

Because there she was.

Epiphany Hopgood was right there in the flesh, in the doorway to the kitchen. Looking . . . magnificent. Morgan felt like he'd been hit head-on by a stampeding bull. What in hell was she doing here? And looking like *that*?

He didn't believe his eyes. It couldn't be her. She was in Buck's Creek, not here. There was no way she could have outpaced him, even as slow as he'd been. It wasn't her. It was just someone who looked like her—maybe a twin, like Kit and Charlie, he thought numbly. Because Pip Hopgood didn't dress this fine. Although, if she did, she'd look exactly like this. Magnificent.

She was in a fancy silk dress so deeply purple that it seemed to glow; it was the color of night just fallen. Against it, her hair blazed like burning coals, a fiery tumble down her back. She looked regal, her features starkly beautiful. The dress clung to her corseted curves, and the low neckline revealed a swell of creamy flesh. Morgan's mouth went dry.

"Epiphany, you ain't gone!" Delighted, Vern Little Horse strode across the room to greet her. For a moment, Morgan thought Vern was going to sweep her up in his arms. He was half out of his chair in protest before he realized it wasn't so. Vern pulled up short, bashful as a boy. "Epiphany! You ain't gone," he repeated joyfully.

Epiphany. The name registered again. He must be addled, Morgan thought. It *was* her. But how?

"Goddamn it, Junebug! Have you been at my dresses *again!*" Willabelle screeched. She threw the empty coffeepot down on the counter in a fit of pique.

Junebug! Morgan scowled, searching for her. There. In the serving hatch to the kitchen. The mop of dark hair, the wide gray eyes. That infernal look of triumph.

Morgan growled, and he saw Junebug flinch. She gave him a wave, and then slammed the serving hatch closed.

"Excuse me, do I know you?" this magnificent Epiphany Hopgood was asking Vern, bewildered.

The boys hooted.

"Are you telling me you ain't even been introduced, Vern?" Frank guffawed. "You want to marry a woman you ain't even met?"

"Marry?" Pip was quite clearly blindsided. Her gaze went to Morgan, and he felt the shock of it. Hellfire, he felt like he'd stuck his hand on a hot stove.

"No one's marrying anyone," he grumbled. He took up his saddlebags and headed over to her. His heart was galloping a mile a minute. He'd forgotten the detail of her, he thought witlessly. For all his dreaming of her, he hadn't got the details right. Like the smoothness of her skin, or the way her eyebrows were long auburn arches, or the high sculpture of her cheekbones. There was a hollow at the base of her neck, where he could see her pulse leap. And she was tall. Taller than he remembered.

"Hi," he said huskily as he reached her. It was a dumb thing to say, but it was all he had.

"Hi," she said back, her chin lifting. There was a look in her yellowy-green eyes that he couldn't interpret. Something hot and cold all at the same time.

"I saw her first, Morgan," Vern protested.

"Vern, my friend," he said, without looking away from Epiphany Hopgood, "that's where you're very wrong." He felt the strongest urge to kiss her, even though they were surrounded by all these people. "I think we need to talk," he said to her.

Her gaze narrowed and the yellow lights in her green eyes blazed. "Why start now?"

Morgan blinked. Right. He probably deserved that. But he'd never made her any promises; in fact, he'd explicitly told her he wasn't going to marry her. The stuff in the creek was just . . . nature. That was all. It didn't mean anything. It was an animal thing.

He was certainly feeling the pull of it now. What was it about her? He stepped near her, and his body felt her pull. It was magnetic. Irresistible.

Except he was going to resist it.

"I need to at least talk to my sister," he amended.

"She's in the kitchen," Pip told him, still giving him that hot and cold look.

Did she feel it too? This pull? She'd certainly felt it that night in the creek.

Morgan was sinking into her sunlit eyes. She felt it now too. He could see it in the way her gaze turned liquid. Christ, she was something.

Willabelle gave a gusty sigh. "Do you two need some privacy?"

"Sure looks that way." Vern was salty at Morgan interrupting his proposal.

Morgan snapped his gaze away from hers and flushed. He was making a fool of himself.

"Don't get yourself in a knot, Vern," Willabelle told him, "that's his mail-order wife."

"Wife!" Vern was outraged.

"No, she ain't," Morgan snapped at Vern.

That was enough. Morgan took Pip's arm and dragged her to the kitchen. They weren't continuing this in public.

"What is it with you McBrides manhandling me?" The redhead pulled away from him.

The kitchen was a catastrophe of smoke and steam and spitting grease. Morgan was astonished to see Pip's grandmother at the stove and Sour Eagle attempting to slop eggs onto plates. And was that Thunderhead Bill covered in soapy water in the corner?

"What the hell is going on?" he snapped.

"Junebug's outside, she'll explain," Sour Eagle told him waspishly. "Cain't you see we're busy?"

What the hell had Junebug cooked up here? Whatever it was, it was completely insane. "After you," Morgan invited shortly, gesturing for Pip to go first.

She gave him an imperious look and gathered her skirts up above her knee, to keep them off the filthy floor. Morgan wished she hadn't, as he saw a distracting eyeful of stocking-clad legs. There was something about the combination of the silk stockings and her clunky black boots that fired up his blood.

But, hell, the woman could probably wear a flour sack and he'd get fired up.

He followed her out to the yard, but there was no sign of Junebug. He wasn't surprised. The kid was wily. She'd make this as difficult as possible for him.

"How did you beat me here?" he demanded of Pip. But as he said it, he realized his stupidity. The train. Of course they'd come by train. He swore. "Very clever," he said. "Heading me off like this."

"This may come as a shock to you," the redhead said acidly, crossing her arms and regarding him like he was a bug who'd flapped in her face, "but I am not in Miles City because of *you*."

Morgan snorted. "Sure you ain't. Miles City is your second home, I'm sure."

Two spots of jagged color bloomed in her cheeks. "You really are the most self-centered man," she said coldly.

Morgan's temper was pricking now. Hunting him down like this was one thing; lying about it was another. "I am, am I?"

"You are," she insisted. "You make everything about you."

"So, you didn't come for me?" he goaded her. "You didn't show up in my life, unannounced, expecting to marry me? That's my imagination, is it?"

Hell, why couldn't she have the decency to look ugly when she was mad? What was it about her? The color in her cheeks, the sharp glitter of her yellowy eyes, the heaving of her chest . . . she only looked better angry.

"Unannounced?" Her breasts strained at the neckline of her gown as she gasped. "*Unannounced?* I think you'll find from my perspective, Mr. McBride, that I was well and truly expected and announced. I think you'll find that I answered an advertisement attributed to one Morgan McBride, *in good faith.*"

There she went good-faithing him again.

"And I entered into repeated correspondence with said man *and* was met at the train station by his kin. If anyone was faced with an unexpected shock, it was *me.*"

"That so? You want to talk shocks? Try going for cake and coffee and finding yourself face-to-face with a stealth wife." He mimicked her pose, folding his arms. His saddlebag got in the way, which ruined the effect. He shrugged it off and it landed on his foot. He swore.

"I didn't know that you didn't know about me," she said through clenched teeth.

Morgan's blood felt like moonshine racing through his veins. Arguing with her felt just as arousing as kissing her. "You ain't denying that you wanted to marry me, then," he said, feeling on the cusp of winning the argument.

She flinched, and now the color was draining from her face.

"No," she said. "I won't deny that." Her chin went up and a look of icy pride dropped over her striking face. "That was very much why I came."

"Aha!"

"To *Buck's Creek*." She flared up again as she realized where he was leading her. "Not to Miles City. I most certainly didn't come *here* for the purpose of matrimony."

"But you admit you came for matrimony." He could still win this. "And that you were unexpected and unannounced—to me. I never made a secret of that. And yet you wouldn't take no for an answer, would you?" His mouth was running away from him, the way it did when his temper was up. But also, it was running because he was in a mess. He could barely think straight with her there. It took all his energy to keep from kissing her. "I said no, and you still threw yourself at me." If she hadn't kissed him by the creek, they wouldn't be in this mess, he thought furiously. "You chased me up the hill to Buck's Creek, you proposed to me in the meadow and when I said no you had to push it and go throwing yourself at me in the creek that night. How's a man supposed to react when a woman has her . . ." He gestured at her body. ". . . assets on display? And when I left, you came chasing after me again. And now here you are! And you have the gall to say that I'm making this about me? It *is* about me, lady."

She had nothing to say to that, did she? Because he was right. He wasn't the one who'd knocked her into the creek, was he? *She'd* kissed *him*. "And now you're telling me that you're in Miles City by accident?" He was scornful. She was clearly here for him. They both knew it. And the thought was like fire through him. He was sore tempted, too, God help him. He wasn't going to say he wasn't.

She'd gone very still. "Are you finished?" she asked, very quietly. She waited to see if he had more to say.

He didn't. As far as he could see, he'd won.

"I'm here for the train to Nebraska," she told him stiffly. "And if you'd bother to listen once in a while, instead of talking all the time, you'd know that. Your slippery little sister and my meddle-some grandmother tricked me into coming here. If it weren't for them, I'd be home by now. Back where people are *sane*. I would have found a train to Nebraska, not one to this dusty sin pit."

Morgan scoffed. Like she couldn't have found a train to Ne-braska in Bitterroot, or in Butte. That was the weakest argument he'd ever heard. Tricked? That was her excuse? "What did they do, tie you up and throw you on the train to Miles City?"

Her mouth fell open. And then snapped closed, her lips thin-ning to an ominous line. "Now, Mr. McBride . . ."

He wished she wouldn't call him that. It was somehow sexy as hell.

". . . I have one last thing to say to you, and it would behoove you to listen." She took a step closer to him and tilted her head back to look him dead in the eye. Goddamn, she was something. "I would like to apologize to you." Her voice was frigidly mannered.

Well, that floored him. It was the last thing he expected.

She spoke with the icy precision of a winter's day. "I am deeply sorry that I answered that advertisement. You cannot possibly know how sorry. And I am even more sorry that I ever fetched up in Buck's Creek. I am sorry that I intruded upon your perfectly happy life, and I am sorry that I mistook your attention for more than it was."

Morgan blinked. Wait. What?

"I would also like to offer my most sincere apology for my behav-ior by the creek that night. And *in* the creek that night. If I could take it back, I would. I am sorry"—she bit out the words—"for, how did you put it? Throwing myself at you? I didn't mean to re-pulse you to the point that I chased you out of your home."

Repulsed? Wait, what?

Now, hang on a minute. The infernal woman was turning his words all around on him. He'd not said anything about being re-pulsed. He was talking about her using his goddamn weakness against him, damn it. He was talking about her manipulations! Not him being repulsed by anybody. He was talking about the way he'd been tricked into thinking she was honest, into admiring her for being forthright, and then she went and chased him to Miles City and entrapped him with this purple dress. It was the kind of stunt Junebug would pull and he was disappointed in her, damn it!

"Now, if you'll excuse me, I have business to attend to," she said stiffly. "I wish you well, Mr. McBride. I don't expect we'll meet again."

Morgan shook his head at that. "I expect we will, given how small this place is, and given that you're with my sister." And given how badly she wanted him. All that nonsense about being tricked here. Damn it. Did she think he didn't remember the way she'd wrapped herself around him in the creek? He remembered. Hell, he couldn't forget it.

"I'm not *with* anyone," she corrected him sharply. "There is only me. And I won't be here for long."

And with that she was gone, and Morgan was left feeling like he'd done something horribly wrong. What, he wasn't sure. But it was aggravating, all the same. His stomach was churning, and his palms were sweating. He felt like he'd committed some kind of crime.

He'd hurt her, he realized. That was what was behind the chilliness. He'd hurt her feelings with all that throwing-herself-at-him talk. Why, Morgan didn't know. Because she *had* thrown herself at him. It was just a plain fact. And if he'd been in the market for a wife—which he wasn't—he would have caught her happily. Because, damnation, she was something.

"Behoove was a good word, wasn't it?" a familiar voice observed.

Morgan looked up to find Junebug hanging half out the open window of the upper floor, enjoying the show. He scowled. "Get your ass down here," he snapped. "I've got words for you."

"Now, I don't think that would be in my best interests, do you?"

"Your best interests are back in Buck's Creek, not up there," he said in disgust.

Junebug cocked her head and fixed him with a dark look. "About that," she drawled. "What in hell were you thinking leaving me back in Buck's Creek?"

"Junebug," Morgan sighed. "You knew I was leaving."

She blew a raspberry at him. "That's what I think of that."

Morgan hated to admit it, but it was good to see her. He'd missed her, even though he'd been away for only a week. He unbuckled his saddlebag and yanked out the neatly folded pages he'd written in the dining hall. "I wrote you a letter," he said, holding it up.

"You did?" She brightened at that. "What's it say?"

"Come down and get it." He waved it at her.

"Ha. What do you take me for?" She rolled her eyes. "I got no intention of being within arm's reach of you for quite some time."

Morgan found himself wanting to grin. God, she was annoying. "You're impossible."

"Thanks." She leaned her chin on her hand. "So, how's the trail treating you?"

"Great. It's great."

"That bad, huh?"

He shot her a sour look. "I only just started. It'll take me a while to ease into it."

She nodded. "What if you don't ease?"

"I'll ease," he told her shortly. Although he wouldn't, would he? Because he was damn well dreading getting back on that horse, and sleeping rough by a campfire, and going without a wash for weeks at a time. And he hated writing letters. If he went, he'd have to write them every day, so Junebug would know what he was up to. And then he wouldn't sleep for not knowing what *she* was up to. Because look at the scrapes she got into when he wasn't around.

He conveniently ignored the fact that she got into just as many when he *was* around.

"Oh, you'll ease? Like you eased into that conversation with Pip just there?" Junebug said archly.

"You've got a bad eavesdropping habit." He glowered at her.

"No, I've got a good eavesdropping habit. I have it down to a fine art." She gave him a disapproving look. "And I must say, you would be behooved to think about what she just said to you."

He was, damn it. He couldn't get her voice out of his head, or that chilly-hurt look off his mind. He shouldn't have accused her of throwing herself at him. That was mean. True. But mean.

"She's right, you know. She didn't come here for you," Junebug told him sternly. "I did."

Morgan didn't believe that for a second. He'd felt the redhead's passion in that creek. She wanted him. "Sure, and that's why she was all dressed up like that," Morgan said dryly.

"That weren't for you. Not on her part anyway. It was on my part—I still reckon you should marry her—but she was just looking to restore her pride after you stomped on it."

"I didn't stomp on anything."

Junebug snorted. "Get off. You stomp on everything. You're like a bull elk in fighting season."

"Fighting season ain't a thing."

"Mating season, then. Same thing. And you're doing it again. Stop stomping and start listening."

Morgan was weary of this conversation. He propped his hands on his hips and regarded her darkly. "Hurry up and say your piece. And then we're getting you home."

"Ain't you curious about why we're all working in Willabelle's hideous dining hall?"

He was. But he didn't want to give Junebug the satisfaction of asking now.

Turned out she didn't need it; she was going to tell him anyway, and what came tumbling out of her was truly horrifying. "*How* much debt are they in?" he asked, dreading the answer.

"I don't know. But enough to keep them paying off the interest every night. Turns out Sour Eagle ain't quite the card sharp he claims to be."

Morgan groaned.

"Pip managed to get us room and board here, so long as she cooked for it." Junebug pulled a face. "And then she made me wash dishes."

"Good for her." Something niggled him. "Why are she and her grandmother stuck here? Her ticket should have taken her all the way home, shouldn't it?"

Junebug got her cagey look. "I might have wanted her to be here long enough for you to turn up."

Morgan swore. "How do you make everything so all-fired complicated?" he complained. "You take the simplest things and tangle them up in knots."

"I do not," Junebug said indignantly. "If anything, I cut through the knots. You're the one all knotted up. Spit, Morgan. How hard do things have to be? You love us. You love Buck's Creek. You're falling in love with this woman. And all you can do is run off to Texas?"

"Falling in love," he scoffed. He wasn't falling in love. He barely knew the woman!

"You know what she's doing now, because of you?" Junebug said. "I'd lay bets that she's off selling her horse, which she loves, in order to get as far away from you as she can." She glared at him. "How did you take a woman who was all fired up to marry you and drive her away so fast? And she's a good one too! They don't come along every day, you know."

"What do you mean, she's selling her horse?"

"Well, she'll have to pay for train tickets somehow, won't she? Hey! Where are you going?"

Morgan was glad Junebug was upstairs. It gave him a decent head start.

Eighteen

"What in hell are you doing?"

Pip closed her eyes and wished for patience. She needed it, because she was plumb out. But then she turned to see Morgan McBride holding the reins of her horse, the same horse she'd just sold, and any chance of holding on to her patience evaporated. What did he think he was doing?

"I'm going home," she said stiffly. "Just as soon as I've rounded up Granny and collected my luggage." She wasn't going *straight* home, of course. No, that would be too simple. She had to go to Chicago on a cattle train first, and from there she would get a train to Joshua, via Omaha. It was a ridiculously roundabout way to go, but it would get her out of this hellhole first thing tomorrow. And she couldn't bear being here for another minute longer than she had to.

Morgan McBride was standing next to the railway platform, squinting into the sun. He had Sadie's reins dangling loosely in hand. With his hat tilted back on his head, his belt riding low on his hips, spurs on his boots and his long muscular legs sheathed in tight denim, he looked every inch a cowboy. Pip resented his easy good looks. Couldn't he look dusty and worn like everyone else in this place? She'd been outdoors for less than an hour and was already sheathed in a patina of red dirt.

Pip felt like her horse was giving her a reproachful look over his shoulder. Sadie whickered and Pip's heart pinched. It had torn her apart to sell Sadie to the man at the livery, and she felt guilty as heck. But what choice did she have?

"I would have bought you a train ticket." Morgan McBride sounded stupidly wounded, especially for a man who had been yelling at her less than an hour ago.

Pip kept tight hold of her tongue. She hadn't wanted him to buy her a train ticket. She didn't need his help, or want his help, and she most certainly didn't need to explain herself to him.

And yet here he was, standing out front of the train station, holding Sadie's reins, demanding an explanation and acting like he had every right to insert himself into her business.

"I got your horse back," he said. He looked like he was waiting to be thanked.

"She's a good horse," Pip said, avoiding looking at her. It hurt too much. "I'm sure you'll love her as much as I did." She stiffened her spine and started walking back to the dining hall, clutching her train tickets tightly. She would not cry in front of him.

"I'm not keeping her." He sounded horrified at the suggestion. "She's yours!"

"Not anymore." Pip kept walking.

"Look, this is going wrong on me." Morgan McBride's long stride closed the gap between them, and Pip could hear Sadie's reins jingle as she broke into a trot to keep up. "I'm trying to make it up to you." He fell into step beside her. Pip wished he wouldn't. She was done with him. Why couldn't he just go away? Wasn't that what he wanted, anyway? To get away from her? So why in heck wasn't he doing it?

"Make what up to me?" she said, striving for calm, but unable to stop the causticness from leaching through. "I thought every-thing was my fault." That awful fluttery sick feeling of shame was back. Pip pushed it aside. She was done with being ashamed. This was who she was, and if people didn't like it, then they could go to hell.

"You're turning things upside down," Morgan McBride com-plained.

"Am I?" she said dryly. The man was impossible. Pip remem-bered the first day she'd met him, when he'd charged right over her, not listening to a word she said. He'd just done it again outside the dining hall, and now he was doing it *again*. He couldn't even play nice when he was trying to. Thank goodness she wasn't mar-rying him. Imagine living with this for the rest of your life.

"I never said everything was your fault," he defended himself. "I mean, clearly Junebug is to blame for most of it."

"Most of it," Pip echoed in disbelief. She picked up the pace. She couldn't believe the nerve of him. She was still reeling from his accusations earlier. Mostly because they were true. She had pur-sued him. She had proposed to him. She had, quite literally, thrown herself at him. It was humiliating to look back at it. Still, she hadn't heard him complaining at the time.

"Look," Morgan said, matching her step for step. His legs were longer than hers, so she was unlikely to get away. But the quicker she walked, the quicker she could get to Willabelle's and close the door on him.

"I was out of line," he said. "I've got a temper on me; I know it. I shouldn't have said some of those things."

Some of them. Pip rolled her eyes. She couldn't wait to get out of here, away from each and every McBride. "I've bought Junebug and the trappers tickets back to Buck's Creek too," she told him shortly. "I'll make sure she gets on the train before I go. It leaves in an hour."

He missed a step at that. "I can look after Junebug," he protested.

"From Texas?" She was being waspish. She didn't want to be. She wanted to be cold. Reserved. Untouchable. If she could force a cool smile for Samuel Arcross and his horrid parents, surely she could do the same for Morgan McBride.

Samuel never kissed you.

Pip flinched at the thought. It was true that the kissing made it harder. And not just the kissing, also the bothersome feelings that flittered around inside of her whenever Morgan McBride was around. Even when he was being impossible, he made her shiver. It was his woodsy smell, and the shadow of his stubble, and that sandpapery voice, and . . . Ugh. She had to get away. It was untenable to be attracted to such an irritating person.

"That ain't fair." Morgan stepped in front of her, his hand touching her elbow. "I made sure she was well cared for before I left," he insisted. He seemed offended.

Pip had forgotten what they were talking about, she'd been so caught up in her thoughts. She wished he wouldn't touch her. His hand on her elbow sent cascades of warmth through her. She tugged it away. Junebug. They were talking about Junebug. "Yes, well. She evidently wasn't cared for enough, given that she's here, and not there. Would you mind letting me past?" She set off again.

She heard him make a frustrated sound and then he was blocking her path again. Now she made the mistake of looking up. And it *was* a mistake, because she went tumbling headlong into his turbulent gray eyes. God, he had long eyelashes. She'd never noticed before. They were long sooty sweeps, and they made the gray of his eyes even more startling.

"Pip." He threw his hands up. "I'm an idiot." He made an inarticulate noise. Then he thrust Sadie's reins at her. "I'm sorry."

Pip didn't take the reins. "Why exactly are you an idiot?" She hated herself for the way her heart leapt. She should know better by now. It was only a matter of time before he started insulting her again.

"I think I hurt your feelings earlier."

Pip flushed. Her heart was hammering away like a woodpecker. His hair was riffling in the breeze, the curls brushing against his high forehead. It was painfully unfair that he was so good-looking. If only he'd been plainer, maybe this would have worked out.

Sure. Just like with Old Man Millard, Pip thought sourly. Pretty or plain didn't matter a bit.

"Take the horse," Morgan McBride insisted. "I don't want us to part on bad terms."

But he did want them to part. Just not on bad terms.

"No." She wasn't taking anything from him. Pip steeled herself and maintained eye contact. She could withstand his misty gray eyes. She was strong. "I can't be in your debt," she said firmly. "You've accused me of chasing you, and hounding you, and . . ." Oh, this was getting her riled up again. ". . . and molesting you. I won't have you accusing me of taking handouts from you too."

A mess of emotions contorted his pretty face at that. "I'm being nice!" he bellowed.

Pip lifted a dubious eyebrow. He flushed.

"Take the damn horse," he growled. "It ain't a goddamn hand-out. It's yours."

"No, it's not." The hotter his temper flared, the cooler she got. Pip supposed she should thank him for that. The unsteadier he grew, the steadier she was. "I sold her. You bought her. Quite clearly she's yours." Pip evaluated him. "What is it you want from me, Mr. Mc-Bride? You want to stop being chased; I'm not chasing you. Here you are, instead, hounding me. So, what can I do to make you stop?"

"Hounding you?" He was outraged. "Well, if that don't beat all. I'm just trying to be nice, goddamn it! Junebug said you loved this horse."

Sadie whickered.

Damn him. Didn't he know how hurtful it had been to leave Sadie behind? And now she had to do it again. "So?" she said.

He blinked, astonished. "What do you mean, 'so'?"

"I mean, so what if I love the horse?" Pip felt tears coming as Sadie lowered her head and gave her a sweet stare. "That doesn't change anything, does it?"

Morgan made a horrified noise. "Doesn't change anything? Damn it, woman, you don't go leaving things you love!"

Pip pinned him with a razor-sharp stare. Who did he think he was? "Oh no?" she said softly, feeling mean. "Just like you never left anything you loved? Or anyone?" She meant Buck's Creek. She meant Junebug and his brothers. She certainly didn't mean *her*. So she was flat-out astounded by his response.

"Goddamn it all to hell!" He ripped his hat from his head and waved it at her. "I didn't know you were coming," he told her fiercely. "I planned this for *years*. You got no idea how the thought of it got me through bad times. There were times I didn't know how to manage. You ever tried to raise a pack of kids all by yourself? And they weren't easy kids! You got any idea how many times they almost got killed? You cain't know how many nights I didn't sleep, how many times I didn't eat so they could, how goddamn lonely it was, being the one responsible. And I got through it because of *this*." He gestured at the dusty squalor of the street. "At the thought of being free one day. Of getting to go back to my life. Of being responsible for no one but me. You want to talk about leaving things you love? I loved this, damn it." He had up a full head of steam and showed no sign of slowing. "How was I to know Junebug was ordering *you*? And that you'd come right when I was leaving Buck's Creek? Hell, lady, I don't even know you." He ran his hand through his hair, his gray eyes stormy. "All I know about you is that you drive me wild. You're about the best-looking woman I've ever seen or could ever hope to see. When you're not around,

I dream about you." He swore. "But that ain't anything for a man to hang his hat on, is it? What if I give it all up—again—and all I get for it is more of the same?"

Pip was too shocked to speak. His words pelleted her like sleet. They bounced off, too hard to stick.

He thrust Sadie's reins into her hand. "Take your damn horse. It's meant to be a goddamn apology." He jammed his hat on his head. "I was never repulsed," he told her, towering with frustrated feeling. "But I was always going to leave."

And then he did it again. He left.

And once again she was turned all upside down. How did he *do* that?

"Pip, I don't rightly know how to broach this, so I'm going to speak plain." Granny Colefax took Pip's hands in hers. Her brown gaze was frank. "I wouldn't go back to Nebraska in a blue fit."

Pip closed her eyes and stifled a groan. Why was nothing ever easy? She was still reeling from that bizarre encounter with Morgan McBride in the street. She felt battered by it. *When you're not around, I dream about you.*

And now Granny was being difficult too.

"What are you talking about?" Pip sighed. She didn't have the energy for Granny right now. Her head was spinning. What did he mean, he dreamed about her? *I was never repulsed . . .* The thing was, when he was right in front of her, she *knew* he wasn't repulsed. She could feel their attraction like a bodily force. His gaze turned steamy and roamed her body restlessly. And, holy crow, she'd been over that night in the creek time and time again in her head. Her old insecurities could rear up and whisper insidious things about her forcing herself on him, but the thing was, she hadn't had to force herself. He'd been a very willing participant. *Do you want to try that again?* She remembered the slow tease of his tongue, the feel of his hands running over her, the way he'd kissed her neck, sucked her . . .

"Epiphany, I'm staying here."

Pip tried to focus. She was having completely unsuitable thoughts. She looked around Willabelle's spare room, trying to focus on what Granny was saying. "You want to stay here?"

"Well, not *here*. But in Montana. I'm going back to Bitterroot with Junebug and the boys this afternoon."

Pip tensed. "You're not serious." And *boys*? Those trappers were practically geriatric!

"I am. I never planned to go back." She squeezed Pip's hands. "Why would I? What's there for me there except a corner of an upstairs room, with a view of a cornfield? I'm of no use there. Everyone treats me like a bit of old furniture to be stored up in the attic. I'm not furniture, Pip."

No, she certainly wasn't. Granny had more fire in her than anyone Pip knew, save Junebug. And Pip completely understood not wanting to go back. She was dreading it herself. But where else could she go? She didn't want to stay here in Miles City, cooking for Willabelle. And she didn't want to go with Granny to Bitterroot, where she'd have to live with the memory of her latest nonmarital disaster for the rest of her life.

"But what about me?" Pip asked in a small voice. She felt terribly abandoned all of a sudden. She'd told Morgan McBride she was all alone, but she hadn't really meant it. She'd counted on Granny being with her.

"You'll be fine," Granny insisted, giving her hands another squeeze. "I'll give you my derringer. If anyone gets fresh with you, shoot him."

"I think I have enough money for you to buy a ticket to Bitterroot," Pip capitulated, "so long as I only eat at the half-dime places on the journey home."

"Oh, don't fret. We can trade in the ticket to Chicago for it."

"No, we can't. It's against company policy, remember?"

Granny pulled her hands away, looking slippery. Pip groaned. They were such liars. And she was such a fool for believing them. Still, at least she wasn't further out of pocket, if you wanted to look for a silver lining. And soon Granny and Junebug would be on a train and out of her life, she thought with a pang. There wouldn't be anyone lying to her or leading her on wild-goose chases across the country. There would just be the staid predictability of home. Her old sacky dresses, baking in her mother's kitchen, passing the bowl of peas around the table at Sunday dinners. Everything would be back to normal.

What a thought.

Once they were packed, Pip walked them all as far as the station but stopped dead when she saw Morgan McBride pacing the platform. Of course he'd want to make sure Junebug got on the train.

"I'll say goodbye here," Pip said, stepping back into the lee of a building, out of his line of sight.

Each and every one of them gave her a look that told her they knew precisely what she was thinking. But they didn't. Not even Pip knew what she was thinking. She was still all discombobulated by his speech earlier. *I was never repulsed. But I was always going to leave.* What did that mean? That he wanted her but was *still* rejecting her? Somehow that felt even worse than when a man rejected her because he didn't want her.

"It's been a right pleasure knowing you, Epiphany Hopgood." Junebug thrust her hand out for Pip to shake. The kid hadn't kicked up a fuss at all about being packed off home to Buck's Creek. Pip didn't trust it, even though Junebug swore black and blue that she never wanted to wash another dish in her life and was just glad to get away from Willabelle. But Junebug was Morgan's responsibility, not hers, Pip told herself, and he was right there to make sure she got on the train.

"It's certainly been interesting," Pip said dryly, taking her hand. "If not at all what I expected."

Junebug pulled a face. "Yeah, I'm sorry about that. He's a stubborn old cuss. I did try and tell you in the letters." She gave Pip an encouraging smile. "Don't count him out just yet though. After all, the romance of Miles City might still work its magic." She laughed at Pip's expression. "I still got hopes of seeing you in Buck's Creek one day, sister. Take care of yourself. And go easy on my stupid brother. For all his bluster, he's a tender sort really." And then the kid was running off, skipping up the steps to the platform and cannoning into her brother.

"Here's the derringer, Epiphany." Granny Colefax said her goodbyes next. She had bullets to go with the gun and a list of instructions for both how to shoot it and how to care for it. Pip had no intention of ever using it. "You be careful tonight, this is a rough town. Don't be shy about shooting any molesters. And you lock the door at night." She stood on tiptoe to press a kiss to Pip's cheek. "You were always my favorite." She gave Pip a sly look. "And if you should decide to stay in Chicago and not head all the way back to Joshua, well, you'd have my blessing." She took a step and then turned back. "Write to me, won't you, girlie? I want to know what grand adventures you have next." She gave her foxy grin. "And I'll write and tell you mine."

Pip laughed, even though she had tears in her eyes as she watched her grandmother go, escorted by her devoted trappers. Pip stood in the shadows and watched as they fussed with their baggage and said their goodbyes to Morgan McBride. He was a tall silhouette, hard packed and graceful. Pip shivered from the inside out as she watched him with Junebug.

There were times I didn't know how to manage. You ever tried to raise a pack of kids all by yourself? Pip had been curious about him since she first saw that blunt advertisement in the *Matrimonial News*. But now, after that flood of words this morning, her curiosity was as sharp as a blade. He was so big, and so masculine; he looked like he could haul a mountain off the ground with his bare hands; he was always capable; he had fervent views on everything and was prone to talking over people in order to air them. But until today she'd never known that all of that hid a flood of emotion. He was just roiling with pain and love and conflict. As she watched him see Junebug off, she wished things had played out differently. Maybe if they could have met without the pressures of marriage . . . Maybe if they could have been friends . . . had a conversation. Gotten to know one another. Maybe if she could have known what made him tick . . .

But there was no point in barking at a knot, as her father would say.

Pip jumped at an eruption of frenzied barking, feeling like she'd conjured the sound from thin air with her thoughts. And then Willabelle's dog came tearing down the street, long fur flying. It scrambled up onto the platform and threw itself at Junebug. Well. Maybe Father had got that wrong, Pip thought, as she watched Willabelle lose her dog to Junebug McBride. Maybe sometimes it was worth barking at a knot.

Nineteen

Morgan made sure he saw Junebug onto the train. And he threatened Sour Eagle and Thunderhead Bill with grievous bodily harm
if they failed to deliver her to Kit. They were both shamefaced and
abjectly grateful to him for paying off their debts, so assured him
they would.

"We won't let her out of our sight," Sour Eagle promised.

"You'll have Kit to face if you do," Morgan warned him. "And
you keep in mind he's bigger than me."

Morgan waited on the platform as they boarded and took their
seats, that ridiculous dog joining them. Morgan hated that dog. It
had a penchant for biting him.

Junebug opened the window and leaned out so she could wave
him off, and the dog stuck its head out, too, growling at him. No
matter how it growled, Morgan wasn't leaving until he'd seen
Junebug go. He didn't trust her an inch. Especially when she was
being this amenable.

"Here," Junebug said, thrusting something at Morgan through
the open window. "This is for you."

"What is it?" Morgan was suspicious.

"A letter." She grinned. "Read it when I'm gone. It's so you don't miss me so much."

But it wasn't just a letter. On top of the thick wedge of folded paper was a train ticket. To Chicago. He frowned.

"Just in case you decide you'd rather spend some time getting to know a certain someone," Junebug suggested breezily. "You know, if you finally figure out that she's a sight more entertaining than a bunch of dumb cows." Her grin was so big it looked fit to split her in two. "I reckon you could get to know someone mighty thoroughly on a long train journey."

The whistle sounded, a sharp blast in the late summer air.

"Where the hell did you get the money to buy this?" Morgan demanded. Train tickets weren't cheap.

"It turns out I've got a talent for cards." Junebug raised her voice to be heard as the train shrieked on the rails, lurching forward.

"A talent for . . ." He scowled. "Junebug McBride, you better not have . . ."

"Did you know you can win even if you've got a bad hand? You just need people to *think* you can win." She was too pleased with herself by half. "I'll see you back home," she called, waving gaily as the train pulled away.

"Don't think we ain't talking about this when I get there!" Morgan bellowed after the train. Goddamn that kid. She was going to be the death of him.

He opened the letter as soon as the sound of the train had faded on the dusty air.

Morgan, it read, *sometimes it's powerful hard to know how to talk to you. You're possibly the worst listener I ever met. And that's saying something, because Kit is so bad that I have to write to him. But if there's one thing writing complaints to Kit taught me, it's that if you put things in writing, people have to listen to you.*

Well, they didn't, Morgan thought, feeling contrary. They could stop reading, couldn't they? But he didn't stop reading.

So listen up. You are the best father a girl could have.

Morgan felt like he'd been belted square in the nose.

I only ordered you up a wife because I wanted you to stay. You know that but you don't <u>know</u> that. And I never could quite find a way to get it through to you. I need you, you big idiot. And the thought of living in Buck's Creek without you makes me wish I was under that chokecherry tree with Ma and the girls. It ain't home without you. And that's because <u>you're my home</u>.

Morgan's eyes were hot and prickly, and his chest hurt. He felt something inside him twist. Damn that kid.

I know you didn't ask for this, me needing you like this. I know Ma dumped us on you by up and dying, and Pa was useless to boot. I know you regret coming back that time, because it meant you got stuck with the raising of us.

Regret? No. That wasn't the word he'd use. He'd been bitter at times, sure. Because it wasn't fair, getting stuck with all that responsibility when you never asked for it. But regret? Never. Morgan felt the truth of it in his bones.

But I don't regret it. And the boys don't neither. I know you feel like you've been hard done by, Morgan. But your hard done by was our best fortune. I am glad every single day that you came back, and that you stayed. Pip once asked me why I didn't just let you leave and work things out for yourself. Because you will work them out, you blockhead. You're just a bit slow on the uptake. But you do always get there in the end. And so, I've decided to try it out to see if it works. So off you go. Do what you need to do (it better be getting onto that train to Chicago, though, and not following a bunch of dumb cows all over the place). You be as free as you need to be, until you can come home without feeling like we're caging you up. I am mostly certain that you'll be back sooner rather than later. Because you don't need to tell me you love me for me to know it. I know it because of all those days you stayed, when you would rather be elsewhere. I knowed it when I was little and you scared off my nightmares. I knowed it when you taught me to fish. And I guess I even know it now by the way

you won't marry Pip, just to punish me for ordering her up. Consider me
punished. I'm out of the mail-order bride business.

But on that front, see the pages included with this letter. They were
always meant for you anyway.

Your loving sister,

Junebug Everleigh McBride

p.s. I figure I got nothing to lose by letting you go, because if you don't
come back soon, I'll just come and hunt you down.

p.p.s. Don't tell the boys I got mushy.

Morgan had to sit down on one of the benches outside the train
station and reread the thing. And when he turned the page, he
found more letters, but not from Junebug. The top one was a letter
from Pip. And beneath it there were more: lots of letters from Epiphany Hopgood of Joshua, Nebraska. They were the letters she'd
written in answer to that damn advertisement. Morgan sat there
on the platform long after the train had left, reading and rereading
the fat sheaf of papers, postmarked Nebraska.

He didn't know what to think.

He headed for the nearest saloon. He needed a drink.

He found a table in a quiet corner so he could pore over those
letters. They didn't make a lick of sense to him. *I shall tell you my*
qualities plain, she wrote in the first one. *No one has ever labeled me*
beautiful, but I'm not homely neither. Maybe no one had ever called
her beautiful, Morgan thought, because the word just didn't go far
enough. It was too soft for Pip. Too indefinite. She was unique—
she needed a more unique word. There was a lot of comparing
herself to her sister Naomi in the letters, and Pip always seemed to
come out the worse for it. She talked about her mother a lot, too,
and Morgan got a picture of a pinch-faced narrow woman who
fretted a lot and needed to loosen up. Pip did a hard sell in those
letters: she listed her housekeeping skills, included descriptions of
dishes she could cook, promised she'd bring good egg-laying hens

and a productive milk cow and assured Morgan of her virtues, which included hard-won patience.

What wasn't in these letters was Pip herself. The only trace of her sharp tongue, or her gold-lit greenish eyes, or her goddamn exceptional talent for driving a man wild, was one brief line: *I am not always an easy woman.*

Pip and Junebug seemed to have promised each other stark honesty, and while Junebug had been lying with a free-flowing pen, Pip had been honest to a fault. Or rather, honest only about her faults. Had she been deliberately obfuscatory, or did she sincerely not know her worth?

It had something to do with all these rejections, Morgan thought, ordering another drink and flipping to the pages about all the times she'd not got married. God, she had been forthright. He winced as he read through all the men who had rejected her. *The thing is, Mr. McBride, every time it came down to my looks.*

Well, that made no damn sense. Morgan had a vision of her in the creek. His stomach clenched. *I don't believe I'm repellent, but I'm not the kind of woman men lose sleep over.* Morgan snorted. Well, he was living proof that that weren't so. He couldn't close his eyes without seeing her gold-lit gaze, her brassy hair, those incredible swollen . . . damn. What was wrong with those men in Nebraska? Were they all nearsighted?

Please don't expect me to be dainty. I'm broad of shoulder and hip and I lean toward fleshiness. Of the best kind, he thought fervently, remembering the feel of her against him. None of this added up. But then he remembered meeting her at Rigby's hotel and how she hadn't impressed him at all. Hell, he'd thought she was plain. He racked his brain to remember how she'd looked. A pile of floury red hair. Big. He'd thought she was stocky, he guessed. He couldn't remember what she was wearing. An apron? It was shapeless anyway, because he'd had no idea of her incredible figure until she'd turned up in Buck's Creek in that green dress. God, that green dress. It featured heavily in his dreams, particularly those buttons that ran from the high neck all the way down the front. He was sweating just thinking about it.

Morgan took a sip of his beer and tried to concentrate. He guessed she'd never worn that green dress in Nebraska. He folded the letters up. But even without the dress . . . Jesus, what about those eyes? Her lips? The way her expressive mouth showed everything she was feeling? All he could conclude was that Nebraskans lacked good sense. Either that, or they were scared. A woman who could ignite your blood that way could be damn intimidating. He surely felt it. But intimidating could also be hot as hell. It was arousing as all get-out to find a woman tall enough to look you in the eye, bold enough to kiss you before you kissed her, sharp enough to put you in your place when you were being an idiot. And he was an idiot a lot. His temper ran quick and hot, and he was prone to saying things he regretted. And slow to apologize for them.

Although, on the subject of apologizing, he was still irked by the way she'd refused to accept her horse back. He didn't apologize often. She should have been touched, not goddamn offended. Morgan drummed his fingers against the table. He still felt pretty stupid for speechifying in the street. He'd spouted a whole lot of nonsense at her, most of which he could barely remember. She'd stood there, magnificent in that low-necked purple dress, looking like the best day he'd never had, watching him like he was an un-folding disaster.

He would give anything to know what she was thinking.

"Hey, Morgan." It was Frank. He was deep in a whiskey bottle, drinking through his pay now that the beeves had been shipped off to Chicago. "You need company? You look lonely."

"I cain't go with you to Texas," Morgan said abruptly, rising from the table. "I've got business in Chicago." Or at least on the way to Chicago.

Frank wasn't happy. "I ain't going to lie, losing you and Vern in the same day is a wicked blow."

Losing Vern? Morgan's heart seized up in his chest. Vern wanted to marry Pip. Pip had never been able to find a man to marry her. Hell. What if she was desperate enough to say yes? He didn't know if she would—because he didn't know her. Who knew what she was thinking? Not him. Damn it.

"Hey," Frank protested when Morgan headed for the door. "What about your drink?"

"You have it," Morgan called over his shoulder. "I don't need it no more." He was getting on that damn train with her. Because Junebug was right, a train journey was a great chance to get to know someone. And, God help him, he couldn't marry a stranger, could he?

Twenty

Pip was early for her train the next morning. She was in her green dress and fanciful hat, having left Willabelle's purple on the bed, wincing at the inch of red dirt she'd left baked into the hem. She was not sorry to leave Willabelle and her dining hall, and its hellish kitchen, behind. And she wouldn't be sad to see the back of Miles City either.

The station was a tumult of activity again today, as the ranchers brought their herds in to be shipped off to Chicago. A vast cloud of dust hung over the town, turning the sunlight red. The train had arrived and sat hissing to itself on the rails, as activity swirled around it. Pip watched as the porters loaded Sadie and her cow and carted off her trunks. All those trunks she'd packed so excitedly, thinking they were taking her to her future. Now she was headed straight back to her wretched past . . . which was going to be her eternal pea-shucking present.

"Ma'am?" The stationmaster broke into her thoughts. "You might want to wait in your carriage. It's about to get a whole lot dustier out here as they load up the herds." He escorted her to the train.

"Oh." She stopped him as he kept walking past the third-class carriages. "I only have a third-class ticket . . ." She fished out her ticket to show him.

"It's been upgraded, ma'am," he said placidly, continuing on his way.

Upgraded? Pip frowned. Why?

"I think there's been a mistake," she said, catching up to the man.

"No mistake, ma'am. I can't see another tall redhead on the platform." He gave her an amused look. "The gentleman thought you'd be more comfortable away from all the cowhands. It gets pretty rough back there in third class."

The gentleman? Pip's stomach squeezed as the stationmaster opened the door to the Pullman car for her. *Morgan.*

Only it wasn't Morgan McBride. It was the big, bashful cowboy who'd accosted her in the dining hall the day before, when she'd been wearing Willabelle's purple dress. Pip blinked. She'd quite forgotten about him, after Morgan McBride had dragged her out to the yard to yell at her. And then she'd been so upset about selling Sadie, and then Morgan again . . . Oh, would she ever stop thinking about Morgan McBride?

"Good morning, ma'am." The bashful cowboy was standing with his hat in his hands, shifting from foot to foot and looking up at her shyly through his eyelashes. He was burly and dark eyed, with a gentleness that contrasted starkly with his size.

"Um." Pip stood awkwardly at the open door, which led to the first-class drawing room, which was a wood-paneled and plush forest-green oasis of luxury. "I think there's been a mistake . . ." she said again.

"There's no mistake." The cowboy gave her a sweet smile. He looked nervous in the extreme. "My name is Vern Little Horse," he said, speaking quickly, as though he might lose his gumption at any minute. "I upgraded your ticket when I found out you weren't in first class. You don't want to be back there today, ma'am," he assured her, "it's not a pleasant place to be when everyone has just got off a long drive, and they're freshly paid and liquored up."

No. That didn't sound ideal. "That's very kind of you," Pip said carefully, "but it wouldn't be appropriate to accept."

"Appropriate or not, ma'am," the stationmaster chipped in from behind her, "I'm afraid the choice is out of your hands now, as we've sold our last ticket for third. There won't be room for you back there anymore."

Oh heck. But Pip didn't want to give this Vern man ideas.

This was a unique position for her, she thought. Not exactly an unpleasant one though . . .

"You owe me nothing," Vern Little Horse told her hastily. "I won't take advantage of the situation. My intentions are honorable."

His intentions were honorable. Pip suppressed a smile. He really was sweet. She stepped into the carriage, a little overwhelmed by its grandness. There were plush mahogany benches and bunched curtains with gold fringes, which could be drawn around the benches for a sense of privacy. Etched glass lamps hung from the tall ceiling, and there were large windows letting in floods of dusty-red sunlight. The floor underfoot was even carpeted. Pip had never been anywhere so fancy. It certainly beat third class.

Vern gestured toward a bench and Pip obliged, sliding into it. Oh my, it was comfortable, springy and cushiony and just as welcoming as heck. Pip could get used to this.

"This is very, very kind of you," she told Vern, feeling more than a touch shy herself.

"Would you mind . . . ?" He indicated the bench opposite.

"Oh, please." Although she was feeling mighty awkward. He was rubbing off on her, she thought dryly. He was about the nerviest man she'd ever met. As he looked at her, his Adam's apple bobbed madly. Lord, was this what it was like to have a suitor?

"What do you mean, she's up that way?"

Pip stiffened as she heard Morgan McBride's cracking voice through the open door.

"What's she doing in first class?"

Pip felt a flare of anger. What was he doing here, and why did he care which carriage she was in? Across from her, a frown flickered on Vern Little Horse's face.

Morgan McBride appeared in the doorway. Pip's heart kicked up, the way it always did when he was around. She felt her cheeks flush as he stared at her. And then he saw Vern and his face looked like the shadow of a storm cloud had fallen across it. She saw his lips move as he swore under his breath.

"What are you doing up here?" he demanded.

Who the hell did he think he was, taking that tone with her? Pip gave him the coldest, most imperious look she could muster. "Excuse me? Are you speaking to me?"

He gave an irritated huff and then disappeared. The next thing she heard was the crack of his voice again, hollering over the din of the cattle. "Hey! You! I want to upgrade to first class!"

Pip had the queerest urge to smile, even though she was furious. What was wrong with him? And what was wrong with *her*? Something had leapt inside her at the sight of him. Something that felt like hope. It was pointless and self-defeating, but there it was.

Pip glanced over at Vern Little Horse, only to see that he looked crestfallen. Oh dear. She smiled at him. That cheered him a bit.

But even that bit disappeared when Morgan McBride came through the door into the first-class carriage. He'd dressed up, Pip noticed. He was out of his denim, and into a pair of tight black trousers. He had a jacket on, too, although it was rather crumpled. It looked like it had been rolled up in his bag for a while. His white shirt was open at the neck, revealing that tantalizing V of caramel skin that gave her shivery feelings. He tucked the newspaper he was carrying under his arm and took his hat off. His dark hair did that tumble it liked to do. Pip went warm all over at the sight of him.

"Vern," he said, hooking his thumb into his belt and regarding Vern warily. "What are your intentions?"

"They're honorable," Pip said quickly, before Vern could answer.

Morgan didn't like that. His black brows drew together, and his gray eyes went stormy. "How honorable?"

"We haven't got that far." Pip shot Vern an apologetic look. "And it's honestly none of your business," she told Morgan.

"Marriage," Vern blurted. "I got marriage in mind."

Morgan swore. "Now, look," he said to Pip, crossing the carpeted floor and dropping onto the bench beside Vern. "Don't do anything hasty."

Pip blinked. What?

"I know you came to Montana with marriage in mind, but you got options. You don't have to marry just anyone."

Pip's mouth dropped open. How rude. To everyone involved. "I'm so sorry," Pip apologized to Vern.

"That's it, let him down gently." Morgan relaxed back into the cushiony upholstery.

"I'm apologizing for *you*," she said tightly.

"No need. Vern and I go way back." Morgan regarded the burly man with a genial look. "I get why you're smitten, Vern, I really do. But this one is out of your reach."

"Morgan!" Pip was outraged. The man had been nothing but sweet to her. Whereas *he* was just plain infernal.

"You don't want Vern," Morgan told her. "He's on the trail all the time. You want a man who'll stay put."

Pip couldn't believe what she was hearing. "Like you stay put?" she needled him.

"If you look at my track record, I think you'll find I have a history of staying put," he argued. "It's only my recent history that's spotty. But I wasn't necessarily talking about me."

"I'd give up the trail," Vern interrupted. "I'd settle down."

"You weren't talking about you?" she echoed. Of course he wasn't. *I was always going to leave.*

"I'm talking about the man you ought to say yes to," Morgan said firmly. "He should stay the hell put, not go traipsing around after cows."

"I'll give up the cows," Vern insisted.

"He should also think you're the best thing he's ever seen."

"I think that," Vern said quickly.

Pip blinked. There were other people arriving in the carriage now, but Morgan and Vern didn't pay them any attention.

"He should *beg* you to marry him." Morgan's gray gaze was that mix of intensity and amusement that was so bedazzling. "You shouldn't have to convince him of anything. He should do the damn convincing, Epiphany, not you."

"Pip," she corrected sharply. "Only my mother calls me Epiphany."

"Your mother and me. I like Epiphany. It's got a ring to it."

"I bought a ring." Vern fished in his pocket.

"Damn it, Vern." Morgan swore when Vern pulled out a diamond ring.

Pip almost swore herself. This was moving too fast. Holy crow, she'd pictured a long boring ride to Chicago, and all this was happening and they hadn't even left the station yet.

"All aboard!" The stationmaster was blowing his whistle and doing his rounds, closing doors. And Pip was trapped in here with these two fool men.

"That's quite a ring," Morgan admitted. "Much nicer than the last one. Whatever happened to that girl you were going to marry back in Abilene?"

"I married her," Vern said.

"You're already married?" Pip frowned at him. Honestly.

"Not anymore. She left me on account of I was always off driving cattle."

"See," Morgan said triumphantly. "You want a man who'll stay put."

"I'll stay put this time."

"You divorced yet?" Morgan asked him.

"I'll get divorced."

Pip glowered at them both. "Excuse me, I think I'll find another seat." As she stood up, the train jerked forward and she almost fell in Morgan's lap. He caught her by the hips and she felt like she'd been struck by lightning.

Oh no. She didn't know what his game was, but she wasn't playing. Pip straightened, knocking his hands away and heading for another bench.

"Don't worry, Vern, I'll reimburse you for the upgrade," Morgan told him, standing to follow her. He dropped his newspaper on Vern's lap and Pip saw the masthead as it landed. The *Matrimonial News*. "Here," Morgan said, clapping Vern's shoulder. "Happy hunting."

Pip unhooked the curtains from the wall and snapped them closed around the pair of empty benches she'd chosen. She heard Morgan make an annoyed grunt. And then he just barged right on in.

"Hey!" she protested.

He sat himself down and regarded her. "I won't bother you. Unless you want me to."

Pip took a deep breath and stared out the window. The train was gathering speed, leaving Miles City behind in its cloud of dust. Pip was painfully aware of the intimacy of their curtained nook. Their knees were almost touching. She heard rustling and glanced his way.

He was unfurling a square of paper. He caught her looking and his dimples flickered. Lord, he was good-looking. It was hard not to stare. And Pip's body was singing to be so close to him. Close enough to smell his woodsy scent.

Pip tore her gaze away and pretended to watch the landscape flash by. From the corner of her eye, she could see him lay his hat on the bench next to him and stretch his legs out. More rustling.

"What's your favorite time of day?" he asked out of the blue.

Pip startled and looked over. He was staring at her, his gray eyes clear and curious.

"My favorite time of day?" she echoed.

He nodded. "Yeah. Do you like mornings? Or midday? Or evenings?"

Pip blinked. No one had ever asked her that before. She thought about it. "I like bedtime." Oh. No. That sounded suggestive. She saw the dimples dent his cheeks. "I mean, I like the end of the day," she amended hastily.

"The bed end?" A smile flirted at the corners of his lips.

Pip swallowed. This was ridiculous. "What are you doing here?" she demanded.

"I'm taking the train to Chicago." He smiled. She wished he wouldn't. His dimples became deep grooves.

"What happened to Texas?"

"It's still there, as far as I know."

She glared at him. "Why aren't *you* there?" she asked tightly.

"Because I'm here."

Pip could see where Junebug got her infuriating slipperiness from. Fine. If he wasn't going to talk straight, she wasn't going to talk at all.

He glanced down at the square of paper he was holding. "What's your horse's name?"

"What?"

"Your horse. What's her name?"

What on earth had got into him? And what *was* he doing here? "Sadie," she said slowly.

"Sadie. Right." He looked back down at his square of paper.

"Is that a list of questions?" she asked, astonished.

He ignored her question and asked another. "Where in Nebraska are you from?"

That square of paper he was holding was positively covered with writing. On both sides. "How many questions are there?" she asked.

"A few." His gray eyes had a sparkle to them now. "Where in Nebraska?"

"The southeast. A town called Joshua."

"Did you like it there?"

Why was he asking her all this? Pip frowned.

"I'll take that as a no," he said thoughtfully. "Now. Favorite color? Do you snore? And what are you looking for in a husband?" The last was said abruptly, followed by sharp silence. Pip saw him dart a glance up at her and then look firmly back at the page.

"Gray," she said. "Not so far as I know." And then she paused. "Kindness. Reliability." She bit her lip. He was staring resolutely at the page. "Someone who appreciates me."

His gaze flickered up at her again.

"Someone who wants me."

At the word *want* his gray eyes turned smoky.

"How many brothers and sisters?" he asked, his voice doing that sandpapery thing.

Pip's chest felt tight. What was he doing? "Eight," she said softly. "Five brothers, three sisters."

"Do you ever dream about me?"

Oh God. That sandpapery voice saying those words . . . Pip felt herself quiver from head to toe. "Do *you* dream about *me*?" If he could ask questions, so could she.

"Yes," he said huskily. "I already told you I do."

She lost her breath.

His smoky eyes held her gaze. "Every night." His voice grew warmer. "And sometimes during the day." He got a glint. "Your turn. Do you?"

"Yes," she whispered, her heart pounding. She flushed, feeling exposed.

Time seemed to slow down as he moved across to her bench, sinking down next to her, his arm along the back, behind her shoulders. Pip couldn't take her eyes off him.

"What are you doing?" she breathed.

"Getting to know you," he said. His fingers ran along the back of her neck, and she shivered.

"Why?"

"Because I don't know you." He inched closer.

Oh goodness, that scent. And that look in his eyes . . .

"And you don't know me," he continued. His fingers were tracing circles on the back of her neck now. She could feel it through her body, all the way to her toes.

"But, Epiphany . . ." How did he make her name sound so seductive? "I *want* to get to know you."

Pip felt light-headed.

"And I want you to get to know me." His fingers had migrated up to her nape, where they toyed with the loose curls that had tumbled from her badly pinned coiffure.

"Why?" She didn't trust this.

His thigh was warm against hers. She could feel the heat of him through their clothes. "Because of this," he sighed.

"Because of what?" She was having trouble focusing. His fingers were driving her to distraction.

He smiled, wolfishly. "This." And then he leaned in and kissed her, light as snow falling.

Pip tingled and clenched and shivered and sparkled—all of it at once. His kiss grew firmer, deepened. Her eyes slid closed. She felt like she was catching fire. Her hand lifted of its own accord to rest against his cheek. He was fresh shaven and silky smooth. His mouth moved on hers.

Oh, she'd forgotten how good he tasted, how good he felt.

"That," he sighed as he pulled away. He looked drugged.

Pip didn't want him to stop.

"That is why," he told her huskily, resting his forehead against hers.

"What's *your* horse's name?" she breathed.

"I have three." He didn't remove his forehead from hers. They stared into one another's eyes. "Arthur, Duck, and Porridge."

Pip giggled.

"Junebug named them."

"Favorite color? Do you snore? What are you looking for in a wife?" Her hand was still against his cheek. She rubbed her thumb over his silky skin. She felt a pulse deep down in the core of her, with every stroke.

"Green with yellow bits. Probably. You."

Pip jumped. She pulled away, her hand dropping from his face. He didn't seem troubled by her reaction; he just kept watching her with those smoky eyes.

"You don't want to get married," she reminded him.

"No. I *didn't* want to get married. But then I met you." His intensity was mesmerizing. "Epiphany Hopgood from Joshua, Nebraska. With a horse called Sadie, five brothers and three sisters, whose favorite color is gray. That's an odd color choice, by the way."

"I used to like blue," she admitted. "But gray won me over."

He smiled. "How about a game to pass the time?" he suggested. "I hear it's a long way to Chicago."

Pip felt like melting into the bench as his fingers toyed with her hair.

"I'll guess things about you, and if I get them right, I kiss you."

"What if you get them wrong?"

"You kiss me."

Pip liked the sound of this game.

"Let's start easy," he murmured, leaning so close she could feel the warmth of his breath. "You made that dress yourself."

Pip nodded.

"One for me," he whispered, kissing her lazily. "I have dreams about this dress," he confessed breathlessly, before kissing her again, his tongue slipping against hers. "Dreams about unbuttoning these." His free hand pressed against her breastbone, covering the small black buttons down the front of her chest. Pip let out a small involuntary noise against his lips. She felt him smile into their kiss.

"Two: you thought I didn't want you when I left Buck's Creek."

Pip froze. That hateful feeling of shame came flooding in.

"I have wanted you ever since I first saw you in Buck's Creek." He dropped his head and pressed a kiss to her neck. His tongue swirled against her skin. "I couldn't look away when you turned up in the meadow." His breath was so hot as he spoke. Every word was punctuated by a kiss, up her neck toward her ear. "And when you bent over in the vegetable patch . . ." He groaned. "And then dancing with you felt like catching sparks from the fire."

Pip's eyes fluttered closed. His words were just as arousing as his kisses. She'd never known what being wanted felt like before Morgan McBride. It felt *good*.

"And in that creek . . ." His mouth closed around her earlobe, searing hot, giving it a playful suck.

She felt that suck in the far reaches of her body. Her breasts were swollen and heavy, longing to be touched. She shifted uncomfortably on the bench. More, she thought. *More*.

"You came to Miles City to chase me."

"Wrong," she gasped, pulling away, feeling a stab of yesterday's anger. Then she saw the teasing glint in his eye.

"Oh no," he said wickedly, "I guess that means it's your kiss." He reclined on the bench, spreading his legs and waiting for her to come to him.

"I didn't chase you."

"I know. That's why it's your turn." He bit his lower lip, taunting her.

Pip drank in the sight of him, long legged and lazy as he waited for her to kiss him. She swiveled on the bench. The way he watched her, expectant, was arousing beyond belief. She took her time, appreciating the way his eyelashes trembled as she inched closer, and the way his breath hitched. He was flushed, too, she noticed.

He wanted her.

Pip kissed him slowly. He melted into the bench, his head resting against the plush green cushion, his eyelids sliding closed. He opened his mouth beneath her; Pip accepted the invitation and slid her tongue between his lips. He met her with his. Pip could see his hand gripping the arm of the bench until his knuckles turned white. She played with the collar of his shirt as she tasted him, until her fingertips found that triangle of caramel skin below his throat. He was so warm. She felt the soft whorls of dark hair just below the buttons. He moaned softly, his hand coming up to cup the back of her head. Pip ran her hand down his chest, feeling his muscles clench beneath her palm. When she pulled away, he opened his eyes, the gray hazy with lust.

For her.

"Pip," he whispered, hauling her closer, until she was practically sprawled on top of him. Pip braced herself with a hand over his heart. "Let me know if I guess this right," he said. The hand on the back of her head descended, tracing her spine all the way down to her waist, where it came to rest, large and promising. "If I ask you to marry me, you'll say yes."

Pip could feel his heart hammering under her hand.

"Please," he whispered. "Please say yes?"

"If I kiss you now, doesn't that mean you got it wrong?" she breathed.

"Only if we're still playing the game." All the teasing had dropped away. Pip could see the naked vulnerability in his eyes.

"But I like the game," she confessed, rearranging herself so she was sitting across his lap. He gave a soft moan. She could feel him pressing into her derriere, hard.

"I like this dress," he said in a pained voice. "No bustle to get in between us." His gaze dropped to her breasts, which were in his eyeline now. "I like everything about this dress."

"You guessed if you asked me to marry you, I'd say yes," she reminded him.

He nodded, hypnotized by her.

"According to the game you kiss me now."

He registered what she'd said. "That's a yes." He looked like he'd just caught the moon.

This time when he kissed her there was no softness. He hauled her down to him and kissed her with something akin to desperation. He was fierce. Hungry. Unleashed. Pip felt wild. She plunged her hands into his dark hair, loving the feel of it between her fingers. His tongue entered her as his hands found her breasts. By the time they broke apart, they were both breathing hard, and aching with desire.

"Chicago," he said, burying his face in her neck. "We're getting married in Chicago. And then we're renting a goddamn hotel room."

Pip felt a wave of euphoria. She didn't care about weddings anymore. All that mattered was that she was here, held tight in Morgan McBride's arms, and that he didn't want to let her go.

"I have a question of my own," she told him, resting a finger in the dent of his dimple.

"Yes, anything."

She laughed. "When did you know?"

"Know what?"

"That you liked me."

"Honey, I don't like you." He gazed at her as he stroked her face. "I am goddamn flat-out head over heels in love with you."

"But . . . how?" She shook her head. It went against everything she'd ever known.

He laughed. "I'll show you," he promised. "Just as soon as we get to that hotel."

Pip wasn't sure she could wait that long. Idly, she ran her fingers over his chest, feeling the hard point of his nipple through his shirt. His sharply indrawn breath made her tingle. "Have you got more questions for me?" she asked, circling his nipple with her fingertips. "We've still got a long journey, and you said you wanted to get to know each other."

He sighed happily, surrendering to her touch. "If I'd known marriage could make a man this content, I would never have put up a fight."

"Don't get ahead of yourself, Mr. McBride. You aren't married yet."

But it was only a matter of time. Because Epiphany Hopgood was resolved.

Twenty-One

Chicago, Illinois

Compared to the ordeal of obtaining a marriage license and waiting the required time before the ceremony, the wedding itself was
quick as a heartbeat. Morgan and Pip were itchy from the delay
and impatient to get it done. They'd checked into the hotel as husband and wife on arrival in Chicago, but had refrained from sharing a bed until they were wed. Well, Morgan had refrained. It drove
Pip to distraction, but Morgan was as stubborn as all heck about
it. He unfurled his bedroll on the plush carpet of the Palmer House
hotel room the first night and turned his back on her.

Honestly. Here they were, alone, and he wouldn't so much as
touch her. Why on earth had he booked them into the fanciest hotel
in town, with the biggest, plushest bed, if he wasn't going to make
use of it? Holy crow, if he was going to sleep on the floor, a cut-rate
boardinghouse would have done just as well.

"You know the bed is big enough for both of us," she told him,
trying to sound seductive. She could tell by the stiffness of his body
that he was listening, but he didn't respond.

"Morgan . . ."

"Not a good idea."

Pip could have kicked him. The whole journey here he'd kissed her senseless and now they were here, on the verge of marriage, and he'd gone cold on her.

Pip considered the giant mahogany bed, which loomed in the center of the room beneath the brass chandelier. The electric light was bright as midday; the whole hotel was wired with electricity, the first place of its kind Pip had seen. The blazing light made the marble floors in the foyer shine and the gilt on the ceilings glow; everywhere Pip looked there were brass and crystal sconces and chandeliers. It was like being inside a jewelry box. Pip had protested at the extravagance of the hotel, but Morgan had said she deserved the best, and he'd earned a lot of money and hadn't been able to spend it anywhere, so why not enjoy themselves?

But they weren't enjoying themselves at all, Pip thought testily. She missed the train, and their dim cocoon behind the curtains. Her skin felt like it was on fire, she wanted to be touched so bad. Peppery with displeasure, she stalked to the dressing screen, where her trunk had been deposited. "You didn't even kiss me good night," she grumbled as she struggled to get her green dress off.

"If I start, I won't be able to stop," he sighed.

"So *don't* stop. What does it matter, if we're going to be married anyway?"

"We're doing this right." He was immovable. "Turn off the light once you're in bed. We'll go sort the marriage license in the morning."

"What does it matter if we do it now or later, if we're going to be married anyway?" She'd learned the habit of repeating herself until he *listened*. Pip pulled her nightgown on.

"What does it matter?" He was sitting up in his bedroll when she came out from behind the screen. He was still fully dressed. The only items of clothing he'd removed were his boots and his coat. She saw the way his gaze lingered on her uncorseted body under the thin cotton of her nightclothes, and her heart did a long slow squeeze.

"It'll matter plenty if I get you in the family way," he said quietly. "What if I get you pregnant and then get hit by a cable car before the wedding? You got any idea how hard it is being a woman alone with a kid? An *unwed* woman alone."

"Couldn't you just *not* get hit by a cable car?"

"What if I die of ecstasy in your arms," he said dryly. "Where would you be then? A dead naked man on you, and no marriage certificate."

"Do they ask for a marriage certificate when they find a dead man?" He really was impossible. Pip wriggled into the bed. The sheets were cool and fresh against her bare legs. She felt enjoyably unclothed in her nightgown. She'd dropped her wrapper on the floor in front of him, but he'd refused to take the bait. "I won't be able to sleep." She pouted, flopping back against the pillows. She'd been ready for this moment for years. And kissing him unlocked something in her, something hungry and elemental. Something impatient as all heck.

"So, do something else until you get tired. Write to your folks. There's hotel stationery and a pen set on the desk." He sounded surly.

"I really don't see what the fuss is."

"The fuss is: I don't want you to end up like my ma," he snapped.

Oh. Pip hadn't considered that. So much of his thinking was still a mystery to her.

He ran his hands through his hair. "You know what happens when a man and a woman get friendly? Babies. And no kid of mine is going fatherless. When we do this, it's going to be done right."

Pip heard the weight of feeling in his voice. Well. He was serious about the baby thing. And about getting hit by a cable car and leaving her disgraced. She pulled the covers up to her chin and gave the matter serious consideration. Children. Of course she knew they came with marriage. But abruptly it seemed very real. Maybe too real.

"You want children, then?" Pip said awkwardly. It was mighty strange to feel like you knew someone, but also didn't really yet at all. Think of all the years they had to learn about each other, she thought, feeling a glow at the idea. She remembered his list of questions on the train. She should probably compose some questions of her own.

"I don't know that it's a matter of wanting . . ." His voice got quieter. "They come with the territory, don't they? Kids. One thing leads to the other." He cleared his throat.

Pip really thought about it. She had always just taken it as a given, that she'd get married and have children. But *did* she want them? She remembered trying to keep Junebug in line back in Miles City. Oh Lord, that had been hard work. And just think, Morgan had raised *four* of them. Pip remembered her nieces and nephews back in Joshua; the babies, the toddlers, the yelling kids tearing around the yard. And then she remembered the hushed conversations in the kitchen, and the advertisement for "Mother's Friends" her sister-in-law had passed to Naomi.

"They don't *have* to come with the territory . . ." Pip said carefully. She didn't know the details, but she knew there were things you could buy that meant babies were less likely.

She felt Morgan's stillness.

"I mean, my sister-in-law . . ." Pip cleared her throat. Oh my. This felt very odd. Abruptly she reached over and pulled the light cord, plunging them into darkness. There, that was easier. "My sister-in-law used something, so she wouldn't . . ."

"You don't want children?" Morgan sounded cautious. But she thought she also heard something else.

"I do," she hurried to assure him. Because she did. Just maybe not straightaway. "Eventually."

"Eventually?"

"I mean, we barely know each other yet," Pip admitted. "And we haven't had time to . . ." She blushed, glad that the darkness hid her embarrassment. "To enjoy ourselves." Pip pulled one of the pillows over her face. Had she actually said that aloud?

Morgan gave a startled laugh.

"I mean"—she pulled the pillow higher, so her mouth was free—"it would be nice to have some time, just you and me. To get to know each other. Properly."

"And *enjoy* ourselves?"

Oh, he was loving this. His surliness had broken, replaced by amusement. At her expense.

"Yes," she said tightly. She scrunched her eyes closed and pressed the pillow closer, her mind full of ways she'd like to enjoy him. "Do *you* want kids?" she blurted.

There was a long thoughtful silence. "I don't know. I just assumed it came—"

"—with the territory," she finished for him.

"Yeah," he agreed. "I know there are ways around it, but I thought you'd want them. Kids, I mean."

"I do," she reminded him.

"Eventually." He lapsed back into silence.

"There's no rush, is there?" she asked nervously. "I thought you might have had your fill of child-rearing . . ."

Morgan gave a full-body groan that was half laugh, half agonized cry. "You have no idea."

"You've probably earned a rest." Pip pulled the pillow off her face and rolled onto her side. The glow from the street outside fell in a thick shaft through the parted curtains. He was still sitting up, she saw. Staring at her, his shadowy face impossible to read.

"I don't plan to do much resting," he warned her, his voice husky with repressed desire.

Pip felt the warmth of his voice through every last inch of her. "What do you plan to do?"

There was a flash of white as he grinned. She bet that dimple was winking. "It'll be worth the wait to find out," he promised. He lay back down. She heard his breath, uneven, hitching. He wanted her. It was arousing beyond belief.

Pip ran a hand down her own body. This was torture.

"Now that I think about it," Morgan said pensively, "there's a lot we could do."

Yes. This was more like it. Pip's breasts grew heavy as she brushed her hand over them. Her nipples pebbled under her palm.

"You know what I liked about running cattle?"

What? Pip's hand paused. Really? He wanted to talk about cows?

"I liked seeing new places."

Pip dropped her hand to her side. How could he talk about seeing new places when she was right here, in this bed, hot and ready for him? Unless these new places were places on her body . . .

"You know, there's nothing that says we have to go straight back to Buck's Creek." The wretched man had propped his arms behind his head and was gathering steam. "I got a bank account full of money and nowhere I've got to be. We could spend some time riding the rails."

Pip would be more than happy to go back to trains if he'd go back to touching her.

"What do you say? You and me, Mrs. McBride, taking a little wedding tour."

"Only if you get in my Pullman bed with me," Pip said sourly.

"Honey, as soon as I get that ring on your finger, you'll never get me out of your bed."

"Morgan," Pip warned him. "If you don't get into this bed right now, I'm coming over there."

"Good night, sweetheart."

Oh, she could kill him.

They got married on the first day they were legally allowed to after obtaining the license. They were out of the hotel at the first hint of day and barreling down to the courthouse. Morgan bought Pip a bunch of flowers from a flower seller who'd set up in front of the courthouse. She clearly knew trade would be brisk in couples who were in a rush.

"Roses and carnations for love," the woman told them cheerfully, handing over a bunch, "and hydrangea for perseverance."

"You'll need that," Morgan told Pip, passing her the bouquet. "I only get harder with time." He registered the double meaning and flushed. "Come on." He took her by the arm and hurried her into the courthouse. "I'm out of stamina."

So was Pip.

Fortunately, the wedding was a swift exchange of promises and a signing of the register, and then they were back out in the sun, blinking like moles.

"He didn't even tell us to kiss," Pip complained. She looked down at the plain gold band Morgan had slid onto her finger. She barely remembered it happening, it was so quick.

"You need someone to tell us to kiss?" Morgan asked.

But before she could answer he yanked her to him and kissed the life out of her.

"God, I've wanted to do this for days," he moaned. Then his tongue slid into her.

Vaguely, Pip heard catcalling and realized they were still on the street. "Bed," she ordered, propelling him down the street. Morgan McBride didn't need to be asked twice. Their heels clicked a frantic staccato on the marble as they crossed the vast foyer of their hotel, and then they were dashing up the carpeted stairs to their floor. The moment they reached their corridor, Morgan hauled Pip off her feet and carried her the last few yards. They burst into the room, and Morgan just about threw her on the bed. He locked the door and snatched the curtains closed.

"Don't!" he snapped when she reached for her buttons. "Don't move a muscle."

Pip obeyed, her heart skittering in her chest.

"I've fantasized about undoing those buttons," he admitted. He stared down at her, breathing hard.

"Well, what are you waiting for?"

Morgan McBride grinned, his dimple a deep groove in his cheek. "I always loved a bossy woman."

Pip aimed to please. "Unbutton me." She stretched her arms above her head, giving him full access to her body. She was quivering from head to toe.

Morgan braced his hands on the bed on either side of her head and lowered himself to kiss her. "Epiphany McBride," he murmured as he pressed his lips to hers.

Oh. She liked the sound of that. Especially in that sandpapery voice he got when he wanted her bad. "Yes, Mr. McBride?"

"You are more than I deserve." He kissed her deeply.

How was this her life? Pip was overwhelmed. She'd answered that ad, never imagining in her wildest dreams that she'd find herself married to a man like Morgan McBride. It wasn't just his looks; it was everything about him. Beneath his gruffness, he was the sweetest man she'd ever known. He was kind, and thoughtful; he just didn't seem to want people to realize it.

Pip arched her back as she felt his hands move to the buttons at her throat. He nipped her lower lip as he pulled away. He rolled onto his side and propped himself on one elbow, so he could drink in the sight of her. Lazily, his fingers flicked the tiny black buttons through the buttonholes. Pip felt her heartbeat thudding through her. She kept her gaze fixed on his face, hypnotized by the stark appreciation she saw there.

Half a dozen buttons down, Morgan traced a fingertip into the naked hollow of her throat. Oh, this was agony. Pip closed her eyes. It only increased the sensations that roiled through her like floodwaters. She felt the air swirl against her skin as he finished the buttons and slowly parted her bodice.

For some reason, Pip had never imagined lovemaking would be slow like this. She didn't know what she'd imagined—something more animal, perhaps. This was slow as honey dripping. Her thighs were twitching and her nipples pinching. Long spirals of heat were uncurling in her lower belly. She moaned.

"I haven't stopped dreaming about that night in the creek," Morgan said huskily, as his fingertips traced the skin just above her chemise. He was a tease. "Do you want to try that again?"

"Yes," Pip breathed. "Oh yes, please."

He bent to place a kiss on the column of her throat. His mouth was hot. The tip of his tongue slid down her throat and across her collarbone, down to her exposed upper chest. His teeth grazed the swell of her breasts and she shuddered with pleasure.

"You better get used to this room," he told her, his warm breath against her damp skin causing a cascade of shivers. "Because we're spending at least a week in here."

"Only a week?" Pip bit her lip as his mouth moved south to her nipple. "Oh God."

His tongue flicked and swirled until she was wild. His hand slid down her body, over rib cage and belly, around her hip. "There's too much material," he complained, breaking contact.

"Oh, don't stop." Pip's hands clenched around the bedspread.

Morgan grinned, his dark hair tumbling over his forehead as he gave her a sly look. "Honey, I'm just getting started."

He really was. Pip had no idea such pleasure could exist. He took his time peeling her clothes from her, his hands and mouth exploring each square inch of skin as it was revealed. Pip's teeth chattered as she shivered.

"Cold?"

"No," she moaned. If anything, she was burning up.

She should feel embarrassed at being naked, she thought witlessly, as he slid her stockings from her, leaving her completely bare. She'd not been naked in front of anyone since she was a child. For a moment, the memory of Samuel Arcross and his revulsion intruded, but it had no weight anymore. Not when Morgan McBride was looking at her with wonder. And hunger.

"Hell, you're a sight for sore eyes." He was flushed and breathing quick, his gaze riveted to her.

Languorous with desire, Pip stretched, watching his eyes widen. "I don't think it's fair that I don't have anything to look at."

"Is that right?" The dimple flickered. He rose to his feet and put his hands low on his hips. "What do you want to see?"

"Everything," Pip sighed happily.

He laughed. "What first?"

She curled around to get a better view and saw him take a long look at her legs, and the curve of her behind. She might never get dressed again, it felt so good being looked at like that. "Surprise me," she purred.

God, he was gorgeous. Look at those thighs. They bulged as he bent to remove his boots. He threw the boots in the corner. Then he was unbuttoning his shirt and *holy crow*. Pip could barely breathe as she watched the caramel skin appear, and the line of dark hair that speared through his hard-packed muscles, down to the waistband of his trousers.

"Wait," Pip said, when he moved to the buttons at his waist. "Not too fast." She gestured him closer and rose to her knees. She didn't want to waste this moment. They only had one first time.

He was trembling, she saw as she came close enough to touch him. He was as velvety as he looked, warm and smooth under her fingertips. His small dusky nipples were hard. Following her instincts without thought, Pip pressed a kiss to his left nipple. She felt him jump under her lips and wondered if it felt as good for him as it did for her. Judging by his moan as she traced her tongue around the firm jut of his nipple, he felt just fine. He tasted salty and sweet. Up close, the woodsy smell of him was intoxicating. She ran her hands down his back and around his stomach, feeling his muscles tensing. She ran the flat of her tongue over his chest, enjoying the taste of him.

She wanted to see more.

Pip slid her fingers down to his waistband. There was a bulge beneath it. Playfully, she brushed it. Startled, she felt it twitch, as though it had a life of its own. She glanced up, to find Morgan mesmerized. His eyes were shining under heavy lids.

Pip took her time slipping the buttons free. His underwear was pale cotton, and she could see the outline of him through the cloth. Her breath caught as he hooked his thumbs in the waistband of his underwear and slid them off, trousers with them. His cock leapt free, swollen and rising hard from black curls.

Oh. Pip's heart seemed to have forgotten how to keep a beat. It was racing and stopping and stumbling over itself. She was wet between her legs, and aching.

Pip touched him. He was warm and silky. She curved her hand around his shaft; he throbbed. She saw his stomach muscles clench as she gave him a soft squeeze. He moaned.

It was the sexiest sound she'd ever heard. She wondered if kissing worked here too. There was only one way to find out. She heard Morgan make a weak noise as she bent forward to kiss his ruddy tip. He was burning hot. Pip gave him a slow lick, feeling the firm curve of him against her tongue. He was wet. He tasted good. She circled the head of his cock with her tongue, resting her hands on the bones of his hips and pulling him toward her. She could feel him trembling as she slid his cock into her mouth.

"Pip," he protested in a broken breath.

But he didn't ask her to stop, so she didn't. She gave him a lazy suck. The ache between her legs was growing painful.

"Whoa," he gasped eventually, pulling away. "I can't hold on if you keep doing that."

"Do you need to hold on?" she asked.

He gave her a rueful look. "I got no plan to let my bride down on her wedding night."

"Who said you'd be letting me down?" Pip wrapped his cock in her hand. He was hard as rock and throbbing.

"Nuh-uh, honey. It's your turn now." He disentangled himself from her grip.

Pip felt a nervous rush. But whatever was about to happen couldn't happen quick enough. She was wet and hurting with wanting him. She scooted back on the bed as he joined her.

He chased her, claiming her mouth, his tongue slipping straight into her. His hands were on her breasts, and then sliding all over her. Wherever he touched, she burned. And then his hand slid between her legs, and she almost jumped out of her skin. His fingers slipped along her wet thighs, parting her. She felt him slide right inside of her. And it felt *good*.

"Don't come yet," he whispered against her mouth as he felt her shudder.

Pip didn't know what he meant. She moaned with disappointment when he removed his fingers. He eased her back down onto the bed.

"You reap what you sow, honey," he said in that sexy sandpaper voice. And then he was between her legs, *right* between her legs, his breath swirling against her most intimate places.

"Morgan!" She came off the bed when she felt his tongue. Oh

my *God*. He was slow and measured; meticulous. His tongue was a delirium of pleasure. She felt her hips rocking of their own accord against his mouth. And then, somehow, she was quite insensible to how, his fingers were inside her, too, pushing into the pulsing depths of her as his mouth licked and sucked and drove her wild.

Just when she thought she might explode, he pulled away and she wanted to cry.

"Hold on," he begged. "Wait for me."

Hold on? Like she was capable of going anywhere. She could barely breathe.

He was leaving the bed. "What are you doing?" Her voice came out thick, drugged.

"You said you wanted to wait for babies." He came back, with something in his hand. "Until we're ready." He gave her a sideways smile and then bent over his swollen cock, rolling something onto it. "It's a rubber," he explained when he saw her confusion. "You still want to wait?"

"For babies, yes. For you, *no*." She hauled him back to her. She felt his sheathed cock curiously. "How does it feel for you?"

He shrugged and gave her a cheeky grin. "It will make me last longer."

That was all well and good, but Pip wasn't sure she had longer in her. She was wet as hell and longing for release. She kissed him, reveling in the full-body press of him against her, the smell of him, the taste. She wanted all of him, forever.

"This might hurt," he said gently.

She felt the hard press of him and opened her legs. God, the brush of him felt good. Right *there*. His hand slipped between them as he kissed her, toying with her, slicking his thumb down her aching swells. She widened her legs and lifted her hips. Oh God, when his fingers went deep like that . . .

"You're so wet," he said shakily as he broke the kiss. "And hot."

"Now, Morgan, please." Her fingers dug into his arms. *"Please."*

And then he was sliding into her, and it was *heaven*. He filled her, a pulsing width, so deep and—sharp pain.

"It won't last long," he promised, his breath labored. He stopped after that painful thrust, holding still so he wouldn't hurt her. "I hope." He pressed a kiss to her parted lips. "I think, anyway. I ain't never been with a virgin before."

Pip swallowed. It hurt. But then his hand returned, as he held himself still inside her. His fingers parted her as he found her nub and rubbed it slowly, gently. He rested on his elbow, his mouth lowering to her breast to kiss her nipple, to suck, as his fingers played with her. Oh, the feelings. Pip nearabout forgot who she was, it felt so good. Before long, she was rocking beneath him, moving her hips as he moved inside her. And it didn't hurt so bad. Not enough to distract from the ecstasy of his hand and mouth. And then he began to thrust, slow as syrup, his hips moving in gentle waves. Oh my *God*. The slowness was incredible. A pressure built in the depths of her, like a tide coming to shore. Pip gasped, and then heard herself moaning. She wrapped her legs around his buttocks and thrust back.

"Hell, Pip, I cain't wait," he groaned.

She couldn't speak.

His thrusts grew frantic and something started fizzing inside of her, like gunpowder igniting. Shudders broke through her and the most explosive, exquisite pleasure erupted. It was a wildfire. And then she was screaming, arriving at a pleasure she never could have imagined.

She felt Morgan go rigid as he let out a growl, and then his cock pulsed hard, which made her shudder with aftershocks so strong they were another wave of intense pleasure.

"Morgan," she whimpered as she came sparkling back to earth. She was limp, drenched in sweat, her heart racing like she'd run up a mountain.

"Yes, honey?"

"The ad didn't say anything about *that*."

He laughed, nuzzling her neck. "I should hope not."

"Will it always be like that?"

She felt his grin against her skin.

"No, honey. That was just a practice run. Wait until we know what we're doing."

Oh God. She wasn't sure she would survive if it got better than that. But she'd be willing to try.

She threaded her fingers through his tumbled dark hair and gave a shaky, happy sigh. "You want to ride the rails, you said?"

"Once we're through with this bed," he said lazily. "Which might be a while."

"You think it's this good on a train?" Her mind had drifted to that curtained cocoon, and the shudder of the train.

"I think we should find out." He propped himself up and gave her a sly look. "Anything else you want to find out?"

"So much," she told him fervently. She lifted a hand to trace the line of his jaw.

"Well, Mrs. McBride, we got nothing but time." He kissed her fingers as they trailed over his lips. "And I reckon the two of us are going to fill that time just fine."

Pip thought he was probably right. For a change.

Twenty-Two

Junebug could have kissed Purdy Joe when he brought her another postcard from Morgan. She didn't, though, because he'd got funny around her since he'd seen her in a dress. He got all blushy and shy and had a tendency to offer her compliments that lacked poetry. One time he told her she looked pretty as a nugget. There were plenty of things Junebug didn't mind being compared to, but nuggets weren't one of them.

"Looks like Morgan ain't coming back just yet," Purdy Joe said, blushing the color of a July sunrise as he tried to keep her talking.

"Looks like it," she agreed, not wanting to talk. She left him on the porch and went inside the trading post to read the postcard in peace. It was from Nebraska.

Hey, Bug, the wife and I are in Lincoln, and heading for Joshua so she can show me off to her folks. I reckon that visit will require a letter rather than a postcard, just to make sure you get the flavor of it. We'll head home after that. Don't burn down the cookhouse while we're gone. Mushily yours, Morgan.

She grinned and pinned it up on the wall next to the others. The first one he'd sent her had a cow on it. Smart-ass. On the other side of the cow were three words: *Just got hitched.*

Sometimes Morgan went and proved you wrong and showed you he wasn't a total idiot after all. Junebug had told the boys they better get to work on another big house, because she didn't fancy living with another married couple smooching and making her sick to her stomach. The boys were dragging their feet on it though. None of them much enjoyed building houses.

Junebug frowned as she heard rustling noises up in the loft of the trading post.

"Hey," she called. "Who's up there?" It couldn't be the trappers, because they were down in Bitterroot mooning over Martha. Beast gave a sharp bark. "Good idea," Pip told him, pulling the rifle out from under the trading post counter. "Whoever it is, you'd best tell, or I'll fill you full of buckshot."

"It's a rifle, not a shotgun, you ninny." Beau's voice came drifting down from the loft, exasperated. "And put it back. You know you ain't allowed to touch it."

Junebug dropped the rifle and flew up the ladder. What was he doing up there? That was where she kept her private things. "What are you doing?" Junebug wasn't pleased to see Beau sitting cross-legged on a stack of hides, ransacking her secret stash.

"I'm looking for those newspapers," he said, undaunted.

"What newspapers?"

"Aha!" He held one up. "These ones!"

He had one of her *Matrimonial News*es clutched in his sweaty paw. Junebug scowled. She didn't like this, not one bit. "What in hell do you want that for?"

"What do you think? I want to find a woman."

Junebug felt like he'd whipped the ground out from under her. "You what?"

Beau unfolded the paper. "I'm a red-blooded man, ain't I? And there ain't no women up here, so I thought I'd see if I could order one up. And then I got to thinking about all the ads in here. I can probably find one who's already looking."

That was Beau in a nutshell, wasn't it? Too lazy to even write his own damn ad.

"You don't want to answer those. They ain't no good. You have to hunt for ages to find a decent one. You're much better off writing your own specifications; then you can get exactly what you want." Junebug sat beside him and pulled out paper and pencil. "Here, write down what you want, and I'll show you how to get in the paper." Junebug peered over his shoulder as he put pencil to paper. This was great. She'd promised Morgan she wouldn't order up any more unexpected wives—but he hadn't said anything about expected ones.

Good-looking guy seeks gal for fun, Beau wrote.

"That ain't an ad for a wife," Junebug said, disgusted. "That's for a whole different kind of relationship."

"I'm open to it."

"You can't go inviting just anyone into the family," Junebug protested.

"Sure I can. Who I marry ain't no one's business but my own."

"I could find you a better woman than you could find yourself," Junebug insisted. "You'll pick someone for short-term fun. That's no way to go about it. When I do it, I make sure they know what they're getting into, with a view to long-term happiness."

Beau didn't buy it, she could tell. But that was only because her first two wives hadn't quite worked out as she'd planned. You couldn't expect a girl to get it right without some practice. And Kit and Morgan were happily married, weren't they? So, she had a perfect record, even if the process was messy.

"There ain't no way you could find a better woman than I can,"

Beau disagreed. "You don't have a clue what a man wants in a woman."

Well, that was flat-out untrue. She'd married off two brothers already, and they were sickeningly happy.

"Here, what about this?" Beau held out the paper.

Junebug thought his ad was stomach turning in the extreme:

Charming gentleman seeks beguiling woman to warm the long Montana winters.

"That makes it sound like you want a whore," Junebug protested.

Beau didn't look displeased at the notion.

Junebug had a suggestion. "What about: *Good-looking layabout seeks frontier bride. Be warned: he's well aware of his own charms and would just as soon kiss a mirror as a wife. The ideal woman would fill his empty head with some book learning and take him down a peg or two. But he does come with a nice patch of land and a good singing voice.*"

"No decent woman is answering that ad." Beau was disgusted.

"Wanna bet?" Junebug said mutinously.

Beau's eyes narrowed. "A bet?" He got that piratical look he had when he leapt headlong into trouble. Beau got into more trouble than anyone Junebug knew. Save herself. "You want to make this a bet?" he asked. "What kind?"

Oh, this was getting good. Junebug was beginning to see how this could work to her advantage, on multiple fronts. "It's simple. We both advertise, and we see who hooks the best wife." Junebug knew she'd win. It wasn't even in question.

"And what are the stakes?" Beau's dark eyes were gleaming. He liked a good gamble. Not that he won much, but that didn't seem to deter him.

"If I win," Junebug said, "you take me to a circus."

"A circus?" Beau looked at her like she'd grown a second head.

"I've always wanted to see a circus. We might have to go to

Iowa or somewhere though. From what I can tell there ain't no circuses in these parts."

He shook his head. "You get the daftest ideas in your head. What about if I win?"

"I'll buy you a mirror?"

"Get off it." He swatted her with the paper. "How about you take over mucking out the stables from me? For a year."

"A year!"

"Well, you want me to take you to Iowa—that ain't cheap," he sniped.

Junebug thought on it. "Deal." She held out her hand for him to shake. "May the best McBride win."

"I plan to." He gathered up as many *Matrimonial News*es as he could and tucked them under his arm before he headed down the ladder of the loft. "I'd best read up on these ads, so I can write the perfect one." He disappeared. And then his head popped back up. "And, Junebug, not a word of this to the others."

Junebug snorted. What did he think she was, stupid?

She grinned as she considered the kind of wife she'd need. Hell, soon she'd have another wife, have beaten the pants off Beau and have gone to the circus to boot.

Life was looking good.

ACKNOWLEDGMENTS

I would like to acknowledge the Blackfoot, Crow and Bitterroot Salish people of Montana, and to pay my respects to their elders, past, present and emerging, and to recognize their spiritual connection to the country I write about in this book. I would also like to acknowledge that I write on the lands of the Kaurna people, lands never ceded, and to recognize that this Country is a place of powerful storytelling and knowledge. I pay my respects to elders, past, present and emerging. These lands are steeped in ways of storying and knowing that I recognize and respect—and I give thanks.

This book was written in a maelstrom of busyness, and it all seems a bit of a blur now. It was crammed in around work and kids and life and all the rest of it—but Buck's Creek was always a fun refuge to run to and I've loved spending time with the McBrides.

This book is dedicated to my grandmother Tess, whom I miss dearly and think of every day. She was a big figure in my life and the most loving person you could meet. And it's dedicated to my grandfather, whom I never met, but who was the love of her life. Grandma outlived him by almost forty years but was buried in her wedding band, which she never removed. He was the enduring love of her life, and she never got over him. I hope they're together now.

Thank you to Jonny, the love of *my* life, who is in many ways the template for Morgan. Some of Morgan's lines are verbatim from Jonny ("I'm being nice!" bellowed at full volume springs to mind). I love you, J. Thanks for raising my kids with me, and being responsible for things that you didn't have to be responsible for; thanks for being a reliable (and very opiniated) partner; for being larger than life; for being ridiculously fun; and for taking me seriously when others don't. I appreciate you. I am deeply thankful for the everyday acts of support when I'm writing (the cooking, the cleaning, the yard work) and for the pep talks when my confidence wobbles. You believe in me—and that's a powerful thing.

To my kids: you are the meaning of life and I love you.

To my parents: thank you for the flowers and champagne; thank you for the everlasting love and support; thank you for buying bookshelves full of copies of my book (just in case you need another ten of them after you've read the first copy?); and thank you for the laughs and perspective in times of crisis.

To the wider family: Gerald and Ash and my in-laws (in their infinite variety), thank you for being there. It matters.

Lynn—disco sister. Wise friend. Thanks and love.

SARA gals, we've been meeting for fourteen years, and you've been my fairy godmothers as I seek my HEA as a writer. Thank you!

Tully, Sean, Alex and the CPA peeps at Flinders University: thank you. There are days a message from you keeps me sane or reenergizes me when I'm depleted. Thanks to the College of Humanities, Arts and Social Sciences for valuing Creative and Performing Arts, and to Assemblage Centre for Creative Arts for fostering new research and creativity.

Also, my huge and heartfelt thank-you to my students—my postgrads and Honours students, who are just about family now, and to my undergrads, particularly the students of CRWR2002 Love and Death over the past few years, who have been part of my journey in thinking through romance. They are always inspiring, and I learn something every single time I step into a classroom (whether IRL or virtually). I won't name anyone specifically because once I start, I won't be able to stop, and this will get as thick as a phone book!

Sarah Younger, thank you!!!!!! You rock. And thanks to the whole team at NYLA, who are not only amazing professionals but welcomingly kind in all correspondence.

Kristine Swartz, you are my perfect reader, and I am so deeply thankful to have worked with you on so many books. Your insight is rare and nuanced and always spot-on—and the books are always better for your input. Thank you!! And thank you to Mary, Jessica, Tina, all the copy editors and designers and everyone at PRH who worked on the book. Superstars, all!

Lastly and most importantly, thank you to everyone who read this book. Especially those who love Junebug and her brothers. I hope to see you in Buck's Creek again soon!

Keep reading for an excerpt from

KIT McBRIDE GETS A WIFE

Available now!

Buck's Creek, Montana, 1886

Well, spit. How was Junebug to know flour was flammable? It was *flour*. You cooked the stuff, for Pete's sake. It wasn't gunpowder. Only somehow that great big sack of flour had blown the belly out of the cookhouse, she marveled as she watched her older brothers try to save the outbuilding.

"You could have killed yourself!" Morgan raged as he threw buckets of creek water at the snapping flames.

She *was* rather singed. And her rear end sure did hurt from where she'd landed in the woodpile. But she was fine. And what a thing to see. All that flour floating about in the air and then *wham*, no cookhouse.

"You ought to be tarred and feathered for this," Beau grumped, sloshing water on Junebug's bare feet as he jogged up from the creek.

"Well, *spit*," Junebug said, "it ain't like I set fire to the cookhouse on purpose. Not this time *or* the last time." If this was anyone's fault, it was Morgan's. He'd been the one to dump that great big sack of flour in front of her and shut her up in the cookhouse to bake, rather than let her go fishing. If it had been up to *her*, she'd be stretched out in the meadow, pulling a few fat bull trout from the creek, and their cookhouse would still be standing. But no, *Morgan* had to go force her into an apron and lock her in the dark little hut for the afternoon. If anyone was to blame for this, it was definitely him. Not that she was game to tell him that yet; she'd wait till he cooled off some. She'd at least wait until the fire was out. Morgan was worse than a grizzly coming out of hibernation when he was in a mood. And he was pretty much always in a mood.

"How do you burn a *stove* down?" Jonah asked as they watched the remains of the cookhouse smolder. "Surely the whole point of a stove is that it's fireproof."

"Junebug could burn down hell itself," Kit sighed. He and Morgan had that mountainous look they got when she was in trouble. They went all immovable and stony, and she knew there was no way around them.

"It wasn't my *fault*," she reminded them.

"It never is." Morgan looked madder than usual.

"But this time it *really* wasn't."

They weren't listening. They never did. Not for the first time, Junebug wished she had a sister. A proper live one. Technically she had three of them, but they were all bundled up under the chokecherry tree, no use to her at all. *Sleeping with the angels* was written on their gravestones, but Junebug never believed it. Why would you sleep if you got to see angels? No, she was certain those three little girls were having a time of it, flying about, instead of being here to help Junebug deal with their brothers. And she sure did need some help.

With the cooking, for a start. Those four could eat more than a herd of buffalo. And they were fussy as hell, always complaining that she'd burned this, or put too much salt in that. Where was it written that she knew how to cook just because she was a girl? Nowhere, that was where. And she *hated* cooking. Almost as much as she hated doing their laundry, and she hated *that* something fierce. Those boys *stank*. After winter, their long underwear was fit for burning rather than cleaning. And did they thank her when she took the trouble to burn it? No. Morgan just shouted at her about the cost of new underwear.

"They were *unwashable*," she'd tried to explain, but that had been another prime example of a time when he didn't listen to her.

"Don't just stand there." Kit thrust a pail at Junebug. "You made this mess; you help clean it up."

Junebug followed him down to the creek. "I told you, it was Morgan's fault."

"You're just lucky we were smart enough to build the cookhouse close to the water and away from the woods. The last thing we need is a wildfire." Kit scooped up creek water.

"It was *my* idea to build it close to the water," she reminded him, filling her own pail. "So I wouldn't have to haul water so far."

"I swear, Junebug, you're as lazy as a house cat."

"*Lazy!*" Oh, Junebug could have dumped the whole pail over his head, and she would have if he weren't already halfway back to the smoking cookhouse. Lazy! She did nothing *but* work. She scrubbed and cooked and mended and fed the animals and gathered eggs and did the work of seven women. At least. Maybe *ten* women.

But did they give her any credit?

No!

Instead, it was *you can't pick blackberries, you have to milk the cow; you can't go wandering, you have to darn some stinky socks; you can't go fishing, you have to bake bread with all this stupid flour.* And when Morgan's deadly flour blew itself up, it was somehow *her* fault. And she was also to blame for how slow they were to put out the fire.

Well, she wasn't taking that.

"No!" Kit said flatly as she stalked up behind him. "I don't want to hear it."

"But—"

"*No.*" He kept his back turned on her, like she was nothing more than an irritating mayfly. "You know the rule. You got something to say to me, you write it in your book," Kit told her shortly.

"I will," she promised his great big slab of a retreating back. "You just wait."

As soon as the fire was out and Morgan was done growling at her, she marched straight down to the trading post. It was a ramshackle log building down by the creek, older and more substantial than the cabin they lived in. The trading post was the chief reason the McBrides were in Buck's Creek at all; their father had been sure he'd make his fortune trading with the trappers, and with the Nez Percé, Blackfeet, Bitterroot Salish and Crow, who took a well-established trade route right through the mountains. The McBrides' wide mountain meadow was a pleasant camp spot for travelers, with fresh flowing water and abundant game. And it did good business in fair-weather years. Good enough that the McBrides had settled in, building a cabin farther upriver, on the rise near the tree line, and a barn and forge. In the beginning Junebug's pa had dreams of Buck's Creek being a proper town, but it was too high up and got snowed in through the heart of winter. Instead, the town of Bitterroot sprang up four hours down the mountain, just far enough away to be wretchedly inconvenient, in Junebug's book.

Junebug loved the trading post and would have spent all day, every day working there, rather than cooking and laundering and being the general workhorse that she was. Interesting people blew into the trading post—you never knew who you'd meet. Or what they'd bring with them. Once she'd almost taken possession of a stuffed beaver from a man named Garneau; the beaver was marvelous, frozen in a look of perpetual surprise, its mouth open, showing its two jutting teeth. But the best thing of all was that Garneau had dressed the beaver up like a gunslinger. It had a little bandolier around its beaver chest, and a cowboy hat perched on its beaver head. And it even held a gun, carved out of aspen and painted to look just about real. It was the darnedest thing. Junebug would have bought it for sure, if only her brothers hadn't been right there, complaining about how Garneau had ruined a perfectly good beaver skin. Someone, somewhere, now had the pleasure of that beaver, and her brothers had never recognized how nearsighted they'd been. They just didn't know a good thing when they saw it.

As she reached the trading post, Junebug climbed over Thunderhead Bill's snoring body and headed inside, yanking her book off the shelf on her way past. She reached for the inkpot and sent splatters of ink across the page as she scrawled her complaints into the book. She stumbled a little over the word *irascible* and eventually crossed it out and wrote *blockheaded* instead.

Kit didn't take complaints in any form except written. He'd laid down the law on that when she was knee-high, and had even taught her to write so she could follow through. He stocked up on ledgers when he went to town, and made sure she had ink. All that trouble just so he wouldn't have to listen to her moan. Junebug was supposed to put her complaints in the book, and he was supposed to read them after she'd gone to bed. Every day she'd check the book after breakfast, only to find he'd gone through and corrected her spelling. Now and then he bothered to write a response to her complaint. Usually listing all the ways in which she had things upside down and backward, which she didn't appreciate. It was an unsatisfactory arrangement, to say the least. But if it weren't for the book, he'd get away without ever getting a piece of her mind. So at least it was *something*.

As she wrote, Junebug was dimly aware of Roy and Sour Eagle sidling up to the counter. She heard the rustle of newspaper as Sour Eagle folded his old reading paper away and tucked it under his arm. Their companion Thunderhead Bill was still snoring out on the porch. The three old trappers had blown in with the last storm of winter and hadn't seen fit to leave yet. They'd taken a shine to sitting around the porch of the McBrides' trading post all day, gossiping like old women. Not that Junebug knew any old women, but Morgan said they were just like 'em, and Morgan wasn't prone to falsehoods.

"Whatcha writing there?" Roy asked.

Junebug ignored him. She didn't like Roy in the slightest. He was uncouth. Not that Junebug was quite sure what *couth* was, but whatever it was, Roy wasn't it.

"That your complaints book?" Sour Eagle prodded, although he knew perfectly well that it was.

Junebug liked Sour Eagle a sight more than she liked Roy. He was dignified and gentlemanly in his ways. Sweet too. What's more, he told some mean war stories, complete with all the details Morgan said she was too young for. "It is," she agreed, slamming it shut, "and it's just between me and Kit. It ain't for the likes of you. Why, it'd sear your eyes right out of your sockets, the fury in those words."

Sour Eagle respected the power of words. He gave her an understanding look. "You burn the cookhouse down again?"

"It was Morgan's fault." She put the book back where it belonged. No one would dare touch it. Not when there'd be Kit to face if they did. Why, Kit had scared the wits out of Roy just yesterday when Roy had tried to put his hand in the jar of sweet strap candy without paying for it first. Junebug had never seen a grown man cry before. Roy had honked like a goose, his face all red and scrunched up, and Kit hadn't even touched him. Just the idea of Kit's anvil fists had been enough.

"Junebug, are you still in the letter-writing business?" Sour Eagle asked, tactfully changing the subject away from the fire as he watched her rub the wet ink from her palms onto her overalls.

"Well, spit, you know I am."

"Roy here needs a letter writ."

Junebug narrowed her eyes and looked Roy up and down. "He does, does he? Can he pay?" She didn't believe a man like Roy Duncan had a cent to his name. Or that he had anybody to write to. Although she supposed every man had a mother. She'd had a ma, too, once, although her ma was out of mail reach now; Junebug would have given anything to be able to write Ma a letter and tell her how these boys were using her up with chores. Her gaze drifted to the open door and the fenced-off plot by the slow-moving creek. The cross that marked her ma's grave was leaning toward the creek in that wonky old way that it had. What good did a dead ma and three dead sisters do her, she thought, feeling a stab of bleakest misery. Couldn't there be *one* woman to help her?

Junebug had been nine when her mother died. Old enough to remember her, although her memories were bitsy and jagged, like clay smashings after you'd dropped a pot. Just lots of bits of broken clay that couldn't carry water no more. That had been a fearful bad year, the year Ma died. First Maybud had died, and then Ma. And Ma hadn't gone easy. She'd moaned and sweat and scared the wits out of Junebug with all the noises she made in the night. After she died, the boys had buried her next to Maybud and the other girls under the chokecherry tree. Pa must have helped, but Junebug didn't remember it; she didn't remember much of Pa at all. The thick minty smell of his chewing tobacco, the sound of him cracking his knuckles, the way he'd drawl, *Well, now* . . . when you asked him a question he didn't want to answer. That was about it. He'd run off not long after Junebug's ma went under the chokecherry tree. And the less said about that, the better; Pa was a touchy subject around here.

Junebug didn't wish Pa back, but she sure as hell wished Ma and those girls back.

And it wasn't just about the chores. Sometimes she got so lonely—

"I got money," Roy said bullishly, interrupting her thoughts.

Spit. There was no use wishing for what couldn't be.

"I *do*," Roy insisted, his nose all out of joint as he took her silence for disbelief. "Honestly earned."

Junebug fixed him with a calculating look. She reached under the counter and pulled out her sign: "Junebug McBride, Public Letter Writer." "I charge twenty-five cents a page," she told Roy sternly, "and I require payment in advance."

"Is she worth it?" Roy asked Sour Eagle suspiciously. "I cain't be paying for no substandard letter, not in this circumstance."

Junebug took offense at that. "I'll have you know that you cain't find better in these parts. I'm *loquacious*."

Roy blinked. She assumed he had no idea what *loquacious* meant. She wasn't too sure herself, but it was a word Kit used to describe her letters, and it sounded plenty fancy. One of these days she'd get around to looking it up in the dictionary.

"You'd have to be the best," Roy said as he fussed in his pockets, "you're the *only*."

Junebug took in the summer grasses and the shine of the creek through the open door behind the trappers. Beyond the broad meadow the highest peaks of the mountains rose, still snowy tipped, even in the middle of August. There wasn't another homestead for miles, and Bitterroot, the closest town, was a four-hour ride down the mountain. She *was* the only. The only girl on a mountain of men. It was enough to make you want to scream. "You want this letter or not?" Junebug had half a mind to refuse Roy's business if he was going to get lippy with her, and her thoughts had her all out of sorts anyway.

"Sure, I want it." Roy brandished a sweaty handful of coins.

"This a long letter or a short one?" Junebug reached for the paper. She loved writing a good letter.

"Short. I ain't paying for extra words, you hear? I just want to answer the advertisement."

"Advertisement?" Junebug slapped the paper down on the counter and climbed up onto the stool. She peered down at Roy, enjoying the height the tall stool offered. She leaned forward on her elbows. "What advertisement?"

"This one!" Sour Eagle untucked the newspaper from under his arm and unfolded it. He spread it out on the counter.

From where Junebug sat it was all upside down. She turned it around. The *Matrimonial News*. Junebug had never heard of it. She'd seen scraps from various papers as trappers and travelers passed through. Usually the papers were woefully out-of-date, but she sure did like some of the illustrations. She hoped Sour Eagle's paper had some illustrations. Maybe he'd let her have a look once they were done with all the letter writing. Sometimes she got to keep a page or two. Up at the cabin she had pages from papers like the *Chicago Daily Tribune*, which Kit told her was in Illinois (she didn't really know where Illinois was, but she liked the sound of it), and the *Lynchburg Virginian* from Virginia (which was nowhere near here). She also had part of a copy of the *Iron County Register* from Missouri, and even a page from the *Sun*, all the way from New York. Once a trapper had left behind most of a *Wichita Daily Eagle* and, another time, she'd found a few pages of the *Yorkville Enquirer* from South Carolina. And the last time Kit had taken her to town, Junebug had talked him into buying a copy of the *Dillon Tribune*, which was printed all the way over in Beaverhead. That was out-of-date, too, but not by as much as her other papers. Junebug liked thumbing through the ratty pages, reading about places so far off they might as well be on the moon.

The *Yorkville Enquirer* even had a column advertising a circus. It was a double show, with six lady performers and five clowns; the circus had come to Yorkville on April 16, in the year before Junebug was born. There were four little pictures down the side of the column, of people doing tricks while standing on the backs of horses. The horses looked frisky. Junebug would have given anything to see those lady performers and horses. But Buck's Creek was a long way from Yorkville and was unlikely to see a circus in Junebug's lifetime. South Carolina must be quite a place . . . maybe one day she could go see it for herself. Until then, she'd find out more about this Matrimonial place. Maybe they had circuses there too.

Only, as she looked at the newspaper, she found it wasn't like any newspaper she'd seen before. It was nothing but advertisements. And they were all advertisements for *people* . . .

Photograph by Sia Duff

Amy Barry writes sweeping historical stories about love. She's fascinated with the landscapes of the American West and their complex long history, and she's even more fascinated with people in all their weird, tangled glory. Amy also writes under the names Amy T. Matthews and Tess LeSue and is senior lecturer in creative writing at Flinders University in Australia.

CONNECT ONLINE

Amy-Barry.com

🗗 AmyBarry.AmyBarry

🐦 AmyB_AmyM

📷 AmyBarryAuthor

Ready to find
your next great read?

Let us help.

Visit prh.com/nextread